THE FALL OF VALENNA

THE FALL OF VALENNA

A. M. PORTMAN

Contents

To My Dear Sons,
Ares and Athan

Dúr Andolin.
Solhiel aynot
Hadur ha nym.
Kehirmund a tol.
Narhaälla ghotd
Ar haramund.
Karhanta mí.
O Pelkimund!

Dear Andolin.
Your spirit calls
from yonder glen
and sea of foam.
A secret told.
Wolf of the Sea.
will come to thee.
Oh Pelkimund!

~ Song of Andolin

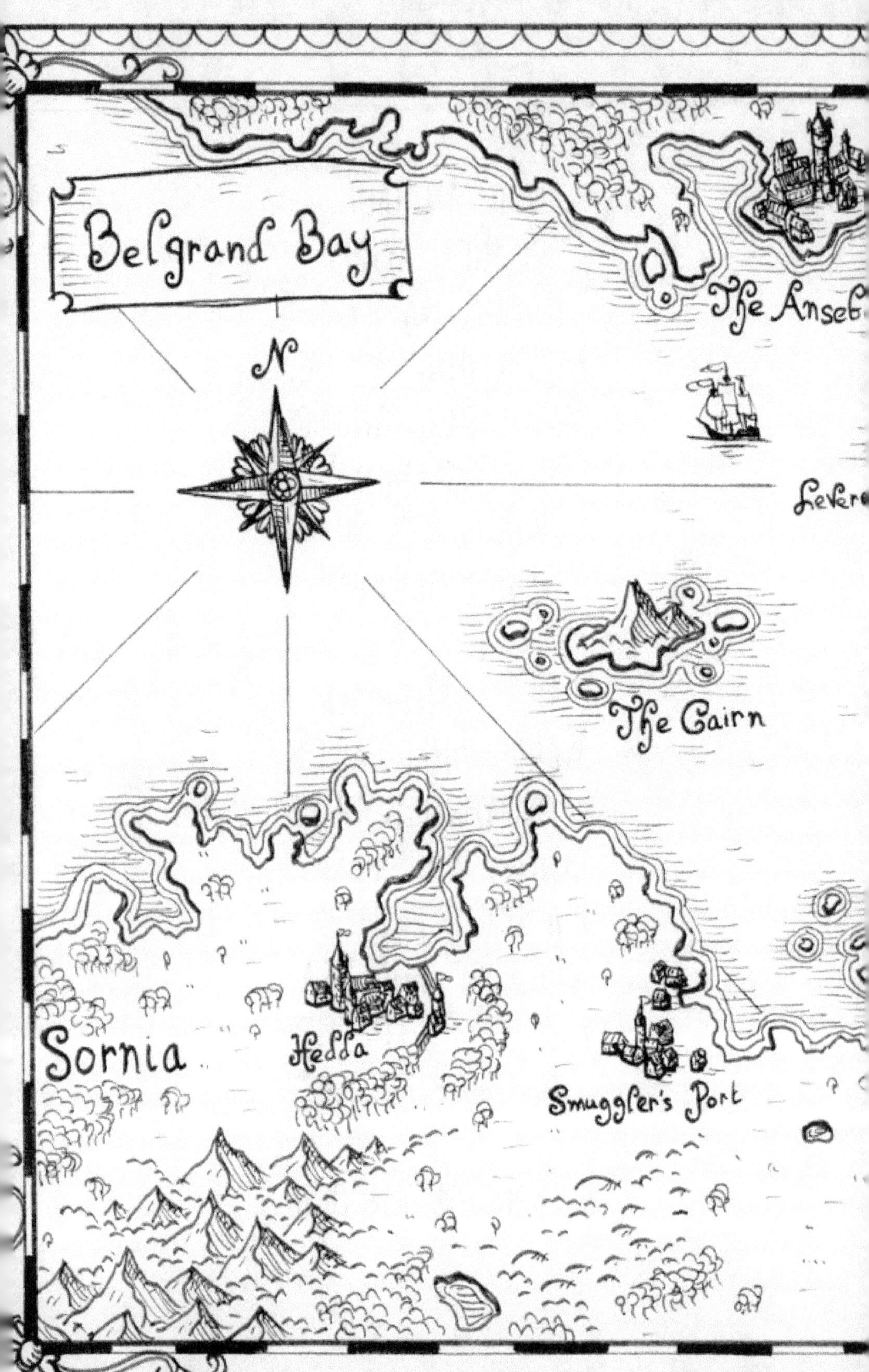

Belgrand Bay
N
The Anse
Levere
The Cairn
Sornia
Hedda
Smuggler's Port

Pentz
Folly
The Isles
Valenna
The Teeth
Raymouth
Figurehead
Elldon
Pass Point
Campos

The Coming Storm

The strange light that hung over the stormy harbor illuminated the deck of *The Tigress* in stark contrast, casting every shape in tints of green. Through the driving rain, Adella spotted two figures across the ship, their blades locked in combat. One, in his broad captain's hat, she recognized immediately. *Captain Declan.* Again and again, the captain crashed his cutlass against the other's, furiously hacking at his opponent.

The other man, barely holding out against Declan's onslaught, pressed against the rail, grabbing the shrouds to keep from falling to the rain-slick deck.

Ragged shouts carried on the wind, indecipherable amidst the downpour, save for one word that carried through the storm. "Traitor!"

It was Declan's voice. *So who's the traitor?* Something about the other man's silhouette, his familiar movements, made her stomach sink. When he shoved the captain away and drew to his full height, her fear was confirmed. The man Declan faced was Kol.

Adella let out a gasp. Frozen in confusion, she watched helplessly, unsure what to do. Lightning flashed on metal as the two dealt blow after blow, frantically parrying each rapid strike that darted through the rain. Finally, Kol shoved the flat of his cutlass into Declan's chest, forcing him back. Seizing the momentary vulnerability, Kol launched a quick jab at his belly.

Heart beating hard against her ribs, Adella ran toward them.

Declan deflected the strike with a gliding parry. Stepping in close, Kol drove his elbow into his face, striking him hard in the jaw and knocking him backward. With the captain briefly dazed and his guard down, Kol pulled back his cutlass, preparing to deliver the final blow.

"No!" she shouted, nearly upon them now, but her voice drowned in a clap of thunder. A blinding crack of lightning turned the world suddenly white. When all returned to shades of green and black, Kol was left standing weaponless. *He's unarmed!* Her pulse thrummed wildly through her veins.

Declan raised his sword high, blade aimed to kill.

Lightning cracked the sky once more, and steel plunged into flesh. A ragged scream tore through the night.

1

Lady Grimless

One Month Earlier

"I've never trained a woman before," Kol admitted, rubbing the back of his sun-bronzed neck.

"That's fine," Adella replied with a smirk. "I've never been trained before, so it evens out."

His dark eyes softened. "Your father never did?"

Adella lowered her brow. "No..." she muttered absently. Once comforting memories, now full of pain, flitted through her mind. While her father had taught her many things—how to ride, hunt with a bow, identify edible plants in the wild—he'd never seen fit to teach her to wield a sword. As a skilled swordsman himself, it must seem to Kol an egregious oversight. "Valenna had been at peace for over a hundred years," Adella explained, eager to defend her father, "after Sornia walled itself away. We no longer needed to learn to fight. While the cavalry had their excursions among the rebellions to the northeast, that didn't concern every noble house." She tucked back strands of auburn hair, blown loose by the gentle breeze rustling the trees above. "After that, the laws of inheritance were allowed to change."

"And that's why you were able to take on your father's title," Kol asked, rubbing his chin, "as a woman?"

She laughed. His question hadn't stemmed from a reproof of her father, she understood now, but merely from cultural differences. "It must seem so strange to someone from Sornia," Adella replied warmly, "but here, the roles had become hardly more than ceremonial. We had no need for warriors." Her smile fell away. "That is, until now..."

Adella drew a deep breath; the perfume of late-summer herbs scented the morning air, though it held a certain crispness, a remnant of the cooling nights. The trees and meadows surrounding the estate were still verdant, but hints of autumn appeared here and there, with patches of red and orange in the boughs, and carpets of brightly-colored fallen fruits beneath. In the distance, cranes trumpeted as they took flight, their pale, grey wings flashing brightly in the blue sky. Metal rang softly as she drew her late father's saber from its hilt at her side.

"What must they think we're doing out here?" Adella mused, knowing the people of Elldon were likely just waking in their tents. "Alone."

"Probably exactly this," Kol replied with a yawn. "It's too early for anything more exciting."

"Hm," Adella muttered. She couldn't agree; she preferred mornings, with the brisk air and the thrill of a new day ahead.

"Remember, we're just working on your form today." Kol gave a wry smile as he leveled his cutlass. "Don't take a swing at me."

"Right." Adella stepped forward to mimic his stance. "Like this?"

They had come to the fields west of Greywood Manor and Captain Holcomb's cavalry encampment to practice privately. As the new Lady Governor of Elldon and Equess Primorri, First Knight of Valenna, Adella hadn't wanted anyone to witness her lack of skill with a sword. Kol was undoubtedly the best swordsman she knew, so asking him to train her seemed only natural, even though he'd led the Sornian attack on her town as a stranger and enemy six months earlier. Even though he'd tried to kill her people, he'd come to realize it wasn't right. To make up for what he'd done, he changed sides, choosing to help her instead. They'd grown closer during their summer travels over Belgrand Bay. His presence was a comfort, even after his recent admission that he loved her.

Guilt dug at her at the thought, but there was nothing for it. By the time Kol had confessed his feelings, taking her entirely by surprise, she had already resumed her old relationship with the captain of *The Tigress* and her former betrothed, Rogero Declan. Adella hadn't yet had a chance to tell Kol; at the time of his confession, he had forestalled her reply. She wasn't sure why, though she had assumed it was due to nerves.

They were alone now, though. Meeting his gaze, she looked steadily into his dark eyes, finding warmth and kindness there. *If I could just work up the courage to tell him...*

"Higher," he said, interrupting her thoughts. "Lift from the elbow, not the wrist. Good, now lunge," he ordered. She stepped forward. "Again," he continued. "Come on, pretend you're stabbing me."

At his cues, Adella darted forward on her leading foot again and again, practicing her swordsmanship for what seemed like hours, alternating between the right hand and the left. The sun mounted higher over the fields, warming the air, and the buzzing of insects surrounded them as Adella's arms grew tired and her legs sore.

"Ohh," she huffed finally, rubbing her shoulder and shaking out her hands. "Can't I try something else for a moment? Something more generally useful."

"Well..." He scratched the black stubble on his jaw. "You should also learn how to grapple, in case you're disarmed."

"Right," Adella replied, catching her breath. "Let's do that, then."

"Because of your small size, you should learn to escape from a hold," he reasoned thoughtfully. "To start, I'll take hold of you, and you try to get out."

She nodded, setting her saber down. In an instant, he grabbed her wrist and spun her around. Her breath squeezed from her lungs as Kol pinned her in his arms. She gasped, suddenly frightened at the unexpected strength pressing in on her to think this might be what she'd have to face on the battlefield. Straining against his tightened muscles, she tried to break free to no avail.

"What are you doing?" he laughed, his breath warming her skin. "You've got to try harder than that."

Adella inhaled deeply against the brutish pressure around her chest and tried again to pull his arms away, but they held fast around her. She struggled, the stubble of his jaw brushing her cheek. His body pressed against hers, and suddenly, all thoughts of the battlefield fell away.

"Look for the weak points," Kol instructed. "Like the thumb or fingers. Use your opponent's body against itself."

Pulse quickening, she tried to focus on his words rather than his breath on her neck, the brush of his lips on her ear. Heat rose in her face, and even he seemed to pause, lingering in the moment while he waited for a response, a movement from her.

"Stay my hand," he whispered against her skin. His broad palm moved up over her bodice toward her throat. Adella was no longer sure if he was still instructing her in self-defense or if he could sense the goosebumps rising along her back. She reached for his hand, intending to do as instructed, but her fingertips met his rough, warm skin, and she wavered.

"Lady Grimless," a voice called out from close by, startling her so much she gasped.

Instantly, Kol released her and stepped aside to reveal Captain Holcomb reining his chestnut gelding to a halt.

"I can see you're both very busy," Holcomb said archly, lifting a brow, "but I have some news to discuss with her ladyship at the map, when you're able."

"Yes, Captain," Adella replied. "I'll be right there."

With a nod, he spurred his horse and trotted away.

When he was out of sight, Kol gave a loud chuckle.

"How embarrassing!" Adella grimaced, taking up her saber. "I wanted to come out here to *avoid* this very situation." She sighed heavily. "Oh well. Shall we pick up at the same time tomorrow?"

"I think that would be best," Kol replied. "You... haven't quite got it yet."

Adella gave an embarrassed smile. "Right," she said with a laugh.

"You know," he began, pulling a dusty oxblood jacket over his patched linen shirt, "you shouldn't care so much what people think. I don't."

"I wish it were that easy for me," Adella sighed, sheathing her saber. "Unfortunately, it's part of the job." She eyed the bits of hay clinging to his sleeve. "And it might not hurt you to care just a little," she added playfully.

Inspecting his jacket, he brushed it off with a smirk.

Adella turned and plodded through the wiry grass to where the horses grazed. With his soft muzzle, Shy, her little bay gelding, snuffled gently in her hair while she crouched at his forelimbs to untie the rope hobble.

"I wanted to talk to you about something," Kol said, tightening the saddle girth on his large, black mare.

Adella straightened. "What is it?" Trying to hide the sudden tension rising within her at his words, she absently stroked the white blaze of Shy's muzzle.

"Since I've taken on the Royal Westward Trading Company," he began, stepping in closer, "I've been looking over Martin's old business plans. You know how I've never really felt at home anywhere, except here in the Campos..." He held out his hands, fingers laced, to offer her a leg-up.

Adella gathered her skirts, which she lately wore over riding breeches for convenience, and placed her knee in his palms. He lifted her into the saddle. "Go on," she said, taking up the reins.

"And you being the person I should talk to about such things… though I've no idea how to…" He trailed off as he hoisted himself up onto Madigan's saddle. "You see," he said, apparently starting over while they rode, "Martin's old shop was on the eastern side of town before it was destroyed, and that's quite a ways from the Campos—and it will need to be completely rebuilt anyway, when the fighting is over—but the deed is for that particular location."

He stopped as though his point had been made, and Adella strained to understand what he was getting at. "Oh!" she said at last. "You want to rebuild the shop elsewhere?"

"Yes," Kol replied. "Here."

She turned to look him in the eyes. "Closer to Greywood?"

He nodded. "Yes." Kol kept his gaze lowered, not meeting hers. "Closer to Greywood."

Finally, she understood the meaning behind his words. *Nearer to me.* Adella was touched at the request, then the guilt hit again and she wondered if he'd regret it after he learned of her and Declan. "Of course," Adella replied with a shrug, trying to keep her tone casual. "That's no problem; we can look over the cadastral maps and find you a new parcel. I think there are some available just northwest of the manor house."

As she turned to continue onward, a tall, white flower brushed against her skirt amid the other wild shrubs and grasses, catching her eye. "Comfrey…" she muttered pensively as she recognized its large, broad leaves. The prairie plant didn't grow in Valenna proper, only in the Campos, but the people of Elldon had come to discover that it made a potent poultice for broken bones. Her thoughts turned to poor James, lying on the sofa. She jumped down from the saddle and, as she bent to pluck the herb from the soil, her forearm brushed another plant beside it. It pricked her skin, stinging the flesh deeply like the venom of a wasp.

"Oh!" she gasped, clapping her hand over the pain.

"What is it?" Kol asked.

"Nothing," she muttered, stuffing the comfrey into her haversack. "Just some nettles or some such..." She eyed the offending plant; it looked almost like a small elderberry shrub, though the leaves were distinct enough that she knew it was something new.

Kol eyed the foliage dubiously. "I've never seen that one before."

"No, I haven't either." Inspecting her forearm, she could find no mark. Adella shrugged to herself and climbed back into the saddle.

They rode the short distance to Elldon in silence, the sun shining warmly on the fields and their faces while the chill of the morning dissipated. As they drew nearer to what remained of the town after the attack that spring, Greywood rose up on its hill like a sentinel. It pained her to see the tall, majestic elms that once sheltered the manor house now in the process of being cut down, but there was nothing she could do. They needed the timber to build a palisade around the estate to protect the townspeople within, since Elldon didn't have enough people or horses to take them from further afield. The drastically altered view struck her with sorrow every time she saw it. Now, the open sky above Greywood's dark slate roof was a bitter reminder of all that she'd lost, and all that was still at stake. Her home would never look the same, but at least it was still standing.

They passed one end of the semicircle of rough-hewn timbers, with their tops carved to a point. The palisade was still in construction, and Adella could only hope it would be finished before the Sornians mounted another major attack. While they had just enough trees for the felling in and around the grounds; it was hands to build it that were growing scarce.

Adella and Kol entered the spacious parlor of Greywood Manor, which was empty save for James, who lay with his injured leg propped up on pillows. After his leg was badly broken in the recent mounted charge against the Sornian army, there was nowhere else for him to go; his own home had been destroyed, and he was in far too much pain to risk moving him again, and so he'd become a permanent fixture on the sofa, with everyone pitching in for his care. His familiar snoring filled the room while Adella approached the large map on the wall. Pinned to the top was the Queen's letter of commission to her, conferring onto her the authority to organize and lead a band of civilians into a militia group of rangers, which the people of Elldon had affectionately dubbed the Queen's Rangers. The overseeing of that group, along with Captain Holcomb's recently-hired cavalry troop, put more responsibility on her shoulders than she'd ever imagined when she'd agreed to take on her father's title. It was Valennian custom to pass titles through the line of inheritance; with her older sister Margo having declined already and their brother Lucas having defected to Sornia, Adella couldn't let their father's legacy dissipate like the morning dew.

"I hope Holcomb's brought good news, for once," she muttered to Kol beside her. The map, drawn by her own hand, depicted the Campos, the contested territory of wilderness and prairie that stretched between her homeland of Valenna and the neighboring country of Sornia to the west. *Kol's homeland.* It was strange to think that they'd begun as enemies from disparate sides of the map, yet the unpredictable and incredible circumstances of their lives had led them to stand together at its center.

With a deep breath, Adella steeled her nerves. "Kol," she began, turning to face him. "There's something I've been meaning to speak to you about—"

Boots rapped sharply across the floor as Holcomb approached, his riding crop still tucked under one arm. "M'Lady," he greeted her with a bow of his head.

Adella winced, still unaccustomed to her new title and his staunch formality, which seemed so out of place here at the frontier. Captain Holcomb, however, was from Pentz, and things were done differently there. "What is it, Captain?" she asked.

Holcomb's eyes shifted briefly up at Kol, who towered over them both. The cavalry captain was hardly taller than Adella.

"Mister Kol is in my confidence," Adella reminded him. "You can speak freely in front of him."

"Your rangers—The Queen's Rangers," Holcomb amended, "asked me to relay information to you from the field. Firstly, they wish you to know they have discovered fresh tracks of Sornian riders not far to the southwest, and advise you to keep a close watch from that direction. Secondly, they asked me to inform you that, rather than returning today as anticipated, they will follow the trail onward, in the hopes of finding Misses Asher."

"Hm," Adella muttered. "As tracks don't last long in the Campos, I suppose that was the logical choice," she conceded. "But it's a risk; they will be on their own. This was Jacoby you spoke with, I'm assuming?"

Holcomb's freckled brow furrowed. "Remind me?"

"Large but rather young," she replied. "Light brown hair, blue eyes, rosy complexion. Misses Asher's youngest son."

"That's the fellow," Holcomb attested. "Oh, by the way, there was a sailor looking for you out front. I directed him to wait in the dining room."

"Must be my cousin with the post," she guessed. "Thank you, Captain."

He nodded curtly. "You'll be joining us for games tonight, won't you?"

"Games?" Adella scrunched her brow.

"It's a tradition for our troop, started by Lord Endlebridge. Every Saturday night, games, music." He shrugged. "Nothing much, just a little pastime to keep our spirits up." He raised his eyebrows hopefully.

"Well, I..." she began hesitantly. The idea of enjoying such diversion while Misses Asher was still in enemy hands turned Adella's stomach, but she couldn't think of a gracious way out of it. There was nothing to be done until Jacoby returned with his news, at any rate. *I'll give him one more day, before I head out there myself...*

"Of course," Holcomb added, interrupting her thoughts, "you are welcome to bring the Sor—" His eyes darted toward Kol as he cleared his throat. "Soldier. And your rangers."

"We'll be there," Kol interjected.

"Excellent!" Holcomb replied. "See you both tonight." With a curt nod, he left.

"You surprise me," she said, turning to Kol.

"I think the cavaliers will appreciate their patron's presence," he replied. "I know I would've, but such things are unheard of in Sornia." There was sadness in his voice, as though the memories pained him.

"I hadn't thought of it like that," she said softly. Her stomach rumbled, reminding her that they had begun the day with only a bite of cold bread and water. "I bet you're hungry, too," she guessed. "Come, I'll make something. What would you like?"

He raised a brow. "To eat?"

"You think I can't cook?" she asked defensively.

"Well..." he trailed off, looking away.

"Go on," she prodded. "Pick something."

"Toasted bread, with butter and honey," Kol replied finally. "You take a slice of bread, and put it on a gridiron over coals until—"

"I know how to make toast," she laughed, feigning offense. While it was true that Adella had grown up with servantry, given the state of things, she no longer had that luxury now. Like everyone else, she'd been fending for herself in the kitchen lately. Even so, she was relieved to hear him ask for something so simple.

Adella brought the heavily-laden silver tray into the dining room, where Kol and the young sailor from *The Tigress*, Yul Childric, were already seated.

"It's good to see you again, cousin," Yul greeted her. He pushed back the large blue cuff of his jacket and rifled through his haversack. "Let's get this out of the way," he began, pulling letters out and setting them down on the table, "as I don't have much time. You've no idea how badly things have gotten in the watery parts of the world." Leaning over, he took a piece of toast and bit into it.

"What do you mean?" Kol asked.

"The water—" Yul mumbled through his food. "It never retreated seaward; it creeps further and further ashore with each rising tide." He paused to swallow. "Pentz is completely gone; you'll have to update your maps. Raymouth seems to be next, with the high tides coming up to the streets now. And though we no longer have reavers to worry about, the sea beasts have become far worse."

"Do you mean the sea serpents?" Adella asked. "The *pelkimund*," she remembered aloud to herself, using the Old Andolinian word for the strange creatures that had lately invaded Belgrand Bay. The sea had always been teeming with sharks, but the *pelkimund* were another matter entirely.

"Yes, right," he replied with a dismissive wave, pulling a stack of letters from his haversack. "Whatever you call them. They're a constant plague, snatching sailors from ships and fouling the waters with blood," he went on darkly. Adella shuddered at the thought. "Add to that, without the bounties won from fighting reavers, *The Tigress* is struggling to stay afloat—quite literally. The coffers are so light now, we can hardly afford to make repairs." He pushed the letters across the table toward her. "I still haven't been paid for our last voyage."

"I'm sorry to hear that," she replied, frowning. "That's awful."

"Yes, quite. Oh," Yul carried on enthusiastically, "My friend has finally spilled what he knows about the man who burned the ship belonging to the Belgrand Bay Company over the summer—*The Poesy*, I think it was named—who the locals have been calling the Wolf of Raymouth. Apparently, he's involved with the Royal Westward and has been seen now and then in town, lurking around the business district."

Adella darted a glance at Kol. "You don't say..." she muttered, a sinking feeling settling in her gut.

Shuffling through the letters, she paused at one addressed to a Kol Seaborn. The surname, she recalled, was also borne by the reaver ship

Declan had mentioned in the letter he'd finally delivered to her that summer after years had passed, in which he'd recounted the murder of his father. She wasn't sure if the two were related somehow, but the thought made her queasy. "Seaborn?" she asked, raising a brow at Kol, who only hid his face in a teacup.

Reluctantly, she turned back to Yul. "How is the Captain?" she asked.

"The Captain," he replied, taking another piece of toast, "asks that you visit him at the Ivy Crown soon, as we'll be docked in Raymouth for some time."

"Oh." Adella furrowed her brow. "Well, I can't leave Greywood, obviously. He knows that."

"To tell the truth," Yul went on, "we're all glad the two of you have made amends." He gave a crooked grin. "I heard you passed the night together. He told us of your betrothal some years ago; I hope to call my dear cousin 'Misses Declan' before long, so that I can be jealous and happy at the same time."

Adella's face burned. When she'd spent an intimate night with Rogero Declan as they sailed from Pentz to Raymouth, she'd hardly considered it would be fodder for the crew's scuttlebutt. "Is nothing private on a ship?" she managed to utter.

"Nothing," Yul affirmed chipperly. "Anyway, I'm afraid I must be off now." Holding out his open palm, he cleared his throat.

It took Adella a moment to understand. "Oh, right..." She fished around in her skirt pocket for some copper coins and set them in his waiting hand.

"Thanks," he said, gratitude evident in his smile. "I'll see you again soon, I'm sure." With that, he gathered up his things and, taking a final piece of toast with him, left.

Silence filled the room. Glancing up at Kol, Adella caught a sour look on his face.

"Declan?" he asked at length, arms crossed tightly. "Really?"

Adella's face warmed again. "I had meant to tell you—but never mind that. When were you going to tell me *you're* the criminal wanted for the destruction of *The Poesy*?" she demanded.

"I tried to," he countered. "It was an accident—"

"And now you're going by 'Seaborn?'" she interrupted. "You just met this man, and you're already using his name? Are you sure that's wise?"

"You don't know what it's been like for me, Adella," Kol replied sullenly, looking away. "You've always known who you are."

"I just don't want you to get mixed up in a stranger's affairs," she said, tone softening.

"And just when were you going to tell me about you and Declan?" he shot back. "He doesn't care for you the way you think he does." His teacup clanked on its saucer as he rose suddenly, bumping the table. "He left you for dead on *The Accord,* remember?"

"He did what he had to," she snapped, anger rising at the accusation. "You said it yourself, 'Some things are more important than just one person.'"

"Depends on the person," he replied, snatching up the last piece of toast. "And who you're asking." He spun on his heel and headed toward the door, throwing a dark glance over his shoulder. "You're just another victory to him."

His cutting remark struck her so deeply, her heart stuttered. After all they'd been through, she hated to think that Kol would think badly of her. He'd been the one to save her when Declan hadn't, jumping into the stormy sea when she'd been swept off the foundering ship despite his deep-seated fear of the water. And yet, he was wrong about Declan; of course he loved her. He'd told her so himself. The year that he had disappeared after asking her to marry him, and she'd been so angry at him, thinking the worst—it had all been a misunderstanding. Adella opened her mouth to reply, but Kol was already gone. "Damn..." she muttered, burying her face in her palms. *He took that badly. I should've told him myself before now.*

Shaking off her guilt, she let out a loud sigh. It was a relief to be alone for a moment. Propping her feet up on the table, she allowed her thoughts to roam. "An entire city, completely gone?" she murmured at length, scratching absently at a tingling sensation on her forearm. "Underwater? It doesn't make sense..."

Reaching into her skirt pocket, Adella pulled out a small, pearl-handled pen knife and paused. *To think it was only a few months ago...* Lucas had given her the knife as a gift the night he disappeared. *The night Elldon was attacked.* It felt like ages since then, the moment her life had changed forever. *The only reason I'm here now as Lady Grimless is because he left.* The family always assumed Lucas would be the one to take on their father's title. As he was the only son, it was rightfully his according to tradition. Though the laws had changed, allowing for women to inherit estates, their older sister had never wanted to contest for it. Margavita had made it clear she had enough responsibilities in the Capital, as the wife of a high-ranking lord with his own estate and political affairs to oversee. Adella had always assumed she'd follow the same path. But with their parents gone and Lucas having defected to Sornia, it was up to Adella to take up her father's duties and carry on his work. *To make him proud...* Someone had to continue his legacy; only she was left.

Adella stared at the little blade, remembering her brother, his heinous treason, and all the lives lost because of his actions, and her stomach turned. *Wherever you are, Lucas, I hope you get what you deserve.* She slid the blade beneath the seal of one of the letters and sliced it open. Unfolding the paper within, she read:

Miss Adella,

Still working on my mission. I won't let you down. Cannot find the Queen. Don't you worry, I've written to Miss Margo; she'll know what to do. Will write again when I have more news. Be safe!

~ Ben Armand

Adella chewed her lip. *Can't find the Queen? What could he mean by that?* Perhaps Queen Ellinora was too busy with her official duties. After all, the country was still recovering from the recent plague, the passing of King Harrian, and now faced a burgeoning war with Sornia. She had asked Armand to investigate the ancient lockbox they had recovered from the Sornian vessel, *The Accord,* out of a growing sense that the ancient legends of Andolin might be more than myth. But she had also wanted to send the old man far from the battlefield. Armand had been Lord Grimless's lifelong friend after being assigned as his valet in the cavalry, and he'd served as their butler for their household for many years. It was her duty to ensure he lived to enjoy his retirement. Whatever he was up to in the Capital, he would be safer there than at Elldon.

* * *

In the parlor, Kol leaned forward in the chair and pushed a stray black curl from his face. Lately, he'd been wearing his hair tied back in a Valennian queue, but it still wasn't quite long enough to remain in place and out of his eyes. "So there I was," he went on enthusiastically, "surrounded by swamp rebels, alone and armed with only my knife—"

"You already told this one," James sighed. He lay with his broken leg propped up on the back of the sofa, his accustomed position wearing a dent in its crimson brocade. His brown hair lay untied and strewn across the plush sofa arm.

"No, it happened twice," Kol replied. "Just listen."

Closing his eyes wearily, James rubbed his forehead. "Do I have a choice?"

"Right," Kol continued undeterred. "So, there I was—"

"Wait," James interrupted, putting a hand in the air. "Nature calls; help me up."

"Uh..." Kol slowly rose to his feet. "I'll go get someone—"

"No, I can't wait." James winced, his eyes crinkling. "It's urgent."

Kol shook his head. "I really don't—"

"Listen," James ordered. "I've been a captive audience to your war stories for the past hour and a half; you owe me your assistance. Now, give me a hand."

Kol looked around for someone to beg help from, but, seeing that the room was otherwise empty and no footsteps could be heard from the adjoining hallways, he let out a breath in resignation. "Fine. Let's get you to the privy."

"Privy?" James blinked at him in disbelief. "I have a broken leg, for goodness' sake! There's a chamber pot beneath the sofa."

Kol groaned but felt too sorry for the poor fellow not to help. After he had steadied James by the arm and his business was done, Kol helped him back onto the sofa.

"I think I know the real reason why you're here," James began.

"That wasn't it, I can assure you," Kol retorted.

James rolled his eyes upward. "I'm referring to the fact that you seem to be avoiding Miss Adella. Or she, you?"

"That's not the case," Kol said quickly, straightening the sleeve of his jacket. "Contrary to what you may think, I don't need to be at her side every moment."

"What's it about?" James prodded.

Kol frowned. "Did you know about her and Declan?"

"Ha!" James said triumphantly. "So I was right; it *is* about Adella. No, I hadn't, though I've heard the name more than once. A sea captain, isn't he?"

Kol nodded. "A privateer, they say. Though I think he's nothing more than a reaver."

"And you're jealous," James said flatly.

"No," Kol replied defensively. "I just don't like the man. I think he's a scoundrel in a fancy coat."

"Privateering is dangerous work," James said with a shrug. "Maybe he'll die."

Kol laughed loudly. "I like the way you think. We could be friends."

"No, not friends," James assured him with a good-natured smirk. "I just can't escape."

At that moment, Adella entered, and Kol rose so suddenly at the sight of her that he nearly tripped on the leg of his chair. "Adella," he murmured as she approached.

"How's your leg, James?" Adella asked, ignoring Kol.

"Forget the leg," James replied. "I'm losing my mind, stuck on this sofa."

"I'm sorry." Adella shrugged helplessly. "You'll have to bear it a little while longer. I can bring you some new books?" she offered.

"Good heavens, no more books." He waved toward the large stack of cloth-bound hardcovers on the little table beside him. "Thank you; you've brought me plenty already."

Smiling politely, Adella nodded. She turned and caught Kol's eye. Her smile fell, but she said nothing. Kol watched helplessly as she strode across the room and disappeared down the hallway.

"It's more serious than I thought," James remarked.

Kol groaned, rubbing his face.

"Oh, cheer up," James replied. "It doesn't really matter, does it? It's not like you had a chance with her anyway."

"That's not helping," Kol growled, making to leave.

James grabbed the tail of Kol's jacket. "Listen," he began, "whatever your personal feelings, please don't let it get in the way of helping save my mother from the Sornians." His grip tightened, pulling on the fabric. "You were one of them; you know their ways. Please," he pleaded. "Do for her what I cannot."

2

Omens

Matei gasped, eyes opening wide. A tickling sensation made its way down his lip.

"Are you sure you want to do this again?" Lucas asked. "Clearly, it takes a toll."

Matei pressed the rag to his nose, soaking up the crimson blood that trickled from one nostril. "I want to keep going," he said, setting the cloth on the floor beside him. "I'm almost there."

Again, he closed his eyes, feeling the cool facets of the crystal against his palm. *The Corelimun. The Heart of the World.* He focused on the words like a prayer. He knew the power was there within the stone, and his for the taking; he just had to tap into it. He'd easily learned to embody and control animals; animating human forms was the next step. *Lucas.* In an attempt to connect their minds, Matei envisioned his friend's face, recalling the time they'd met. A thrumming pounded his brain and sounds and voices began to swirl. From the mist, Lucas's voice emerged and grew clearer. *A memory...* As the sensations gained vibrancy, Matei could hear Adella's muffled voice reply indistinctly. *Focus, Matei!* He held out a hand, trembling as he tried to force the movement into Lucas's flesh and bone, mere feet away from him. *Flesh and bone...* The connection snapped together, and Lucas's hand was suddenly his to control. Matei lifted the arm, so much stranger and lighter than his own, into the air. *I've got it!*

Frantic images flooded his mind—Lucas riding a red and white horse, sneaking away from Greywood in the dead of night, hiding from Adella in the busy port at Raymouth. As the emotions mounted, he felt his power over Lucas's body begin to ebb. *No...* Pushing the thoughts away, Matei poured his entire energy into Lucas's arm, feeling the tendons twist as he turned the wrist, the muscles contract as he lifted the hand.

'*You stayed a while in town,*' Adella's voice echoed as Lucas's memories surged over him again. '*Where did you go...*' The scent of lavender and the clinking of porcelain overwhelmed his senses. Matei groaned, straining to push Lucas's mind aside and maintain his connection with the body, but his muscles shook with the strain until he could no longer sustain the effort. The floor beneath him snapped and shuddered, the stone walls around them grating and rumbling.

Matei released his hold, collapsing onto the carpet, and the tremors died away. A sharp pain stabbed his eye; the trickle that ran from his nose now spewed like a fountain.

"What was that?" Lucas asked, looking around the dark room with widened eyes.

"You felt it, too?" Matei winced, rubbing his throbbing temples.

"Of course. Are you alright?" Lucas pressed the rag to Matei's face. "Good heavens, your eye!" He recoiled, a look of horror on his face. "It's completely bloodshot."

"I did it," Matei muttered, brushing Lucas's hand away. "I moved your arm!"

"Yes," Lucas conceded. "A little."

Matei sat up, pinching his nostrils together beneath the cloth. He had succeeded, but the effort required even to do that much had been enormous. Still, it had been the first time he'd used his own will to control another person. "It's so much easier with animals," he grumbled, voice muffled through the cloth. "The human mind is so strong..." He pulled the rag away to see it was soaked through with bright red blood, staining his fingers. "It's the mind that gets in the way."

"You're going to kill yourself," Lucas pleaded. "Take a rest; you haven't been getting much sleep."

"Sleep?" The word struck Matei with an idea. While controlling another person's waking mind was proving difficult, perhaps it would be easier to do when they slept and their defenses were lowered. He pointed a finger at Lucas emphatically. "Why didn't I think of that?"

"Whatever you're thinking," Lucas replied, putting his palms in the air, "that's not what I meant..."

Matei looked across the solar room toward the open balcony. Dark clouds cast an inky pall over the ports of Hedda, with the roar of the sea its constant song. He had let the weights of the tall-case clock spend their chains entirely as the pendulum came to a rest, ending its regular, distracting chiming. He could only guess that it was still morning; it hadn't seemed that long since sunrise. "Teressa is still asleep, I take it?" Matei asked, not meeting his eyes.

"I'm sure she is, but—" Lucas's brow furrowed. "Matei, up until now, you've been working on willing participants..."

"If she's asleep, she can't object," Matei replied. "She won't even know it, I promise. I need to figure this out. Lucas—" Matei grabbed him by the shoulder, looking him hard in the eye. "This is for the glory of Andolin! Don't you want to be a part of it?"

"I do," Lucas said quickly. "Of course I do."

"We'll explain when she wakes," Matei reasoned. "She won't mind."

Lucas winced. "I suppose..."

"Great!" Matei rose, and his head spun wildly. He grabbed Lucas's elbow for support. "Take me to her."

Sitting in complete darkness, Matei squeezed his eyes shut, his grip tightening around the crystal as he grappled with his senses to find Teressa's mind. Hers was much quieter than Lucas's, whose thoughts were loud and colorful, flashing quickly and impossible to grasp. Teressa's, so far as he could see, were muted, soft, and malleable. He reached out a hand toward the bed where she slept, pushing through the stone's thrum that filled the ether around them. *I think I've found her...*

The crystal grew warm against his other palm; even through closed eyelids, he could sense the glow emanating from it. In his mind, he saw her seated beneath an apple tree, pink petals falling softly upon her shoulders. In the half-world of dreaming where he found her, he stepped closer.

"Matei!" she uttered in surprise, her voice hollow and faint, as though from a distance. She rose at his approach, brushing petals from her apron. *"What are you doing here? I was waiting for Lucas..."*

He reached toward her, but she drew back. *"Don't worry,"* Matei replied, his voice echoing strangely. *"He's here, too."*

"Is this real?" she asked, a sudden clarity brightening her eyes.

"Yes." He smiled at her recognition of what was happening. *"I think I'm onto something big here."*

Back in the waking world, Teressa stirred. Matei slammed back into his own body, reeling backward as the glow of the crystal in his hand suddenly darkened and he found himself swarmed with her overwhelming thoughts, drowning out all other sensations. Desperately, he strained to pull away from her consciousness, caught between the push and pull of sensation and memory until finally, with one last, exhausting effort, he drew his mind back from the discordant images and broke the connection, returning to the respite of his own mind.

"Lucas?" Teressa called breathlessly, the bed creaking as she moved.

"I'm here," Lucas replied. "It's all right."

"And Matei?" she guessed.

"Yes," Matei answered.

"For heaven's sake!" she snapped. "You could've warned me!"

At the fireplace, Lucas raked old coals back to life, bathing the room in a warm glow.

"If you had expected it," Matei replied flatly, "it might not've worked."

"So it was successful?" Lucas asked.

"Not entirely," Matei admitted, "though it was much easier to connect to her sleeping mind than yours since it was disconnected from her body." What he'd discovered so far was interesting and would certainly prove useful, it wasn't quite what he was searching for. He wanted to force his will upon another's person; to inhabit another's physical form completely. *What I need is a body without a mind...* He blotted the blood from his nose with his sleeve, and an idea came to him.

Lucas stoked the hearth and the small bedchamber grew brighter, bringing their features to light. Teressa turned her attention toward Matei in the corner, and let out a gasp. "Your—" She put a hand over her mouth, eyes widening. "Your face!"

* * *

Adella ran from her tent as its poles rocked precariously around her. Outside, the encampment was in chaos; the land beneath her feet shook, its deep rumblings carrying through the soil and up into her legs, into her very bones. Though the tremors had become more frequent, this one seemed different. There was something ominous about its sudden intensity. The clouds that had gathered low overhead had a strange, greenish cast to them, the color of an impending storm.

Near Greywood, a crowd of people gathered beneath the darkening sky, their dim silhouettes congregating around the manor's stone well that sat north of the stables. *That's strange.* The well had gone dry over the summer; she wondered what the interest could be. As the manor was always their regrouping location after major events, Adella figured they simply didn't want to risk the tall fieldstone building coming down upon their heads, and had decided to meet at the well instead.

As she strode quickly across the property, the quaking slowly abated. "What is it?" she asked, approaching Rosalind. Her gaze roved from face to face, each fixed on the well with a look of fear or open-mouthed confusion. They stared at the water, fetid and brackish with the smell of fish. Burbling over the stone lip, bringing up ferny strands of brown seaweed, it pooled on the ground, wetting their shoes. A shiny, silver-bodied fish slipped over the smooth stones and flopped helplessly, shimmering in the grass at her feet.

They looked at each other, wide-eyed and speechless, as a nauseating sinking feeling hit Adella in the gut. *The sea, surging up from the well...* She shook her head in disbelief. *That's... impossible.* Suddenly, the water dropped, disappearing back down into the depths with a loud, gurgling suction. She leaned over the void to get a better look.

A cold spray smacked her hard in the face, pushing her breath back into her lungs as water burst again from the depths, this time with such force it made a veritable fountain over their heads, splattering down in a sheet and drenching them thoroughly.

Coughing up brine, salt stinging the back of her nose, Adella looked around at the others, each too stunned to speak.

Finally, Rosalind broke the silence as she pulled a frond of seaweed from her sleeve. "There's something unnatural at work here," she said darkly.

It was cool inside Greywood Manor now that autumn was setting in; the chill of night lingered in the stone walls, no longer dissipated by the warmth of the day. In her bedchamber, Adella stepped around some wooden crates filled with dry goods and opened the old oak wardrobe adorned with carved vines and flower baskets that her family had brought with them from the Capital. She tried to avoid coming upstairs where she felt her family's absence most keenly. The rooms were now filled with painful memories in addition to the dry goods. Her room, like every other in the manor, was now mainly used for storage, but she was running out of clean clothes in her campaign tent. Grief, anger, loneliness, and shame met her here in the dusty spaces, echoing loudly in the halls and in her heart.

"The Campos, the sea," she muttered to herself as she pulled a linen shift, pink floral gown with a split-front skirt, and a white petticoat from her carved-oak wardrobe. "Elldon, the tremors..." Her thoughts flitted from place to place over the map in her mind's eye. Rosalind was right; it was unnatural, and Adella was sure it all had to be connected. *But how?* Of course, there were the sea caves along the coast that tunneled deep beneath the Campos. That had been a recent discovery. *But how far could they go? Could the sea lie beneath our very feet, here at Elldon?* She changed quickly, draping her damp clothing over a tower of tea crates, and turned to leave.

Across the hall, something seemed to call to her from the open doorway of her father's study. It was the only room that she hadn't allowed to be used for storage, remaining mostly the way her father had left it. *Mostly... except for one thing.*

Entering the study, Adella padded softly across the wood floor, her gaze passing over the dusty blue shelves filled with old, leather-bound books. Past her father's desk, which now contained her own work papers within its drawers, a large tome sat high on an empty shelf. It seemed to beckon from its perch. *The Codex.* The ancient text, written in the forgotten Old Andolinian language—the precursor to the Modern Andolinian common tongue of both Valenna and Sornia—had mysteriously survived through the ages, with Modern translations added to it here and there over time. When her concerns with the Sornian army in the Campos had taken priority, she had safely stored it here, putting it and her translation work out of mind. Seeing it now, something tugged at her from within the pages. "Oh, all right," she muttered, retrieving it from the shelf. While balancing the Codex on her hip, she pulled her work papers from the writing desk and tucked them safely inside the cover.

Lugging the heavy book, Adella returned across the storm-darkened field, now filled with people rebuilding their tents, to her pavilion. As she stepped beneath the canopy, the aged, dust-slick leather tome slipped and fell to the ground at her feet. Its pages fluttered briefly in the rising wind. Splayed open, an illustration spread across the pages, its pigment faded with age but the drawing was still crisp and clear. A crystal, double-pointed and glowing with golden rays radiating from it in gilded lines, floated above a battlefield; below, men and horses waged war, their blood spilled out in vermilion ink. Looming over the scene were towers of indigo, bending inward over the fray, threatening to drown them in water. From those blue pillars, wreathed in white foam and seaspray, rose the spiny, black figure of a massive creature, its size unlike any she had seen before. Its vast, arching coils spread over the scene, dwarfing the castles and trees below.

Crouching, Adella ran her fingers over the pages. Her mind buzzed with an intense, fraught foreboding, like the sensation of being watched in the night, or danger approaching in tall grass. While she stared at it, the dark creature seemed to grow, eclipsing her thoughts; the jagged teeth of its gaping maw grew larger and larger, as if to swallow her whole.

"Lady Grimless," came a voice behind her, startling Adella so hard that she screamed. Shutting the book quickly, she turned to see Captain Holcomb standing behind her.

"I didn't mean to frighten you," he began sheepishly, "but I wanted to remind you about tonight. We're all looking forward to seeing you there."

"Yes, of course," she replied, quickly closing the Codex and scooping it from the ground. "I'll be there; thank you."

3

Pickled Eggs and Switchel

Outside the manor house, Kol trudged through the grass, scattered with the gold and brown of fallen leaves, past the stables and toward the swath of tents where Holcomb's troops, as well as many of Elldon's newly formed rangers, now camped. His own small tent, from Martin's supplies, had been recently erected. Staked on the western edge, it was removed a bit from the others, but not far from Adella's open-air campaign tent. It had seemed a logical place since he'd initially been hired as her guard. However, his duties as the new owner of the Royal Westward Trading Company were taking up increasingly more of his time, especially when he had to go to Raymouth's port. *She doesn't need me here as a guard,* he noted. *Not now that the place is crawling with cavaliers.* As he passed her pavilion, he could see her moving within. The sight of her after their disagreement stung him with regret.

Inside his tent, Kol removed his cutlass scabbard, set it on the washstand, and flopped down onto the cot. Of all the places he'd lived, Elldon was the first to truly feel like home. Adella meant everything to him; she had been the first to show him kindness, she'd vouched for his character and the Queen had made him a Valennian citizen, and she had made him feel welcome when the others only saw him as the enemy. *I should have told her sooner...* He wondered if being honest about his feelings for her from the beginning would've made a difference. *Would she still have chosen Declan?*

His thoughts returned to their sparring earlier that morning. He cared for her safety, yet he had no say about the choices she made, so he'd wanted to teach Adella to be able to protect herself. To show her how to escape if an enemy soldier caught her was the best he could do when he couldn't be there. But he couldn't ignore how his heart raced when he'd taken her in his arms. *Did she feel that way, too?* The catch in her breath, the arch of her back, the way her hand lingered on his—he couldn't help but wonder what it meant. Perhaps she was confused about what he was asking or had hesitated due to a lack of confidence. *Or perhaps...* Perhaps she was fighting her feelings like he was. The thought brought heat to his face. For a moment, he imagined how things might've gone if they hadn't been interrupted, his hands remembering the softness of her body, and his heart ached.

He pushed the thought away. *Doesn't matter, now.* The harsh words he'd said to her gnawed at his conscience. *I should've kept my mouth shut about Declan.* His stomach knotted. *After all, her personal affairs are none of my business.* That emotional outburst had cost him the only person he truly cared about. Groaning, Kol rubbed his face with his palms. *How could I be so reckless?*

Beside him sat the antique copy of *Blood Island* that Adella had lent him. The book, with its faded cloth cover and gilded lettering, seemed to beckon him, the fantastical story inside promising distraction from the pain in his heart. The last time he read it, he'd left the character Jonny Reddin-Black caught in the middle of a war between the family of tigers that raised him and a group of shipwreck survivors recently stranded on his desert isle home. By comparison, his own problems seemed smaller, and Kol opened the book eagerly, hoping to lose himself in the pages.

As he came to the end of the book, marked with a promise for future installments, a violent rumbling drew him back to the present. His tent shook around, threatening to come down on his head. Grabbing his cutlass, he threw back the canvas flap and stumbled out over the quivering ground. The sky had turned a lurid green, casting the landscape in a sickly tinge. The ring of tents surrounding the encampment shuddered, several collapsing in a heap of canvas as people rushed from them with shouts of surprise. In the distance, the few trees remaining shook their leaves, and in the surrounding paddocks, the horses ran to and fro, tossing their heads and bucking.

The quaking slowly died away as Kol crossed the field toward Greywood, making sure that no harm had been done to the fieldstone manor and its outbuildings. Unexpectedly, Kerchaw made his way toward him over the grounds. Kerchaw had become his agent at the Royal Westward Trading Company after the murder of Henry Martin, Kol's friend and the Company's previous owner.

"Kerchaw?" Kol asked, brows knitting, and wondered if he'd forgotten something important.

"Sir," Kerchaw greeted him, pulling off his black wool hat. His small, dark eyes darted around at the chaos. Behind him, a loose horse galloped briskly by, followed by several panting cavaliers trying to catch the rope dragging from the animal's leather halter. "What the hell is going on here?"

"Just tremors," Kol replied casually. "Did we have plans to meet?"

"No, I came straight away." Kerchaw set the hat back over his receding hairline. "I need you to come with me urgently. We've been offered a rare deal on a ship for the Company—its owner has come into hard times and needs to sell quickly. A top-class ship," he added, smacking his lips with relish. "Just needs some work. But he wishes to speak with the Company's owner immediately, or we risk losing our chance."

Kol searched the grounds for Adella. She was by the manor's well with a few others engrossed in its depths. He likely wouldn't be missed; Adella was the only one who seemed to care for his presence anyway, and they currently weren't on speaking terms. Raymouth was only a short ride away; he could be back by evening. "I'll get my horse ready."

"No need," Kerchaw replied. "The carriage is waiting."

Kol followed Kerchaw, who had shown himself onto the property, likely wandering back to the encampment when his knock at the door went unanswered. They went past the side of the manor house and came to the gravel path that approached Greywood's entrance, where a coach, freshly lacquered in a dark oxblood and bearing the crest of the Royal Westward Trading Company, waited with a team of sturdy greys.

"We have a coach now?" Kol asked, voice brightening.

"I purchased it some weeks ago," Kerchaw explained tentatively, "and had it refinished. You gave permission for it; don't you remember?"

"Right." Somewhere within Kol's mind, the vague memory tried to surface. It wasn't that he was careless, but the attacks against Elldon took up the greater portion of his thoughts, especially since he relied on Kerchaw to handle most of the Royal Westward's business.

Kerchaw opened the door and they climbed in, Kol adjusting his scabbard to sit comfortably. Kerchaw quickly signaled to the driver, and the carriage lurched forward. Soon, the team broke into a trot and they passed briskly through the stockade gate with its posted cavalry guards, down the path toward Raymouth. They rolled through the remains of the town, down lanes of ruined houses destroyed by the Sornians earlier that year. Piles of rubble stood like grave markers for the lives lost, and shame burned in Kol's heart, as it did each time he came upon the sight. His leadership had brought the soldiers there that stormy spring night. *And yet...* He didn't regret where his actions had taken him. He couldn't. Guilt panged him at the thought, but given the chance to relive his life up until that point—up until the attack—he'd have done everything the same. *After all, it brought me here.* Before defecting to Valenna, he'd never imagined he would be anything more than a soldier, anything more than Blackburn's lackey. Now he owned the greatest mercantile on the Bay, though he'd be more proud if it wasn't because of Martin's death. The sight of his friend's open throat, blood spilling down his white shirt, still plagued him, resurfacing during quiet moments to unsettle his mind. He blinked the thought away.

At Raymouth Bridge, several scarlet-clad cavaliers stood sentry, brass saber hilts gleaming at their sides. The River Ray divided Elldon from the rest of the country. It was so wide, its banks so steep, that the only way across was the massive timber bridge just north of town. Kol was glad to see it guarded. It was the only way to get supplies to Elldon and a major strategic vulnerability in their defense of Valenna's western frontier.

They rolled past the guards and over the weathered planks with the roiling, roaring river below. Kol wondered how long the bridge would last. The water was much higher and more turbulent than last he'd seen it; its deep blue frothed angrily with white as it buffeted the wooden trusses. The passage across was precarious, with no rails to keep travelers from falling to the depths. Kol shuddered as he watched the thundering river rush beneath, imagining what it would be like to be swept away. He let out a breath when the carriage wheels finally touched soil again.

They approached the bustling port city of Raymouth, and found the streets flooded, the cobblestones submerged under a layer of ankle-deep water that splashed beneath the wheels. "What's going on?" Kol asked, glancing at Kerchaw.

Kerchaw shrugged. "The water has been rising the past few days."

Kol lowered his brow. "The tide?"

"I suppose." They traveled further into the city where the water rose higher, sloshing against the sides of the townhouses and up over the low steps to the doors, creeping over the thresholds. "Probably made worse by the storms and tremors," Kerchaw said. Though his tone was light, his brow furrowed. "Should recede soon."

"Hm." Though he'd lived in the Sornian seaport of Hedda for much of his life, Kol had never seen high-water tides encroach on streets like this before. He rubbed the stubble on his jaw. *Then again, things have been strange lately.* And he was new to Valenna. At any rate, Kerchaw apparently thought it was safe enough, at least for the time being.

Rolling through the murky, debris-littered water, their carriage came to the part of the city that Kol had lately become familiar with. He spotted the high slate roof and distinctive clay chimneys of the Ivy Crown Inn rising above the other buildings. They weren't far from his townhouse, bequeathed to him by Martin after becoming his apprentice. He wondered if it had the sea at its doorstep.

The rising water didn't deter the city's residents. They passed quite a few people going about their daily tasks undaunted, simply trudging through the filthy water as they visited the bakeries with baskets in-arm and towed wagons of goods in the direction of the ports. Kol tried to imagine how much higher the water must be at the docks, where the ground lowered toward the sea. He didn't have to wonder very long, however. When the coach emerged into the market square leading to the front entrance of the inn, the lead-grey water of Belgrand Bay came into view to the west, churning dully in the distance. The wooden docks that once crowded the harbor were now lost to sight beneath the waves. Beyond, a forest of masts with sails furled rose up from the many ships that lay at anchor offshore, with the small boats shuttling back and forth between them and the city their only means of contact.

They stopped at the entrance of the Ivy Crown. Kerchaw opened the coach door and waited. Stepping down into the flooded street, Kol wished he hadn't neglected waxing his tall riding boots. Already, the cold water seeped into his stockings, chilling his toes.

By the time they waded to the front steps, Kol's feet and lower legs were thoroughly soaked. "We're meeting the seller here?" he asked dubiously.

"Mhm," Kerchaw grunted. "The captain is also the owner; he lets a room here for when he's ashore doing business. We're to meet him upstairs."

Kol followed him inside. The inn's interior was dim, lit only by the sunlight from the dingy windows. On the far side, pooling water crept onto the brick hearth, and the door to the kitchen wafted open with the flow. The place seemed abandoned.

"Are you sure—" Kol began. The ceiling beam above their heads let out a loud crack, and a cloud of dust and bits of plaster sprinkled down on their shoulders. He cast an uneasy look at Kerchaw.

"Just the building settling," Kerchaw remarked, and trudged up the dark staircase. Reluctantly, Kol followed. At the top, their creaking footsteps sounded down the long, dark hallway and the water from their boots pooled onto the floorboards.

Kerchaw stopped before a door and, removing his cocked wool hat, rapped sharply. Kol swallowed, his throat dry with anticipation. Finally, a muffled voice answered, "Come in."

Inside, a broad figure standing before a writing desk turned to greet them, silhouetted against the light from the casement window. As they approached and Kol's eyes adjusted to the brightness, his stomach dropped. The man before them, with blond hair tied back in a disheveled queue and his sea-blue coat trimmed in cream jacquard, was Captain Declan.

Kol's brow furrowed. "There must be some mistake—"

"Are you the owner of the Royal Westward?" Declan demanded with equal surprise. "*You?*" He pointed a finger. "A Sornian?"

"Yes," Kol replied curtly. The last thing he wanted was to explain himself to this man.

Declan turned to Kerchaw. "What is this? Are you serious?"

"Do you—" Kerchaw stammered. "Do you two know each other?"

"We've met," Kol snapped.

"We're here to do business," Kerchaw replied coolly, turning to Declan. "If you've changed your mind—"

"Let's go," Kol interrupted, not waiting to be insulted further. Turning on his heel, he dragged Kerchaw by the elbow toward the door.

"Wait!" Declan blurted out, voice sharp with desperation. Clearing his throat, he smoothed the wrinkles from his jacket. "Wait," he repeated, composing himself. "Please, sit." He motioned toward a pair of small medallion-back chairs along the wall.

"Just hear him out," Kerchaw whispered to Kol, raising his eyebrows encouragingly.

Taking a long breath, Kol reluctantly took a seat. Like the chairs, the furniture in the small chamber had once been very fine but were now dust covered and a bit battered. A humble four-post bed occupied one corner, its blankets sun-faded but primly folded, as though it didn't get much use.

Declan leaned against his writing desk, palms gripping the edge. "Look," he began pointedly, drumming his fingers on the dark mahogany. "I'll be frank with you; I'm in a tight spot. After the King's passing, my commission expired, and the Queen has yet to renew it. Even if there were any takings to be had at sea right now, I'd be out of luck. As much as I hate the idea, I need to find a patron for *The Tigress* in order to pay my debts."

"Eh..." Kol opened his mouth to speak, but wavered.

"You need a ship, don't you?" Declan asked matter-of-factly. "I need a lot of gold quickly. You won't find a better deal on one than this, especially now—" He paused as the boards beneath their feet groaned and a brass pencil rolled off the desk behind him, migrating across the floor. "It makes good business sense."

"How much?" Kol asked, crossing his arms.

"Sixty-five," Declan replied.

"Sixty-five thousand gold cobs," Kerchaw muttered, leaning toward Kol.

"Right." By now, Kol was well familiar with Valennian money. As they were once colonies of the same empire, they used a similar system in Sornia. *Sixty-five thousand gold pieces...* There was a time when that much money seemed impossible for him. Even now, it was a lot. "And what are your terms?" he asked flatly.

"I would remain captain, of course," Declan replied. "With the appropriate wages. And I must have the right to buy her back when I have the funds again."

Kol shook his head. "I don't—"

Kerchaw widened his eyes meaningfully at Kol, and the word *if* could nearly be read on his face.

"One moment," Kol said to Declan, standing abruptly, and pulled Kerchaw into the hall. He tried to close the door behind him, but it no longer fit into the door jamb. Peeking through the crack, he could see Declan hurriedly stuffing things from his desk into the ditty bag. "Are you out of your mind?" Kol whispered.

Kerchaw raised his brows emphatically. "It's a hell of a good deal."

"Why would we agree to let him buy it back?" Kol countered, arms flailing with exasperation.

"We can negotiate that part," Kerchaw reasoned. "He's desperate; we can ask a higher price, plus repairs and interest. If he does buy it back, we'll make a profit."

"Why is he so anxious to sell?" Kol asked, lowering his brow. "Seems suspicious."

"I had the ship inspected," Kerchaw replied. "It's seaworthy, but needs repair. The captain can't afford it."

"So he wants us to fix it for him," Kol commented.

"But *we* can afford it," Kerchaw reasoned. "We'll just take it out of the buy-back price."

Kol frowned. "And he wants to be captain."

"So?" Kerchaw shrugged. "We'll need to hire a captain anyway. And a crew."

Kol chewed his thumbnail. Though he didn't care for the man, he knew Declan to be highly capable, as well as his crew. He hated to admit it, but it *was* starting to make sense. "No..."

Kerchaw shrugged. "Why not?"

"I—" Kol began. "I don't like him."

"You don't have to like him," Kerchaw whispered, leaning in. "He's right; you won't find another deal like this. We'll be making out like bandits whether he buys it back or not."

Kol took a deep breath. "I don't know—"

"Let's at least see what we can negotiate," Kerchaw reasoned. "If you don't like what you hear, we'll walk away."

Kol groaned. "Fine."

"The buy back," Kerchaw said loudly as they entered again. "Let's say, purchase price plus twenty percent? With a three-month limit."

"Ten," Declan countered, tying the ditty bag closed. "And six months."

Kol looked Declan up and down, glancing at the hair that hung loose from his queue and the salt stains on his sleeves, and narrowed his eyes. His thoughts turned to Adella and what the sailor Childric had said about the two. Unbidden, the image of her and Declan together, bodies pressed against each other, flooded his mind, and his stomach turned. He shook his head to clear it away. "Forget it," he replied, making to leave.

"Please," Declan pleaded, reaching out toward him, his thick brows drawn upward. "Help me save *The Tigress*."

Kol wavered. Somewhere in the back of his mind, the idea of taking Declan's ship from him—his prized possession, the thing he loved above all else—gave him a sense of dark satisfaction. *No...* Kol swallowed, burying the feeling deep inside. *If I bought* The Tigress, *I'd be doing him a favor.* Though he hated the idea of helping the man, Declan clearly meant something to Adella. She would appreciate it if Kol assisted him in his time of need. *The Royal Westward needs a ship regardless, and I'm already familiar with this one. Perhaps it does make good business sense...* The smug satisfaction of taking Declan's beloved ship for himself resurfaced. Somehow, the act felt like revenge. He remembered the young sailor who'd come on Declan's behalf to warn Kol to stay away from Adella; the arrogance of the captain in sending his lackey to give him orders rankled his pride even now. It would feel good to take the man's ship.

"Fifteen," Kol replied. "And four months."

Declan grinned. "Twelve and five months."

Kerchaw leaned in to whisper into Kol's ear. "We could talk him down on the purchase price as well—"

Ignoring him, Kol rose and offered his hand to Declan. "I accept."

Declan pressed their palms together. "Then we have an accord!" he said cheerfully. "I'll have the paperwork drafted right away. Meet me aboard *The Tigress* in..." His eyes rolled upward as he thought. "Three days, as this place may well be underwater by then." He chuckled. "Let's say by morning tea, at ten? I'll send for the notary to make it official."

Kol nodded. "Fine."

"Five months should be more than sufficient, at any rate," Declan commented to himself with a smirk.

"You have something planned?" Kol couldn't help but ask, suspicion growing within him.

"Indeed," Declan replied. "Oh," he added suddenly. "Will you be returning to Elldon today?"

"Yes, of course," Kol replied brusquely, casting a nervous glance around as the ceiling let out a loud creak. "Why?"

Declan retrieved something from his desk. "Deliver this for me, will you?" he asked, pressing a letter into Kol's hand. It was addressed to Adella. "Please."

"Certainly," Kerchaw answered on Kol's behalf. From the wall beside him, a small painting fell to the floor with a sharp crack. "Looking forward to doing business with you," he said quickly, nudging Kol toward the door.

Outside the Ivy Crown, the sun came out from behind the clouds and warmed their shoulders. A gull cried shrilly as it descended and floated in the street beside the carriage.

"You're not so good at haggling," Kerchaw commented, putting his hat on his head. "Leave it to me from now on, eh?"

Looking down at the letter, Kol's stomach dropped as he read Adella's name again. "That slimy reaver," he muttered. "What's he got planned?"

"We'll find out soon enough," Kerchaw replied wearily. "He's your slimy reaver, now. You shook on it and everything."

"Ugh," Kol groaned, hoping he wouldn't come to regret his haste.

"Well, it's a good time to buy a ship, at least," Kerchaw noted wryly, casting a glance at the water around them.

Kol let out a small laugh. "I just wish I knew what he meant." He brought his thumbnail to his teeth, tapping distractedly. "What's he up to? How could a man like him come into so much money in so short a time?"

Kerchaw shrugged. "Gambling? Blackmail?" He chuckled to himself and added, "Marry rich?"

Kol's blood ran cold as he stuffed Declan's letter in his bag, wondering what was written inside. "I need to get back to Elldon," he said, trudging toward the carriage.

"Of course," Kerchaw began, opening the coach door. "But first, you should retrieve the Company records from the townhouse, just in case. I haven't been there in days, so I don't know the state of it."

"Right," Kol replied, taking the warning.

"I have more errands to run in town," Kerchaw went on, "so you'll be making your return trip without the pleasure of my company. See you in three days." Tipping his hat, he nodded a goodbye.

As the carriage, now up to its axles in dirty water, rolled through the streets, Kol's stomach twisted into knots, his mind distracted by the letter in his bag. When he finally arrived at his townhome, he waded up the front steps and paused at the door, eyeing the small brass plaque proudly embossed with the name of the Royal Westward Trading Company affixed to it. The sea crept over the threshold, lapping beneath the green-lacquered door. Already, the paint at the bottom was rippling. Kol took a deep breath, preparing himself for the damage to the furnishings within.

Inside, his boots squelched on the soaked carpets in the dim, musty interior, illuminated only by the daylight filtering in from the dirty bay window behind the sofa. The water around him was just beginning to pool here and there on the floor; the bedrooms upstairs would be safe for some time yet.

Passing the hearth, which held only soggy ashes, he sloshed to the basement door and, opening it, felt a waft of dank, briny air hit his face. As expected, the steps disappeared downward beneath dark water. He groaned to himself as he shut it again. He headed for the staircase, and the boards above his head gave a loud creak. Pausing, Kol looked about nervously. *Could be nothing,* he reasoned. Even so, his hand moved instinctively to his sword hilt as he continued up the stairs.

He passed by the open door of Martin's old bedchamber, and froze. The room was strewn with belongings he didn't recognize: a wool jacket lay across the bed, a faded grey cocked hat hung from one of its posts, and large cuffed boots slumped on the floor. "What in the—" Kol muttered to himself. Kerchaw had mentioned he hadn't been to the townhouse in days, and, at any rate, he wouldn't leave his things behind. Kol drew his cutlass and, as quietly as he could in his waterlogged boots, padded toward the study at the end of the hall.

As he crept up to the door that hung ajar, a sharp creak came from behind it. Heart pounding, Kol touched the tip of his blade to the heavy oak door and pushed it open, ready to strike.

Groaning loudly on its hinges, the door swung slowly open, and metal flashed toward him. He jerked his cutlass up in time to parry the edge of a blade, steel clashing just in front of his face. The large figure before him, silhouetted by the daylight from the windows at his back, leaned forward, pressing into his cutlass. Kol's wet boots slipped on the smooth wood flooring, and for a moment, he thought he would be overpowered.

Rallying from the surprise, he drew a deep breath and shoved his blade forward. The man stumbled backward, and Kol drew his cutlass back for a strike.

"Son?" a gravelly voice broke the silence.

Kol froze again, brow furrowing. "What?"

"'Bout time you showed up!" The other man laughed heartily.

Kol squinted as his eyes adjusted to the light. "Father?" he asked, his voice barely a whisper. He slowly lowered his cutlass and the man stepped forward, wrapping his arms around Kol and squeezing. Before he could react, the man released him and stepped back. Kol found himself looking into the grizzled face of Adamas Seaborn, his iron grey hair hanging limply. Kol blinked at him. "What are you doing here?"

"Ehh," Seaborn dithered, sheathing his sword. "I thought I'd surprise you."

"Well, you did," Kol replied, putting his cutlass away.

"Sorry," Seaborn muttered and nodded toward Kol's cutlass. "Thought you were a soldier. Told you I'd come for a visit, remember?"

Seaborn turned toward the large desk by the window of the little study, which was laden with an assortment of jars and pitchers from the downstairs kitchen. "Pickled egg?" he asked, lifting one large jar and holding it out toward him.

"Uh..." At that moment, Kol's stomach growled. "Sure." He took an egg from the jar. "How did you..." Watching Seaborn stuff a whole egg in his mouth, Kol considered his words. "Get here?"

"Hitched a ride on a fishing boat," Seaborn replied, yolk crumbs falling from his mouth. "Found your place, picked the lock. Not difficult." He swallowed, and held out a pewter tankard to Kol. "Switchel?"

"Thanks," Kol muttered, and took a swig.

"Just like the breakfasts we'd have on the old ship when you were little. Do you remember?" Seaborn asked, a hopeful gleam in his eye, but Kol only shook his head. Seaborn went on with a note of sadness in his voice, "Nah, you were too young, I'm sure."

Kol wanted to comment that it was much like the quick meals he'd had while in the Sornian army, but then he remembered his father's dislike of soldiers. He took another drink instead, savoring the ginger tang, sweetened with honey. It'd been a while since he'd had switchel—they didn't seem to drink it in Valenna—and the taste brought to mind the flowering fields of his past while stationed in the Campos, often sleeping in the open under the summer stars. *The Campos...* The thought reminded him he'd told Adella he'd go with her to the cavalier camp for games that night. He intended to keep his word. It would be a good chance for him to apologize for his behavior earlier. He briefly considered inviting his father to Elldon with him but, as he wasn't sure Seaborn was the sort of man he'd want Adella to meet, he put the thought away.

"I thought we could spend some time together," Seaborn said at length. "Get into some trouble..." He smirked, the lines around his mouth creasing. He took the tankard from Kol and gestured at the window. "Is this place always under water?"

"Look," Kol began reluctantly, "I just came by to get my ledgers; I have to get back to Elldon." He pulled a stack of leather-bound books from the shelves that lined the walls and set them on the edge of the desk. "Why don't you look after the place for me until I return?"

"But—" Seaborn began, his expression falling.

"I'll be back three days, at the latest," Kol quickly replied. "I'm buying a ship—*The Tigress*," he added proudly. "I'll be meeting with the captain to sign for it then. We can celebrate together after; I'll show you around the ship. Right now," he explained, shifting the books to one arm, "I've got to get these ledgers someplace dry. If anything happens to them, the Company will be in trouble."

"Right," Seaborn sighed.

"I'll come back sooner, if I can," Kol said, trying to sound optimistic as he headed for the door, leaving his father alone in the dark townhouse.

Kol let out a long breath as he settled onto the coach's leather seat. He hated to brush off his father, but his visit was unexpected, and there were more pressing matters. He'd told Adella he would be there tonight; after insisting she go, he didn't think it would be right for him to not show up. *Even if she is still angry with me.*

When the carriage finally rolled through the northern stockade gates and halted in front of Greywood Manor, Kol took a deep breath and stepped down. Returning to the manor house, with its sturdy fieldstone walls and gabled windows looking cheerily down on him from beneath the roof slates, felt like coming home.

Passing through the foyer, he made his way upstairs to the library, hoping Adella wouldn't mind him storing the ledgers there for a time. There was certainly no chance of the sea ruining them there, at least.

Returning downstairs, he strode through the long hallway, his reflection moving from glass to glass in the gilt mirrors that lined the walls. He hoped to see Adella in the large gathering room, but found it quiet and dark, aside from James, snoring softly in his usual place on the sofa. The letter Declan had given him felt like an unbearable burden in his bag. Though he knew he should deliver it in person, he grimaced at the thought of conveying a love letter between the two of them. Just the idea of seeing her open it in front of him hurt. *Propriety be damned,* he decided. *I'll leave it on her desk.*

Kol's wet stockings squished audibly in his boots as he approached Adella's writing desk and pulled out the letter. Staring blankly at her name written in Declan's bold handwriting, he paused. It would be so easy to just stick it back in his bag, to keep it to himself. *Or burn it.* Adella never needed to read its contents, whatever they were.

And yet... Whether he liked it or not, he'd agreed to do business with Declan. *I knew what I was getting myself into.* This was the consequence of his hastiness; he'd brought it on himself. If he and Declan were to be business partners, Kol needed to act in good faith, even with something so personal as this.

Groaning, he set the letter on Adella's writing desk, propped up on an ink bottle to catch her eye. It was the best he could do.

4

Dreams

That evening, as the sun lowered behind heavy, dark clouds, Adella made her way across the western fields of Greywood Manor, guided by the music coming from the group of tents in the distance. Ahead, a bonfire blazed, with people silhouetted against its bright light.

An odd sensation crept over her as she joined them. The once-quiet meadow was now alive with voices, laughter, and music, and the flurry of activity engulfed her. The past and present clashed in her mind; memories of her once-quiet home overlaid the crowded military encampment she stood in. Beneath the starless black sky, surrounded by people she hardly knew, an intense loneliness overwhelmed her. She yearned for loved ones lost and days long gone, for the feeling of belonging and familiarity she'd once known. She wondered if she would ever experience them again.

"Our Lady Governor has joined us!" a voice called out, breaking her trance as a murmur of welcome traveled around the fire. Adella looked to see if Kol was among them, but didn't see him. Eventually, she spotted Captain Holcomb, offering a pewter tankard as he approached.

She nodded her thanks and took a drink. "I appreciate you inviting me."

"But of course," he replied. "You didn't bring your Sornian?" he asked, looking around. Though the comment sounded playful, there was a hint of condescension in his tone that put her on edge.

"Mister Kol may look and sound like the enemy," she began, keeping her words measured, "but I assure you, he's one of us. Though his manners may be different, a better man I've never met."

"Indeed," he replied sheepishly. "I will bear that in mind." He took a long draught from his tankard. He asked at length, "Care for a game of cards?"

"Not cards," a nearby cavalier, still in his scarlet jacket, interjected. "I think she'd prefer to dance." He was young and trim, with piercing eyes and a long, red scar running down one side of his face. *A saber cut,* Adella noted. She knew the sight well; her own father likewise had borne such tales written on his flesh.

"Pay no attention to Lieutenant Lewis," Holcomb laughed. "He's drunk already."

"It isn't true." The lieutenant bowed and offered his hand. "Lady, would you do me the honor of joining me?"

"I suppose," Adella agreed, taking his hand hesitantly, "but I don't know this tune—" Before she could finish, he pulled her away; she barely had time to pass the tankard back to Holcomb.

The music was fast, lively, and of a style more popular among sailors and soldiers than the gentry she'd grown up with in the Capital. She could barely keep up with his quick steps and the rapid bowing of the fiddle as they made their way around the fire, spinning so often she grew dizzy. Adella was glad she'd put long skirts on rather than breeches as they helped hide her missteps, but after a time, she grew accustomed to the movements. She noticed others had joined in, dancing in pairs, a mix of cavaliers and people from Elldon.

"Did he say you were a lieutenant?" Adella asked breathlessly, trying to keep the pace. "I thought Captain Holcomb mentioned there were only captains and cavaliers."

"An honorary title," he replied, his long scar stretching as he smiled. "I was captain of another troop in Pentz, but I wanted to come to help on the frontier. After what happened—" His voice lowered as his smile fell away. "I didn't have enough men left to make up a troop, so I merged mine with Holcomb's."

Goosebumps raised on Adella's neck as her thoughts returned to the floods at Pentz and the day the Governor's mansion had filled with rushing water, pulling her out to sea with the tide. She suppressed a shiver as she recalled her terror. "I see," she said softly, looking down at her feet. "I'm sorry."

"Enough about that," he replied, forcing a lighter tone. "Mulling over sadness—that's not what a dance is for." Taking her by the hand, he spun her to the rhythm of the music until she was so dizzy, she couldn't help but laugh.

* * *

Kol passed by groups of cavaliers, many still wearing their scarlet and sabers. Shrill fiddle-playing and a blazing fire greeted him. He felt uneasy about the commotion and had to remind himself the Sornians already knew where Greywood was located. An attack while Elldon slept would be far worse than if the Sornians had attacked now, when everyone in earshot was wide awake. Besides, the enemy had been lying low lately after being beaten back in the last skirmish. *The enemy...* That word still felt strange to say of the Sornian army, which had only some months ago been his whole world, little and bleak though it was. *And yet, even when I was one of them, that's how it felt.* He'd never been good at making friends; enemies came easy.

He glanced over the faces that gathered for card games at makeshift tables of planks stacked upon crates. *Adella should be here, somewhere...* Finding a table where one cavalier was just beginning to cut a deck, Kol joined in. "Room for one more?" he asked, jingling the coin pouch in his haversack to be sure it was there.

"Please," the cavalier replied, waving a knotted hand. He was old enough to be Armand's father, judging by the white beard.

"What is it?" Kol asked as he took a seat.

"Pounce," the old man said, shuffling the cards loudly. "Do you know it?"

Kol nodded. "I've played it."

"Ellicot," the man said plainly. Kol looked at him in confusion. "Meriwether Ellicot."

Realizing it was an introduction, Kol blinked at the name. "Kol," he replied, but the old man still waited expectantly. "Kol... Seaborn," he went on, though Adella's earlier warning about using that name gnawed at him. "Though I prefer just Kol," he added quickly.

"Hm," Ellicot muttered, dealing out the cards. "Well, Just Kol, prepare to have your purse lightened!"

"We'll see about that, Grandpa," Kol replied, helping himself to a wine bottle as a few of the other cavaliers at the table chuckled over their cards. He was surprised to see Captain Holcomb take a seat beside him, with a tankard of ale in each hand. Kol raised an eyebrow at him. "Captain."

"Good of you to join us," Holcomb replied.

Kol, having been dealt a bad hand, eventually grew bored. He watched absently as the others at the table took their turns until his attention wandered toward the figures dancing at the bonfire. The cavaliers found it amusing to dance with each other, scarlet sleeves interlocking as they stomped and turned; even from where he sat, he could hear their coarse laughter each time one forgot who was leading and tripped over the other's boots.

There were a couple of women among them, as he could see by their long skirts; one he recognized as Adella, judging by her small frame. She danced with someone in uniform who seemed to be good at it. The cavalier drew her closer, and Kol wished it was him instead. The news of Adella and Declan's relationship pained him still, but there was one consolation: *Declan isn't here.* And likely never would be; the renowned sea captain certainly couldn't be bothered to set foot out here on the dusty frontier, not even for her sake. *Don't know what she sees in him...* He shook his head slightly at the thought.

"Why don't you go out there?" Holcomb asked, surprising Kol out of his thoughts. The captain's eyes followed Kol's line of sight, and he nodded in that direction. "I'm sure Lewis won't mind if you cut in."

"I don't think she'd want me to," Kol replied sullenly.

"Don't say that," Holcomb rebuked him. "She thinks very highly of you."

Kol looked down into his cup. "I doubt that."

"Mm," Holcomb muttered pensively. "I think I see the problem; it's because she's one of them."

"One of what?" Kol asked, puzzled.

"Highborn," Holcomb replied. "An aristocrat."

"She's the only one I've really known," Kol admitted.

"Well, I have a lot of experience with their kind, and..." Holcomb tilted his head to one side, considering his words. "They live differently than we do. Born to serve the Crown, raised to bear public scrutiny; they are expected to keep a tight seal on their emotions. Stoic, you could say."

"Like horses?" Kol mused.

Holcomb laughed. "Something like that."

"I've seen her really angry," Kol countered.

"I'm sure," Holcomb said with a smirk. "'None of us play our part in this world perfectly.'"

"I know those words," Kol replied. "That's from Jonny Reddin-Black."

"Ah, you've read it?" Holcomb's freckled face lit up. "Forgive me, but it seems you're more of a Valennian than I thought."

"And I'd be surprised if you're not a gentleman yourself," Kol commented. He took a drink and knocked on the table to pass as his turn had come around again.

"Born a bastard," Holcomb replied, setting a silver piece down. "With a foot on both sides." He sipped his drink quietly for a moment.

"I don't know either of you very well, but I know a bond between two people when I see one. It would be a shame to let that go to waste because of misunderstandings."

Kol pressed his lips together. Holcomb was right. His feelings for Adella had always been more than friendship, but even knowing that was all it could ever be, he couldn't let it end this way, with hurt and anger lingering between them. No matter how her relationship with Declan pained him, he had to try to speak with her again.

Finishing off his wine, Kol tossed his cards down. "Thanks for the advice," he said as he rose, leaving his money on the table.

* * *

Adella continued the dance as best she could. When the tune shifted and the others all turned to switch partners, she did likewise, facing one with golden curls and a bright smile.

"Rosalind!" Adella exclaimed, taking her hands. "I'm glad you're here."

"Of course," Rosalind said, grinning. "I love this dance. No, no—like this," she instructed, bunching up her skirts to show the steps. Hooking her elbow in Adella's, she laughed as they twirled.

Adella, out of breath and light-headed, slipped free mid-turn and stumbled, stopping only when she ran into a warm solidness. She steadied herself on what felt like an arm as she waited for the world to stop spinning. "Oh!" she said, seeing Kol looking down at her in amusement.

Much to her surprise, he put a hand on her waist and pulled her along.

"What are you doing?" she asked tentatively.

"Dancing." Kol shrugged. "Isn't that why you grabbed me?"

"Right," she muttered, not wanting to admit to her clumsiness.

"We could stop," he offered.

"No—" The word came out a little too quickly. "No," she repeated, lowering her voice. "It's fine. I think I'm getting the hang of it."

The tension in Kol's arms seemed to pull her gently toward him as they moved, his fingertips pressing against the small of her back. Dancing like this brought to mind the time they had spent in the Capital, and their travels before that—the times she'd fallen asleep, travel-weary, wounded, wherever they found themselves, with no thought to her safety because he was there. *What must he think of me? Especially now...* She clutched his sleeve, her gaze roaming over his chiseled features, and her breath quickened. Black curls had fallen loose from his queue, framing his dark eyes, and, for a moment, Adella couldn't help but wonder what would've happened if he'd told her of his feelings sooner. *Would I still have chosen to be with Rogero?* She recalled the night she'd spent on Rogero's ship with him, and the pain on Rog's face when he'd finally given her his old letter. *To have gone through all that he did, the pain and terror of losing his father that way...* Guilt struck her at the thought, and she looked away.

Kol stared at her, watching the emotions play on her face. "There's something I wanted to say—" he began.

"Listen," she interrupted, the memory of his accusations earlier rekindling her anger, "if you're going to complain about Rog again, you can stow it."

"No, I—"

"I know you don't like him," she continued.

Kol tilted his head in concession. "That's true—"

"But it's really none of your business," she interrupted again, her grip inadvertently tightening again on his sleeve.

He turned away, his features falling momentarily into shadow. "I know—"

"I'm sorry you had to find out that way," she went on, cutting him off again, "but there's no need to take it out on me."

"I was just surprised you have time to fool around with men," he commented under his breath.

"Don't be silly," she snapped. "Who doesn't have five minutes?"

Biting his lips, Kol snorted. "Forget it," he finally managed. "Let's not talk about it anymore, if it upsets you."

"I'm not upset!" she insisted, then stopped to look around. The music had ended, and the others had gathered at the tables for games, leaving the two of them alone and standing closely, with his hand on the curve of her back. Suddenly, she found herself very aware of his proximity. Their shadows still danced together in the warm firelight, serenaded now only by crickets and the crackling of embers, and as she watched the flickering light play on the rugged angles of his face. The memory of when he'd confessed his feelings for her in Greywood's dining room came flooding back. It had caught her completely off guard, but now, looking back, she could see there had been signs, moments where his gaze, his touch, had lingered. *Moments like this...*

Dropping her arms, Adella cleared her throat and stepped back. "Where is Holcomb with that ale?" she muttered. "I could really use it about now."

Kol laughed quietly, and they made their way back to join the others.

By the time Adella had retrieved her tankard from Holcomb, she'd lost Kol among the groups of people. Some were playing cards or dice in the light of the lanterns, others sat by the fire telling tales. Soon, she spotted Rosalind seated on a log by the fire, wrapped in a shawl against the rising wind. Gathering her skirts to one side, Adella sat beside her. Rubbing her forearm, she was surprised to find a blister had formed where the strange plant had pricked her skin earlier. Her fingertips brushed the little mark, and it burned to the touch.

"Are you enjoying yourself?" Rosalind asked.

"Yes," Adella replied. "At least, I think so."

Rosalind laughed. "I know what you mean. It's hard to relax."

Adella nodded, wrapping her arms around herself. "I can't help but think, what if the Sornians attack now? What if they're hurting Misses Asher at this very moment? What if—" She shrugged helplessly.

"That's exactly why we need times like this," Rosalind replied. "Otherwise, there's only the bad and never the good. If I had known how soon he'd be taken from me, I would've wished for more evenings like this with Tristan." She drew her shawl tighter around her shoulders as the scent of rain carried in on the wind.

"Your husband?" Adella guessed. She had heard Rosalind's heartbreaking story before, but it was the first she'd heard his name.

"It's never easy to go on alone," Rosalind continued wistfully, as if to herself, eyes turned toward the night sky, "but finding a love like that was worth it." Though her face darkened with grief, there was a faint smile there, too.

"How did you know it was love?" Adella asked curiously. "Did you know right away?"

"It happened slowly." Rosalind looked down at her hands, where a thin gold ring glistened in the firelight. "First, I noticed his face was always the one I searched for in a crowd. Whenever I had news to share, he was the one I wanted to share it with. When I was sad, or hurt, he was always the one at my side, to comfort or help me, and eventually, I realized that's what love is."

Is it? Adella wondered, tucking back a strand of hair that blew across her face and thinking of Rogero. *Is that what we have?* There was no doubt he was handsome, with a physique seemingly carved from stone; it was difficult not to melt in his arms. He likewise had an impeccable reputation, one any Valennian man would strive to emulate. The two of them seemed a good match—indeed, she had agreed to marry him once before—and being with him reminded her of better times, before she moved to Elldon, before she lost her parents, and before Lucas's betrayal. Not to mention, he was the only man she'd ever been with, and there was a comforting familiarity in that. *But is that love?* Adella wondered. She took a long draught of ale; far on the western horizon, lightning flashed silently behind dark clouds.

That night, as Adella lay on her cot in a scratchy wool blanket, sleeping fitfully to the sound of rain on her tent, her mind wandered across the peculiar landscapes of her dreams: the shadowy emerald forests of the Cairn, with its unfamiliar bird calls; the undulating waves of a fathomless, indigo sea; the wide, wind-swept prairies of the Campos beneath stormy skies.

The dark, silent halls of Greywood Manor beckoned. Creeping along the patterned carpets with only a chamberstick to light the way, she entered her bedchamber. Devoid of the crates and flour sacks that crowded its floor in the waking world, a dark silhouette waited, sitting cross-legged on her canopy bed. In the figure's lap, cradled in both hands, lay a strange, angular object that gave a cool, steady light, wholly unlike the warm, dancing flame of her candle.

"What's this?" she muttered. "Who are you?"

The figure rose and approached. "I can't believe I've done it," said an oddly familiar voice in a strong Sornian accent. A thin, silver circlet glinted on his brow. He pocketed the object, and she caught a glimpse of the shape in his hands. It looked to be a large jewel or crystal.

Adella tried to remember where she'd heard the voice before. As he approached, his features came into the light. Ash-brown hair, cropped short rather than tied in a long queue, hung over hard, storm-grey eyes. *Matei!*

"I've been looking for you." His cruel smile twisted a face too cold and void of expression to ever be called handsome. He leaned in and gripped her chin with his fingers, forcing her to meet his eyes. "Now there will be no hiding from me." His mouth was so close to hers that she could smell his foul breath, which reeked of rot and death.

"Get back," Adella said, shoving his hand aside. "I'm not afraid of you."

"Not yet, perhaps," he replied, his grin growing into a strange grimace. "But you will be." His words echoed as the darkness around her grew until it swallowed her completely.

Floating in a sea of black, amidst the constant roar of crashing, unseen waves, stars appeared one by one. A thin crescent moon, glowing pale among the darkness, formed like a crack in the heavens. It grew wider, rounder, until a golden orb hung before her in the night sky. A slit of black cut through the center as a serpentine pupil formed, and the great, shimmering eye turned its gaze toward her.

Heed the Codex.

The voice, inhuman in its depth and coolness, boomed in her mind, shaking her to the bone as deeply as the ground tremors had done in the physical world. Plummeting through the darkness, she suddenly plunged into water so icy it felt like daggers in her flesh. She opened her mouth to give voice to her surprise and fear, but frigid brine surged in, filling her lungs.

You've brought this upon yourself, scribe... the voice thundered in her head.

The sea filled her ears, drowning out all sensation. Her limbs seemed to fall away from her body, numbed by the cold, and she became one with the ebb and flow of invisible tides.

Now fix it!

Adella awoke with a gasp, clutching her wool blanket. The harsh words of her vivid dream still echoed loudly in her mind. Throwing back the covers, she sat up, her linen shift clinging to her sweat-soaked form. Crickets chirruped in the darkness outside her tent, but a faint, growing light told her dawn was not far off.

"Ugh," she groaned, rubbing her face as the visions from the night slowly replayed in her memory. *Why did I dream of Prince Matei?* Her stomach clenched as she recalled the stench of his breath. *What's wrong with me?* Slowly, the rest of the dream returned, and the full words of the disembodied voice came back to her. *The Codex!*

Adella dressed quickly, pulling on a sea-blue petticoat and matching jacket bodice over her damp linen shift. While dawn began to paint the east in a gold wash, and the rest of the camp still lay in silence, she sat at her campaign desk and looked down upon the ancient tome. Reverently, she passed her hand over the gilded glyphs embossed into the cracked leather cover. They seemed to call to her.

Her fingers moved from one golden shape to the next, and the culmination of months of translation work struck her with a sudden clarity. She finally understood their meaning: *Legends of Andolin.* A chill crept over her, sending shivers down her back.

Pulling the book open, the pages once again fell to the same place as before. She studied the image in the dim morning light, her eyes settling on the angular shape depicted with gilded rays that loomed over the field of battle. It appeared to be the same object Matei had held in her dream. Below the image was an inscription in Old Andolinian glyphs. *Corelimun,* she read. *The Heart of the World...* Kol had once told her the legend of Leveret, how the Heartstone, or *Corelimun* in Old Andolinian, had bestowed upon him strange abilities. Somehow, its use had also unleashed the cataclysm that had destroyed the Andolin Empire a millennium ago.

It seems the same events are happening once again, at this very moment... She flipped through the pages until she found one in particular. Her finger followed over the pictographs as she read: *Plague, rising tempests, the pelkimund and haramund, the sea filled with fire...* Her stomach dropped as she realized all that had come to pass, just as described in the ancient tome. *Could Matei have the Heart of the World?* Perhaps he'd survived the sea battle, like Lucas and Teressa had, and had taken the crystal from the box during the fray. *After all, he had Leveret's Key on him, along with the lockbox.* Perhaps that's what her dream was trying to tell her. *Did we bring the lockbox to the Capital empty?*

Upon the pages, one passage in particular caught her attention. *A turning of the minds of her people... of those nearest to her waters.* She furrowed her brow. *Madness.* That was one omen she hadn't seen, yet. Perhaps there was still time.

She tried to recall how Leveret's story ended. *Oh, that's right...* Kol had recounted the tale during their first trip through the Campos, and she'd accidentally fallen asleep before the end, even though it had been her turn to keep watch. She'd woken up to find herself lying beside him, using his arm as a pillow. Adella's face flushed at the memory, but she quickly brushed her feelings aside. She had to see Kol and find out how the legend ended. *Oh, that's right!* Groaning, she smacked herself on the forehead. *I was supposed to meet him for training this morning!*

Outside her tent dawn broke; raised voices and rapid hoofbeats punctuated the morning silence. Adella shut the Codex and stepped into the brisk air as a group of riders galloped toward camp from the western fields, their horses blowing and lathered with sweat. One by one, they dismounted and headed toward the stables.

"Jacoby!" Adella called out, grabbing her skirts out of the way as she ran toward them. "What is it?" she asked, chest heaving as she finally caught up.

"We've found them," Jacoby said equally breathlessly, leading his piebald horse in-hand as he turned to meet her. "We couldn't get very close, their scouts were everywhere. But we know where their camp is."

"And your mother?" Adella asked. "Was she among them?"

"Yes," he replied. "We could hear her—" His voice broke, brows furrowing. "Even from where we were."

The meaning of his words hit her, and Adella's gut turned. *He heard her... Screaming.* They had to save her before it was too late. She nodded curtly. "See to your horse, then meet me at the map."

5

Tea With A Horse

With a rag in his hand, Kol pulled the tin kettle off the coals and shook some tea into it from a canvas pouch, the bits of dried leaves swirled in the bubbling water. Soon, Adella would be riding up on Shy for her morning instruction, with her father's saber on her hip. This was the first time he'd come early, bringing the tea-making things carefully packed into his saddle bags. He wanted to make amends, and knew she wouldn't have time for breakfast beforehand. Covering the pot with the cloth, he looked around; the sun was much higher than her usual arrival time. *Where is she?*

He'd meant to apologize to her last night, while they were dancing, for the way he'd acted before, but she'd been so quick with her temper and her words, he hadn't found a chance. The tea might help his cause; she liked tea. His mind kept returning to the way she'd looked at him in the firelight, the way she'd gripped his arm, pulling him closer. Moments like that, and there had been many since they'd met, burned brightly in his mind. *No one's ever looked at me that way, aside from her...* It was as though she saw past the dirt, weapons, and rough manners to see him for who he truly was. She never flinched at him like others did.

The liquid steeped, growing darker as he waited, but still, there was no sign of her. His black mare, Madigan, whom he had left tethered to graze close by, wandered over toward him in curiosity.

"Get back." Kol pushed her muzzle gently away from the broad fallen log that served as a table, then poured tea into a cup. *Adella must still be angry with me.* The thought hurt. Whatever the nature of their relationship, he'd believed it would've survived a few harsh words, and even if she was upset, it was unlike her to miss her morning lesson. *It must be worse than I realized.* He frowned. *But I was only being honest...* Once again, Madigan snuffled at the tea things, licking her lips, and he gently pushed her face out of the way. *Perhaps I've ruined things forever. Or worse—* The thought struck him sharply in the chest. *What if there was never anything between us at all? What if I only imagined it?* His stomach knotted.

"I don't think she's coming," Kol said dejectedly, resting his jaw on his hand. "I guess it's just me and you, girl." Heart aching, he poured tea into the other cup for Madigan, who lapped it up sloppily. Kol took a sip of the strong black tea mixed with lavender buds from his own cup, but the delicate flavor was lost on him. His mind was elsewhere. Porcelain clinked sharply as Madigan knocked her cup from its saucer, spilling tea onto the ground. "You need to work on your table manners," he commented, pulling a piece of hardtack from his haversack and dipping it into his tea.

"I don't know what to do," he muttered, brow furrowing. "I've never felt like this before." He bit into the hard biscuit he had gotten from the stores at Greywood. Hardtack had been a staple of his soldier days, and though it was always barely edible, today it seemed especially tasteless. Even the tea couldn't soften it. He gave it to Madigan instead, who seemed to appreciate it more. "Perhaps I should go find her and talk to her?" he asked the mare, rubbing her face, then groaned as his anxiety about the situation flared, knotting his stomach. "Or not..." He uprighted Madigan's teacup and refilled it, then watched as she grabbed the rim between her teeth. "No, you're right. I need to stay calm. Get that out of your mouth—" He grabbed the cup from her and set it back down. "But what if she marries him, Maddy? How could I bear it?" Heaving a sigh, he began to pack up his things.

Kol returned to camp, trudging through the grass with Madigan in-hand. Past the unfinished palisade, he found the place bustling with commotion. Passing between the tents and cookfires, he searched for Adella.

"What's going on?" he asked, catching the eye of Elldon's carpenter, Mister Giles, who was working at a sawhorse nearby, carving the point on one end of a log before it would be added to the fortification.

"Eh," the old man began, lowering a bushy white eyebrow as he squinted. "Young Jacoby's returned with his ranger party." He pointed a knotted finger toward Greywood Manor. "He's gone to meet with Lady Grimless. Oh, if you're heading that way," he added, bending to pick up something from the grass, "give these to Jamie-boy for me, will you?" He handed Kol a pair of freshly carved crutches. "He'll be glad to have 'em."

Kol found Adella, Jacoby, and Captain Holcomb inside Grey-wood's spacious gathering room, standing before the map on the far wall. The once opulent and impressive space, with high ceilings and ornate wainscoting, now seemed dark and stuffy with its boarded-up windows. Without a housekeeper, dirt sullied the large floral carpet and dust dulled every surface except the sofa, upon which James still lay like another fixture, sleeping soundly. Kol's boots rapped softly as he crossed the room, leaning the crutches against the sofa arm for James. He passed Adella's writing desk and winced with guilt when he saw Declan's letter still sat on it unopened. He had to tell her soon that it was there.

Holcomb waved a riding crop idly behind his back. He always seemed to have it on his person; it seemed to be part of his uniform. Jacoby looked unusually pale, though his eyes were still bright, the same shade of sky blue as Armand's. His queue had come untied, and his brown hair hung loose on his shoulders, clumped with sweat and dust. Adella, with her long, auburn hair pinned up in a hasty bun, tapped her lip as she squinted at the map, deep in thought.

"I'm glad you're here," she said to Kol. "I need your advice." Her ruffled sleeve slid back as she pointed to the map, revealing a cluster of small, red-ringed blisters on her forearm.

"Your arm—" he began, voice edged with concern.

"It's nothing," she muttered dismissively. Sweeping her hand across the map westward toward *Compass Point* at the center, she stopped halfway between it and Elldon. "A small group of Sornians, led by Blackburn, have broken away from the main camp and gathered in an outpost here, on a rise in the land just beyond our caltrop field," she explained, referring to the military obstacles they'd deployed in the area earlier that year.

Kol scratched his stubbled chin. "They're using our own devices against us."

Adella nodded. "Apparently so. It's odd, they've avoided every surprise we've set for them, though we've never seen their scouts out here. It's almost as if they've had a bird's-eye view..." Adella gazed into the distance, then cleared her throat. "Anyway, that's where they're holding Misses Asher. It's only a day and a half ride from Elldon, but we can't delay. Jacoby—" She prompted with a wave of her hand.

"Our rangers further afield have discovered Sornian reinforcements on their way," Jacoby explained. "Troops fresh from Hedda coming from the northwest, as well as an outpost from the south that have broken camp, are all heading toward their main encampment in the shadow of Compass Point."

"So that's why it's been so quiet," Kol replied. "They're waiting."

"It's their answer to our new cavalry," Adella went on, "and it's more than enough to sweep us off the map, if you take my meaning. So we don't have much time. We have to get Misses Asher out of there quickly, or not at all." She lifted her hands helplessly. "But according to our scouts, Blackburn's outpost is well guarded; they can't get close enough to sneak her out. Now, we could simply mount an attack, and try to rescue her in the diversion—"

"In which case," Holcomb interjected, "we would lose many in a rushed attempt to save one person. Which I can't agree to."

"Right." Adella pressed her lips together. "That leaves us with only one other option."

Something in her tone sounded like a warning. "What are you suggesting?" Kol asked, raising a brow.

"I want to negotiate with the Sornian general," she replied, and looked at him expectantly. "And bargain for her life."

"You're asking if that's possible?" Turning his gaze back to the map, Kol bit his thumbnail. "Their troops often go without needed supplies, and they're always short on horses," he admitted. "I don't like the idea, but it's the better option. Aside from—"

Adella shot him a pointed look. "I think I know what you're going to say, but we have to try. We can't just leave her."

"Then negotiating is the best course," Kol sighed.

"It's settled then," she said, clapping her hands together. "Now, how do I meet with him?"

"You?" Kol asked, much louder than he intended.

"Yes, of course." She shrugged. "Who else?"

"Right..." Kol suddenly regretted agreeing to the deal. He hadn't realized Adella would be directly involved, though he could see the responsibility fell on her shoulders. "Forget it," he recanted. "It's too risky. They could take advantage of the situation and just kill—" He stopped, unable to say the words out loud. "Adella, think this over," he pleaded. He saw the determination on her face and knew it was already a lost cause. Still, he had to try. "You Valennians—yourself, Captain Holcomb—hold yourselves to standards of behavior that Sornian officers don't. There's no reason to expect Blackburn to—"

"We'll arrange to meet, Blackburn and I, unarmed and unaccompanied between our two locations," Adella interrupted, tapping the empty space of open field on the map. "If it appears he isn't keeping to the terms of our meeting, I'll simply retreat to the safety of Elldon." Pulling her gaze from the map, she looked up at him, brows raised.

Her eyes, a stormy blue-green that brought to mind the turbulent seas of Belgrand Bay, pleaded silently with him in a way he couldn't refuse. The desperate hope, mingled deeply with sadness, that shone in them pierced his heart, and Kol wanted to reach out to her, to sweep back the stray lock of hair that brushed her cheek. He let out his breath in defeat. "Write your message to Blackburn, and I'll see that he gets it."

"Wonderful!" she replied with a sigh of relief. "And how will you do that?"

"I don't know," Kol admitted, shaking his head. "I'll figure it out once I get there and see things for myself."

"I'll go with you," Adella said over her shoulder as she hurried over to her writing desk nearby. "This needs to be done quickly because if it doesn't go well," she went on, opening the drawer and pulling out supplies, "we'll need all the time we can get before their reinforcements arrive." Declan's letter, which she had failed to notice, was soon buried beneath the stack of blank papers on which she prepared to write.

"Uh—" Kol began, again cringing at the thought of telling her about it.

"Captain," Adella said, taking no notice of Kol's utterance as she looked across the room at Holcomb, a goose quill pen in hand, "I shall leave you in charge."

"If it's the same to you, Lady Grimless," Holcomb replied, "I'd rather come along. I'll leave command of Elldon to Lieutenant Lewis. He's capable, and we can be sure the Sornians won't make any advances in the meantime."

"I'm coming with you, too," Jacoby interjected. "I'll take my party back into the field; we'll be close by in case something goes wrong."

"But you just returned," Adella countered. "You all must be exhausted and sore."

"We'll manage," he replied. "We'll change horses and head out after you." Adella opened her mouth to protest, but Jacoby cut her off. "Please."

Sighing, she looked up at Kol. "You know the Sornians better than I; what do you say?"

"You can't let them see you until the terms are agreed on, or they'll think we're mounting an attack," Kol instructed, turning to Jacoby. "You'll need to remain far back and out of sight. Our lives depend on it."

Jacoby nodded, and Adella finished writing her message. Taking a pewter chamberstick from her desk, she lit its candle in the coals of the nearby hearth, then, returning to her desk, heated a bit of wax above the flame in a little spoon. She sealed the letter with the gold signet ring on her finger. "All right," she said at last. "Let's be off."

The others gathered around her, ready to return to the stables, but as they headed for the door, James rose suddenly from the couch. "Wait," he called out, putting all his weight on his good leg as he tucked his crutches beneath his arms. "I'm coming with you."

"No, Jamie," Jacoby interjected. "You know you can't."

"I'm sorry," Adella said gently. "But that's not possible. Your leg hasn't fully healed."

"Lady Grimless," James began. "Adella," he added, the informality invoking their younger years at Elldon together. "Please, I must go. It's my mother, for goodness' sake! I can't just sit here any longer." Though he grimaced, face reddening at the prolonged effort, he stood resolute.

Adella frowned. "I appreciate the sentiment, but there's no way you can ride. And if you fall—" She shook her head, voice thick with regret. "You have to stay here, James. I'm sorry." Reluctantly, she turned and left, with Holcomb and Jacoby following closely behind.

Kol paused. There was a wild emotion in James' eyes that he couldn't quite name, though it felt all too familiar. He searched the other man's face, and a feeling of foreboding welled up in his gut.

"Please," James urged again, taking a faltering hop forward. "Bring me with you."

Kol felt for the man, but he shook his head, turning to follow the others.

"Let me come with you!" James begged from behind him. "Please!" His voice, ragged with desperation, pulled Kol to a halt once more, and he winced. It stung to leave the injured man behind, helpless and fearing for his beloved mother, but there was nothing for it. There was no way the man would make it. He had to know that.

Resignation slowly crept across James' features at Kol's silence. He slumped back, returning to his spot on the couch. "At least," James pleaded as Kol walked away, "could you send for Rosalind? I could use her help with something."

"Sure," he replied over his shoulder. It was the least he could do for him.

6

A Little Diplomacy

Squinting over the wide plains with the early autumn sun glaring in her eyes, Adella drew her horse to a halt. The bay gelding threw his head up and down, jangling the snaffle bit as he mouthed impatiently. "Shh," she whispered gently, patting the sweat-soaked coat of his neck. Though the bond between her and Shy had been forged through years of trust and affection, his patience had its limits.

Like every horse at Greywood, the little gelding had received full cavalry training by her father and Armand over the years, but she didn't like riding him in the wilds of the Campos. He tended to be nervous so far from home, and he wasn't the fastest horse in the stables. He also had a habit of planting his feet when he didn't want to go any farther, but above all, she didn't like to place him in danger. His unwavering trust in her stung every time she risked his life. *This is a diplomatic errand,* she reminded herself. *Nothing more. It will be fine.* Taking a deep breath, she tried to steady her pounding heart.

From her vantage atop a rise, she caught a glimpse of movement along the edge of the trees in the distance. *Scouts.* Emerald jackets retreated, blending into the green of the foliage. *Theirs.* Certainly, they could see her on the rise, outlined against the clear blue sky. *But there'll be no sneaking about at a time like this...* Adella swallowed, her throat tight and dry.

Kol and Captain Holcomb halted on either side, and Adella passed a look to each in turn. Then, the captain pulled a large, white kerchief from his waistcoat pocket and pressed his lanky chestnut horse onward, treading steadily through the tall grass ahead.

Adella watched breathlessly as he approached the trees wherein the Sornian soldiers hid, holding the white kerchief high aloft as a flag of peace. Across the open field, a man emerged from the gloom beneath the boughs, then two. Soon, several figures came out from the shadows, hastening toward Holcomb.

Adella narrowed her eyes. "Are they—" she began as the soldiers across the field drew weapons. "Oh!" she gasped. She'd just begun to urge her horse forward when Kol leaned over and grabbed Shy's reins.

"Wait," he said quietly, keeping a steady gaze on the scene ahead.

Adella quickly pulled the spyglass from her haversack. *Come on...* Jaws clenched, she peered through the lens as the men surrounded Holcomb. *Give the message...* One grabbed his horse by the bridle and it paced nervously in place, jostling into them. Then, Holcomb reached into his waistcoat. *The message.*

She let out her breath. "Thank goodness!" she sighed, tucking the spyglass away as Kol released her reins, tension visibly falling from his shoulders.

Suddenly, a shout carried over the field and Holcomb's horse reared, pulling free from the enemy hands. The pounding of hooves filled the valley as green-clad riders emerged from beyond the trees to the north, breaking into a gallop as they rode straight toward Holcomb. Tearing away from the Sornian soldiers, Holcomb spun his horse on its haunches and bolted back up the rise toward Adella and Kol.

"Go," Kol ordered brusquely, shoving her horse's neck away to urge it in the other direction. "Go!"

Adella kicked her heels into Shy's flanks and sped away, his hooves throwing clods of dirt in the air. Looking back, she saw Kol galloping behind on Madigan, yet she couldn't see Holcomb. *He should've caught up to us by now...*

"Holcomb!" Adella shouted as she reined Shy around in a tight circle, drawing up beside Kol as he slowed Madigan to meet her. Shy mouthed the bit as she steadied him, foam dripping from his lips. "We need to go back for him!"

Kol opened his mouth in protest, but Adella kept her gaze resolute. "Damn!" he swore under his breath. Kicking Madigan's sides, he followed her over the rise.

While they rode, Adella searched the vast green below for a sign of movement. Just beyond the trees, dark figures darted westward, with Holcomb in his bright Valennian scarlet at the front. He had apparently circled to the northwest, leading the soldiers away. *He's trying to protect us.*

"Ready your crossbow, but don't shoot unless I say," Kol ordered over the sound of their horses' pounding hooves.

Adella nodded and, resting the reins on Shy's neck, pulled the crossbow strap from over her shoulder. With the toe of her boot in the weapon's metal stirrup, she pulled the string back and locked it in place, careful not to release it in the jolting of the horse's strides.

"Flank left," Kol instructed. "I'll take right."

Adella pulled her horse to one side as she galloped toward the group of riders just ahead. Shy tossed his head, showing the whites of his eyes as she overtook one at the back, drawing up beside the soldier in emerald. He threw a quizzical glance in her direction.

"Good day, Miss," he said mockingly, tipping back his cocked hat as wrinkles creased around a feigned smile. "Out for a pleasure ride?"

"What are you doing?" Adella demanded. "This is a diplomatic—" She bit her tongue as a sudden force knocked her sideways in the saddle. The Sornian had reined his horse into her, the animal's shoulder crashing hard into her knee. Pain shot through her leg, and as Shy stumbled at the impact, her heavy crossbow dropped to the grass, disappearing behind them. "Damn!" she spat. The man belted out a harsh laugh as she fell back and he left her behind.

"That is so uncivilized..." Adella grumbled to herself, looking around to mark the spot in the landscape in hopes of retrieving the crossbow later. Not far to her right, Kol grabbed the reins of another soldier's horse and yanked it hard backward. The animal halted violently, throwing its head down and tossing the soldier from the saddle. He hit the ground with a dull thud. Even over the sound of hooves, she could hear Kol laugh in satisfaction. "I think he's enjoying this," she muttered wryly.

It suddenly struck her that the soldiers weren't releasing any arrows, nor swinging any blades yet. Even so, she knew things could take a bad turn at any moment. Rallying Shy with a series of tongue-clicks and heel kicks, Adella pressed onward.

Drawing level with another green-clad Sornian whose horse had begun to tire, she reached out to grab his reins like Kol had done, but a hand clapped down around her wrist. "Enough with the games," she said impatiently, trying to pull her arm free. "Take my message to Blackburn."

"How about I take you instead?" The soldier was quite young and small-framed, but his grip was like a vice as he pulled her sideways toward him.

Adella's thoughts turned to the bolts in the quiver on her belt. *No, no weapons yet,* she reminded herself. *Kol hasn't given the signal.* Whatever it was that held them back from it, she didn't know, but didn't want it to be her own actions that incited violence. With her other hand still gripping Shy's reins, she pulled hard to the right and barreled into the soldier's horse. Once again, her leg was buffeted against the animal's side, foot slipping from the stirrup, but the impact was enough to toss the soldier off balance; he fell sideways, yanking Adella by the arm until his weight wrenched his grip free and he toppled to the ground on the other side with a shout of surprise. Her chest lay over his now-empty saddle, and for a moment, the space between the horses widened, the grass below her passing by in a blur as she slipped, inching slowly downward toward the ground. The damp green scent of torn grass and freshly turned soil wafted up from beneath rapidly coursing hooves.

Reaching up with her rein-hand, she wove her fingers through the long black hair of Shy's mane and pulled herself back into her saddle. Behind her, the soldier's horse slowed to a trot and stopped.

"Get her!" he shouted indignantly from the ground beyond the horse. "She's got a bounty on her head!" he called, his voice fading as the group rode on.

Kol veered left, riding up beside Adella, just as something hissed through the air between them, so close to her head that the wind from its passing blew back a strand of her hair.

Kol's dark eyes widened. "I don't think they're playing anymore," he said, glancing over his shoulder as a soldier only a few strides away knocked another arrow on his small horsebow. "Go! Find Jacoby's party, get to safety." Reaching over his shoulder, Kol drew an arrow from the quiver at his back and leveled it on his bowstring. "I'll get Holcomb."

With a nod, Adella reined Shy around and sped off in the other direction.

When she came to the spot where she'd dropped her crossbow, she slowed Shy to a trot and searched through the meadow, looking closely along the trails of trampled grass left by the horses. She didn't want to lose something so precious and hard to come by on the outskirts of Valenna. She searched the area; soon, a metallic glint in the grass caught her eye, and she dismounted.

"Thank goodness," Adella sighed, relieved to find her weapon none the worse for wear. Even the string was intact. Pausing to sling it over her shoulder, the reins suddenly ripped from her hand and Shy bolted towards home.

"What in the—" Adella began. Hoofbeats sounded behind her; she spun to find a rider in green galloping toward her, raising a long saber in the air. "No," she groaned with despair. She was horseless and alone; it was just her and the lone rider, out in the open. He approached quickly, already nearly upon her. She had no time to load the crossbow; he would cut her down before she even had time to raise it. She could draw her own saber, but the rider had the clear advantage of height and speed; he'd cut her down in an instant. Adella froze, unsure what to do.

* * *

Kol pressed his heels into Madigan's flanks and pulled her to the left, slowly overtaking one of the soldiers who rode after Holcomb. Drawing back the arrow on his bowstring, he took aim, but as the rider turned his head in his direction, Kol was surprised to recognize the face. He lowered his arrow and, drawing their horses shoulder-to-shoulder, reached over and grabbed the rider's sleeve.

"Tovey?" Kol asked in disbelief. The rider was no more than a child; he couldn't have been older than fifteen. It was about the same age Kol had been when he'd joined the military himself, and he remembered meeting Tovey because of the commonality. "What are you doing? You know the rules of the white flag."

"Aren't you that traitor?" the boy asked snidely, wrenching his arm free. Apparently, the boy hadn't remembered him. "The one that escaped. You know when they catch you, they'll burn you alive." He let out a sharp laugh, his wide grin displaying crooked teeth. "I reckon you've only got days to live. A week at most."

"You little shit," Kol growled. In one quick move, he reached from the boy's sleeve to the back of his jacket and yanked hard. He fell from his horse, landing with a yelp in the grass. The loose horse fell back to a trot and then lowered its head to graze.

As he watched the boy stumble to his feet over his shoulder, a shadow flashed in the corner of Kol's eye. He turned just in time to catch a glimpse of the brass butt of a cavalry saber catching the sunlight as it hurtled toward his face.

* * *

Adella darted sideways and sprinted toward a grove of trees not far off. There was no way she could outrun a horse, but she could possibly outmaneuver a rider. A quick glance over her shoulder showed that her sudden change of direction had left the Sornian galloping away from her for a few strides before he could react, but soon enough, he circled around again, coming for her with sword drawn.

Hooves beat the ground behind her, outpacing the rhythm of her panting breath. She ran as fast as she could will her legs to go, her boots pounding as she stumbled over the uneven landscape. Beads of sweat formed and trickled down her brow; her muscles burned and ached as her lungs tightened with exertion. Behind her, the hoofbeats grew louder until she felt the hot breath of his horse on her neck; a glance back revealed the silvery edge of a blade slicing through the air toward her, the rider close enough to see the red tint of veins in the whites of his eyes.

Adella threw herself down, falling so hard that her head jarred against the hard-packed ground, the gritty soil scraping her cheek and elbows as the sword whistled over her head. Jumping back up quickly, heart hammering in her throat, she darted toward the treeline while the rider circled his horse around.

Though her lungs seared and sides cramped, Adella forced herself to keep running. With every footfall, the crossbow crashed against her back, bruising her skin until, finally, the safety of the trees was nearly within reach.

She scrambled beneath the foliage just as a loud crack sounded close by. From the saddle, the rider had swung hard, hacking his sword into the tree trunk beside her. It was wedged so tightly that he struggled to pull it free.

Under the cool, dappled shade of the trees, Adella unslung her crossbow and set her foot into its metal stirrup. Pulling a bolt from her quiver, she readied the weapon just as the rider freed his blade. His horse champed its bit, but no matter how the rider kicked, it refused to enter the thicket. Adella leveled her crossbow and aimed at the man's chest. His eyes met hers and a foul, goading smirk spread over his dirty, red-bearded face. Indignation flashed through her, and her finger found the cool metal of the lever.

A small, nagging feeling stopped her hand, and she groaned inwardly. *Diplomacy,* Adella reminded herself. Her party had come under a white flag, a promise of peaceful negotiations. *I can't be the first to draw blood.* She stepped toward him, weapon still carefully aimed.

"Is this how Sornians negotiate?" she shouted, her sharp words ringing through the trees as she advanced. The soldier's dark, foam-streaked horse danced nervously backward, throwing its head as she slowly came out from the cover of the foliage.

"Just you wait," he scoffed. "You'll find out soon enough." He spun his horse on its haunches and galloped off. Adella resisted the urge to put a bolt in his back.

"Bastard," she muttered. Then she let out a long breath to steady her nerves. With the threat of immediate danger gone, her hands trembled. "Ugh!" She slumped into the grass, rubbing the sweat from her face. With no horse, it would be a long walk back.

The sound of a loud snort in the distance brought Adella cautiously to her feet with her crossbow again at the ready. Over the rise, a rider appeared, silhouetted before the blazing sun, and her heart began to hammer again as he trotted his horse toward her. Squinting painfully against the brightness, she aimed as he drew nearer, the figure growing larger until the color of his clothing became visible against the light. Beneath a cocked hat, heavily-powdered hair had come untied, streaming freely over a gold-trimmed, scarlet jacket.

"Captain Holcomb!" she called out with relief. Carefully, she unloaded her crossbow and slung it over her sore shoulder. He trotted toward her and, leaning down, offered a hand. "Thanks," she said as he pulled her up onto the horse's back.

"Your horse?" he asked as she settled behind the saddle.

"I think he's gone home," she sighed, grabbing the sides of Holcomb's jacket when he urged the horse forward again. "What about Kol?"

"Lost sight of him," he replied over his shoulder.

"Go back," she ordered. "We have to find him."

He nodded, and, clucking loudly, sent his horse into a trot.

Adella and Holcomb returned to the area where they'd last seen Kol, but the field was empty, with no sign of riders now. Holcomb slowed his horse to a walk as they searched the tall grass, eyes scanning the landscape until Adella caught sight of a dark shape moving in the distance.

"What's that?" Holcomb asked.

Adella narrowed her eyes. "A... horse," she guessed. "I don't see a rider—" A frantic neigh sounded over the field as the approaching animal picked up its pace, and Adella's heart pounded. "Madigan! That's Kol's horse!" she said, voice ragged as panic gripped her chest. "He's fallen..." Her words trailed off, mind coursing through the dire possibilities.

"He must be nearby," Holcomb replied, lowering the brim of his hat to shield his eyes as he searched.

Adella dismounted as Madigan came toward them. She caught the mare by the reins as Holcomb spoke. "Lady Grimless," he began darkly. "Look there, in the grass." He nodded westward.

Following his motion, she spotted a dark shape on the ground. Her heart fell into her stomach as she passed Madigan's reins to the captain. *No,* she pleaded silently, breaking into a run, *don't let it be Kol...* Drawing nearer, she could see his familiar faded, black shirt and doeskin breeches. Her legs grew unsteady, threatening to give out beneath her.

"Kol!" Adella shouted. Falling to her knees at his side, she gently turned his head to face her, but he didn't respond. His body was limp, eyes closed; black hair clung, wet and matted, to his blood-stained forehead. "Kol," she repeated under her breath, shaking him by the shoulders. "Please, wake up."

He remained motionless, a strange pallor swallowing the usual bronze of his face. She put an ear to his chest, but there was no sound or movement. *He's not breathing!* Prodding two fingers at his throat, she searched for a pulse, but her own heart was beating so wildly, it was all she could feel. For a moment, visions of her life without him flashed in her mind, and it felt cold and empty.

"Kol, wake up!" Adella shouted, tears springing into her eyes. "Don't leave me here alone! Please..." she muttered, hands trembling as she clutched his shirt. "I can't do this without you." She was dully aware of hoofsteps at her back, then Holcomb knelt beside her, putting his fingers to Kol's neck. "Is he—?" She couldn't say the word.

"Come on, man," Holcomb pleaded through his teeth. "Get up."

Adella watched breathlessly as Kol's face took on a sickly, ashen cast, blue tinting his lips. "Kol!" she shouted, voice breaking as she frantically shook him by the shoulders. "No!"

7

Masquerade

Armand strode through the Ansebulet's vast hallways as the bright sunlight streamed in from the high, arched windows, passing beneath brass chandeliers that hung from a ceiling painted with clouds. Though he had promised Miss Adella he'd verify the presence of Leveret's lockbox in the treasury, he'd been unable to contact Queen Ellinora to ask her permission. He'd spent weeks in the suites they'd been given that spring, sitting among the opulent furnishings and gaudy gilt moldings and enjoying the deliciously seasoned meats and colorful pastries the Capital was known for. But a response from the Queen never came. Now, he was done waiting patiently. Thankfully, he had another ally in the palace he could call on.

The vast hall's marble floors supported great, fluted columns which held a high, domed ceiling. Armand watched the well-dressed courtiers who milled about the hall, and scarlet-clad guards at their posts, looking for Miss Margo. She'd responded to his letter only that morning, requesting to meet him outside the throne room immediately. He turned this way and that, scanning the space.

"Armand," a bright, familiar voice called out, and he turned. A young woman in a scarlet jacket and petticoats, with chestnut hair pressed into ringlets, embraced him.

"Miss Margo," he greeted her. It felt like ages since he'd seen Lord Grimless' oldest daughter, who was as dear to him as his own flesh and blood. "What—" He raised an eyebrow at her military-style jacket, trimmed with brass buttons and gold braid. It reminded him somewhat of the officers' uniforms from his days in the cavalry. "What are you wearing?"

"Oh," she said, brushing her hands over her skirts as she looked down at her clothes. "It's the fashion now, inspired by a certain Lady and her cavaliers on the frontier. It's meant to show our support for those at the warfront." She flashed a quick smile, hiding an underlying look of concern. "How *is* my sister? And Lucas?"

"She's well," Armand replied. "At least, she was when I last saw her..." He cleared his throat. "Your brother and Teressa ran off together. Heaven knows where they are now, but I'm sure they're happy."

"Is that so?" she asked with surprise. "Strange; he didn't write. But how are things at Greywood?" she prodded, shaking it off. "I've heard only rumors; is it true Adella hired the Pentz Standing Cavalry?"

"Yes," he replied proudly. "They'd just agreed to it last I saw her. That's when she sent me here, to the Capital. And how are things here; how are the little ones?" he asked quickly.

"Not so little anymore," she replied, the smile briefly returning to her pretty face. "I wish you could see them." Taking his elbow, she leaned in to whisper. "Rolan is taking them to stay at his parents' estate outside the Capital. Something is going on around here, though I don't know what. Come," she said, eyes darting around as she pulled him along. "We can't speak here."

Turning a corner, they came to an empty hallway. "The Queen is missing," Margo said pointedly, her voice low. "No one knows where she is. Or they're not saying."

"How long?" he asked.

"I'm not really sure." She shrugged, pouting sadly. "But, as some still consider Lord Hollen to be next in line, her absence puts us in danger of having him placed back on the throne. He went missing after the Queen's return, but something tells me he hasn't gone far."

"That treasonous bastard?" Armand frowned. "They can't put him in charge."

"Unless another option is brought forth," she replied with a shrug, "they very well might."

As much as he hated Lord Hollen, Armand had a more pressing matter for which he needed her ear. "Listen, Miss Margo," he began frankly, leaning in. "I need your help with something urgent. I made a promise to Miss Adella I'd find a way into the treasury to make sure the Heart of the World was still safe, and I intend to keep it. But as I haven't been able to get the Queen's permission—" Though they were alone, he lowered his voice to a whisper. "I'll have to do it without."

"Into the treasury? And without the Queen..." Margo pressed her lips together. "That's not an easy task. But of course, I will help you and my sister however I can." She paused, tapping her chin. "We're going to need a plan." She paced down the hall, then turned abruptly and strode back. Sticking a finger in the air, she opened her mouth to speak, then shut her mouth and strode away again.

"What if we—" Armand began.

"Shh," she interrupted, waving her finger. Margo stood for a moment, as still as the shadow she made in the sunlight of the window, then turned suddenly and hurried back to him. "I've got it," she said finally. "There's an event in the ballroom Saturday night. Queen or no, the Harvest Ball will go on just the same." She rolled her eyes upward in displeasure. "That's our chance. I'll meet you at your suite with supplies—" At the sound of footsteps, she shut her mouth.

A woman turned the corner, her dress completely covered in lace frills and pink bows. Her face was heavily powdered; her glossy black hair was pinned high on her head and adorned with large feathers and pearls.

"Lady Margavita," the woman muttered, failing to stifle a smirk as she approached. She hid a glower behind a small, painted fan. "I thought that was you."

"Lady Joy," Margo countered. "What a surprise to see you here." Though her tone was polite, the look in her eye suggested the surprise wasn't a good one.

"Who is your..." Lady Joy's grin was nearly a sneer as she looked Armand over. "Companion?"

"An old friend of my father's," Margo replied coolly. "Armand, this is Lady Joy Fadley, of the Hartwick Fadleys. She likewise resides at the Capital. We run into each other often," she added, clipping her words primly.

Lady Joy bowed slightly at the introduction. "Well, aren't you two a conspiracy, whispering here in the hallway alone?" she said teasingly, the drawn-on mole on her cheek bouncing with every word.

"Just taking a stroll and catching up," Margo replied. "Will we have the pleasure of seeing you at the Harvest Ball?"

"Oh, I wouldn't miss it." Lady Joy smiled broadly. "I hope to see you and *Lord Rolan* there," she added, emphasising the name. Then, with a wave of her fan, she turned and continued down the hallway.

"Ugh," Margo groaned when the interloper was out of earshot. "How I hate that woman! She'd better not get in our way."

"Her?" Armand chuckled. "She seems harmless enough."

"That's what you think," Margo retorted. "Let's go before she decides to come back and annoy me again. Don't forget to be in your suite Saturday evening before the ball," she reminded, wagging a dainty finger at him. "I'll meet you there."

Returning to the suite, Armand plopped down on the jacquard sofa. It felt good to finally make progress on fulfilling Miss Adella's request, though he wasn't sure what Miss Margo had planned. Once again, thoughts turned to Elldon and Greywood Manor, as they had so often since he'd been in the Capital, and he wondered how his young friends were faring. It had been clear to him for some time now that the Sornian, Kol, whom Armand had come to regard like a son, had developed feelings for Miss Adella. Unfortunately, she was too besotted with the handsome Captain Declan to see it for herself. Armand couldn't help but wonder if there had been any developments on that front while he was away. Declan didn't need Miss Adella, and though she'd yet to realize it, she didn't need him, either. But Kol was new to Valenna and without a friend in the world. *He's the one who needs her.* Likewise, she needed someone to look out for her now that she was on her own, and Kol clearly wanted the job. *Unlike Declan.*

"Ehh," Armand muttered to himself, waving the thoughts away. "Young people's problems." He had his own problems to worry about. A bottle of strong brandy would sort Kol and Adella's situation out quick enough, but his was more serious than that.

When the day of the Harvest Ball arrived, Armand remained in the suite, fearing to leave even for a moment and miss the appointed meeting. He had spent the past few days keeping to himself in the rooms of the Ansebulet to avoid any outside attention. Laughter and conversation issued from the hallway outside all the morning as people made their way through the palace in preparation. He had dressed for a ball, wearing a silk cravat and embroidered waistcoat, its buttons straining from too many days spent in leisure with good food.

He sat on the sofa, staring at the tall-case clock in the corner. The hours crept by, each chime bringing new degrees of anxiety. Outside the balcony, the autumn sun lowered as evening crept over the Bay, its waters darkening to iron in the twilight.

Finally, a knock at the door broke the silence of the room and he jumped to his feet. Rushing over, he opened it and, much to his surprise, a Royal Guard in scarlet pushed past him, carrying a large canvas sack in front of his face.

"Uff," the guard huffed, dumping the bag onto the sofa to reveal an assortment of clothing.

"Uh," Armand began, the door falling shut behind him. "What's going on?"

Ignoring him, the guard rifled through the clothing scattered on the sofa, throwing waistcoats on the floor before finally holding up a red jacket. Spinning, the guard measured it against Armand's chest, and a smile spread across the smooth, youthful face. "Ah ha!"

"Listen here, boy—" Armand began. Then he stopped himself. The guard's hair, tied back in a queue beneath a large cocked hat, shone a familiar shade of chestnut; together with the full, pink lips and delicate nose, the realization finally struck him. "Miss Margo!" he said, then furrowed his brow. "You can't go to the ball dressed like that."

"Put this on," she ordered, pressing the jacket into his arms. "Quickly." He obeyed. Passing him a sword-belt and hat, she pulled him into the hallway.

He had just finished buckling the belt onto his waist when a well-dressed group of ladies with jeweled masks hanging above their painted lips approached, chatting amongst themselves. Seeing the two of them in their uniforms, the ladies looked them up and down, giggling behind their hands and making faces as they passed.

Armand turned, watching them make their way down the hallway. "I should've become a Royal Guard ages ago," he said, a grin spreading across his face.

"Don't get distracted," Margo chided. Pulling him along, she shot him a half-smile. "It's me they're looking at, not you."

Soon, they came to the Great Hall outside the Throne Room, its spacious vaulted ceiling hung with banners of russet and gold above crowds of opulently dressed courtiers. They pressed through the groups, tripping now and then on long skirts and pointed shoes, through a dizzying array of color and texture, of gold jacquard, feathers and lace, the air heavy with the varying scents of pomanders, perfumes and hair powder.

They elbowed their way through one large group, raucous with laughter. Margo pulled her hat lower over her brow to shield her face. A black and gold masked woman eyed them sharply.

"That woman," Margo whispered to him after they'd passed. "Is she still watching us?"

Glancing over his shoulder, he was relieved that the woman turned back toward her companions. "No," Armand replied as they continued onward. "I don't think so." He looked back again, this time to her picking up her pace along behind them, her long, ruffled black and gold skirts swishing side to side with each quick stride. He frowned. "Yes. Damn. She's following us."

"Go quickly," Margo urged under her breath, hastening her steps.

They hurried down the crowded hallway. Sweat beaded on Armand's brow as he struggled to keep pace with Margo. The old injury in his knee, incurred back at the Cairn that spring, began to ache, hobbling his movement.

"Over here," she whispered, pulling him down a narrow side corridor. Their shoes echoed on the bare stones as Armand limped to keep up. Coming to a recessed doorway, Margo pressed her back against the door, motioning for Armand to do likewise.

He squeezed himself as tightly as he could against the door to hide behind the stone ledge.

"Armand," Margo whispered sharply, widening her eyes at his gut. It stuck conspicuously out from behind the wall.

Taking a deep breath, he sucked in his belly as far as he could. His face pulled into a grimace as he flattened himself into the alcove.

Footsteps echoed down the corridor. Glancing around the ledge of alcove, he caught a glimpse of black skirts rustling past as the woman continued down the hall. He let out his breath, letting his belly hang free again.

The footsteps stopped abruptly. Then, they grew louder, gaining speed as they returned. Armand squeezed his eyes shut and pulled his stomach in again, holding his breath as he pressed himself desperately flat against the door. If they were to get caught impersonating Royal Guards, it would surely be treason, and with the Queen missing, there'd be no explaining their way out of it. He'd be no help to Miss Adella locked in a tower.

The steps quieted, then faded away entirely.

"Armand," Margo whispered, but he could hardly hear her over the beating of his pulse. "Armand," she repeated louder.

Opening one eye, he looked carefully to find they were alone. He let out his breath in relief. Their pursuer had returned the way she'd come.

"Let's go," Margo said, pulling at his sleeve.

They made their way down several more side corridors, through passages that Armand, though he'd lived in the Capital with the Grimless family years ago, had never seen before. At the top of a dark stairwell, sparsely illuminated by glass-paneled lanterns that hung along the wall, Margo grabbed one from its hook and descended.

His heart hammered as he followed her down into the musty, damp air of the stairwell. The pain in his knee grew sharper with every loud, shuffling step, while their black shadows danced in the flickering orange light of the lantern.

Soon, voices carried through the darkness ahead. They came to a subterranean tunnel, lined with arched stone passageways, some of which were barred by iron grates secured with heavy locks. Water dripped from the raw rock ceiling, collecting in pools here and there on the floor. He followed Margo into one passageway, and a familiarity suddenly struck him: Though they'd entered from a different direction, he'd come this way months ago as he accompanied Queen Ellinora to the treasury. *We're almost there.*

Lanterns illuminated the far end of the passageway, which ended in an iron door. Two Royal Guards in scarlet stood on either side, the sword hilts on their hips gleaming gold. While one stood at attention, the other sat, crouched against the wall, leaning his head back against the damp stone, a wine bottle in one hand. He rose at their approach, hiding the bottle behind his back.

Armand swallowed his fear, sweat dripping down his nose despite the coolness of the air. He hoped Margo had a good plan up her sleeve.

"We've been sent to relieve you," Margot said, deepening her voice. "Captain's ordered half-watches for the Harvest Ball."

"Oh, thank goodness." The younger guard, who'd been sitting, sighed as he stretched his legs. "I was afraid we'd miss it entirely."

The other guard narrowed his eyes, gaze passing slowly from Margo to Armand. Then he nodded a brief salute and turned to go.

"Ah," Margo said, stopping them with an open palm. "The keys."

"Yes, of course," the younger guard prompted, tilting his head in expectation.

The other moved his hand slowly toward his belt but hesitated, eyeing her dubiously again.

"Go on, then," the young guard urged. "I'd like to make it in time for some dancing."

The other guard wavered with his hand over the keys, glancing from Margo to his companion. Finally, he took them from his belt and set them in her hand.

With a final salute, the two guards disappeared down the corridor.

Margo let out a sigh of relief once they were out of sight, then passed Armand the lantern. Turning toward the iron door, she began shuffling through the keys, trying one and then another in the large keyhole. Soon, it unlocked, and the door opened with a grating squeal.

"I can't believe that worked," Armand laughed as they entered the room, where many shining, glittering objects sat on dusty shelves locked behind protective bars.

"It's the Harvest Ball," Margo reasoned. "No one is sober."

Striding toward the back of the space, he came to the far wall and lifted the lantern to search the shelves. His heart sank. In the place they'd left Leveret's lockbox months before, the shelf sat empty, with only the memory of its shape left behind in the dust. "Oh, dear," he muttered.

"What is it?" she asked, stepping beside him.

"The Heart of the World," he replied breathlessly, staring at the void on the shelf. "It's gone."

"Are you sure?" She picked up the lantern and looked around. "What does it look like?"

"Just an iron box..." he trailed off, his eyes searching the shelves. "No," he uttered finally, shoulders drooping. "It isn't here. It's gone." Miss Adella had given him only this one task, and he'd failed.

"Well," she reasoned, patting his shoulder, "we'd better not linger. Let's go."

They stepped out of the treasury door and into the passageway. Emerging from the shadows, hands grabbed them roughly, pulling their arms behind their backs.

"Yes, that's them," a sharp voice spoke from the darkness. Stepping out of the shadows and into the lantern light, a woman lifted a black and gold mask over her brow, revealing the face of Lady Joy. "I knew they were up to something. Guards, lock them in the tower," she sneered with satisfaction, "for stealing from the royal treasury."

Margo passed a look to Armand as the guards pulled her along, the astonishment and fear clear in her widened eyes.

"No!" Armand called out, fighting against the arms that held him. "Let her go, it was all my idea!" One guard dealt a blow to his stomach so hard that it knocked the air from his lungs. Doubled over in pain, he gasped helplessly as they dragged him through the passageways and back up the stairwell.

They wound through hallways, prodding him up many flights of stairs until, finally, the guards shoved him forward. He fell to his knees upon the hard stone floor of a prison cell, cringing at the sound of the lock sliding into place behind him. Though it was dark, a chill breeze wafted in. Searching the wall above his head, he found a square of night sky, dotted with stars.

Turning around, he moved forward until he found the prison bars. Grasping them, he called out, "Miss Margo, are you in here?"

"I am," she replied softly.

Tears sprang into his eyes. "I'm so sorry," he groaned miserably, "for dragging you into this. It's all my fault." Leaning against the bars, he buried his face in his hands.

8

A Reckoning

Kol heaved, finally pulling air into his burning lungs. His head spun, stars twinkling before him, while he tried to recall where he was. His vision slowly cleared, and a figure came into focus, leaning over him, silhouetted against the blue sky. He squinted, trying to make out the features. *Adella?* His thoughts swirled with confusion.

"Oh, thank heavens!" Adella sighed as she threw herself over him. Wrapping her arms around his neck, she buried her face in the hollow of his shoulder.

Kol groaned, pain throbbing through his skull. Grass tickled his skin. Across his chest, Adella's body trembled against his ribs. *She's shaking...* Unable to muster his voice, he set his hand reassuringly on her slender back. Soft, auburn hair fell over his face as he drew another deep breath, inhaling the scent of rosewater.

"Are you hurt?" she asked, sitting up.

Kol rolled over, coughing as he propped himself up on an arm. His head pounded violently; he could hardly think. Putting a hand to his forehead, it came away wet and sticky, fingers glistening scarlet.

"What happened?" she asked, rising to her feet.

Gingerly, he sat up. "I don't—" he began hoarsely. "I don't know."

"You must've hit your head," she replied, voice strained.

Kol blinked at her. *That's right...* he realized, flashes of images suddenly returning; *I fell off my horse.* His pride didn't allow him to admit it aloud.

"How long were you lying there?" she prodded.

"Not long." He rubbed the back of his head and felt a large knot forming. "I think."

"Glad you're still with us," Holcomb commented warmly, offering him a hand.

Seeing their concerned expressions looking intently down on him, Kol's face grew hot. "What are you two staring at?" he muttered as Holcomb pulled him to his feet. "Just got the wind knocked out of me, that's all."

"You were unconscious," Adella countered sharply, wrapping her arms around herself.

Kol searched her face, his gaze tracing the lines that worry etched into her expression. He hated to be the cause of her pain, but he knew there would be more for her yet. Their attempt to negotiate had failed; she'd have to give up on rescuing her friend.

"Let's head back," Adella said dryly, turning away.

Kol was taken aback; he hadn't expected her to say it first. He opened his mouth to speak but couldn't find the words.

"We gave it our best," Holcomb reassured her gently, putting a hand on her shoulder. "You can't save everyone, no matter how hard you try. I'm sorry."

Adella drew a deep, shuddering breath and nodded.

Kol wished he were the one consoling her, but his head still pounded, muddling his thoughts. "We need to go quickly," he managed, the urgency in his tone carrying the warning that they were still in enemy territory.

* * *

Adella's heart ached as she, Holcomb and Kol headed homeward. Out of a sense of politeness, Holcomb had lent her his horse, while he walked beside them. Cresting a ridge, they spied plain-clothed riders watering their horses at a small stream below, beneath the sprawling arms of a great oak.

"Sornians?" Holcomb asked beside her, halting his horse, which he led in-hand while she sat in the saddle. When the two sides wore the same dun homespun, it was difficult to tell them apart at a distance.

Adella shook her head. "I think those are our people."

From the haversack at his side, Holcomb drew a small spyglass and peered through it. "Yes, you're right," he said, putting it away. "Their long hair is tied into queues."

"That means that's Jacoby's ranger party," Adella added, her expression falling. Her stomach knotted. She wasn't looking forward to telling Jacoby they'd failed. *After everything Misses Asher—Beatrice—has done, for Elldon, for Greywood, only to have to leave her behind now...* But in trying to save Misses Asher, she'd nearly lost Kol. The thought of weighing one life against the other turned her stomach, but seeing him lying motionless in the grass, head stained scarlet with blood, had struck her profoundly. Though she'd certainly seen him injured before and often worried for his safety, he'd always seemed too quick-witted, too hardy, too stubborn to die. She'd never seen him vulnerable like that. *I can't lose him.* The sudden realization struck her like a knife to the heart. *I can't do this without him.* They continued on toward the group. Adella drew a deep breath to steady her nerves, then dismounted Holcomb's horse, passing the reins to him.

"Where's Jacoby?" she asked as she approached the group, her boots sloshing through the shallow, trickling stream. The shade beneath the outstretched boughs of the massive oak cooled her sun-flushed skin as she looked them over, all clothed in drab browns and tans.

One man stepped solemnly toward her, leading a dappled grey. He pulled a wide-brimmed wool hat from his head to reveal a familiar, stout face from beneath its shadow.

"What happened?" Jacoby asked, voice low as his gaze flitted anxiously from Adella to Kol and Holcomb at her side. "Did you meet with them?"

"I'm so sorry, Jacoby—" Adella began, throat heavy with the weight of her words. Before she could finish, his eyes widened and settled in the distance behind her. She turned to see what had caught his attention. Behind her, a broad silhouette on horseback overlooked the valley, standing motionless on the western ridge. A tall, plumed hat added height to the already imposing figure. *General Blackburn.* Adella's pulse quickened as two other riders joined him. One raised a pole skyward; streaming from it, a pale patch of cloth fluttered on the mounting breeze. *A white flag!*

Seeing her horseless, Jacoby passed his reins to Adella. She nodded in thanks and climbed into the saddle.

"There may be more waiting beyond the ridge," Holcomb warned, turning his horse to follow.

"I know," she replied quietly, her back straightening. She looked to Kol as he drew up beside her on his black mare. He gave a small nod of encouragement, blood still glistening on his brow, and the three of them rode back out the way they'd come.

Halfway across the field between the stream and the ridge, Blackburn broke away from his escorts, leaving them on the rise as he rode down toward them.

Adella understood the cue. "Wait here," she instructed. Kol and Holcomb obeyed, halting their horses. She continued alone, closing the distance between herself and the general. At his back, storm clouds gathered in the west, darkening the horizon.

"I got your message," General Blackburn grumbled loudly as he halted on a large draft bay. His voice was deep and gravelly, resounding through the massive barrel of his chest. "Not sure what you think you can offer me," he added, disdain tinting his words.

"Supplies. Money. Horses," she replied plainly, drawing back her reins.

"You're willing to strengthen your enemy for the sake of one old woman?" he scoffed, lines creasing around his broad mouth as he twisted it into something resembling a smile. "She must be very valuable to you."

"My reasons are sentimental," Adella replied coolly, all too aware of the danger in appearing overeager. "Are you interested in a trade, or not?"

"You understand that it's only a matter of time before my troops wipe your little holdout off the map?" he asked, though his tone made it clear it wasn't a question. "Everything you have will be mine. All you can offer me in the meantime, is a little amusement." His grin deepened as he rubbed his wide stubbled jaw. "I'll trade you," Blackburn offered, voice booming over the field so loud it was clear he wanted the others to hear, "a life for a life."

Adella's mouth went dry, pulse quickening. She hadn't expected him to put her in such a dilemma. Supplies she could part with, but to trade people like dry goods was out of the question; she'd have to find another solution. Her expression turned into a scowl. "Forget it—" Her horse began to prance nervously in place, and she glanced back to see what upset it. Before she uttered another word, a plain-clothed rider burst into the negotiations, flanked by Kol and Holcomb.

"I'll do it," the rider shouted, pulling free as Kol and Holcomb grabbed for the reins of his horse. "I'll make the trade." James halted beside Adella, his piebald lathered with sweat. Her mouth fell in disbelief seeing him upon Misses Asher's horse, Bixby. "I offer myself captive in her place," he announced.

Adella's stomach clenched at the sight of him. A rope held James in the saddle, tied around his thighs and waist. His injured leg, bare and sickeningly swollen, the skin a deathly purple, dangled free from the stirrup iron; his face was blanched and beaded with sweat, pain written clearly in his fraught grimace.

"What are you doing here?" Adella snapped. From the depths of her memory, she heard Armand's voice; *Promise me you'll keep an eye on them at Elldon. Beatrice, and her boys...* Adella shook her head frantically. "No, James! Go home!"

Watching her reaction, a smirk of satisfaction spread over Blackburn's face. "We have a deal," he replied. Placing his fingers in his mouth, he let out a shrill whistle, and the Sornains waiting on the ridge rode down toward them.

"No!" Adella yelled. She urged her horse forward, but Kol reached for the reins and held her in place.

"Take him," Blackburn ordered, pointing. The men surrounded James, throwing ropes over him and his horse, and led him away.

"Stop!" Adella shouted.

Kol steadied her horse again. "He made his choice."

"We have no reason to think Blackburn will keep his word," Adella countered, pushing his hand away, but it wouldn't give.

"Too late now," Kol muttered darkly. "It's done."

From beyond the rise, a pale horse came into view, led by an emerald-clad soldier. Upon its back, a figure slumped, head bobbing with each stride; a skirt draped over the saddle.

Adella let out a gasp, hand rising to her mouth. "Beatrice!" she uttered under her breath, her stomach twisting into knots.

Kol charged forward on Madigan, dismounting quickly as he came up the slope, and pulled the insensible woman from the saddle. The Sornian retreated with his horse as the old woman slunk lifelessly into the grass at Kol's feet. Lifting her limp body, he placed her gently upon Madigan's back.

Adella directed the men to put Misses Asher on Jacoby's horse, and sat awkwardly behind the saddle, holding up the half-conscious woman. They needed to travel as quickly as possible if they were to return to Elldon by nightfall, so they took turns walking and trading horses to keep from slowing the group down.

By the time they had reached the western fields of Elldon, Adella's muscles ached. They crossed the cavalier encampment, with the cavalry horses in their make-shift paddocks, constructed after the spring fire destroyed the stable fences, and passed through the wide gap in the palisade, which was nearly complete. As it was of the utmost importance in defending the town, all had to do their part in its construction, even as they prepared for the coming battle. Soon, the final gate would be put into place, forming a stockade around the Greywood Estate to protect its people from attack. *Hopefully it's finished before the Sornians arrive.* They were certainly going to need it.

When they reached the manor house, Kol and Captain Holcomb pulled Misses Asher carefully from the saddle. As they placed her on the ground, her legs buckled beneath her and she slumped into the grass. Letting out an anguished wail, she turned away on her side. Sweat glistened on her brow; her forearms were mottled purple, and dried blood caked her fingernails.

"What's wrong with her?" Adella asked fretfully, brows knitted.

"I don't know," Kol replied. "She's delirious. It could be camp fever." He shrugged. "Outbreaks are pretty common in the close quarters of the Sornian encampments. But the bruises..." An unusual graveness settled over his features.

Adella's heart panged at the unspoken possibility. *Torture.* She brushed the damp grey hair from Misses Asher's face, fingers sweeping over eyes that stared absently into the distance. A cold raindrop hit Adella's cheek. "Let's get her inside."

She held the door of Greywood's rear entrance while Kol and Holcomb carried Misses Asher's light frame, stretched out between them, one at her shoulders and one by her feet, into the manor. Shuffling their way carefully through the dim hallway, they brought her into the spacious parlor room, where the high, ornate ceiling sheltered Adella's writing desk and the sofa that had been James' recovery bed since his injury.

"Set her here," Adella instructed, moving a scattering of belongings from the cushions. They lowered her gently onto them. Scant light filtered through the chinks in the boards that covered the tall casement windows, still unrepaired and shutterless from the Sornian attack that spring. Outside, thunder rumbled, and rain began to patter loudly on the slate roof.

Glancing up at the boarded windows, Adella wondered if she'd ever see Greywood Estate restored to its former beauty. All around her were remnants of the life she'd once had; treasured heirlooms sat, now dust-covered, on the mantel: her mother's antique clock, her father's cavalry portrait, Lucas's pewter horse figurine from when he was a child. With everything that had happened, she knew her life could never be the same. She looked at the frail Misses Asher lying on the sofa and thought of James, now in the hands of the Sornians. Her brother, her parents, Teressa, even Armand, all were gone now. Even though the circumstances varied, she felt each absence keenly. She couldn't help but fear that each person at Elldon would slip away, one by one, until no one was left and only ruins remained.

Rosalind's soft voice jolted her from her thoughts, coming from the far side of the room where she lingered like a shadow in the doorway. "Where's James?"

"He's not here," Adella replied, her voice straining through the lump that formed in her throat. She swallowed to clear it. "Could you look after Beatrice for us while we see to things?" she asked before Rosalind could respond, trying to keep her tone light. "Perhaps some tea…" she trailed off, heart sinking at the futility of her request. Adella turned her head away, tears blurring her vision.

Outside the manor house, the air had turned cool. A thick blanket of dark clouds hung low over the landscape, pelting their faces with droplets as Adella, Kol, and Holcomb made their way to the western camp where the rangers were untacking their horses. Adella scanned the grounds for Shy in hopes he'd made it safely home. Passing by scarlet-clad cavaliers tending to the horses, she searched for his distinctive markings among the bays in the paddocks.

"Lieutenant Lewis," Adella called out, catching his attention while he brushed down a grey gelding. "Have you seen Shy?"

"Lady Grimless." He turned to greet her, revealing a long red scar on one cheek, then pressed his mouth as he thought. "Little bay, wide blaze?" he asked, and she nodded. "I believe he is—" A loud squeal pierced through the sound of the pouring rain.

Adella spun. There, at the gap in the palisade wall, a horse galloped in from the western fields, calling frantically for its herd. Through the gloom of the drizzle, she saw the black and white markings of the horse's coat, with a rider clinging onto the saddle. Panic stabbed Adella's gut like a knife.

"That's Bixby!" she shouted. There was something odd about its fitful movements, as though the rider had no control. *What's wrong with the rider?* She squinted at the dark form in the saddle.

"James!" she screamed, running forward. The rider's shape seemed strange, too small to be James. *Perhaps he's hunched forward?* Bixby slowed to a trot as cavaliers approached, crossing the grass between paddocks and tents to corner the animal, and Adella broke into a run.

Kol caught her after a few strides, and, grabbing her arm, held her back. "Adella, don't." There was an edge in his voice. "Get inside Greywood."

"Why?" she asked breathlessly, looking up at his eyes, then back at the horse. The cavaliers surrounded Bixby, grabbing the reins; the dark form sitting on the horse's back lurched alarmingly sideways but stayed in the saddle. Adella pulled against Kol's arm. "Something's wrong. He needs help!"

Kol shook his head slowly, but didn't loosen his grip on her arm. Ahead, Bixby spun his haunches around while cavaliers tried to calm him. The white markings along the animal's side were stained a bright crimson. Adella gasped. *Blood!*

"Kol, let go!" she ordered as Bixby broke free from the cavaliers and trotted wildly through the encampment, heading their direction.

Neighing madly, his head high in the air, Bixby came toward them. Jame's body was lashed to the saddle, with his hands tied to the martingale strap. Between his shoulders, where his head should have been, protruded a ragged, raw stump of flesh, white bone peeking through the red cascade of blood that flooded down his pale shirt.

Adella screamed, and Kol quickly wrapped her in his arms, pressing her face against his rough wool jacket. But it was too late. The image seared in her mind, her limbs shaking as he pressed her forehead into his chest.

Her empty stomach churned. Pushing away from him, she fell to her knees, retched, and spat acrid, yellow bile onto the grass. "Why?!" she demanded hoarsely between her sobs, throat burning and mouth sour.

"They're trying to intimidate us," Kol replied through gritted teeth. "To get us to act rashly."

"Damn them!" Adella pounded her fist into the dirt. "Damn those Sornian savages!"

Kol reached toward her, but she recoiled, eyes wide and insensible, mind reeling from the sight of her mutilated friend. Raw nerves made her hands tremble as she brought them to her face. She took a shuddering breath and slumped forward to the ground, cradling her head in her palms.

Kneeling down beside her, Kol took her hands in his, his steady gaze drawing her back to the present. "Adella, stand up," he whispered, glancing around at the crowd that surrounded them. The entire encampment had gathered around the body, their shouts of shock and anger growing louder.

She shook her head. "Leave me be."

"Lady Grimless," he said sharply, and the sudden formality caught her attention. "You must get up," he hissed between his teeth. "All eyes are on you."

My people. Spurred by his words, Adella drew a deep, shaky breath, then tentatively rose. "Give me your arm," she whispered, back straightening though her legs trembled beneath her. She blinked, trying to see through a blur of tears. "Guide me to the house. Please."

He led her by the arm into the silent refuge of Greywood's darkened parlor. "Losing people..." Kol began softly, voice trailing as he searched for words. "It's a consequence of war—"

Adella rounded on him. "Is this how your people make war?" she snapped.

"Adella, please—" He raised his palms, the hurt clear in his voice. "I'm not one of them. Not anymore."

Seeing his wounded expression, she let out her breath, the tension falling from her shoulders. "I'm sorry. I—" She sat down in the little chair beside her writing desk, shoulders slumping as she leaned against the back. "I forgot myself."

"It's all right," he replied under his breath.

"Dear James," she said thickly, her voice sticking in her throat as her tears overflowed again. "What did they do to him?" she asked blindly. The sight of his disfigured body tied to the saddle still burned in her mind like a branding iron.

Slumping onto her writing desk, she buried her face in her folded arms and sobbed. With each ragged cry, she let go, releasing all the emotion she'd been trying so hard to keep inside ever since she returned to Elldon without her family.

Standing silently beside her, Kol placed a hand on her shoulder. In the midst of her inconsolable sorrow, his touch felt comforting and strong, as though he could somehow hold her together even while the world fell apart.

* * *

As the moments passed into hours, Kol stood by Adella, crumpled in tears. It had been many years since he'd felt as she did about the loss of a fellow soldier. James' death stabbed at his conscience, too, but it was something he could bury deep, like all the others. Perhaps he'd grown callous over the years. Having never been good with words, he had none to quell her pain. All he could offer was quiet company, a reminder that she wasn't alone.

After a time, Adella wiped her face on her sleeve and looked over at Misses Asher, still unconscious on the sofa. "Should we wake her and tell her?"

"No," Kol replied softly. "Let her be, for now." His gaze shifted to Declan's letter, mostly buried beneath the sprawl of papers on her desk, save for part of her name. The sight of Adella's name written in another man's hand twisted his gut. Though he knew the timing couldn't be any worse, he couldn't put off telling her about it any longer. Perhaps reading a letter from the man she loved would ease her pain a little. He let out a breath of resignation. Hesitantly, he reached out for the letter, fingers twitching briefly in the air before snatching it from beneath the papers. Whatever was between her and the captain, it didn't change the way Kol felt about her, no matter how much he might wish it, and as he stared blankly at the letter in his hand, his jaw tightened with resolve. *This is going to hurt.*

"What is it?" she asked, brows raising.

"I'd meant to tell you—" Despite his attempt to sound casual, there was an edge in his voice. "You have a letter from Captain Declan."

"What...?" she whispered as he set it down before her. Quickly, she broke the seal and unfolded the paper.

Realizing he'd been looking over her shoulder, Kol turned to leave, his boots rapping sharply over the wood floor as he made his way across the room.

"It's a marriage proposal," she said softly from behind him.

Her words stopped him in his tracks, cutting straight through his heart. Glancing back, his eyes met hers briefly as she looked up at him from across the room. His throat tightened, breathing quickening as he turned hastily, not wanting her to see his expression breaking. His rapid footsteps echoed through the parlor, then the hallway, as he gave Adella her privacy.

9

A Long-Awaited Moment

It rained softly the following morning when James was laid to rest beneath the great oak that sheltered the fields of his family's smallholding. The same plot that had held barley seed in the spring, had been burned in the raids, and which had lain fire-fallow since, now gently cradled his desecrated body in its cool, dark soil.

We work the land, and it feeds us, Adella reflected silently as the rough pine coffin was lowered slowly into the ground, *and when our days are done, our bodies feed it in turn.* No matter how long or brief a man's life might seem, it was still only a moment to the mighty oak. The broad trunk of the one that protected James' grave gave testament to an age marked in centuries, not decades. She looked up, noticing that the leaves that shuddered in the wind high above her had just begun their autumnal change, the ends of green boughs heralding the close of another year with somber shades of russet.

The encampments were quiet that day. Each person took to their tasks solemnly, many sharpening their blades and repairing tack for the days to come. Though everyone understood the imminence of the danger that awaited outside the unfinished palisade walls, it was not fear that moved them; their bleak despondence, like a fresh wound, was foremost in mind. Perhaps it seemed selfish to care too much about one's own life when that of a friend's had just been taken, succumbing to a fate that might await them all.

Each time she thought of James, guilt tore through Adella, nearly bringing her to her knees again and again, just like the first time. *It's my fault...* She'd been the one to suggest a negotiation, despite Kol's warning. She'd been arrogant to think she could make a difference with diplomacy. *James was under my care.* The people of Elldon were her responsibility, each one; she had sworn an oath. Worse, she had promised Armand. *I was stupid to think I could do it. Stupid to think I could fill my father's shoes...* All morning, her thoughts echoed relentlessly in her mind, and though she did her best to keep her face from betraying her composure, her heart felt like lead in her chest, sinking down ever further toward her gut.

Trying to keep her mind busy, Adella returned to her translation work, opening the Codex on her campaign desk inside her tent and throwing herself into it so greedily that even before midday, she had turned the last page. The task that had once seemed impossible was now complete. Each glyph had its translation recorded in her dictionary of Old Andolinian, the papers of which she tucked gently into the back of the tome; they would be useful now for translating other inscriptions she might come across in the future, and she was eager to find out what the symbols she'd captured in charcoal rubbings on Paloma's tomb meant.

Completing the work felt like a small victory in itself, which touched her with a slight sense of accomplishment. But now that she was done, there was once again too much room in her mind. In addition to James' death, Declan's proposal gnawed at her; though she'd once been elated for him to ask for her hand, she couldn't help but notice that now, his offer didn't bring her the same joy. Instead, for whatever reason, her heart ached to think of it. *Marrying Rog...* When she tried to picture that life for herself, it only stung. There was no denying she'd take her place in his heart after *The Tigress*, after the sea, and after glory. *Perhaps even after gold,* she thought bitterly. As she sat at her campaign desk, staring blankly at the final page of the Codex and listening to the raindrops pattering dully on her tent, the realization slowly came to her: *I don't want to marry Rog.*

She had to face the truth; if she never saw him again, her life would largely remain unchanged. He'd been absent for too long for it to make a difference. The thought didn't pain her nearly as much as the way she'd felt when she'd found Kol unconscious in the field. *Kol...* The memory of his ashen face painted with blood made her stomach lurch. *How close I was to losing him! What would I do, then?* Surely, she'd carry on, doing her part to defend the frontier until the bitter end; and yet, the bitter end would likely arrive much sooner without him there. Rising each day without looking forward to seeing his rugged face that always held a smile just for her, or being able to discuss their hopes and sorrows, making jokes over tea—a life without him would be bleak, she was sure. He was the only one she could let her guard down around; all others expected greater from her than what she felt she truly was. Kol had met her when she was merely Adella, before she'd become Lady Grimless. *And to think, when he told me of his feelings for me, my thoughts were only of Rog...* How callous that reaction felt now! She wished she could tell Kol how much he meant to her.

Wait a moment— The thought struck her like a thunderbolt, so suddenly that she stood from her seat, smacking her palms onto the desk. *It's not Rogero I love; it's Kol!* As the realization settled in her mind, resonating in her bones, her eyes wandered back to the Codex beneath her fingertips. A war scene, etched in fading ink, sprawled across the pages, wherein soldiers in strange armor bore lances and glaives against each other. Studying the linework of the little drawings closely, the armor on some caught her eye with its odd shapes and pale hue. Black circles gaped where eyes should be, their grim teeth bared. Some were missing limbs, or even heads, yet still readied their spears for striking. Searching the margins of the illustration, she found a set of glyphs written along one side, entwined in the border formed by the coils of an elongated, decorative *haramund* that framed the scene.

"In the hands of Leveret, the Heart of the World sang with power..." she read tentatively, flipping back and forth to reference her hand-written dictionary. "And at the end, while Andolin fell unto the sundering sea, the dead were seen again." Adella bit her lip. *One of the Twelve Calamities,* she recalled reading earlier in the tome. *But the dead can't return,* she mused, trying not to think of James. There had to be another meaning.

* * *

Kol paced the small area inside his tent, her words twisting in his gut like a knife. *A marriage proposal...* Adella still wore the little coral ring given to her by the captain earlier that year; he'd seen her fidget with it often. Perhaps it really was intended to be an engagement ring, after all. She certainly seemed to be taking it for one.

He'd been stupid to think he had a chance with her. But even now, he couldn't let the thought go. When she'd been captured by the Sornians, he crossed the sea to find her; he'd do it again and again. He'd never felt at home anywhere until he'd met her, and he couldn't let that go. *But I must, now. I have to.* She'd made her choice. Kol wasn't sure how he could stomach seeing Declan again, knowing now that he'd lost Adella to the captain. *Damn!* He smacked himself on the brow. *I almost forgot... I have to meet him in Raymouth in the morning to sign for the title.* It stung to think that Declan would have Adella, and Kol would only be left with a ship to fill the hole in his heart, but as far as he could see, there was no way around it.

Before his thoughts could take him any further, loud voices issued outside through the pattering of rain. Throwing on an oilskin cloak, he stepped out to see what it was.

* * *

Adella left the seclusion of her pavilion, restless but uncertain what she intended to do next. She wandered through the wet grass, lost in thought. She had worn her best clothes for James' funeral earlier that morning, a gold jacquard jacket-bodice and matching skirt that did little to keep her warm now in the rising wind. Rain spattered her face and shoulders as she twisted the gold and coral ring on her finger. Her mind was awash with emotions, her stomach pitted with anxiety. It had been some time since Kol had told of his feelings for her; she had no surety he'd still feel the same. *And after the way he found out about me and Declan...* She couldn't forget how he'd lost his temper; he thought very little of Rogero, and probably now of her as well. That certainly would've ruined whatever feelings he still had for her. The thought stung. *He deserves better.*

She sighed. There was nothing she could do about what had passed between her and Kol, but at the very least, Declan's proposal needed an answer. She wanted to write to him now, with her clear determination. Though she had her small campaign desk in her tent, with its collapsible legs and folding cover, it didn't contain all of her supplies, and for serious matters like this, she preferred the larger desk in Greywood's parlor. Deciding to also check on Misses Asher while she was there, she turned her steps in the manor house's direction.

Drawing the hood of her cloak tighter under her neck, Adella crossed the soggy fields under the evening sky with the rain pelting her eyes. As she approached the manor house, a voice called out for her.

"Lady Grimless."

Turning, she found Holcomb riding quickly toward her, the rain making a haze around his shoulders as it rebounded off his oilskin coat.

"What is it?" she asked as he halted the chestnut gelding beside her.

"The Sornian army is on the move," he said breathlessly, his freckled cheeks patched with red from exertion. "The main group is approaching from the west, and two more from the south and northwest."

"So they're closing in," she stated plainly. "How long do we have?"

"Days," he replied, his tone as grim as ever she'd heard it. "Three or four, perhaps."

She pressed her lips together. "And the palisade?"

He shook his head, water pouring from the corners of his cocked hat. "Work has stopped with the weather." He shrugged helplessly. "It can't be done in the mud."

Adella let out a breath, shoulders drooping. Even if the rain stopped now, it would take longer than that to complete the construction. "Make all preparations," she ordered. "Organize your troops. Let's be ready for them by tomorrow night. Thank you, Captain."

He nodded and, turning his horse, trotted off into the darkening fields.

Inside Greywood, Adella found Rosalind setting a stack of clean, folded blankets on a chair beside Misses Asher, who still lay upon the sofa. It pained her to see her old friend still lying, hand dangling limp, face pale, in the same place for so long.

"How is she?" Adella asked as she approached.

"The same," Rosalind replied quietly, draping a blanket over the old woman. "But she feels cold."

"Yes, it is cold in here..." Adella noted, wrapping her arms around herself. "I'll get the fire going," she said, tilting her head toward the hearth on the far side of the room. "But let's move her upstairs to my chamber; it's too drafty down here."

Rosalind nodded. "I'll go and get help."

"Thank you," Adella replied.

Rosalind made her way toward the hallway and paused, lingering in the threshold. Casting a pained look back at the sofa, she opened her mouth to speak, but shut it again quickly. The guilt on the woman's face mirrored that in Adella's heart. *Was it she who helped*

James into the saddle? He couldn't have done it on his own. Before Adella could ask, Rosalind disappeared down the hallway.

Kneeling on the sheepskin rug, Adella set to making a fire in the hearth, then warmed her hands in its growing glow. On the mantel above, her father looked down on her from his cavalry portrait. "Oh, Father," she muttered, her eyes meeting his within the picture, "I fear I've made a mistake." When she'd taken on his title, she had no idea what she'd have to face. She'd tried, but she couldn't do it. "It'll all be over soon," she said to herself, her words barely a whisper in the vast, dark parlor. With the palisade unfinished and enemy forces surrounding them, they didn't stand a chance. "Should I give up?" she asked softly, looking back up at her father's image. "Abandon Elldon? Save what lives I can?" Her father stared blankly back at her, offering no answer.

Yes, she realized. *If Sornia wants the Campos so badly, let them have it.* Elldon was isolated from the rest of Valenna due to the sea cliffs, the River Ray, and the great span of the Campos. The bridge was the only means of contact between the town and the rest of Valenna. If they fell back to the northern bank, they'd be able to hold the Sornians off at the bridge. It would be easy enough to defend, even with their small numbers. *It's not what Father would have done...* There would be no glory in retreat; some would surely call it cowardice. *But I'm not my father. And my people will live.*

The thought of losing Greywood made her heart sink. *My home... My family's home.* The manor house was intended to be passed down through the generations. Though it had only been built some years ago with the rest of the town, it was meant to last forever. It was supposed to be the home of her children, her descendants, and it was her duty to protect it. The fact that she couldn't would be a mark of disgrace she'd bear the rest of her life. *I'll give up my title.* It would be the right thing to do; she didn't deserve it now. It would likely be stripped from her anyway, after this. With the Queen missing, she couldn't guess who she'd have to answer to for her actions. Perhaps she'd be punished for desertion, or even executed for treason. *But I can face whatever comes, if it means no more will suffer. Anything, to save them.* She thought of Kol, ever the loyal soldier, ready to die at her side. If they retreated now, she would at least know he'd be safe.

She set about writing her letter to Declan quickly, putting the same care into it as he'd apparently put into hers, which wasn't much. *If he didn't want to be answered by letter,* she figured, *he shouldn't have proposed that way.* Then, she folded it and sealed it with hot wax, pressing her cipher into it with the ring seal on her finger, and left it on the desk to set. For a moment, she paused, looking at the coral jewel on her other hand, and wondered if she should return it. *It wasn't an engagement ring,* she reminded herself. *He called it a token of friendship.* She wasn't sure she and Rogero would still be friends after breaking things off with him; he'd likely be pretty hurt. *Would he even want it back?* She thought about the man she'd called her betrothed once before; when she'd accepted his proposal the first time, he'd suddenly disappeared, and at the time, she'd taken it very hard. Now, though, she felt no need to get even with him. She shook her head. *This isn't about revenge.* She did love the little ring, though. It reminded her more of Kol than Declan. After all, Kol was the one who had carried it with him, wearing it on a string around his neck so he could return it to her safely. *No, I think I'll keep it.* She spun the little ring on her finger, wondering again if it was too late to tell Kol how she felt.

Rosalind soon returned with Benson and a few others, their oil-skins running with rainwater and leaving puddles on the floor as they entered the room. With her recent realizations, Adella's heart gladdened to see Kol among them. Together, they moved Misses Asher to Adella's bedchamber and made her comfortable—as comfortable as possible, anyway. The old woman still tossed fitfully, lost in a fevered sleep, only rising now and then to gasp suddenly, eyes wide, before falling back into the oblivion of her restless mind. When she was dozing again peacefully for the time being, Adella left her to rest. Before heading down, she ducked into her father's study.

By the time she returned to the downstairs parlor, the others had all gone back to the encampment. Only Kol remained, standing at the hearth.

"Kol," Adella began, approaching tentatively as he warmed himself by the fire. She watched as he rolled up his damp sleeves, the sinewy tendons in his arms flexing with the movement. "I wanted to speak with you."

Rainwater had soaked his hair, curling the black strands into glossy ringlets that clung to his brow and cheekbones as he turned toward her expectantly. The scant light that filtered through the gaps in the window boards had completely faded away; only the warm glow of the hearth illuminated the dark space, casting soft shadows on the floor.

"You are," he replied, one side of his mouth pulling into a smirk. It was the same answer he'd given her the last time she said those words to him, in the Cairn that spring. Half a year had passed since then, but it felt like ages ago.

She smiled briefly at the memory, then it fell away. "Holcomb has told me the Sornian troops are closing in around us; we have only days." It pained her to utter the words. "I've decided to abandon Elldon. I'll give the order in the morning."

"Are you sure?" Kol drew his brows together. "But your home..."

His words trailed off, but Adella knew what he meant to say; everything they left behind would be destroyed. She would no longer have a home at all. Many of them wouldn't. Adella shook her head sadly. "I don't think I have a choice."

"There's always a choice," he replied. "But, no matter what you decide... Wherever you go, I will go with you."

Again Adella recognized the words he first uttered in the tavern of the Capital; she hadn't understood then how earnestly he'd meant them, but she could see it now. A heavy silence settled between them, their glances meeting and parting until Adella finally worked up the courage to speak again. "I—" She cast her eyes down. "I've brought you this," she said, handing him a book.

"Drums of War," he read, turning over the faded cloth cover.

"The fourth Jonny Reddin-Black novel," she replied. "It's a bit bleaker than the others, but it's my favorite."

He tucked the book under his arm, nodding, then gave her a searching look. "Is that everything you wanted to say?"

She quailed under his sharp gaze, her courage dissipating. "Yes," she whispered.

His shoulders fell. "Thanks," he replied, disappointment thick in his voice. He turned to leave.

Adella felt her chance slipping away. "I made my answer," she blurted out, surprising herself. "To Declan."

A muscle in Kol's stubbled jaw tensed as he turned back to face her, eyes darting toward the letter addressed to Declan on her desk. "I'm meeting him in Raymouth in the morning," he said flatly as she picked the letter up, "to buy *The Tigress*. I can deliver it for you." He took it from her hands and his fingertips lingered on hers, his gaze falling from her eyes to her lips.

"Kol," she whispered, "I..." Her voice faded as she realized what he'd said. "You what?"

"Business matters," he replied, giving her another half-smile. "Nothing to worry about."

"I wasn't—" She stopped herself, not wanting to argue. "Kol," she began again softly, heart racing as she summoned her courage once again. "Do you still..." Adella let out a shuddering breath and pressed her lips together, her stomach a flurry of nerves.

Moving closer, he searched her face intently, glancing from eye to eye. "What is it?"

She drew a deep breath. "I'm not marrying him," she blurted out finally. "I realized... It isn't Declan I love."

He watched her for a moment. As the meaning behind her words settled over him, his dark eyes softened and his brows raised. "If you're here to tell me it's Captain Holcomb..."

Adella let out a small laugh and shook her head.

Reaching for her face, he swept his rough hand along her cheekbone. His thumb followed the corner of her mouth down to her lower lip, just as he had done that spring in the Great Room of the Cairn. She inhaled sharply; her heart drummed against her ribs as he leaned in, his breath warming the air between them.

"Adella..." Her name was a prayer on his lips, quiet and tender. Then, uncertainty flickered across his face. She wondered if this moment would pass, too, just like it had back in the Cairn. Staring up into his eyes, all the times that he'd made her heart flutter with his touch, the many moments she'd blushed under his gaze, the aching thoughts of him she'd pushed aside out of doubt or guilt, they all came rushing back. Then came the sudden image of him lying motionless in the grass, and, remembering the terror that had gripped her at the sight, she reached for him.

Shutting her eyes tightly against her strained nerves, Adella wove her fingers through the rain-soaked hair that cascaded down his neck as she pulled him close, meeting his lips with hers. She resolutely kissed him, his breath and hers becoming one, and she knew that, at least this time, she was certain she'd made the right choice.

Slowly, tentatively, she drew back. Kol opened his eyes and met her gaze, brows lifting in astonishment, and all of her certainty melted away. Her face burned with embarrassment and she looked down, heart wringing itself painfully as she wondered if she'd misread the situation, if his feelings for her had faded after all.

* * *

From the very first time he'd set eyes on Adella, Kol had longed for this moment, dreamt of it often. It hadn't felt like this in his mind, though. He'd never imagined how his heart would pound, his hands shake, and his breath catch in his throat the way it did now. He hadn't expected to be frozen with the fear of making a mistake, of comparing unfavorably to her past experiences. He'd never admit it aloud, but it had been quite some time since he'd been with a woman, and he tried not to wonder if Declan had been better at this than he was. The thought made him briefly ill until he willed his attention back to the smooth skin of her cheek against his palm. *Don't ruin this,* he reprimanded himself, and cradled her face in both hands. Eyes the color of stormy seas looked up at him, drawing him in like a tide, drowning out his fears. Kol pressed his mouth to hers and kissed her deeply, desperately, as though she were water to his parched lips.

Her hands slipped lightly around his waist, pulling him closer.

Combing his fingers through her soft hair, he moved his other hand down the front of her bodice. Fingertips intertwining the lacing, he pulled quickly, breaking it with a snap. She gasped, her eyes widening suddenly.

I've frightened her... His stomach dropped as he recalled her disparaging comment about the quickness of men. He paused, unsure if he had ruined things with his overeagerness, and drew back.

"Don't stop," she muttered softly, leaning gently into him and tightening her grasp on his waist.

Overcome with relief, he buried his face in her neck. Pressing his lips over her warm skin, he worked his way down her bare collarbone.

10

The Bridge

Kol awoke in a pile of blankets on the sheepskin rug. Adella slept soundly beside him, her long, auburn hair draped over his arm. Faint light seeped through the window boards. He lay there, not wanting to move for fear of waking her and spoiling the moment. He wondered if every morning from then on might be spent together like this, and a sense of peace, of belonging, filled his heart. It pained him to think of leaving Greywood behind; it had come to feel more like home than any other place he'd been, but he knew it was her presence that made it feel that way. Anywhere would be home, if she was with him.

Adella let out a soft groan and rubbed her eyes, then sat up suddenly, drawing a blanket over herself as she looked around. "It's morning?"

Kol let out a small laugh. They'd been lucky no one had come into the manor house yet, but the longer they lingered in the parlor, the more likely that became. "Uh, Adella," he began hesitantly. "Last night, when you said it wasn't Declan you loved, you meant—"

"You," she said, smirking as she shook her head, "obviously."

He laughed. "Right." He'd just wanted to hear her say it.

"Don't you have to be in Raymouth?" she asked pointedly.

Kol smacked his forehead. "Damn it!" He threw the blanket aside. Grabbing his shirt from a nearby chair, he pulled it over his head. "I'm going to be late," he groaned, buckling on his sword belt. "I'll be back as quick as I can."

She nodded. "I'll let the others know my decision. It'll take us some time to prepare for travel."

He pulled on his jacket and knelt beside her. "Just be ready to leave when I return, and stay near the manor. Please," he added, trying not to let his anxieties overwhelm his mind, "be careful."

"Of course," she muttered. "I'm always careful."

"I mean it." He placed a hand on the side of her face. "I'd be lost without you." Then, he gave her one last kiss before departing.

Kol tacked Madigan up quickly and, after checking to be sure he had Adella's letter in his haversack, rode off toward Raymouth. He passed through the north opening in the palisade, with its red-jacketed guards on either side of the unfinished gate, and trotted out into a dense fog. If he weren't already so familiar with the path, nor determined to return as soon as possible, he might've waited for it to clear.

It took some time for him to make his way through the remnants of town, but as he finally approached the Raymouth Bridge, the sound of rushing water thundered through the white mist. As he drew closer, Madigan pricked her ears and let out a low snort.

"Easy, girl," he said, patting her neck. "It's just fog; it can't hurt you." Kol searched the area, peering through the haze, but couldn't see the usual guards at their post. *They must be here somewhere... They* wouldn't leave the bridge unguarded; everyone in Elldon understood it was their only lifeline to civilization. *Perhaps I just can't see them through the fog.* Anxiety stirring in his gut, he drew his blade and pressed his horse onward.

Iron-shod hooves clattered as Kol rode over the weathered planks of the bridge. Crossing the wide span, he glanced down over the ledge; the dark river thundered below, churning violently through the white mist. Madigan snorted again, and Kol swallowed his fear. "Now's not the place to act up," he muttered, pulse quickening.

A dark shape moved ahead, merely a brief shadow through the haze. *What was that?* Kol narrowed his eyes but couldn't see anything more. He urged Madigan forward into a canter, eager to be on solid ground once more, and her hoofbeats pounded over the bridge. *Not very stealthy,* Kol noted with chagrin. When he came to the far end, where he'd thought he'd seen the movement, he slowed to a trot, his grip tightening on his cutlass. Hopefully, it was only the bridge guards he'd seen, but if so, they were on the wrong side of the river. The thought made him uneasy. Striding onto solid ground again, he reined his horse around, searching for the source.

Madigan halted suddenly, throwing Kol off balance as she blew out a loud, rattling snort. At her feet lay a body clad in Valennian scarlet. Blood pooled on the ground around his pale head, his eyes staring blankly out at nothing. Balking, Madigan shuffled backward.

A sharp blow rammed Kol's leg, and he groaned in pain between clenched teeth. Turning, he faced a dark figure that had emerged from the fog to hack a blade into the cuff of his boot. Kol slashed his cutlass across the man's shoulder, and a scream rang through the air.

Hands grabbed at him from the other side; Madigan let out a sharp squeal and reared. Kol gripped her mane to keep from falling, but he began to slip from the saddle. As her forelimbs came back down, Kol kicked out at the attacker's head, boot heel cracking against bone. A familiar, pungent smell permeated the cold air and then behind him, a light blazed, warming his back. *Turpentine?* Yanking the reins, he spun to see a fire spreading over the deck of Raymouth Bridge, flames licking over the planks.

"No!" he shouted. If the bridge was destroyed, it would leave Adella and all of Elldon with no means of escaping the oncoming Sornian army. Kicking Madigan forward, he galloped at the fleeing figure and drove the cutlass into the man's back, the tip of his blade bursting through cloth and skin. Through the fog, a roaring fire mounted, engulfing the bridgehead, the heat stinging his face. "*No!*" he screamed again. He couldn't leave Adella to her fate; if he couldn't save the bridge, he'd at least be with her at the end. Desperation tearing through him, Kol spurred his horse onward, hoping to gain enough speed to run her clear through the flames and make it to the other side before the fire grew larger.

He galloped straight at the blaze. Madigan cocked her head high, eyes ringed with white, as he kicked her sides furiously to keep her going. Just as her hooves came down at the edge of the fire, she slammed to a halt and, dropping her shoulder, spun. Kol fell onto the ground, pain flaring through his body as she bolted away, disappearing into the fog down the road toward Raymouth.

Kol screamed through his teeth, sweat running into his eyes as the flames blasted him with heat. Bracing his throbbing side, he pushed himself off the ground and shuffled away from the blaze.

* * *

Standing in her short linen shift, Adella rifled through the oak wardrobe of her bedchamber. Finding a dusty pair of riding breeches with suede patches at the knees, she buttoned them on quickly, then grabbed last year's winter coat, cut from the same thick, blue wool that the sailors often wore, and pulled it on over her silk bodice, the lacing of which she'd repaired with a hasty knot. She tucked her shift into her breeches and stored the skirts away on a shelf; she wouldn't be wearing them today. Her tall boots would complete her outfit. With her hair pulled back in a queue, she might have passed for a young cavalier from a distance, if it weren't for the color of her coat.

A small creak came from behind her as Misses Asher moved on the bedstead. "Misses Asher," Adella whispered, stepping closer. "Are you awake?" The old woman's head turned on the pillow, but her eyes remained shut. Reaching out toward her, Adella brushed a wisp of grey hair from her chilled forehead. There was no response.

"We're leaving," Adella said softly. "I know you would've stayed until the end, but it's over now. We're going to get you out of here." Though it pained her that it had come to this, it was a relief to think no more would die in defense of Elldon. The Lady Grimless had failed at her duty, that much was certain, but at least they'd all be safe now. "Did you hear, Beatrice?" A wan smile crossed Adella's lips. "We'll all go to the Ivy Crown, have a drink—"

Misses Asher moaned again. Eyes squeezed tightly shut, her face twisted into a grimace as she threw her hands up defensively. "No," she murmured. "No, stop!" Turning fitfully on the mattress, the old woman let out a pained wail, then let out her breath and lay still.

"Beatrice," Adella said, placing a hand on her shoulder, but there was no response. A sinking feeling hit her gut like a stone. "Beatrice," Adella called again, giving her shoulder a little shake. The woman's mouth fell open, her motionless eyes staring placidly at the ceiling. "No!" Adella screamed, jumping up. Grasping the woman by both shoulders, she shook harder. "Beatrice!"

Footsteps echoed from the open door and Captain Holcomb entered, his face drawn and pale.

"She's gone," Adella said under her breath, lowering her head.

"Lady Grimless," Holcomb began, his tone a warning. "Forgive me, but there's something you need to see."

Adella drew back Shy's reins and halted, pulling her coat collar up over the lower half of her face. The surrounding area was engulfed in heavy, dark smoke that stung her throat and eyes, choking out the light of the noon sun. Before her, the charred remains of the Raymouth Bridge still smoldered, the blackened, skeletal structures at the bridgeheads on either side slashed with glowing red coals. The central span had fallen away into the river, gone save for a few scorched stumps of timber piers jutting up from the water.

"It burned so quickly," Holcomb said with a hollow look in his eyes. "Only a matter of hours."

"Hours?" Adella repeated under her breath. "No..." Worry knotted her stomach. Quickly, she pulled a brass spyglass from her haversack and searched through the smoke across the water. Her heart dropped when her view passed a figure lying in the dirt. Hands trembling, she adjusted the lens. The body came into focus, Valennian scarlet showing through the dark haze, and she let out her breath. *It isn't him.* Sweeping the glass, she found another form lying dead on the far side, also in a cavalier's jacket, then three more in emerald. *Sornian soldiers.* Thankfully, there was no sign of Kol. *He must have made it over before the fire.*

She glanced at Holcomb beside her, and her heart panged for him. "I'm sorry, Captain. Your guards..."

"Lieutenant Lewis," he replied. "And Ellicot." His voice was even, but his brow crumpled. Solemnly, he pulled off his hat and placed it over his heart.

Adella watched a precariously balanced, blackened beam crumble into the turbulent water below. A sudden weight pressed on her, dragging down her shoulders. Kol might be safe, but she and her people wouldn't be. "There will be no retreat," she said, more to herself than to the captain. Uttering the words aloud sent an ache through her chest. "They've got us backed into a corner now, and vastly outnumbered. It's over."

Putting his hat on his head, Holcomb raised a brow. "Surely you aren't entertaining the thought of surrender?"

"What choice do we have?" Adella raised her shoulders helplessly. "We are so few."

"You saw what they did to your friend with the broken leg," he replied. "It was unconscionable and unnecessary."

Adella nodded. "And to his mother," she added bitterly. It was clear now the old woman had been tortured nearly to her death. "No, they can't be trusted to act with honor."

"Certainly not," Holcomb replied, shaking his head. "If we put our hands in the air, we'll be promptly butchered."

"I'm afraid you're right," she replied. "Then, the only way out now is through." Bolstered with resolve, her grip tightened on the reins as they turned their horses around. "We'll ride out all together. If we can't find a way past them without a fight, then we'll take as many of them down as we can. If by some stroke of luck we survive, we'll continue on through the Campos to Smuggler's Port." The Sornians would likely chase them down, but if by some chance they made it that far, they could sail back to Raymouth, where she hoped Kol would be waiting for her. *If we survive...* She swallowed to moisten her dry throat.

"I want to be sure you understand the consequences if we do this," Holcomb warned. "I must impress upon you our very slim chances for survival, considering the numbers we'll be facing. And with their many scouts..." He frowned. "They'll know we're coming."

"But at least we'll have a chance," she countered, "right? And we won't be letting their atrocities go unanswered. What do you say, Captain? One last ride over the Campos?"

"If this is to be our last ride," Holcomb replied, voice growing louder as he urged his horse to a trot, "then let's give them hell!"

* * *

Adella steadied her horse on the rise overlooking the western fields as the townsfolk and cavalry of Elldon prepared their horses. With so few people remaining, they decided to saddle the cavalry's spare horses for transport rather than using them to carry supplies, ensuring that no one would have to go on foot. She set a hand protectively on her haversack, with the heavy Codex within; it was far too precious to leave behind. The sun shone brightly from a clear sky, warming the breezes that gently rustled through the branches. The few remaining trees that sheltered the estate were ablaze with autumn color; leaves of gold and scarlet fluttered around them, sweetening the air with their scent as they blanketed the ground. She drew a deep breath, taking it all in. Though the man-made structures of the landscape had changed since the day she'd first arrived at Elldon years ago, the land looked the same; the gentle swells of higher ground, the shallow valleys that ushered seasonal streams of rainwater north to the sea, and the eternal sweep of the horizon would all remain unchanged long after she was gone. *Sometimes I forget what a wonder it is to be alive.* No matter how brief or turbulent life could be, there was no denying its beauty.

Beside her, Holcomb sat in his saddle pulling on riding gloves, a heavy hunting bow strung over his shoulder. Thickly powdered curls were tied back neatly in a large, black ribbon beneath his crisp, felt hat. His scarlet jacket was freshly pressed, without a wrinkle in sight.

"You're looking well turned-out," she commented.

"Thought I'd dress for the occasion." He gave a wide grin. "Where's your Sornian?"

"On the other side of the bridge," Adella replied sadly.

"That's too bad," he replied. "I rather wish he were here."

"So do I," she sighed. It was true; they could really use an experienced soldier like Kol. Yet at the same time, a part of her was relieved he wouldn't have to face what lay ahead. *At least he'll be safe.*

He raised his brows. "Forgive my candor, but we missed you two at camp last night."

"We spent it in the manor," she replied dryly. "I love him, Captain," she added, turning to meet his gaze. She couldn't hide a smile; it felt good to say it out loud.

"Ah," he said with a smirk of satisfaction. She wondered if he had known it all along. "Very good." They fell silent for a moment, watching as their parties readied the horses. "Are you afraid?" he asked at length.

"Yes," she admitted. "Are you?"

"Of course." Holcomb shrugged. "But we can't have courage without fear."

"My father once said," she began slowly, almost to herself as the memory surfaced, "there's a fine line between courage and foolishness."

He laughed. "Yes, in fact they're often indistinguishable."

* * *

Matei sat at the long dining table and yawned, watching the jewels of the courtiers sparkle in the candlelight. The others at the table avoided his gaze; the whites of his eyes were stained a striking crimson, startling even him the first time he'd seen himself in a mirror. He wasn't concerned with what they thought of his appearance, though. Over the years, he'd come to hate most of the people present, save for Lucas and Teressa. They were the only ones who seemed to understand his plan. The meal that evening was particularly extravagant—all of his favorite foods, ordered by his father—which he presumed was an attempt to make up for decades of ill treatment now that he was the Crown Prince. His dead brother's silver circlet adorned his brow. He'd heard the whispers, the rumors and suspicions about him, but he couldn't bring himself to care. The Heartstone weighed heavily in his waistcoat pocket, a reminder that soon, he'd never need to be mindful of such matters again. *Emperor,* he said to himself. *Not prince, not king. That's what I will be.* Emperors didn't care what others thought; they didn't need to. He just needed to figure out how to reach the Stone's full potential, like Leveret had done in the stories. *If he could do it, an ordinary peasant by all accounts, then surely so can I.* The son of a king was born for wielding power, and he was a direct descendant of a long line of Andolinian rulers. The Heart of the World was rightfully his.

He cut into the roasted duck breast on his plate and took a bite, his attention shifting to a little green fly that buzzed around the flames of a candelabra in front of him.

"Of course, I was a lord in Valenna," Lucas was saying beside him. "Or I would've been, if my father weren't still alive. However, I didn't agree with King Harrian's policies on trade..." He continued to prattle idly to an old courtier across the table. Matei wondered if anyone there could even understand Lucas's foreign accent or if he was wasting his breath. Surely, none of them had ventured beyond the Sornian borders like Matei had. Their worlds were small. In his travels, he'd acquired a taste for the whole empire.

He wished his father was dining with them. King Berento had lately taken up a drinking habit—and not just the expensive royal brandy that Matei enjoyed. He'd been filling his days and nights with it since the passing of the late Crown Prince Gio. The king had always favored his older son, but now that Gio was gone, Matei hoped his father's affection would fall on him instead.

His gaze shifted back to the fly buzzing dangerously close to the fire, diving between the tallow candles. With the slightest twitch of a finger, Matei sent his will into the creature's body. Long nights of exhausting practice connecting with the thrumming power of the Heartstone had made such little feats effortless. He sent the fly quickly careening toward the flame. Singed, it fell lifelessly on the tablecloth, its little legs crossed over its belly.

Matei rested his chin on his hand while he picked at the herbed vegetables, the conversation around him too dull and predictable to hold his attention. His eyes settled on the little glossy green body crumpled next to his plate, and his curiosity piqued. Boring his gaze into the little speck on the table, he reached into his waistcoat pocket and felt the smooth facets of the crystal against his palm. It grew warmer as he summoned its energy, and with a sudden burst of will, he sent it into the fly. Its legs twitched.

The little creature buzzed helplessly against the tablecloth for a moment. Then, clambering away on faltering legs, it fell over the edge and disappeared beneath his chair.

With that entertainment gone, Matei turned his gaze back to the extravagant foods arrayed before him: autumnal fruits, thick sauces, tarts, and various seafood pulled fresh from the water that very day. One silver platter on the far end boasted a particularly large and succulent raw octopus, its sinuous tentacles still glistening with brine on a bed of mint. An older woman, her large wig heavily powdered white above a deeply lined forehead, reached for it with her knife. As she cut into one tentacle, Matei focused his attention, fingers tightening around the pulsating crystal in his pocket. Just as her knife tore the flesh away from the rest of the body, the contents of the tray burst into motion, and a swarm of tentacles wrapped around her arm. The woman let out an ear-piercing shriek and fell backward in her chair. Around them, the dinner party erupted into chaos.

11

The Last Ride Over the Campos

Checking their pace to preserve energy, Adella braced her saber through the jostling of her horse's strides. Riding across fields patched with grey-green lavender, their blossoms long since spent, the heady perfume filled her with cherished memories of years past—of her mother, her father and brother, and the lands she called home—and her heart ached for what was gone. By the time they all settled into a steady gait, her vision was blurred with tears. Blinking hard, she wiped her eyes.

It was usually a three-day ride to Compass Point, where the enemy had built their main encampment. By Jacoby's account, they would most likely meet the Sornian forces not far from there. *Unless we can find a way to pass through the area unnoticed.* Though it was unlikely, she tried to retain hope. It was better than thinking of the alternatives.

They were few, now—the people of Elldon. *So very few.* It was a disadvantage, but it made her hope possible. When she'd traveled to Pentz that summer, leaving James in charge, any who weren't fit for battle had been sent to Raymouth, leaving hardly fifty to defend the town. When she'd returned with Holcomb's cavalry troop, they'd bolstered their numbers by sixty-three, but so many had fallen in the field since then. Now, altogether, they were just shy of seventy-five, with hardly a spare horse among them to carry supplies. They'd left nearly everything behind. With so few and traveling light, it was possible they could find an unguarded path through the Campos and make it to Smuggler's Port. It was a small hope, but it guided her onward, like a star in the darkness.

When the sun touched the horizon, they stopped to make camp in the open. Adella was grateful for the clear skies. With the help of the weather, they'd made good time, and by her reckoning, they'd likely meet the enemy troops by nightfall the day after tomorrow. *If we can't get through unnoticed, that leaves us with a night battle...* Though she hated the thought, at least they'd have the full moon to see by, presuming the weather held; even now, she could see it rising, great and round and pale, as the sun slunk below the far horizon.

After they untacked the horses, fed them from what little grain they managed to pack, and watered them at a small brook, they secured them to the picket rope for the night and settled in for a hasty supper. Adella untied her bedroll from the cantle rings of her saddle, spread it out on the dry grass and sat, biting into the dry bread she'd packed in wax cloth in her haversack. Wisps of iron-grey clouds crossed the autumn sky, their cool colors contrasting with the warmth of orange and rust in the trees that interspersed the fields. Already, many had lost their leaves; their dark, bare branches reaching to the heavens like black, skeletal hands desperate with prayer.

She wondered if her parents were up there in the heavens, watching her now. *What would Father think of my choices? Would he have done the same thing in my place?* She wondered if he'd have abandoned Elldon sooner, getting the others to safety, or if he'd simply have formed a better plan of escape. *He'd always had luck on his side,* she recalled, then sighed. *I clearly don't.*

Rosalind sat down beside her, offering a wineskin, and Adella took a draught. "Thanks," she said, handing it back. "Do you think this is the right choice?" Adella wondered softly.

Rosalind raised her brows, glancing over at her. She paused, giving Adella an appraising look, then shrugged. "Sometimes, there is no right choice. But if you're asking if I wanted to stay there and see what the Sornians would do to me?" She shook her head. "Being a woman, I think you understand."

Adella nodded. Her time spent in Sornia had been degrading enough, and she knew that wasn't the worst they were capable of. "It's hard to leave our home behind, though," Adella replied. "In their hands." She hated the thought of Sornian soldiers using Greywood Manor as an outpost, defiling it with their presence. Suddenly, James' headless body flashed through Adella's mind, and her stomach turned. She swallowed the bile that rose in her throat. Rosalind passed her the wineskin again, and Adella took a swig, pushing the memory away.

Jacoby sat down beside them, his expression heavy with grief. As one of their outriders for the journey, he had scouted ahead on behalf of their party. They hadn't seen much of him, save for the times they stopped to rest. Adella wondered how much worse James' death must be for him to bear. *And now he's lost his mother, too... Poor fellow.* He'd lost everything to the Sornians. "How are you holding up?" she asked, her voice heavy with concern.

"Still standing," he replied grimly.

"Do you think we can make it?" Rosalind asked, lowering her voice as she leaned in toward the two of them. "Across the wilderness."

Adella nodded. "I believe we can," she replied. "So long as we make it past their army. But our scouts haven't been this far in days; I'm not sure what to expect." She looked to Jacoby, whose ranger party had been the ones to bring news of the oncoming troops.

"Well, we know their main group will be coming from Compass Point," Jacoby reasoned. "That's dead west. And with the reinforcement troops coming from the northwest, there may be a gap between them that we can sneak through unnoticed in the darkness. At the very least, it may give us a head start before they're alerted to our presence."

"If that happens, can we make a run for it?" Rosalind asked.

"We're traveling light," Adella replied, "and the Sornians are always short on horses. We'd stand a good chance of losing them in the field."

"And then what?" Rosalind asked, hope kindling in her eyes.

"We'll ride to Smuggler's Port; it's only a few days beyond Compass Point, and I know the way," Adella said reassuringly. She was the only one among them who'd traveled that far west. "From there, we can sail to the Capital. I'll meet with the Queen and let her know all that's happened.

"It's a hard thing, losing Elldon," she went on thoughtfully. "But burning the bridge didn't just cut *us* off from Valenna, it cut off the Sornians as well. It gained them the Campos, but they won't get any further now." Despite their sacrifices, it warmed her heart to know it wasn't all in vain; Valenna was still safe.

With her thoughts on the Capital, Adella wondered how Armand was faring. She'd be glad to see him again, if they made it that far. The sting of shame suddenly pricked her heart. *I'll have to tell him I failed...* She could already imagine the disappointment on his face when she told him they'd lost Elldon to the Sornians. *And Greywood Manor...* Everything her father had strived for in his life, his entire legacy, would all be gone. *And when I give up my father's title, Armand will be there to witness it.* After failing to defend the town, she knew she couldn't keep it, but the thought of Armand standing by while they meted out her punishment, however warranted, still struck her heart like a knife. *Even so,* she told herself, steeling her resolve, *I will face whatever awaits me, if I can just get everyone there.*

Lost in thought, her eyes settled on the round moon mounting over the eastward rise. Adella wondered what Kol was doing at that moment. It felt strange to be here without him, returning to the area of the Campos where they'd first traveled together, shortly after she freed him from the Sornian encampment, but knowing that the one person she cared about the most was safe brought her strength. *Though I'm sure he's in a panic...* He wasn't the sort to shy away from a fight, and he'd always been fiercely protective of her; he'd be having a fit somewhere, eaten up with anxiety knowing she was stranded in Elldon, unable to get to her with the Sornian army approaching. Guilt swept over her at the thought, though it was out of her hands. *I hope he's not blaming himself for the way things turned out.* Even if he'd made it over the bridge well before the fire, by now, he'd have tried to return and discovered the bridge was completely destroyed. *Then what would he do?* If she knew Kol, he'd try to get back as soon as possible by another direction. Without the bridge, the only other way would be to sail from Raymouth straight for Smuggler's Port, then cross through the Campos—the same way she'd hoped to take her own people. Perhaps, if her group made it through safely, she'd arrive at Smuggler's Port in time to find him there. She knew it was unlikely, but the thought encouraged her, and she wouldn't allow her mind to dwell on other possibilities.

As the moon spread its gentle glow over the landscape, she wondered if Kol was watching it, too. *Perhaps from the deck of* The Tigress, *with the moonlight dappling the waves...* Though she loved Elldon, she'd often felt a longing for the sea, a deep desire to feel the salt spray on her face and the briny wind in her hair, yet always had to be content with the rain on the prairie. At times, she envied sailors their freedom. The thought of Kol safely aboard Declan's familiar, sturdy ship, taking in the fresh sea air, so far from the dangers she now faced on land, brought her peace. Arranging her few belongings, she lay down for the night, resting her head on her saddle. Even if this was to be her last ride, it comforted her to know the man she loved wouldn't meet the same fate.

* * *

Kol ran the remaining distance to Raymouth. He understood why Madigan had deserted him at the bridge, fleeing from the blaze, but time was of the essence. He had to figure out a way back to Adella—but he also had to meet with Declan, if it wasn't too late. Panting hard with aching lungs, he finally arrived at the port city and waded through the still-flooded streets past the Ivy Crown. *Dammit,* he swore to himself as the sun broke through the clouds. Judging by its position, he was two hours late for his meeting. He hoped he hadn't missed his chance completely. Kol tried to pick up his pace as he strode, struggling against the still-rising currents, now inching up his belly. The tide was much higher than the last time he'd been in Raymouth, and the thought of sharks or other sea creatures passing by, unseen beneath the murk, quickened his pace by another degree.

The water crept up to his chest when he arrived at the docks, or rather, the area where the docks used to be, and he carried his bag on his shoulder to keep it dry and safe. Searching frantically over the Bay, he spotted ships in the distance, and let out his breath, relieved to see *The Tigress* still lying at anchor, her red and black sails furled. The other ships nearby were already getting under way, and *The Tigress* likely would be, too, before long. But it was too far to swim in the dangerous floodwaters.

While he contemplated his options, Kol felt something brush against his boot, unseen beneath the water. His heart leapt into his throat. He scrambled back to the steps of the Ivy Crown, hoping whatever had touched him was only debris floating by. Making his way to the top step, he looked around. The city seemed completely deserted; he couldn't spot a single person among the water-filled streets or in the shop windows. *How am I going to buy* The Tigress *when I can't even make it there?* Kol shook his head. There was nothing he could do; he had failed. Sitting down on the top step, feet still submerged in cold water, he rested his head against his knees, cradling his haversack, and allowed his careening emotions to overwhelm him.

He'd missed his chance to make it to *The Tigress*. Though he certainly didn't regret the reason for his tardiness, he couldn't see how he'd possibly get back to Elldon now. *I never should have left.* He cursed his selfishness in wanting to buy the ship at all, then his stupidity in leaving Adella's side at the worst possible moment. *Now I'll never see her again.* With the bridge completely destroyed and the river impassable, there was no way for her to get out; she'd be killed by the Sornian army, along with the rest of Elldon. Worst of all, he wouldn't be there with her. Despair tore through him, and he buried his face in his forearms.

Water splashed nearby, and he jerked his head up, rubbing his eyes to see a small boat emerge from around the corner of a flooded side street. Two figures in scarlet worked the oars while a small group sat at the stern. Kol's heart leapt at the sight. "Wait," he shouted. Without pausing for a response, he jumped down from the steps into the water. Holding his bag up to keep it dry, he waded over to the small boat, ignoring the voices that raised on his account, until he came to its starboard side.

"Good heavens!" one of the Royal Guards called out. "What are you doing? We're full! We can't take on anymore."

"Let me on," Kol demanded, reaching for the chainwale. "Please."

The man stuck the oar in Kol's face, nudging him away. "Go, you'll tip us!" Something splashed loudly behind Kol, and the soldier's eyes widened. "In the boat!" he shouted, suddenly changing his mind. Reaching out, he grabbed Kol's shirt collar and pulled. "Now! No—" he said as Kol tried to glance back. "Don't look!" The boat dipped precariously to one side as Kol pulled himself into the hull with the man's help, and the people that crowded at the back made room for him.

"Row!" the other oarsman ordered, and the two worked furiously. As they began to move, Kol caught a glimpse of a large, black shape disappear beneath the water, and a chill shivered up his back.

"Those damned things are everywhere," the guardsman muttered between breaths.

Kol was glad he hadn't seen whatever was in the water with him. "Are you heading to the anchorage?" he asked.

The guardsman nodded. Pulling a kerchief from his waistcoat, he mopped the sweat from his brow. "We're getting out of here; most everyone else has gone already. The sea can have it!" he shouted, throwing a sullen glare at the flooding city.

"There," Kol said as they neared the anchored ships, pointing to *The Tigress*. His heart raced to see the anchor already rising up the side of the hull. "Take me to that ship. Please," he added quickly.

The guardsman nodded. When they neared *The Tigress*, he cupped his hands around his mouth and hailed the crew on Kol's behalf, but there was no response. The figures on the ship above continued with their orders, preparing to get underway.

Kol refused to believe he'd made it all this way just to be left behind. Determined, he rose and, hands around his mouth, shouted to the crew himself. There was no ignoring his loud voice as it carried widely over the water. Soon, figures gathered at the rail above them. One of them wore a blond queue hanging beneath his wide hat.

"One more aboard, Captain," the guardsman called out, and a rope ladder unfurled over the side. Kol thanked the boatmen and climbed up.

"You're late," Captain Declan commented as Kol stepped onto the weather deck, distaste evident in his scowl. "What kept you?"

"We've got to get to Smuggler's Port," Kol blurted out frantically, grabbing Declan's sleeves. "The Raymouth bridge has been destroyed, and Elldon is under attack—"

"Calm yourself, man" Declan replied, pulling free from Kol's grip. "We're getting underway as we speak."

"Didn't you hear me?" Kol scowled. "Adella's in danger!"

"Adella is always in danger," Declan muttered, rolling his eyes. "Need I remind you, it was her choice to return to the frontier? There's nothing we can do for her right now," he reasoned with a shrug. "Your colleagues are already aboard, waiting for you. Come—" He motioned aft. "Let's get this over with."

Kol opened his mouth to protest, but Declan escorted him forcefully across the deck, pulling him by the arm. He shook himself free as they entered the captain's quarters, which was familiar from his previous voyage on *The Tigress*. Kol was relieved to see Kerchaw, along with the old notary from Raymouth, who held his spectacles as he bent over a pile of papers at the table.

"There you are!" Kerchaw scolded, rising from his chair. "I've brought you something, but now I think I should've got you a clock instead." He reached under the table, then brought up a model ship, with little sails painted in black and red, and presented it to him.

"It's *The Tigress*," Kol said, raising his brow.

"To commemorate the buying of your first ship," Kerchaw replied.

Surprised by the sentiment behind the gift, Kol smiled. "Thank you."

"Yes, yes," Declan said, shepherding them to the table. "Very touching."

Pulling out chairs, they sat, Kol placing the model ship beside him on the table. They made their way through the papers, signing every place the notary instructed as *The Tigress* lurched into motion. Kol tried to keep his wet sleeves off the parchments. They finished signing and Kerchaw placed the ship's title and the bill of sale carefully into a large leather envelope. Kol let out a sigh, glad that he'd made it aboard in time to complete the transaction.

"It's done," Declan said. Pushing his chair back, he rose. "And it looks like you lot will be coming with us," he said with a smirk. "I'll try to find you some dry clothes, but we've picked up quite a few stragglers from Raymouth, so supplies will be limited. As you're the new owner, this cabin is at your disposal," he continued, eyeing Kol darkly. "I'll have spare hammocks brought up for your people, but please, don't touch my things."

* * *

Adella awoke well before sunrise, huddled beneath her cloak. Her breath rose in white wisps on the air while her muscles ached from two days of hard riding. Though the night had turned cool, she'd slept deeper for it, and by the time the pale sun rose, scattering its wan light over the fields and chasing the moon down below the western horizon, their party had eaten their cold rations and worked quickly to ready the horses.

While Shy grazed peacefully, tethered beside her belongings lying in the grass, Adella took his long, black tail in her hands. Though it had been years since she'd last tied the silky strands into a warknot—a tradition she'd learned from her father before setting out for rough terrain—her fingers remembered the simple movements. Gathering up the long skirt of hair below the dock, she parted it into two sections and, twisting them, tied them together, then looped one end around and slipped the other through. She then poured a little water from her wineskin over the knot to keep it secure during travel. Though it was customary to also fashion the mane into small, secure plaits, she didn't have time for that now. Instead, she worked her fingers quickly through the hair down his neck, interlacing it in a hasty running braid and tying the end with a piece of string. It wasn't very pretty, but it would have to do. Her own hair she pulled partly back, leaving the rest flowing freely over her shoulders, before returning to tacking up her horse.

Barring any unexpected difficulties, they would likely meet the Sornian troops that evening, but despite the impending danger, she found it hard to stay focused as they rode out. Her mind kept returning to her journey across the same land earlier that spring, traveling with Kol over the Campos to bring her brother home. That trek had been an utter failure so far as rescuing Lucas was concerned, but looking back now, she could see that even then, her feelings for Kol had been stronger than mere friendship. She simply hadn't wanted to admit it at the time; after all, he was a Sornian and therefore the enemy. Despite that, though, she'd trusted him from the start. Tending his wounds, riding double with him at times, falling asleep on his arm—the memories from their first travels together no longer made her blush with embarrassment; instead, she'd come to cherish them. Even if the Sornians were to destroy Greywood, it comforted her to know that at least the Campos would always be there, filled with her memories.

They continued on, drawing nearer to Compass Point, and the sun grew warm overhead. They stopped to water the horses at a small stream beneath trees ablaze with autumn colors, scarlet and gold. She marveled at the beauty of her surroundings and with a heavy sadness, wondered if this would be the last she'd see of it. From her saddle bag, she pulled out a handful of oats and offered them to Shy on her palm, stroking his face. It hurt to think how much he trusted her even now, as she led him into danger. *Poor, sweet animal.* He didn't know what they'd soon be facing. Blinking back tears, she leaned in and kissed his soft muzzle.

"Will you ride beside me?" Adella asked Rosalind as they mounted up again, looking over at the woman she'd come to view as a friend.

Rosalind smiled with sadness in her eyes. Her golden curls were tied back in a queue like the others, a bow slung over her shoulder. "Of course."

As the sun lowered westward, Adella crested a rise in the land and drew Shy to a halt. In the distance, a dark cloud of troops sullied the far fields below, with the massive outcropping of Compass Point in the distance. She let out a gasp, her stomach dropping; the Sornian forces stretched end to end, as far as she could see in either direction. *So many...* There would be no passing through unnoticed. She turned to Holcomb beside her, whose eyes widened in horror.

Mouth agape, he shook his head in disbelief. "There must be no one left in Sornia," he muttered. "They're all here."

Adella turned to look across the fields. It seemed like madness to send so many troops over the frontier just to quell their little holdout in Elldon. *Why would they do that?* There was only one person in Sornia she could think of who might be behind it. *Matei...* Adella wondered. *Is this your doing?*

"What now?" Rosalind asked, riding up to Adella's other side. Her voice was brittle with fear.

"We could camp behind the rise tonight," Holcomb suggested. "And have the advantage of the sun behind us in the morning?" A newfound uncertainty dimmed his once-confident demeanor.

Jacoby joined them, already shaking his head. "Look, there." He gestured north across the field, where two figures rode hard down the ridge toward the western encampment. "Scouts."

"They know we're here," Adella said grimly. "There's no way out of it. We'll face them before the sun sets."

12

Sundering

Brushing aside yew branches, Matei stepped out from behind the rusty iron door and into the falling light of evening. A chill hung in the air, forming wisps of mist in the shadows of the formal garden as he slipped the key back into the small patch-pocket of his breeches. The punched tin lantern he carried cast flickering streaks of light on the faces of his companions.

"Come on," he whispered over his shoulder. He was relieved they'd found no one else about at that hour. "Quickly."

"You should stay here, Tess," Lucas suggested, holding the heavy door open. "This excursion might get a little... unsavory."

Wrapping her arms around herself, she shuddered in the cool air and brushed past him, stepping through behind Matei. "It's always been unsavory. I don't want to be left behind."

Lucas shrugged, following her as the door fell shut behind him. "Suit yourself."

"Shut up," Matei interrupted. "Let's go."

He led them through the vast garden and along the stone wall. When he came to the place where he knew the ivy concealed a secret opening, he hid the lantern beneath his cloak. There were soldiers walking the parapet, their forms black shapes against the darkening sky. Though he knew they likely couldn't see him crouching in the wall's shadow, he waited for them to pass.

Feeling for the opening through the foliage, his hands soon gave way. Blindly, he crawled into the tangle of vines. Not many knew about the hidden passage; it was a secret guarded by the few who'd discovered it. Matei had found it the night his wife had died a decade ago. He'd sat alone, unseen in the dark garden, with tears streaming down his face as he silently begged the stars and pleaded to Mundil herself for his beloved Livia's life back. No answer had come, but in the darkness, he'd spied a figure disappearing through the ivy. As he took the same path now, creeping along the packed dirt floor, the pain of his loss came flooding back, his unanswered prayer aching again like a knotted scar in his heart. With tears filling the corners of his eyes, he crossed the short distance through the wall and pushed the covering stone aside.

Emerging from withered, crackling foliage, he waited for the others to come out, then carefully replaced the stone. Keeping the lantern concealed, he led them southeast, scurrying quickly from cover to cover beneath the trees.

"Where are we going?" Lucas asked after they were a safe distance from the walls of Hedda. "Surely the Crown Prince needn't sneak around his own country?"

"We're not in Sornia anymore," Matei replied sharply. "Not officially, anyway. And I don't want anyone to see what I'm attempting now." He knew his earlier trick with the octopus would likely be reasoned away as too-fresh seafood, but this new idea of his would be something else entirely.

"You still didn't say where we're going," Teressa noted.

Matei smiled in the dark, his teeth gleaming. "You'll see."

Soon, they arrived at the southern edge of a field. Before them, pale tents dotted the dark landscape in the light the sinking sun, glowing orange in the sky like an ember.

"Right," Lucas began dubiously, pulling back his cloak hood, his breath visible in the failing light. "What is this?"

"The barrow fields," Matei replied.

Teressa gave a derisive scoff. "The what?"

"The cemeteries of Hedda are full," Matei explained darkly. "They have been for some time, so this is where we bring our dead."

"For heaven's sake," Teressa muttered, holding her nose as a putrid scent carried toward them on the breeze.

"You insisted on coming," Lucas reminded her, pulling his shirt collar over his mouth.

"Quiet," Matei snapped. They followed him through the field, weaving between the tents, their feet crunching on the dry leaf litter that had blown in from the surrounding groves in the rising autumn winds. He approached one and lifted the corner, revealing a pile of bodies stacked carelessly inside. "Try to find one that looks fresh," he whispered. Teressa gave Lucas a disgusted look but said nothing. As they went, a sudden rustling broke the silence, and a small shadow darted from one tent, scurrying off into the wilderness.

Teressa screamed.

"Shh!" Matei hissed. "It's just an animal."

"Ugh," she groaned. "This seems disrespectful. Are there not even any night guards?"

"Not anymore," he replied. "We've sent nearly all our local troops across the Campos."

"Blackburn knows to leave Greywood intact," Lucas interjected. "Right?"

"Of course," Matei lied smoothly. "I gave the orders myself."

"Over there," Lucas said suddenly, pointing across the field. "A wagon. Must be new arrivals?"

"Good eye," Matei replied, quickening his pace. Coming to the unmanned wagon that sat on a rise on the far side of the field, he lifted his lantern and pulled off the heavy tarpaulin. A foul stench—stale urine mingled with feces, rather than the pungent smell of putrefaction—hit his face, and his stomach turned. Reaching into a waistcoat pocket, he pulled out a handkerchief and held it to his nose, inhaling its orange blossom perfume with relief.

"Pull that one down," Matei ordered, voice muffled beneath the fabric as he pointed to a small, delicate body lying on top of the pile.

"No," Teressa pleaded, voice trembling. "Not that one."

Matei groaned. A child would have been easier for what he had planned. "Fine," he huffed, pulling the cloth away from his nose. "Just grab one, then."

Lucas took hold of an arm that hung over the side and, turning his face away, pulled it down. The green-jacketed body landed at their feet with a dull thud, and its face lolled toward them in the lantern light. In place of a mouth, a black hole gaped from a missing jaw, seeping thick, dark blood onto the soil.

Clapping her hands over her mouth, Teressa stifled a scream.

"You shouldn't have come," Lucas muttered sympathetically. "You're going to have nightmares..."

"No, I won't," she whispered. "I'll be fine—" She gagged again as Matei grabbed the corpse's wrist and dragged the body along the ground.

"He doesn't mind," Lucas consoled her. "He's dead."

Matei pulled the soldier through the grass until he was a few paces from the wagon. Dropping the soldier's arm, he sat down at his side, setting the lantern beside him. "I need silence for this," he said, looking up at them pointedly. Seeing that they intended to cooperate, he turned his attention to the gaping face, speckled with orange light from the lantern.

Though he'd been greatly improving his connection with the crystal, building on what he'd learned with each new attempt, Matei still wasn't sure he was strong enough for what he was about to attempt. He wasn't even sure it was possible. Leveret himself had never accomplished such a thing, at least not in any of the versions of the tale he'd come across. And yet, he'd already come so far, there was no telling what he could do with enough effort. The only way to know was to try.

Matei set the Heartstone on his palm. Reaching out with his mind, he connected with the body of the soldier lying limply on the cold ground, and the stone grew warm against his skin. He probed the mind before him, or at least the place among the ethers surrounding the body where the mind would normally be. He felt nothing at all, no resistance other than the sluggishness of cold muscle. Like lightning, Matei's will coursed through the dead limbs, enervating them with his consciousness. The process was simple enough; however, when he tried to compel the body into motion, nothing happened.

Matei focused harder, sending more of his mind into the corpse's brain. His jaw ached, throat burning in the cold evening air as the distinction between his own body and the other began to blur. Soon, strange memories imposed themselves into his head, thoughts of another life recently lived and even more recently ended. The images flashed quickly: the swing of a saber in his gloved hand, the bright sun in a blue sky, the din of hooves and the ringing of steel flooded over him. The pain of the soldier's gaping wound became his. Then came a dark brown blur and a flat-pupiled eye rimmed with white, followed by large, yellowed teeth hurtling toward his face, turning his world to blackness.

His connection snapped, and Matei opened his eyes, gasping for air.

"What happened?" Lucas asked. "Did it work?"

"I was savaged," Matei replied between breaths, "by a horse in battle. I mean, he was," he amended, nodding toward the soldier.

"Ugh," Lucas replied. "Sounds painful." The wind rose and the air around them came alive with the rustling of leaves, blowing across the dark fields under the golden light of the setting sun.

"I'm going to try again." Matei probed the inert mind, his fingers reaching through the ether to find those belonging to the body. Despite some of the bones being broken and the pain echoing in his own hand, he felt the full connection finally slip into place.

This time, the body responded to his command. Leaves crunched as the corpse slowly rolled over, a guttural gurgling rising in its throat. Thick, syrupy blood bubbled and splattered from the cavernous mouth, hitting Matei on the cheek.

Slowly, Matei rose, the crystal in his hand glowing with an eerie green light. Mirroring his movement, the soldier lumbered upward. As it unfurled its full height, the head lolled to one side, liquid oozing down its neck.

Matei smiled, elated at his success, and the crystal's power surged through his arm, sizzling through his veins and invigorating his entire being. For the first time since the Heartstone had come into his possession, he felt as though a veil had been lifted; he and the crystal were one. *Nothing can stop me now!*

Matei dropped to a crouch, digging the fingers of his empty hand into the cool, damp soil, and the stone's energy soared like lightning through his arm and into the land. The ground beneath him trembled, reverberating through his bones, as the air filled with the deep, grating sound of shifting rock. Pebbles emerged from the soil at his feet and began to roll, then bounce violently, as the trembling grew stronger. All about him, an unnatural green light permeated the darkness, emanating from the crystal in his hand.

Retaining his connection with the soldier's form, his mind soared through the ether to the other empty bodies all around them. Still and calm, they gave no resistance to his will; the instant he connected with their flesh, they rose slowly and shambled to their feet. They stood there, shadowy black sentinels in the eerie, viridescent light, as the corpses thrummed with borrowed life.

Suddenly, the sky blazed with a streak of white, cleaving the heavens as a thunderous crack echoed through the air. The instantaneous flash starkly illuminated the dead as they stood silently, awaiting his command, and Teressa's shriek tore through the twilight, ringing over the windswept fields.

* * *

Jacoby drew up beside Adella. "We can't waver now," he said, holding back his horse as it champed at the bit. "Isn't this what we came for?"

"He's right," Holcomb replied. "'The only way out now is through,'" he said, repeating her earlier words.

Adella let out her breath in resignation. "Then, we charge." She knew it was hopeless; given how outnumbered they were, the only way out for them would be the oblivion of a quick end. Still, it was better than leaving their fate in the hands of the Sornians.

Holcomb cleared his throat and leaned in toward her, lowering his voice, "If you should find my body in the field, and my wig has come loose—"

"I'll fix it before anyone notices," she said softly.

He nodded. "Thank you."

"And if I should be captured..." Adella kept her voice steady and her gaze ahead, trying not to betray her emotions. "An arrow to the heart would be a kinder fate." She glanced toward him, raising her brows pleadingly. After seeing what the Sornians had done to Misses Asher and James, Adella shuddered to think what they might do to her. Though the bounty on her head offered some protection, there were worse things than death.

He frowned as he considered her request, then nodded.

"Right then," she said, seeing that the others were ready. "Let's get on with it."

Adella adjusted the crossbow strap on her shoulder and urged Shy forward on the rise, overlooking those gathered below. "Fellow Valennians," she called out. "Neighbors... My friends," she added warmly. "We are cut off from Valenna. There will be no help coming, and we are few facing many." The gravity of her words weighed down her voice. "But there's one thing that matters more on the battlefield than the outcome: that is how it's fought. And as Valennians, there can be no greater purpose than to live and die with honor." Metal sang softly as she drew her father's saber.

"But there, across the far fields," she continued, pointing the blade westward, "are those who know no honor. They attack us in the dark of night like wolves, breaking over a century of peace; they desecrate our fallen and slaughter the helpless. And when they converge upon us, they will do the same to each of us." Her even gaze passed from face to face, taking in their grim expressions.

"It is better to die now, with honor and courage, beating them back even a hair's breadth, than to live long enough in our cowardice to find out what fate they will press upon our bodies—" Her throat tightened. "Like they've done to our loved ones. And when we ride out—" Her voice gathered strength, soaring over the plains; "It won't be for glory, nor victory, but to avenge our families in whatever way we can, and to deprive our enemy the satisfaction of our surrender. So I ask you now, will you ride out onto the battlefield with me, and show them what Valennians are made of?"

Her words were met with a resounding roar. Pulling on Shy's reins, she spun and sent him into a trot, gaining speed down the hill as the people of Elldon all joined her, hooves pounding and soil flying as they rode west toward the battlefield. They rode together, cavalry and civilian alike, the scarlet beside the duns of homespun and canvas, with Captain Holcomb and Lady Grimless at the front.

"Charge!" Holcomb repeated, loud enough for those at the back to hear as he hoisted his bow. "For Valenna!"

"For Elldon!" Adella shouted, sheathing her saber and unslinging her crossbow. Voices rose behind them, and they spurred their horses down the rise.

"Form a line," Holcomb called out as they galloped over the prairie toward the looming rock of Compass Point and the forces gathered at its base. "And keep together!"

Adella pulled a bolt from the wooden quiver on her belt and loaded her crossbow. Across the field, where the golden sun lowered toward the horizon, the flanking Sornian cavalry broke into motion. The murmur of their cries carried on the wind.

Holcomb turned to Adella. "If by some twist of fate we break through, keep going," he ordered. "Don't look back."

Adella nodded, though she thought it was likely he was wasting his breath.

Halfway across the field, a deep rumble tore through the soil, reverberating in their bones. A strange, metallic tang innervated the air, and Adella glanced nervously around, looking for the telltale signs of a coming storm. As far as she could see, the skies were still clear. *No, wait...* On the edge of the western horizon, just below the sinking sun, dark clouds gathered, casting a stormy, green light in the distance. *Fitting,* she thought grimly, digging her heels into Shy's sides to spur him along.

Ahead, emerald-clad riders broke away from the bulk of the Sornian forces and galloped at them head-on, rapidly closing the span between them. "Keep in formation!" she shouted to her companions, hoping their courage would hold.

An arrow flew from the group of oncoming riders and whistled past her head. Somewhere behind her, a horse squealed in pain. With a surge of anger, Adella lifted her crossbow to her cheek and released a bolt over the distance into the oncoming riders, but she lost sight of it amidst the tumult. Beside her, Rosalind's bow twanged as she let fly an arrow of her own.

Bracing the crossbow stirrup with the toe of her boot, Adella quickly pulled the string back into the locking mechanism and reloaded, launching bolt after bolt into the enemy riders. Ahead, bodies fell from horses as the Sornians drew nearer. Though she dared not glance back, she knew they were losing people, too. The cries and faltering hoofbeats were clear enough.

Only a few strides out from meeting the enemy with no time now to reload, Adella slung her crossbow over her shoulder and drew her saber. *For Father,* she told herself, gritting her teeth. *And Mother.*

Red collided against green as Valennians and Sornians clashed in the dying light of evening. At the fore, Adella sent Shy crashing into the line of horses, shoving between Holcomb's steed and those of the enemy. A blade swung at her overhead. Hoisting up her father's saber, she met it with hers, the strike ringing loudly in her ears. She shoved it away. Horses roared their feral battle calls, pressing in on all sides. The Sornian beside her lost his balance briefly, jostled from behind, and, seizing the opportunity, she hacked her saber across his open shoulder. As he fell, the hot breath of his horse warmed the air as it let out a savage squeal, then bared its teeth and lunged at Shy's neck, tearing away a strip of hair. She slashed at the other horse, but her blade missed as Shy reared, and Adella had to grab a fistful of mane to hold herself in the saddle.

A low, ominous rumble shook the earth again, and lightning split the sky. Something caught Adella's eye in the distance. Far beyond the jutting form of Compass Point, beneath the storm clouds she'd spotted earlier, an uncanny green light now rose from the horizon. Before it, darkness spread over the far field, rapidly swallowing up the landscape.

"What in the world..." she muttered, jaw falling slack. She wondered if anyone else saw it. "Holcomb!" she shouted, trying to get his attention as they continued to press through the fray, hacking this way and that. He dispatched the enemy at his side and glanced at her quickly. "Look there," she said, nodding westward.

The color drained from his face. "Heavens, have mercy—" His words were barely discernible above the noise.

"What's happening?" she asked, furrowing her brow. On her other side, Rosalind looked on, eyes wide with terror.

Holcomb cried out as a sudden blow threw him sideways in the saddle. Just in time, Adella reached over and grabbed his coat collar, keeping him from falling beneath the sea of stamping hooves. Groaning under the great strain, she pulled hard against his weight, leaning back. She was grateful he was a small man. If it had been Kol, he'd have been lost.

Regaining his balance, Holcomb pulled himself back in the saddle. Grimacing, he grabbed his left shoulder, and his hand came away coated in blood. The Sornian riders broke from the fray, veering off along the flanks to regroup for another attack.

"Forward!" Holcomb shouted, ignoring his injury and spurring his horse into a gallop. The others followed behind, keeping in close formation.

Adella readied her crossbow quickly. Within moments, their riders crashed upon the Sornian infantry, who'd had little time to prepare for the unexpected onslaught. As they crashed into the wall of emerald green, the soldiers scattered on foot, scrambling to keep from being trampled beneath pounding hooves.

"Hold your positions!" Blackburn's harsh shout soared over the din. Another rumble like thunder cracked through the air, and men fell and horses stumbled as the soil beneath them shook violently. Shy blew a loud rattling snort, eyes rimmed all around with white, and as his forelimbs gave way, his shoulders ducked downward. Unprepared, Adella fell forward, catching herself on his neck.

Behind her, the same sort of strange, turbulent darkness that encroached from the west now spread across the eastern field as well. Rock and soil crumbled, swallowed up in the void, and Adella's mouth went dry as she realized the very ground they stood upon was rapidly collapsing. A roar broke over the landscape, growing louder over the sounds of battle. Turning westward again and squinting against the setting sun, Adella could just make out a shimmer on the darkness, a white spray cresting along the leading edge. *Is it water?* she wondered. The blackness continued to grow, surging toward them as it devoured the crumbling fields. Panic seared through her. *The Campos are falling into the sea!* Desperately, she searched the battlefield, but in every direction, the vast prairie of her homeland was being swallowed up in the dark, surging waters.

Beside her, Holcomb's mouth fell open as he stared at the violent landscape. He shot her a bewildered, questioning look, unsure what to do.

"Forget orders," a soldier ahead of her called out, turning his horse aside. "Run!"

With the ground rapidly falling away around them and the leading edge coming at them quickly, no direction seemed safe. "Get to higher ground," she shouted over the din, pointing with her crossbow to the looming peak of Compass Point. She hoped that the great rock formation would hold out somehow.

The soil beneath her horse's feet groaned, then shifted suddenly. A crack split through the grass, bursting between Adella and Rosalind on her other side. "Go!" she shouted, and they spurred their horses onward toward Compass Point. Glancing back, her breath caught in her throat as several riders disappeared into the ground, swallowed up by the darkness below.

Panic and tumult surrounded her; the shrill screams of terror from riders and horses alike echoed in her ears. Beneath them she heard the permeating grumble and grate of massive rock, and, in the distance, the booming, wild roar of the sea. Again and again, she loaded her crossbow again and released bolts as she rode, trying to clear the path of the remaining Sornian soldiers who, ignoring the greater danger, still ran at them with brandished blades.

Her horse leapt over a writhing body. Just as its forelimbs touched down again, the ground beneath jolted sideways with a loud crack. Shy's hooves slipped and skittered on the sloping rock beneath and, losing balance, Adella tumbled from the saddle. Landing on her hip, eyes watering with the pain that surged through her bones, she covered her head with her arms as the sound of hooves pounded in her ears, striking the ground around her head and grazing her shoulder as the stampeding group thundered past. Coughing, she choked on the rising dust, waiting for the tumult to pass. When she finally looked up, Shy was gone, along with everyone else.

The patch of ground she lay on slipped again, groaning ominously as it began to tilt beneath her. Jumping to her feet, Adella tucked her crossbow under her arm and sprinted toward the dark shape of Compass Point outlined against the lurid green sunset, fighting to stay upright as the ground beneath her feet tipped down toward the growing abyss.

The edge of the rocky platform before her began to dip more precariously, rising up faster and faster. Pouring her last ounce of energy into her legs, she reached the ledge, and, planting a booted foot on the crumbling edge, took a flying leap, hoping there would be something to land upon on the other side.

She crashed onto a hard surface, falling with such force that she tumbled forward, rolling over sharp stones that slashed her clothes and skin but grateful to feel solid ground beneath her. Grabbing her forehead to quell the spinning, she stumbled to her feet and retrieved her crossbow from the ground beside her. At the base of Compass Point not far ahead, a few red-clad figures scrambled up the slope, hoping to find refuge on higher ground. At the base of the rock formation, she was surprised that a few soldiers in emerald still clung to their orders, hacking their blades at any unhorsed Valennians, who were doing their best to fend them off despite their injuries.

Pelting after her fellow Valennians, Adella made her way across the field of chaos toward the base of Compass Point, and stumbled as the ground shifted and slipped beneath her feet. As the tremors worsened, the swath of green soldiers ahead scattered in panic up the rise, save for one large figure who came at her against the flow of bodies, resolute. Raising the stock of his heavy iron crossbow, he pulled back on the goat's foot lever to set the string and placed a bolt into the channel.

Adella glanced about, but there was nowhere to hide. He was too near for her to run; she'd surely get a bolt in her back if she dared try. Facing her attacker, her heart pounded with sudden recognition. Beneath a broad, black hat glowered a craggy face with a stubbled, hard-set jaw. "Blackburn," she muttered, pulse racing.

"You," he growled between clenched teeth, taking a step closer and leveling the crossbow at Adella's chest. His fingers moved toward the lever. "I had orders to bring you back alive," he sneered, his gravelly voice rising over the distant rumbling. "But if it's the last thing I do in this crumbling world, I'm going to take you out of it." With a cruel smirk, he took aim and squeezed.

Just as his finger moved, a sudden crack cut through the air. The ground lurched, throwing him off balance, and the bolt sliced through her wool coat, biting into her arm as it grazed past. Clapping her hand over the stinging wound, she sucked a sharp breath through her teeth as Blackburn reached for his bolt quiver and found it empty. Swearing under his breath, he pulled his saber from its scabbard.

Adella's heart hammered in her ears. The man was so broad, so massive, she had no chance to beat him in combat. Yet she had no choice. As the world fell apart around them, all that remained was the two of them under the dusky, green sky. Taking a deep breath, Adella drew her father's saber, the metal singing softly amid the noise of groaning earth and sea. *Now's not the time to panic,* she reprimanded herself, shoving away the fear that threatened to overtake her mind. *There are worse things than a noble death.* When she'd taken her vows before the Queen, she'd known this could be the fate that awaited her. If this was to be her end, she was ready for it. Drawing a deep breath, she stepped into the defensive position, thinking of Kol. She leveled her blade and tried to remember everything he'd taught her: the position of her feet, how to hold her wrist, where to look for vulnerabilities. Maybe she couldn't win this fight, but her only intention now was to take her opponent down with her. "I promise you," she said, fighting to keep her voice steady, "it *will* be the last thing you do."

Blackburn let out a sharp laugh. "We'll see," he jeered, lip curling into a snarl as he charged, slashing forward savagely. Quickly, Adella parried, the force of his blow nearly knocking the hilt from her hands as it shuddered up her arms, jarring her bones.

The ground cracked again, jolting beneath their feet, and Blackburn stumbled. For a brief moment, his side was left unguarded. Knowing it would be her only chance, with the same swift movement Kol had made her practice so many times before, she lunged forward with everything she had, groaning through her teeth as she drove the tip of her saber deeply beneath his ribs, then withdrew.

Blackburn's eyes bulged, and he doubled over in pain, gasping and grabbing his belly. Slowly, he fell to one side to lie crumpled and groaning on the ground.

Giving the man a final glare, Adella stepped over the uneven, shifting ground toward the rise of Compass Point. The air around her cracked as lightning seared the sky. She paused to take in the sight. Just beyond Compass Point, where the rolling fields of the Campos had been, a vast, endless chasm gaped. A small span of land remained, jutting up to the edge of the chasm in a sharp precipice, but the illusion of permanence was fleeting. Even as she watched, several more large chunks of land crumbled and fell away, crashing into the dark, turbulent waters below, adding to the chaotic currents and creating angry waves, cresting white with foam. Adella froze at the sight, her blood chilling in her veins as she watched the destruction approach.

Just as the growing chasm was nearly upon her, a massive hand clamped around her neck, as strong as steel. Fingers crushed her airway as another hard hand wrenched her wrist up painfully behind her back, and her saber fell to the earth with a clatter. She tried to gasp but only choked, her vision mottling at the edges.

Sour, hot breath warmed her cheek, and Blackburn's leering face appeared in the corner of her eye. He tightened his hand around her throat, his broad form pressed against her back as she fought to stay conscious. Ears ringing, lungs burning for air, she pried at his fingers and the powerful arms that held her fast, but they didn't give at all. Tears flooded her eyes as she realized this would be the end of not just the Campos, but her as well. It seemed fitting, somehow. She was glad Kol wouldn't be there to see it.

13

The Tigress

"What do you mean, 'coming with you?'" Kol asked, rising from his seat as Captain Declan strode away. "Aren't we heading for Smuggler's Port?" There was no answer; he'd already left. Kol turned back to Kerchaw. "We're going to Smuggler's Port, right?" he asked, but Kerchaw merely shrugged.

Kol slumped back into the chair and rubbed his face, letting out his breath. While he knew Adella to be competent, her courage often led her headfirst into danger. Indeed, the Valennians were alike in that way; their sense of honor often seemed to outstrip any instinct for survival. He hoped the Sornian army would take its time in advancing so Elldon's stockade wall would be completed before their arrival. That would buy her some time, at least.

"What's the matter?" Kerchaw asked, drawing Kol from his thoughts.

"My home," Kol replied. "It's in danger. Adella..." Words failed him; he shook his head helplessly.

"Oh, the war; I see," Kerchaw commented, frowning. "You've left your girl behind."

"Ugh," Kol groaned into his palms, pained to hear it put so plainly. "I thought I'd have time to get back."

"Don't be so glum." Kerchaw patted Kol's shoulder, his hand squelching on his damp jacket. "I've heard they've got Endlebridge's cavalry on their side. Those boys are highly trained, you know. Me and Annie go see the parade every King's Feast, up in Pentz. Of course, the place is gone now..." He glanced down at Kol but got no response. "I've sent them to Enth," he went on, changing the subject, "Annie and our little one, to my sister's place in the mountains. Safe as anything, up there in the northeast, far from the coast..." He trailed off at Kol's continued reticence, and silence settled over the cabin. Beside them, the notary bobbed his head sleepily, hands folded on his belly.

Kol rose suddenly, his chair scraping loudly against the wooden floor. "I can't just sit here," he muttered and strode from the room, determined to find the captain.

Water oozed from his boots as he made his way across the weather deck, where Captain Declan busily gave orders to the crew. Though Kol now owned the vessel, the captain still held supreme authority over the ship. He'd have to wait to speak with him until the man was ready. Walking along the larboard rail, he took in the wide, blue sweep of the sea as *The Tigress* changed tack. He'd found himself sailing more this year than ever in his life, and though the fear of open water still unsettled his nerves, he felt more at ease than previously. The salty air brought memories of distant shores, carrying the thrill of adventure on the wind. He now began to understand why some might choose to spend their days upon the sea.

He pushed back the strands of wet hair that blew about his face. Since coming to Valenna, he hadn't cut it. Although it was nearing the length of the customary Valennian queue, the gusts that came in from the Bay always managed to pull his thick curls loose no matter how securely he tied them, whipping them straight into his eyes. The chill cut through his damp clothes as well, raising goosebumps on his arms, but despite the annoyances, being above deck still invigorated his sore and weary limbs. He stared out over the blue depths, and his thoughts turned to Adella. With an aching heart, he wished he had never left her side. *I have to find her.*

A loud group of fellow passengers from Raymouth, including quite a few red-clad Royal Guards who'd come aboard to escape the flooding city, crowded up the companionway from below deck. Each looked, rather like himself, he supposed, bedraggled and dripping with seawater. It was a common occurrence these days, ships taking on those fleeing the dramatic natural disasters that continued to grow more frequent. While he waited to have a word with the captain, a figure in a fine blue coat, somewhat older than himself but beaming with a cheerful disposition, approached him from across the deck. "Nutmeg Jon," Kol greeted him.

"It's First Mate Jon now," he replied with a laugh, "if you please. I wanted to congratulate you on becoming the new owner." Tucked beneath his arm was a bundle of red cloth. Holding it out, he offered a dry wool jacket, scarlet and cut in the style of the Royal Guard.

"Thank you," Kol said, removing his rain-soaked coat. "And to you on your promotion," he added, pulling the jacket over his broad shoulders.

Jon gave a slight bow in gratitude. "I heard you've come into a new line of work since coming to Valenna and have found a good bit of luck in it."

Kol nodded.

"Good for you," Jon replied.

"And I've heard you were one of the crew that vouched for my character before the queen," Kol countered, wringing out his wet coat. "Thank you. I won't forget that."

Jon smiled warmly. "Oh," he added, "there's a man aboard looking for you, one of the stragglers we brought on seeking refuge from the flood. I believe he goes by the name of..." He lowered his brow as he thought. "Skilly?"

"Hm," Kol muttered. "I'll search him out. Thanks."

Jon nodded and gave another slight bow before returning to his duties, leaving Kol to his thoughts. He'd never heard such a name before and was quite puzzled as to who it could be. *Maybe it's Royal Westward business,* he figured. Spying Declan walking alone across the weather deck, Kol shrugged it off and followed after him.

"Just to be clear," Kol began, striding quickly to catch up, "we're heading for Smuggler's Port, right?"

"Listen," Declan began, taking Kol by the arm and pulling him aside as he leaned in close. "Don't make a scene about it, but I have royal orders to sail to a different port immediately."

Kol opened his mouth to protest.

"There's no use arguing," Declan cut him off, lowering his voice, "it's by the queen's command, and there's nothing I can do about it."

"But—" Kol began, but Declan gave him a look of warning, and he let out his breath. "Where?"

"The Capital," Declan said plainly. "I received orders just before you came aboard."

"No." Kol shrugged off the captain's grip. "I need to get to Smuggler's Port right away. I need to find Adella."

"You don't have a choice," Declan insisted.

"If we pass another ship going west—" Kol began hopefully.

The captain shook his head. "It wasn't just *my* orders; it was a royal summons for *every* ship in Valenna."

Heavy dread flooded through Kol's gut. "But Adella—"

"What could you do for her, anyway?" Declan interrupted. "You're just one man. Look, I care for Miss Adella more than anyone. I plan to marry her. But my duty to the queen and country must come first."

Kol bit his tongue. He hadn't delivered Adella's letter; he hadn't even had a chance yet to mention he had the captain's personal correspondence. *Now's probably not a great time to tell him I slept with the woman he thinks he's going to marry...* The memory of Adella's soft skin against his body brought a sudden heat to his face, catching his breath in his throat.

"Are you alright?" Declan asked, narrowing his eyes at him. "You look flushed."

"I'm fine," Kol said dryly.

"Just think about what you're proposing," Declan went on, more delicately this time. "As captain, I can't abandon my ship, so you'd be on your own. It's a three-day sail to Smuggler's Port, then a week's ride through the Campos. By the time you get there, she'll already be captured, or killed, or have fled if at all possible. No matter the outcome," he reasoned, looking him earnestly in the eyes, "you'll be too late. I suggest you try to have a little faith in her, as I must do."

Kol groaned in exasperation, but held his tongue. Returning to the cabin, he paced about, running a hand through his hair. It pained him to admit it, but Declan was right. *Even so, the Capital...* They were sailing in the wrong direction. His jaw clenched as he kicked the leg of the table violently. It didn't budge at all, affixed as it was to the sole, and it stung his toes painfully. Kerchaw, still sitting with his arms crossed where Kol had left him, raised his brows.

"We're not heading to Smuggler's Port," Kol informed him bitterly. "Royal orders. Damn," he hissed, and plopped down on the chair with arms folded.

"What are you going to do?" Kerchaw asked, his pocked brow furrowing.

Kol chewed his thumbnail. "I don't know." There was nothing for it; he'd just have to trust that Adella would be able to take care of herself. Pulling open his haversack, he was relieved to find her letter safe and dry. At some point, he'd have to give it to the captain, but if he did it now, when they were already at odds, he couldn't expect much cooperation from him going forward, and despite how much Kol disliked the man, he had a feeling he was going to need it.

* * *

Blackburn tightened his grip on Adella's throat, and her vision blurred. Faintly, a red form materialized ahead, stepping closer out of the tumult. Blinking to clear her eyes, she found herself looking into the face of Captain Holcomb. *He came back for me?* His expression resolute, the cavalry captain drew his bow and leveled the arrow at her chest. Her head swam as she tried to make sense of it; with Blackburn behind her, her body would serve as his shield. *That's right,* she recalled dimly, thoughts muddled with lack of breath, *I made him promise. If I were to be captured...* Adella squeezed her eyes shut, tears falling down her cheek, and braced herself for the arrow. Yet, her heart wrenched to think she'd never see Kol again.

No! It can't end like this. The thought came unbidden yet vibrant and strong. She wanted to call out to Holcomb, to tell him to give her yet another moment in this world, but her voice was stifled by the hand around her neck. Suddenly, a memory surfaced, one of Kol's arms around her, holding her from behind—similar, and yet so very different from the way Blackburn held her now. '*Stay my hand...*' His words echoed in Adella's mind. '*Look for the weak points.*' Summoning her last dregs of strength, her fingers pried around the loosest of those clenched like a vice on her throat, and, with all her might, she snapped it backward.

Blackburn cried out as bone and tendon cracked, and his grip loosened. Adella slipped free, gasping desperately, and threw herself clear of Holcomb's arrow just as it whizzed through the air to lodge deep into Blackburn's broad chest. He gave a choking groan, and a spatter of blood warmed her cheek as he dropped to his knees, then slowly pitched forward, twitching a few times before finally lying still.

Head spinning, Adella lay on the ground, breathing heavily, then pushed herself up to sit, waiting for her vision to return fully. Holcomb ran over to help her up, lifting her by the arm. "Thank you," she managed to wheeze, voice hoarse with the pain of her bruised throat.

"That was lucky," he muttered. Glancing over her shoulder at the chasm still swallowing up the land, his eyes widened. "No time to wait.

Run!" he shouted over the din of rumbling rock, pulling her by the arm.

Together, they sprinted toward the base of Compass Point, which seemed to sink further and further into the distance as the world heaved and swelled beneath them. An ear-splitting crack tore through the confusion, and Adella screamed as a deep chasm slashed through the ground a short way ahead of them, cutting through their path to Compass Point. Feet still pounding over the uneven terrain, she threw a questioning glance at Holcomb.

"We have to jump!" he shouted as they careened onward over the tumultuous ground toward the rift. She nodded.

As the toe of her boot came down at the ledge, Adella shoved off from the ground, arms flailing wildly as she leapt through dusty air. For a moment, she was suspended over the gaping, black void below. Her heart hammered in her ears. Then, the hard surface hit her in the chest, slamming the air painfully from her lungs. She was relieved to feel land beneath her arms and chest, but her legs dangled precariously over the ledge as the weight of her lower body slowly dragged her down into the chasm.

Her hands scratched and scraped at the dirt as she struggled to find a hold, but there was nothing to grab onto; it all crumbled beneath her fingers. Inch by inch, she lost ground to the emptiness below while her waist dropped over the edge, then her ribs. Hanging by her elbows, she kicked at the steep rock, desperately seeking a foothold. The terror of a dark, unknown fate awaiting below gripped her heart like a vice. *No!* The thought came again. *It can't end like this!*

"I've got you—" Holcomb's strong hands suddenly clamped around her wrist. Groaning under the strain, he dragged her up and back onto solid ground.

"Thank you," Adella said gratefully, stumbling to her feet. "That's twice you've saved me today."

They hurried on, with another thunderous rumble shaking the landscape. A wash of loose rock and debris cascaded down the slope before them, tumbling into the crevasse out of sight. The ground shuddered again, and her heart leapt into her throat as the very ground on which they stood gave way. This time, there was no stopping their fall. Her feet slipped out from under her, and she and Holcomb, swept up with the scree, slid down the plunging slope. Adella's fingernails clawed at the dirt but found no purchase as she fell into the unknown, the world around her a hazy blur of dark sky, soil, and the scarlet flashes of Holcomb's coat. She could hear his cries of pain mingled with her own as they tumbled, unhampered by the rocks that tore at clothes and skin. Finally, as she hit a hard surface and rolled to a sudden stop, her head struck sharply upon stone, and everything went black.

* * *

Colors swirled around her: blue, white, and gold. Little painted birds paused in mid-flight above her head while lively violins filled her ears with a light melody. "I thought you weren't dancing..." she murmured, the touch of Kol's rough palm warming her hand. Smiling couples floated gracefully in circles around them, and laughter tinkled like bells in the air.

A low rumbling drew her out of the beautiful comfort of the dream, shuddering through her body, awakening her to a sharp pain in her head. She tried to open her eyes, but her eyelids were too heavy to lift, and she allowed herself to be pulled back into unconsciousness.

Darkness became a memory of the sea, the serene lap of water engulfing her. Indigo and teal flooded behind her closed eyes, and her legs twitched, startled into motion by the urge to swim. She shifted on the cold rock beneath her, felt pebbles digging into her back and saltwater stinging the blistered nettle-rash on her arm, and realized it was only another dream. The waves crept higher along her body, and she let the vision wash over her, surrendering to the soothing sensations.

Soon, the susurration of water melded into a voice, gentle, deep, and cool.

Each calamity has its cure... The words came to her slowly, distant and dim, arising like a mist through her thoughts.

Daughter of Andolin, you know what to do.

In the midst of the deep blue of her dreaming mind, an image formed: a plant with vibrant green, broad leaves, crowned by a cluster of white florets.

A lesson to be learned...

The words trailed off into stark silence, and an inky blackness grew like a stain over the watery landscape in her mind's eye.

"There you are," a harsh voice broke jarringly into her dream, its tone sharp as knives. "Hm, that didn't go very well for you, did it?" it taunted, so closely that it seemed to come from within.

Amidst the indigo that engulfed her, grey eyes materialized, a face rising from the shadows. "Matei?" she murmured, recoiling inwardly at the unwelcome surprise.

"I've been watching you," he replied, his voice echoing in her head. Though the shadowy features before her were hard to discern, a smile was audible in his voice. "And your little holdout. You should know... No matter what you plan, I'll always be a step ahead," he grinned, teeth appearing like a crescent moon in the darkness. "Come to me willingly," he offered as a pale hand reached out, "and things will be easier for you." Adella shuddered at the thought, but her sluggish mind couldn't muster a reply. Sensing her resistance, his voice hardened. "If you make me waste my energy bringing you to me, I'll be very angry," he warned. In his other hand, emerging from the void, a large, double-pointed crystal emitted a soft light. "Resist me, and I will destroy everything and everyone you hold dear."

"What?" Adella's brain throbbed as she strained to understand. "No. Go away; get out of my head."

"No one tells me no," he replied, his grim expression darkening further still. "I will have what I want. Now *get up*." His last words echoed painfully through her skull.

A bird call, shrill and so much more real than the sounds in her mind, rang through the air, pulling her back to her body. Adella winced, grabbing her pulsing forehead, and blinked open her eyes to find a slate-colored sky pattering her face with light raindrops. High above, a little grey hawk circled on gliding wings, wheeling over her head.

Beside her, a steep precipice rose from the water, a plane of jagged, broken rock cutting her off from the battlefield of the night before. She wondered if anyone from their party was left up there, somehow. Though her memory was hazy, and her head still pounded fiercely, it was apparent that the ground had fallen away for more than just her and Holcomb, sweeping them all down the steep slope to the water that now lay below Compass Point.

She felt cold, so very cold. Water lapped at her feet, that much she knew; she could feel it seeping further up her legs. There was a stinging pain in her forearm. Something tickled her cheek; she swiped it away and blinked at her sticky fingers. *Blood?* Groaning, she rolled to her side and found herself looking into a familiar, freckled face with brown eyes staring dully back at her. A large rock lay across the man's midsection. "Holcomb!" she tried to shout, but her voice came out as a hoarse whisper. Pulling herself over the coarse, wet ground, she dragged her aching body closer. Gritting her teeth, she strained every muscle in her battered limbs to shove the heavy rock away until it finally fell with a splash into the shallow water. Clutching the scarlet wool of Holcomb's jacket, she shook him. "Holcomb!" she screamed, regaining her voice as it pierced the silence. His head lolled to the side, falling free from his rain-soaked wig that clung to the ground.

"No..." She placed a trembling hand on his cheek. It was icy cold. It was far too late to help him now; he was gone and had been for some time. *I must've been passed out for hours, while he—* A sob racked her body at the thought. Shivering in her wet clothes, she reached out tentatively and straightened the wig, still heavy with damp powder, so it once again sat straight on his head. Then, wrapping her arms around herself, she let out a loud cry as her tears began to fall freely. *It's my fault; he died because he came back to help me.* The realization hit her like a blow to the gut, and she nearly retched. *What in the world was I thinking? This has been an absolute disaster; we've lost so many. I never should've...* Her throat tightened, choking out her breath as her face pulled into a tight grimace. *I never should've taken my father's title. It was stupid to think I could do this. It would've been better if I'd never returned to Greywood at all. I've failed everyone...* An anguished cry tore from her throat, and a wave of nausea swept over her. *Everything is lost, and it's all my fault. I should've kept them safe.* She doubled over, heaving with grief.

Eventually, her tears ran dry. Her muscles, spent and aching, relaxed of their own accord, and she lay back, exhausted and empty, with nothing left to do but gaze around at the broken world that surrounded her. The green fields of the Campos that had once waved gently in the wind beneath the shining sun were gone. Only muddy grey waters spread westward as far as she could see. Dark forms—bodies, she realized with a pang of horror—lay among the shallows, limbs bobbing on the surface of the water and scattered over the new shoreline, amongst the boulders and scree that had tumbled from Compass Point.

Her thoughts returned to the strange dream as she rubbed the inflamed blisters on her arm absently, stopping suddenly when the pain flared intensely. If she never saw Matei again, it would be too soon, so it baffled her as to why she'd be dreaming of him. And the other voice, the one that seemed to come from the very depths of the sea itself, she likewise couldn't account for. *I must've hit my head very hard indeed...* She wanted to shrug it all off as the hallucinations of a shaken brain, but the plant from her dream came again to mind. Its broad leaf and crest of white blossoms struck her with familiarity. *Comfrey...* It was the herb she'd collected out in the Campos during one of her first training sessions with Kol, the same day she'd been stung on the arm by the strange weed whose blisters still pained her. *Is it still in my bag?* she wondered, patting her side for her haversack.

Adella unbuttoned the flap and, digging through the contents, was pleased to find the herb still relatively intact. Her gaze shifted to her forearm, where the inflamed blisters had been slowly spreading since she received the injury. The rash was vivid red over her pale skin, the burning sting of it seeping deep through her flesh. *I wonder...*

Tentatively, she crushed the herb between her fingers until her fingertips were coated in a green, fragrant moisture. Clenching her jaw against the pain, she carefully clamped the crushed leaves over the rash and, pressing with her palm, held it there. Gradually, the sting began to ease.

Waiting for it to abate, she stared absently over the water. A dark shape rose to the surface, then quickly sank back down, disappearing beneath the murk. She lowered her brow, watching closely until it appeared again, this time nearer.

The creature was little; that much she could see as it rippled in and out of the lapping waves, snaking its way to shore. Unlike the pointed snout of the *pelkimund* that lately populated Belgrand Bay, attacking ships and devouring sailors, this animal had a muzzle more like that of a horse, with large and bulging black eyes, and lacy, seaweed-like whiskers streaming from its snout. It was a different beast entirely, rather like the creature she'd caught a glimpse of when she'd been aboard *The Tigress*, and the rudder had broken. However, that animal had been enormous, and this one was much smaller. *Perhaps it's young,* she mused.

Reaching the shore, the animal pulled its strange, elongated body onto land, revealing paddle-like flippers as it foundered gracelessly over the rocks like a seal. The crest of weedy whiskers continued down the animal's neck like a mane, and the way it bobbed its head up and down with each galumphing stride reminded her of a horse's canter. *Haramund,* she suddenly recalled the Old Andolinian name. *The Sea Horse.* Unlike the tiny creatures that were sometimes found on the beaches, washed up and dried in the sun, this was a beast of old with a similar name. In the Codex, she'd found a painted illustration of a high king astride the massive, mysterious creature, riding through the waves upon its back.

The small *haramund,* about the size of a porpoise rather than the massive adult she had seen earlier that spring, wandered aimlessly along the shore. It paid her no attention as it sniffed around the rocks and puddles scattered across the low, rocky beach beneath the ridge. Though it had nostrils, a series of fish-like gills swept the sides of its neck, opening and closing with each breath. A long, finned tail, much like that of an eel, dragged along behind it. *It seems to have no fear of people,* she noted, watching as it nibbled the grass clinging to a clump of soil that had, like her, slid down the slope during the quake.

Adella couldn't help herself; so horselike was the little sea animal, and so ungainly on land, that she felt no fear of it, and clucked her tongue in her cheek as though she were calling to her gelding.

The *haramund* jerked its head up, tilting it sideways as it finally noticed her. It made a quiet, burbling sound from deep within its throat, and ambled boldly toward her, startling her fiercely. Her pulse pounded, and she sat frozen, afraid to move a muscle while the little animal snuffled around at her feet, then tickled her skin with wet whiskers as it inspected her hands. Its glossy, greenish-brown body was thick with blubber and gave off the swampy reek of the sea and decomposing vegetation.

The animal sniffed at the comfrey she still pressed onto her arm. Seeing its keen interest in the plant, Adella held it carefully out to the creature. She was surprised that the blisters beneath had cooled, and the redness of her skin had faded significantly. With a sudden jolt, she recalled the words from her dream: *Each calamity has its cure...*

Adella drew a sharp breath as broad, smooth teeth scraped her palm, taking up the herb in one slow, hesitant bite. The *haramund* chewed the mouthful, dropping bits onto the ground, then sniffed at her hands again.

"That's all I've got," she said softly, showing the creature her empty palms.

The *haramund* cocked its head, then turned and bounded away quickly over the rocks. Adella slowly let out her breath. *Stupid,* she scolded herself. *You don't know anything about these animals. Its mother could be out there, watching. Or a whole family of them.* She scanned the dark, placid waters that now formed a sea where the Campos had been. To the west, there was no land visible across the water. Only small islands of broken rock dotted the surface here and there.

A shrill call came from somewhere above. It took Adella a moment to realize it sounded like the high whinny of a horse. Adella turned to the bluff behind her, searching for the source of the call, but water curved around the massive formation, limiting her view in each direction. With sea or stone her only choices, it was clear she'd eventually have to make her way up; she couldn't stay here by the water, and there was no other way to go. But without any idea of what she'd find above, she wasn't sure she wanted to try it just yet. If there were Valennian survivors up there, they might need her help. *But there could be Sornians as well.* She sighed. There was little to be gained in putting it off.

Every part of her ached when she finally stood. Bruises and scrapes seemed to cover every inch of her body. She wasn't entirely sure whether any bones were broken, though nothing stood out more than the rest. Slowly, she lowered herself back down again, groaning and wincing at the pain that bloomed with each movement. *Climbing'll have to wait.* Cradling her throbbing head in her hands, she closed her eyes and shivered in the rain.

The young *haramund* splashed loudly as it plunged into the surf, disappearing. In the distance, from behind a bend in the rocky shoreline, a small ship came into view, bobbing over the waves by the aid of oars. *What in the world...* Adella stood dumbfounded as it drew closer. *Are they Valennian?*

The vessel was long and narrow, with many oars jutting out from the sides working in unison. Only one mast, which was cocked at an odd angle, rose from the open weather deck; it bore a single, large sail, but it was furled up under an unusually long yard. At the prow, the keel curved steeply up into the air, and, though it wasn't yet near enough to see clearly, seemed to be ornately carved, like a figurehead.

Adella held her breath as it drew closer. She'd never seen a ship like it before, neither Sornian nor Valennian. Despite her pain, she rose to her feet. Instinctively, she reached for the hilt of her father's saber, but it wasn't there. Her sword belt was missing, torn from her waist during her tumble. *Damn.*

The ship, propelled by its many oars, drove itself right up onto the rocks a little ways down the beach from her, and several people jumped out. Adella turned and, in a painful, limping run, hurried down the shore in the other direction, hoping they hadn't seen her.

She picked her way over the precarious rocks around Holcomb's prone form, then followed the shoreline around a curve only to find more water ahead, with more bodies littering the shallows. Carefully, she made her way around them, save for one large one that she had to step over, nearly falling upon it as her feet slipped on wet rocks. She caught herself by pushing off from the cold, rain-soaked corpse's broad shoulder. An arrow protruded from his chest. When the body lolled to the side, she gasped. Dead eyes gazed blankly at her from an expressionless face. *Blackburn!* Shoving herself away from him in disgust, she carried onward around the bend. Behind her, the voices grew louder; feet splashed quickly in the shallows. She didn't know who the strangers were, but her stomach clenched with fear.

Ahead, the morning sun shimmered on endless waves. Adella searched the horizon, but there was no more land to be seen. Her mouth went dry, heart dropping into her stomach. *It's an island... I'm on an island.* She doubled over, hands on her knees to catch her breath.

The whole area has collapsed into the Bay! Her beloved fields of the Campos were no more; only the dark, serpent-infested sea remained. Unable to stifle a weary cry, she fell to her knees, overwhelmed by her sudden helplessness and loss. Caught between sea and stone, everything she loved was gone.

When the ship's crew caught up to her, she didn't have it in her to resist. There was nothing left to fight for, nowhere to go. The men, dressed in strange clothes and speaking a foreign language, tied her arms behind her back and pulled her along over the rocks by her elbows.

They shoved her over the fallen bodies, some of the strangers stooping to take trinkets from lifeless necks and fingers. Adella watched them numbly, the broken world around her clouded by her tears. Protruding from the rubble, a golden tassel hung from a fine brass pommel, now dulled with mud. Her fingers tensed with a longing for the hilt. *My sword... My father's sword.* She stiffened, pushing back against their arms.

At her slight resistance, one of the strangers paused and, following her line of sight, stooped to pull the saber from the debris. Wiping it on his sleeve, he muttered something in a foreign tongue and slipped the bare steel beneath his belt.

When they came around the bend of the distance point, another ship broke into view. It mattered little how roughly or gently her captors hoisted her over the low sides of the galley—every place their fingers grasped hurt, though she was grateful to land on a pile of animal pelts. Once settled, she could see two more sailing behind it, one much larger than the rest, a proper ship like those she was familiar with.

Soon, the strange ship got underway and the crew set the large mainsail. The island slowly shrank into the distance, its unique shape and rocky precipice inclining steeply to the north. *Compass Point.* She stared blankly at the familiar landmark, now a stark silhouette above the nothingness of the new empty sea. The rain returned, sapping what little warmth she had left. She shivered uncontrollably. A firm hand grabbed her chin and, lifting it, poured a burning liquid down her throat that hit her belly like fire and made her head swim. She squeezed her eyes tightly shut against the dizziness, burying her face in the pile of soft fur.

14

A Dark Hold

Adella opened her eyes to complete darkness and softly groaned. A gentle, wooden creaking surrounded her, along with the lapping of water. A slight echo suggested she was in a large, enclosed space. Her brain pounded fiercely.

Slowly, her memories returned in patches, of the *haramund*, the strange ship, the people dragging her by the arms. Though she was clearly below deck, she was again lying on a pile of pelts, with fur tickling her cheek, and the stale dank air around her mingled with a warm, pungent fragrance of rare spices.

"Oh, good; you're awake," someone spoke unseen from the darkness. "I was worried they gave you too much."

Adella squinted, trying to see who it was. The voice sounded familiar, with a fine Valennian accent, but she couldn't quite place it in her memory. "What was it?" she asked groggily, rubbing her eyes.

"They call it *gilam*," he replied. "Poppy spirit."

Metal clanked as she tried to rise, but a heavy weight tethered her in place. Groaning, she flopped back down on the pelts. The cold iron edges of a shackle bit into her ankle as she shifted her legs. "Where am I?"

"You're at sea," he answered, a hint of humor in his voice. "Either aboard a ship by the name of *Ukishti*, or else the word has some other similarly important meaning that warrants frequent use." Though there was a strained quality to it, his soothing, eloquent tone brought to mind her travels to Pentz that summer.

"Lord Endlebridge?" she asked in disbelief as recognition struck her. She hadn't seen the man since they'd parted in Raymouth, after requesting the help of his cavalry to defend Elldon and Greywood Manor. "Is that you?" Trying to sit up, she swallowed down another groan of pain that flared with her movements. "It's me, Adella Grimless. Of Elldon."

"Good heavens," he uttered softly. "What happened? How did you come to be on this ship?"

"It's a long story," she replied. A knot tightened in her throat, straining her voice as she tried to push the images from her mind—the shore littered with bodies, Holcomb's blank, staring eyes. She swallowed it all down and took a deep breath. "But the Campos has collapsed into the sea. I was stranded on the rock; that's where they found me."

"I'm sorry," he said sympathetically. She could hear the pain in his response; he'd lost his hometown of Pentz similarly that summer. Endlebridge let out a feeble cough, then quickly sucked his breath through his teeth, and Adella's heart sank.

"You're injured?" she asked, though she already knew the answer.

"Only a little."

She didn't know him well enough to judge if it was a lie, but she suspected his condition was worse than he implied. Adella rubbed her temples. "How long was I asleep?"

"Quite a while," he said, his tone carrying a hint of worry. "A day, at least."

She lowered her voice. "They're reavers, aren't they?"

"I think so," he replied. "They attacked my ship on the way to the Capital. But it's hard to say for certain, since they're Madorran. They could be reavers, or it could be that they've allied with the Sornians against us in the war."

"I hope that isn't the case," Adella replied, frowning at the thought. "We have enough enemies." She'd never seen Madorrans before. Though they sometimes graced the designs of Valennian pottery and book illustrations, little was known about them. The seafaring people had recently arrived in Belgrand Bay, bringing a lot of expensive trade goods with them. Thus far, they'd kept mainly to themselves, staying close to the western mouth of the Bay and the small islands that dotted the area.

Soon, light poured in from the companionway as a figure descended, holding a glass-paneled lantern. Blinking in the sudden light, Adella glanced about to see barrels and crates stacked and secured with cargo nets all around. The lantern bearer approached, revealing a fretwork of large iron grates that boxed her and Endlebridge into separate prison cells on either side of the ship's hold.

The man, short and rotund with a broad cutlass on his hip, set down a small bundle wrapped in cloth at her feet, then held the lantern to her face, inspecting it closely. He wore a long, white beard, which struck her as very much unlike the current fashion in either Valenna or Sornia, which favored a neatly-groomed appearance. Unsatisfied with his appraisal, he pulled a folded parchment from his bejeweled waistcoat and whipped it open. Holding it up to her, he said something in a foreign tongue and paused, apparently awaiting a reply. The sheet bore a charcoal sketch of a woman with delicate features and long hair hanging freely. The figure wore riding breeches rather than a petticoat, wielding a small crossbow. Written upon the sketch was her name, along with the promise of a hefty reward.

Adella furrowed her brow. "Is that... supposed to be me?"

He repeated the words more forcefully, but she could only shake her head in confusion. Something red and lustrous caught her eye above his shirt collar, and she let out a small gasp. Hanging from a gold chain, set into a wreath of gold and diamonds, a large ruby sparkled in the lantern light. She'd know that jewel anywhere—it was her mother's, the payment that she'd given to Endlebridge in exchange for his cavalry troop.

Across the hold, Endlebridge cleared his throat and gave a short answer in a strange tongue. The man stuffed the drawing back into his pocket and left.

"You speak their language?" Adella asked in surprise.

"A little," he replied. "My mother was Madorran, but she left when I was small."

"So what was that about?" she asked pointedly. "The drawing."

"That was the captain," he explained. "You have a bounty on your head."

"A bounty?" she repeated, taken aback. She opened her mouth to speak again, then paused, biting her lip, as Blackburn's words came slowly back to her aching mind. *'I had orders to bring you back alive,'* he'd said. Then, prompted by that memory, she recalled the Sornian soldier, Jais, who'd tried to capture her during a skirmish that summer. He'd said something similar, about gold and how she wasn't worth the trouble. She'd nearly forgotten about that. Adella swallowed hard. Her mouth was so dry that her lips cracked. "Is that where they're taking us? To Sornia?"

"I don't know." Endlebridge's voice grew weary. "I assume they're holding me for ransom as well."

"He's wearing the ruby," Adella commented. "They took it from you?"

"Pulled it right off my neck," he replied, his voice fading. "It looked better on me." He gave a feeble laugh.

She smiled slightly at his humor. While she didn't know how badly he was hurt, it pained her to think he was using up what strength he had left to answer her questions, so she turned her attention to the bundle the Madorran captain had left for her. Untying the cloth wrapping, she found a wineskin filled with water and some ship's biscuits. She drank eagerly, but set the biscuits aside. Though her stomach was long since empty, it still felt too unsettled from the strange poppy drink for her to consider food.

Lying in the dark hold, Adella lost all sense of time, save for the distant ring of the ship's bell from above decks. Presuming they kept the same routine as a Valennian crew, she knew there would be two watches, each taking four-hour turns, plus an evening half-watch. Of course, she knew nothing of Madorran culture or their naval customs, but with nothing else by which to mark the time, it was as good a place as any to start.

She passed the next few watches keeping count, with her only comforts being water, ship biscuits, furs to sleep on, and a chamber pot for relief. But it didn't matter to her. In the hours between each ringing of the bell, her mind was filled with the horrors of the battlefield, and the faces of her countrymen as she'd last seen them—dead, alive, or riding off into the turmoil of the collapsing landscape. Image after image flashed through her thoughts, no matter how she tried to block them out, no matter how tightly she squeezed her eyes shut. Every face remembered brought her pain. The only distraction during the long spans between watches was when one of the crew would come and check on her and Endlebridge, bringing food and drink and emptying their pots into a bucket. Occasionally, she'd try to speak with Endlebridge, but she found he didn't know any more than what he'd already related, and their conversation was taxing for him, so she soon thought better of it. Besides, as her thoughts and fears grew stronger in the darkness, she lost interest in her surroundings. She stopped counting the bells; whether only a few days had passed, or weeks, she couldn't say, nor did she care. The biscuits left for her went untouched, and she hardly drank enough water to bother with the chamber pot. Her world shrank in around her until there was nothing left but the visions behind her eyes and the stabbing pain in her heart.

It had all been my own doing, her inner voice constantly reminded her. There was no escaping the truth of it; it was all her fault. The guilt of their deaths lay upon her shoulders. It wasn't fair that she had survived and they hadn't. *But perhaps my fate had merely been delayed.* Adella licked her parched lips, but it did little good, as her whole mouth had become dry. *Perhaps this will be my end.* A prisoner of war, slowly starving in an enemy ship—it seemed a fitting punishment.

As she lay half-asleep, rocked gently by the ship's motion and the monotonous lullaby of its ever-present creaking, a shape began to take form behind the blackness of her gently closed eyes. By now, the horrors of her imagination had faded into the background of her mind, a constant that dimmed as she became used to it, but this was something new, fire-bright and fresh. At first, it appeared to be just a small ember of white light, but as it slowly grew larger, its planes and angles became clearer, revealing the form of a bright prism suspended in the air. Soon, a hand materialized around it, and a face came into focus somewhat above, shadowed grotesquely in the prism's glow. As the vision grew, the foul stench of rot and death filled her nose and lungs, burning her airways with a sulphurous sting.

"No!" she tried to shout, but her voice was only a strained murmur. "Go away!"

The dream-figure let out a laugh, throwing his head back. Then, stepping closer, he reached out a hand to her, his fingernails lined with black. Heavy shadows darkened the hollows of his bloodshot eyes; the area around his storm-grey irises that once had been white was now a striking crimson. "I'll be seeing you soon," he replied, the fingers of his other hand reaching out, grasping for her.

Slowly, the fog of her mind drew back, revealing strange surroundings. She was in a private bedchamber, or rather, he was. Her form took on the hazy, dream-like quality that he had first appeared in, while his form, like the room they now stood in, took on the brilliance of reality. At his back, heavy curtains billowed in a strong gust of wind, though oddly, she didn't feel it on her skin. The view beyond the open balcony doors showed the wide, indigo swath of Belgrand Bay, as real to her now as ever she'd seen it in waking life. Below, ships clustered about the docks, crowding the busy harbor as more sailed in from every direction.

Around her, well-dressed servants bustled about, passing oddly close to her as they fetched items and packed them in large, wooden trunks. One came striding directly toward her as though he didn't see her at all, his arms laden with folded clothing, and she gasped as he passed right through her, taking no notice of her presence whatsoever.

"What is this?" Adella demanded, rounding on Matei with a scowl. "What's going on?"

"I warned you what would happen if you escaped," he grumbled. He stepped toward her, and his hand clasped painfully around her arm, drawing her closer. She leaned back, trying to get away from the putrid smell that grew stronger as his grinning mouth inched closer to her. "You belong to me." He clipped the words out between clenched teeth, yellow and black with rot. His icy breath, like a blast of winter air, sent a chill over her skin.

Adella awoke with a scream, sitting bolt upright in the darkness. It took her a moment to remember she was locked in the hold of the Madorran ship.

"Are you alright?" came Endlebridge's worried voice.

"Just a dream," she replied, breath heaving. "I think."

"You were talking in your sleep."

"I was?" she asked, rubbing her head. "What did I say?"

"You were..." He trailed off hesitantly. "Muttering."

She groaned, rubbing her eyes. Why she'd been dreaming of Matei lately, she had no idea. *The fall onto the rocks must've damaged my brain.* Nevertheless, the dreams sickened her and left her with a deep sense of unease. Pushing the images out of her mind, she turned her thoughts to Kol instead in search of comfort, but found little reprieve. *If he tries to return to Elldon now,* the thought struck her, *he will find only water and a new sea to cross, not a home to return to.* Her heart ached for him and the pain he would inevitably endure at the discovery.

15

The Fury

Matei slumped into the plush velvet armchair in the corner of his solar room. Across the space, gloved hands poured steaming buckets of hot water into the wooden bathtub he'd demanded the palace attendants carry up the many flights of stairs. Likewise, the water had to be lugged up from the garden well before being heated on the large stone hearth of his private chamber. It was quite an undertaking merely for his pleasure, requiring many hands and much effort.

One of the attendants pulled a small side table noisily across the stone floor toward the bath, setting a sea sponge and a block of soap on its surface. Matei tapped a finger to his chin, staring blankly at the colorful tapestries that covered the doors of his balcony, pulled shut in an attempt to keep out the chill autumn winds. Beside him, the glowing hearth radiated a comforting heat.

"Your Highness," one attendant said as he approached, his bare head bowed respectfully. "You have a message from Valenna." He lowered to one knee and, slipping a hand into his jacket pocket, pulled out a letter sealed with crimson wax.

Snatching it from his outstretched hand, Matei examined the crest pressed into the seal and let out a weary breath. It was yet another correspondence from the Valennian queen, who'd taken up the throne after her son's passing. Harrian had been king of the neighboring country for many years, but he'd failed to produce an heir, and his sudden death had left Valenna scrambling to stabilize. *That's no way to run a kingdom,* Matei thought smugly. When it came his turn to sit upon the throne of Sornia, he wouldn't make such a flagrant mistake. Without bothering to open the letter, Matei tossed it into the glowing coals. The attendant drew a sudden breath of surprise before realizing his error and clapping a hand over his mouth. Matei glared at the attendant, who hurried back to his duties.

It wasn't the first letter he'd received from the old woman; he'd disposed of all the others the same way. As far as he was concerned, the throne of Valenna was empty. *She's nothing but a consort. Sornia doesn't recognize the rule of queens.* Here, the King had his First Consort, who would produce the primary line of heirs, and if that lineage were to disappoint, the progeny of the Second Consort would follow. It went against tradition, but provided for any contingencies. Though his father's First Consort had plenty of daughters, she'd only borne one son; therefore, the Crown Prince Gio's untimely death had made Matei, the only son of the Second Consort, the next Crown Prince. *That had been easily done.* But if something were to happen to himself, the sons of the Third Consort would be next, if she were to have any. This way, the throne would never be left empty. It was undoubtedly an effective system, though it engendered much competition; the current First Consort and her kin had always treated him with suspicion, calling him a bastard and keeping him under lock and key. It also meant that, if his father were to have any more sons, Matei would have rivals for the throne. That thought had been nagging at him ever since Gio's death. Sighing, he rubbed his temples with his fingertips and tried to put it out of mind.

A feeling of being burdened always accompanied the Heartstone's presence on his person. The more he possessed it, the more it seemed to hum with a power and voice of its own. So far, no one else had noticed, or at least, no one had remarked on it, not even Lucas or Teressa. He slipped his hand into his waistcoat pocket. When he held the crystal against his skin, the constant waves lapped at the edges of his mind, threatening to drown out all other thoughts. Its vibrations grew until they reverberated inside his skull like the crashing surf, drowning out the platitudes of the groveling servants. Or perhaps it was the Bay he heard outside, just beyond the city. *Or maybe both... After all, they were connected, the stone and the sea.*

The longer he sat silent, the louder it grew until he could almost hear a voice in the murmur of water, lurking there, waiting for his thoughts to quiet. The strange sound grew stronger whenever he attuned himself to the crystal, and for a moment, he strained his ears, almost able to make out the words again now.

Listen...

Listen...

Listen!

The sudden urgency of the ephemeral command sent a jolt through him, and his gaze shifted to the large gilt mirror on the wall beside him. His own eyes, dove-grey encircled in red, stared dully back at him.

Return the Heart, the voice insisted.

"No," he muttered under his breath. "Leave me alone."

As he stared at the mirror, his reflection came to life, moving of its own accord, and pointed an accusing finger at him. **Return the Heart, you stupid child!** His image in the glass mouthed the words that echoed in his brain. Matei jumped to his feet.

"Shut up!" he screamed, driving his fist into the mirror and shattering his reflection. Glass shards stabbed his knuckles and scattered loudly on the floor. He cradled his hand against his body, blood dripping down his wrist. Finally, all was silent.

Across the room, the servants stared open-mouthed.

"Your Highness—" they began, stepping timidly toward him as fear drew lines around their weary eyes.

"Get out," Matei ordered. Still, they hesitated. "Get out!" he repeated, this time in a feral snarl that filled the room.

They scurried out, closing the door behind them. He exhaled loudly, looking over the damage he'd done, first to the broken mirror that littered the floor, then to his blood-soaked hand. Gritting his teeth, he pulled the largest pieces of glass from his skin one by one. Removing the Heartstone from his pocket with his uninjured hand, he set it on the nearby table. Lifting the silver circlet from his head, he carefully put it beside the stone, then disrobed, strewing his clothes across a chair.

Usually, the royal attendants would do the work of bathing him, but he'd just sent them all away. Matei threw the sponge into the tub, and, gripping the edge, he lowered himself slowly in. Blood wept from his knuckles, staining the hot water in scarlet curls before dissipating. It had been many days since he'd last set the crystal aside like this; it was always in his hand, in his pocket, or beneath the pillow as he slept. Leaning back, sighed, suddenly feeling lighter, as though a long-suffered burden had been lifted from his shoulders. The air around him was notably calm, devoid of the fraught humming that had plagued him mere moments ago. Even his breath came more effortlessly without the stone on him, which seemed odd; as it was small enough to fit comfortably in one hand, it didn't weigh enough to justify the heavy feeling. Reaching for a bowl that had been left on the table for him, he grabbed a handful of fresh cranberries and popped the bitter fruit in his mouth. Taking up a small chalice, with a silver stem and a bowl made from the polished shell of a large sea snail, he took a mouthful of honeyed cordial and set the chalice down empty.

Closing his eyes, Matei sank further into the bathwater, allowing the warmth to ease his tension, and let his mind relax. He took a breath and slipped completely beneath the surface, lying there for a moment, blowing bubbles from his nostrils as water filled his ears. Then, coming up for air, he wiped his eyes and leaned his head back against the tub. His thoughts, like they often did lately, turned toward Adella, and his face flushed with heat. The way she spoke to him—earlier that spring as his prisoner, and since then, whenever he slipped into her dreams—was entirely disrespectful of his status as prince, even more so now that he was Crown Prince and heir of Sornia. And yet, she bore an aching resemblance to his beloved Livia, whose untimely death had left a hole in his life as well as his heart. That the troublesome Valennian captive should behave so outrageously unlike his dear wife, while at the same time reminding him so starkly of her, pierced him with fresh grief and longing even as it turned his stomach. For a while, he'd tried to ignore it, pushing the feelings away whenever he looked at her, but that only seemed to make them stronger. It was a heady and confusing mixture of pain, anger, and, as he understood it, misplaced desire for a face that looked like Livia's. It was nothing, however, compared to the deeper, purer longing to reunite the shattered empire under his own rule. To restore the glory of Andolin and be remembered by all for millennia, not as a bastard but as the rightful ruler, had always been his greatest dream. Now he was so close, he only had to reach out and grasp it, but he would need *her* for that. And, at any rate, she owed him both a lot of gold and her life.

Instinctively, he closed his eyes and stretched out a hand, but he was met with nothing but dull silence. Prodding his consciousness through the ether to connect with another person's sleeping mind had grown all too easy for him, no matter the distance. Still, it'd been so long since he'd last set the Heartstone down, he'd almost forgotten his abilities only came with its possession. Without the stone in hand, or otherwise in close contact with his body, he was as powerless as anyone else. The reminder left a bitter taste in his mouth.

He snatched the crystal from the table. At once, the great, familiar burden settled over his heart like a lead shroud, curdling his grief and longing into a more acrid mix of contempt and malice. It took him a moment of steady breathing to brace himself against the weight, but soon he was effortlessly sending his will soaring over the water, jumping from mind to mind, from fish to serpent to bird. Finally, he alighted upon a ship and began to sort through the minds aboard, seeking one in particular. His earlier connection with Adella had been broken, and he wished to resume it. He picked out her unique energy, a mix of thought and memory as distinct as a signature, from deep within the darkness of the hold, but he couldn't take the connection deeper. *She must be awake.* Not ready to give up, he continued to probe the edges of her mind, searching for a hint of any plans or determinations. The tactic had proven successful before; it was her thoughts that had warned him of her decision to retreat with Elldon's remaining survivors over the bridge to Raymouth. Burning the bridge had solved that problem, and the rest had been easy. *Her thoughts had betrayed her.* Likewise, his expansive view of the landscape through the eyes of a passing hawk allowed him to see the Valennians' every move, played out like pieces on a game board. He laughed to himself. The abilities the *Corelimun* bestowed on him had changed the course of his life, of his entire world.

Returning to his focus, Matei's brow furrowed at the strain as he tried harder to connect, uttering her name into the silence of the room. "Adella..." There was something about a person's name that helped him concentrate on their energy.

"I wish you'd forget about my sister," a voice cut through the silence, drawing him from his meditation.

Opening one eye, Matei groaned to see Lucas standing by with arms folded. "What are you doing here?" he snapped. "I'm in the bath."

"I can see that," Lucas replied. "For some reason, the servants are afraid to come in." He raised a brow at the cuts on Matei's hand and eyed the red-tinged water. "They asked me to tell you that preparations are nearly done, so be ready to sail by this evening's ebb tide."

"Bring me my dressing gown," Matei grumbled. "No, over there," he said, pointing as Lucas looked stupidly around. "On the bed." He stepped out of the bathtub, water running down his legs and soaking the carpet.

"You know, there are other Valennian women," Lucas reminded him, not for the first time, as he handed him the robe.

"Quit," Matei chided, snatching it from. "I have my reasons." Pulling it on, he winced as the fabric brushed over his sliced knuckles.

Lucas's eyes shifted to the broken mirror across the room. "What happened?"

"Nothing." Matei tied the sash around his waist. "Go get your things ready." Lucas turned to leave, and Matei caught him by the arm. "This is it," he said, grinning. "It's finally happening."

Giving him an appreciative nod, Lucas left.

* * *

Grey clouds blanketed the city of Hedda, letting down a haze of fine rain that dampened Matei's face as he walked. The once-beautiful gardens of the little townhouses now looked bare and sere, with dark skeletal branches clinging to wilted brown leaves in the blasting autumn winds.

"Over there," he ordered, pointing to the larger caravel moored at one of the long, wooden docks nestled in the harbor, flying the green-and-orange royal ensign at its stern. Two green-clad soldiers, lugging his heavy cedar trunk between them, nodded and carried it onward. *The Fury* would serve as their flagship. As the bearer of the *Corelimun* and the Crown Prince, his father had seen fit to place him at the vanguard, on the same ship as the naval commander.

"Have you seen my father?" Matei asked as Lucas approached.

"The King is already aboard the *Imperial*," Lucas replied. "You're the last to arrive."

"They wouldn't leave without me." Matei pulled his cloak hood up and continued down the dock.

"Are you sure about this?" Lucas asked, concern in his voice as he followed along. "You don't look well, and you haven't seemed yourself lately. I'm sure the soldiers can handle it." He gave Matei a searching look.

Matei met his strained gaze with determined assurance. "There's too much depending on this. I don't want to leave it in the hands of the navy; we don't pay them that much." His attention shifted to the churning swells of Belgrand Bay in the distance, and he felt a faint tug at his heart, drawing him seaward. Moving his hand protectively over his waistcoat pocket, he felt for the reassuring weight of the crystal. "I need to be there should something go wrong."

They crossed the gang-board, dark waves sloshing momentarily beneath them, and stepped onto the ship. All about the decks, sailors in green and white prepared to get underway while the marine soldiers, distinguishable by their cutlasses and the trim of their jackets, hauled royal luggage aft to the private cabins. It was Matei's first time at sea since the sinking of *The Accord*, when he, Lucas, and Teressa had escaped in the ship's small boat. Luckily, they'd been picked up by Madorran smugglers, though he'd told his friends they were fishermen. In his travels over the years, he'd learned a little of the Madorran language and had been able to communicate enough not only to ask to be taken to Hedda but also to form a tentative alliance with their leader. He promised to instruct the Royal Navy to look the other way when their ships came into port, and in turn, they'd keep him apprised of the goings-on in the Bay. They could also be called upon for assistance when needed, provided he paid them for the trouble.

The sails were set and *The Fury* was well underway, with the entire fleet following in their wake. The man at the helm, with broad shoulders adorned in gold trim beneath the shadow of a large, feathered hat, nodded as Matei walked by. Commodore Gallo was not only the supreme authority on the ship but held command over every vessel in the Royal Navy fleet. After *The Accord*, it gave Matei a good amount of relief to be aboard his flagship, and being surrounded by so many Royal Marines provided an added sense of security. With his father on the support vessel, sailing just off the larboard quarter behind *The Fury* in case of any trouble, Matei couldn't help but feel invincible, ready and eager for what lay ahead.

Soon, Lucas and Teressa joined him at the taffrail. Perched above the water, they watched the sunlight glisten on the waves until a dark shadow rose in the distance. At first, Matei thought it was an island due to its massive size, revealed perhaps from the disturbed sea floor after so many recent ground tremors. However, the more he stared at the shape, the more it seemed to move of its own power, rather than from the change in perspective due to their ship's speed. He held his breath as a portion of the mass arched up from the waves, bending briefly over the sea before straightening like a stalk. Upon its highest end, a long snout jutted out and parted vast jaws, large enough to swallow their ship whole.

Icy terror gripped Matei, and he let out a feeble gasp, unable to utter a sound. Elbowing Lucas, he pointed out the enormous sea beast, but by the time he looked, it had disappeared again beneath the waves.

He couldn't alert the crew; such a sighting would inevitably shake their courage and affect his plans. While *The Fury*, like each ship in their fleet, was well equipped with a large ballista and plenty of stones, bolts, and other projectiles, the thing he'd spotted in the water was something wholly unaccounted for. He'd never seen anything so large. He wasn't even sure what their weapons would do to it.

Closing his eyes, Matei stretched out one hand toward the sea while the other found the crystal in his pocket. Searching the briny depths, his mind flitted from creature to creature, feeling their hunger, their fear, mingled with the sensation of swimming or floating until he found the immense being that he'd seen moments ago. It was moving at a dizzying speed. In his mind's sight, he watched the massive beast undulating through the swells, its dark, sinewy form weaving in and out of the shadows that dappled the surface. Several times, Matei tried to probe its mind, to connect with it, but no matter how diligently he focused, he found its consciousness impenetrable. As he watched the beast, one great eye, placed far on the side of an elongated head, snapped toward him so suddenly that it sent a jolt through his limbs. The eye, completely black except for a thin ring of pale blue around the large pupil, bore down upon him until it engulfed his thoughts. The crash of waves thundered through his head and, though the creature did not speak, nor utter any sound, Matei got the distinct impression that it was watching him in return, searching his mind, questioning him.

Matei gasped, stumbling backward, and the vision was lost.

"Are you alright?" Lucas asked, steadying him by the elbow. "What happened?"

Catching his breath, Matei slipped a hand back into his pocket and was relieved to find the crystal still safely inside. He shook his head. "There's something out there."

* * *

That evening, Matei folded an arm behind his head and lay back on an overstuffed mattress. As a royal warship, *The Fury*'s stateroom was equipped with all the furnishings required for comfort, including curtained berths for the royal family and their guests, leaving the commodore to berth with his officers.

"How does the story end?" came Teressa's soft voice from across the cabin. "Of Leveret and the Heartstone."

"It doesn't," Matei replied. "It just repeats itself. Again and again. Leveret's story is only the most recent version."

"What do you mean?" she asked.

Matei rolled to his side, staring across the dim room in her direction. "This story has happened many times before, in many different ways." His gaze shifted to the green pennant hanging from the bulkhead, with a hare and dove painted in gold around the Sornian royal crest. "Some say that those whose lives in this world end tragically are later reborn so they have another chance at a different fate." Even to his own ears, the words sounded unconvincing.

Shadows danced on Lucas's face as he set a lantern on the table in the center of the cabin and sat, unbuckling his shoes. "Do you believe that?"

Shifting on the mattress again, Matei turned away. "I want to." While his wife's body had been burned after she'd succumbed to the plague long ago, he'd once wondered if the powers of the *Corelimun* could possibly extend so far as to return her to him somehow, to pull her very soul back down from the heavens. Yet now that he held the stone in his hands, the stars seemed even farther. And when he closed his eyes to picture her, it was only Adella's face he saw. It was she who preoccupied his thoughts. Perhaps, she was the closest thing he'd ever find to the woman he'd lost.

Lucas made his way to the other berth, and Matei pulled his curtain closed. With the crystal in his hand, he shut his eyes and sent his thoughts out over the sea, soaring over and under the dark, heaving waves until they alighted on Adella's now-familiar presence, the griefs and hurts of her heart fresher and sharper than his own, but not so deep and cankerous. It was a relief, in a way, to leave himself behind and occupy another mind, like donning fresh clothing after long travel.

Probing her thoughts, he found her in the dreamlike state just before sleep. He saw the image of a man—tall, rough-looking, with black, overgrown hair and a stubbled jawline—and felt a cascade of memories, warm and dear to her. They played through her mind in vivid detail, over and over and with such devotion that the separation between Matei's thoughts and hers began to blur, and her emotions became his. Yet the landscape of her mind had changed; the pain and grief that had always lingered there had grown much deeper, more overwhelming than he expected, threatening to pull him under like a drowning tide. He fought the urge to give in and let himself be swept away. He just had to hold out a little longer; soon, sleep would set in and her mind would become more tractable. Then, he could take the other man's place in her dreams and communicate with her.

Instead, the images dimmed, and he felt his connection begin to slip away. "Adella..." he muttered, trying to draw closer to her again, but her sleep had been disturbed; he'd been cut off.

The curtain of Matei's berth was jerked back, flooding his eyes with bright lantern light. He squinted to find Lucas's face hovering above him. "Did you just say 'Adella?'"

"Ugh," Matei groaned, shielding his eyes. "Get that out of here."

"You need to forget about her," Lucas pleaded, placing the lantern on the floor. "It's not going to happen. She'll never—" He rubbed his face and sat on the foot of the mattress. "She'll never forgive us."

"It's not her forgiveness I want," Matei replied.

"Then what is it?" Lucas looked him steadily in the eye as he awaited an answer.

Matei's gaze shifted down to his hand, where the soft glow of the crystal still lingered, as he mulled over his answer.

"Look," Lucas reasoned gently, "it's all right to admit it. You're not the first man to have feelings for my sister—"

"It's not that," Matei snapped. "She belongs to me! I don't care what it takes; I want what's mine. Now, go." Shoving Lucas off the edge of his bed with his foot, he yanked the curtain shut in Lucas's face.

A disappointed sigh came from the other side of the heavy fabric.

"I said go," Matei muttered, pulling up the blankets and rolling onto his side. Lucas's footsteps retreated across the cabin, and the room darkened as he blew out the light. Tucking the crystal beneath his pillow, Matei closed his eyes and tried to find Adella again. It was no use. The murkiness of her thoughts told him she was fully awake and out of reach.

16

At Sea

Striding across the quarterdeck, Kol's stomach knotted, the meager supper he'd finished in the great cabin churning in his gut. Knowing Adella faced insurmountable odds while he sat helpless and stranded on a vessel headed in the wrong direction made the situation even less bearable than if he'd been able to take any sort of action. Instead, he felt lost and adrift with the tide. Though he was a different man now than he'd been when he'd first met her—as the owner of the Royal Westward Trading Company, he was one of the wealthiest men in the Bay and now had his own ship—he'd trade it all in an instant, become that half-starved traitor again, if it could somehow buy her safety. Without her, nothing had meaning, his accomplishments felt as hollow as his heart.

The crew came out on deck for the night watch while Kol lingered by the rail, looking out to sea. The sun had nearly set below the horizon, a mere sliver of molten gold shedding the last of its warm light onto the waves. He'd yet to see any of the strange sea creatures that had plagued his previous voyages. Given his other problems, they were almost an afterthought now, but he still scanned the dark water, half-expecting to see a long, slinking shadow break the surface.

A throat cleared behind him. Glancing around, at first Kol couldn't find the source until a figure emerged from the dusky shadows cast by the forecastle ladder.

"I've been trying to catch you alone," a gruff voice began. The figure stepped closer, and the light of the setting sun hit the man's deeply weathered face. From beneath a sailor's cap, iron-grey curls framed dark eyes.

Kol blinked in surprise to see Seaborn standing before him. "What are you doing here?" he asked sharply. "Why didn't you tell me sooner that you were on board?"

"Shh, keep it down," Seaborn hissed. Taking him by the arm, he turned their backs to the crew and leaned in. "There are a lot of soldiers on this ship," he explained in a whisper. "I didn't want to use my real name. Given what happened between me and that Valennian sea captain years ago, I think it'd be best if they don't know who I am."

An uneasiness settled over Kol at the reminder of his father's past. Though Seaborn hadn't gone into much detail, he'd made it clear that Declan's father was responsible for the death of Kol's mother and his being lost at sea when he was young. He racked his brain to remember what Seaborn had said. *Something about a mutiny...* Kol didn't like Declan, but he didn't hold the man accountable for his father's horrendous actions. However, he wasn't sure what would happen if Seaborn found out the son of his mortal enemy was on board. Somehow, he was going to have to keep the two men apart for the duration of their voyage. "You're the one who wanted to speak with me," Kol replied, suddenly remembering the first mate's comment from earlier. "Going by the name of—"

"Skilly," Seaborn supplied with a nod. "That's right."

"Come on," Kol whispered, ushering him toward the stern. "Let's get you to the cabin."

He was relieved to cross the deck to the great cabin without attracting any attention from the Royal Guards that milled about. "Wait here a moment," he said to Seaborn, pausing before the door. "I'm going to make sure it's clear."

Inside, he found only Kerchaw, as the notary had stepped out. "Listen," Kol began, voice low, "my father is here, on *The Tigress*." He couldn't lie to his agent about the surname, since he'd already been using it for himself when signing waybills and such. Though he knew it was hasty, he'd been so happy to finally have a family name that he hadn't been able to resist using it. "Being Sornian," Kol explained, "it'd be best if we kept his identity between us, considering our two countries are at war. He's been going by the name of Skilly."

"I see," Kerchaw replied, nodding. "Yes, these are cautious times."

"And," Kol added, "I think it would be best if we don't mention the captain's name in his presence."

Kerchaw raised a brow, then slowly nodded again. Returning to the door, Kol brought his father into the cabin. "Skilly," Kol began pointedly, "this is my agent with the Royal Westward, Barnaby Kerchaw. He oversees business operations on my behalf."

"Very good," Seaborn replied. "So, this is the ship you boys bought, eh?" he said admiringly, looking around at the fine furnishings. "There's a bit of familiarity about it, though I can't quite put my finger on it. What did you say the name was?"

"*The Tigress*," Kol replied, unease stirring his gut again.

"Hm," Seaborn muttered. "Doesn't ring a bell. Nice ship, though."

Surreptitiously, Kol let out his breath. "Thanks. Let's just keep you in the cabin until we make port."

* * *

The following morning, Kol awoke to rain pattering against the gallery windows. Soon, breakfast was brought in by one of the crew. He and his father remained in the cabin as the sky continued to darken and the day wore on. By evening, Kol felt that perhaps they would make it to the Capital without incident; with Declan moving to the officer's quarters, leaving the great cabin for their private use, and the weather turning foul, he could surely keep his father and the captain from crossing paths for the next few days. At least, he hoped so.

To keep his mind off his anxieties, he'd turned to the book Adella had lent him, but as absorbed as he was in his worries, the meaning of the words eluded him. Soon, he tucked the book away and turned to sharpening his boot knife for distraction instead. Each swipe of the whetstone grated loudly in the quiet cabin, the others watching on for lack of anything better to do. When he had worked so long that he had to admit to himself the blade was well past sharp, Kol put it away and turned to drumming on the table with his fingers.

"Why don't you do something to keep your hands occupied?" Kerchaw suggested. "Practice your penmanship, perhaps? Or you could see if Captain—" He swallowed his words as Kol darted him a quick look.

"My handwriting is fine," Kol replied sullenly.

"Hm," Kerchaw muttered, then turned to rifle through his bag on the floor. "Here," he said, setting some things on the table in front of Kol. "Why don't you make something? I like to carve shells on dull voyages."

Kol looked the items over; one was a small, pointed file, the other a thick seashell. "Carve them into what?"

Kerchaw shrugged. "I make trinkets for Annie and Liza. Keeps my mind off my worries."

Without much idea of what he was doing, Kol gave in and began working the file against the shell's edge. The action was similar to that of sharpening his knife, which he found oddly soothing.

After what seemed like hours, a commotion arose outside. Pocketing his things, Kol got up to see what it was about. Just as he reached for the door, it swung open, and Captain Declan burst into the cabin.

"Arm yourself," he said, glancing at the scabbard Kol had left propped against the berth, "and come with me."

Buckling on his sword belt, Kol followed the captain out onto the weather deck, where a harsh wind blew the rain sideways into his face, stinging his eyes.

"There were shoals here, once," Declan commented, his strides slowing as he came to the rail. "Yet now, our sounding lines aren't even reaching the bottom. It's as though the seafloor has completely given way."

Looking out over the billowing, indigo waves, an odd shape caught Kol's eye. Something long and serpentine rose in a dark coil, cresting above the swell before disappearing beneath the surface. The same happened in another spot, nearer to them, then again further out. Then, two of the creatures rose simultaneously.

"A swarm," Kol uttered, a chill creeping over him.

"I've never seen so many," Declan remarked grimly, tension hollowing his eyes and making shadows beneath his brow. "I know you're good with a blade," he said, turning toward him. "We need you on deck should things take a turn for the worse."

Kol nodded. "When traveling to Smuggler's Port," he began, putting a finger in the air as he remembered, "we'd sailed through a nest of them, much like this. The captain ordered the use of buckets rather than the head and pissdales to keep our scent from fouling the water and attracting them. We should do likewise."

"And make *The Tigress* into a cesspool?" Declan retorted, grimacing. "We've already got a fever brewing below decks, with two on their deathbeds. No," he said forcefully, brushing the idea away with a hand, "I won't hear of it."

"We'll have worse problems than fever if you don't give the order," Kol replied, biting back his anger. "I've seen what these things can do."

Declan's eyes narrowed. "You may be the ship's owner now, but I am still the captain," he said, and though he lowered his voice, the iciness of his tone grew all the more threatening. "And it is my decision. Not yours." He turned to the first mate, who had come up beside him. "Ready the ballista, and stand by for orders," Declan shouted to the first mate, who stood nearby. "Load the bolts, not the balls. We'll be needing those later." At the command, First Mate Jon nodded and sprang into action, calling out orders to the crew.

Kol frowned. "Is there something you're not telling me about?" he asked dryly. He wouldn't put it past the man to keep secrets; he had done so on their first voyage together.

Declan shot him a pointed glance. "I could ask you the same thing. Don't think I haven't noticed," he said, eyes narrowing, "that you seem to care for Adella more than is proper for your station. I warned you she's spoken for."

Fists clenching, Kol drew a sharp breath in through his teeth. He knew he'd have to tell Declan the truth sooner or later, and he badly wanted to do it at that moment, just to see the pain on the man's smug face, but he bit his tongue. Now wasn't the time to make an enemy of his captain. "Someone needs to," he replied coolly instead, unable to keep completely silent.

Declan held his gaze, eyes so full of smoldering contempt that Kol could read his struggle to keep composure in his darkening glare. Instinctively, Kol reached for his cutlass's hilt, but the movement was interrupted by a shout for the captain's attention from across the ship. With a twitch of his jaw, Declan turned on his heel and retreated aft, leaving Kol alone at the rail.

Watching the serpents churning the dark waves beneath the murky, leaden sky, Kol let out a long breath. The captain was right; there was much Kol was keeping from him. *The letter, for one.* He'd held back on delivering it, unsure how Declan would take the news of his relationship with Adella, but given his reaction to Kol's one flippant comment, it was clear now it wouldn't go well, and the longer he waited, the worse it was sure to be. But, that was tomorrow's problem; he had more immediate concerns. A knot formed in the pit of his stomach, wondering what they were sailing into.

He stayed on the main deck the remainder of the day and well into the evening, his gaze fixed anxiously on the water as he paced from starboard to larboard and back to keep the blood moving in his toes while the air turned colder. Though he expected an onslaught at any moment, eventually the sightings of the creatures grew fewer, tapering off until he felt the danger had, for the most part, passed.

Despite the chilly weather, he wasn't ready to return to the cabin yet. Leaning against the rail, he took the file and shell out again, letting the soothing work ease his mind.

* * *

In the darkness of the galley's hold, Adella drifted off into an uneasy half-sleep. The sight of Matei's face, ashen and corpse-like with deep hollows beneath his eyes, lurked in the darkness behind her eyelids. Tossing and turning fitfully on the pelts, sweat beaded her brow. *Go away...* she pleaded, but as she fell deeper into sleep, the swirling vision grew clearer.

"Ah, there you are."

At the sound of the voice, Adella turned. A figure materialized from the dream-fog, standing beside her. "Matei?" she asked, narrowing her eyes at the sight of his face. The deathlike pall that hung over his visage cleared, and she saw him as she remembered him from that spring, healthy and whole. The air around him shimmered, as though an illusion had been cast over reality, and she noticed a large, clear crystal resting on his palm, glowing softly.

They stood on the deck of a ship. It was a caravel, unlike the one she currently slumbered on; its sails were rigged in the same manner as *The Accord's* had been. The indigo sea swept all around them with no sight of land, but scattered among the waves were more ships of the same make, though much smaller, sailing together in formation. The crew that worked on the deck, passing close beside her but paying her no heed, all wore emerald coats. The wind whipped vigorously at their clothes, though she couldn't feel it herself. Everything around her seemed so natural, so solid, that she wondered if she was dreaming, or if she'd been transported somewhere else. She turned back to Matei. "Is this real, or merely a dream?"

"Can't it be both?" he replied with a smirk.

"Why is this happening?" She furrowed her brow. "What do you want with me?"

"Listen, I don't want us to be enemies..." The threat in his oily tone betrayed his words, like a dagger behind the back. "But our fates are tied now."

She shook her head. "I don't believe in fate."

"That's too bad." He reached out and grabbed her face, his bony fingers digging painfully into her jaw. The world around her sprang suddenly to life as the cold wind swept her skin and the briny sea air filled her lungs. "Because I have plans for you. You'll either join me willingly..." His voice was an ominous whisper as he leaned in, the stench of his rancid breath filling her nostrils. As he did so, the flesh of his face sank in, returning to the skeletal husk of tightly drawn, death-grey skin. "Or I'll make you wish you were dead." He pressed his icy, withered lips against hers, and the taste of rot filled her mouth.

Adella jerked awake, her stomach heaving. Throwing her hand out into the darkness, she felt around for her chamber pot and yanked it toward her, vomiting into it until there was nothing left to bring up but foamy bile. "Dammit!" she cried, pounding a fist into the furs.

"What's the matter?" Endlebridge whispered.

Adella winced with guilt. She hadn't meant to wake him. "I keep dreaming of the prince," she replied groggily, thoughts still muddled from the terror.

"And that makes you ill?" he asked quizzically. "Most women I know like to dream of princes."

"Not this one." She wiped her mouth. "He's a nightmare."

"Which prince?" he asked. "Gio of Sornia?"

"His half-brother, Matei Azbarian," she replied, a shiver crawling over her as she said his name aloud. "He held me captive in the spring, before my friends came to my aid. I don't know why I keep dreaming of him..." She trailed off, considering it. Perhaps there was more to it than the delusions of a damaged brain. "I feel there's something unnatural going on," she finally admitted.

"It was only a dream," Endlebridge said gently. "He can't hurt you now."

"Right," Adella muttered, recalling the vivid images as she wiped the sweat from her brow. "Just dreams." Slowly, she lay back down. *Perhaps he's right.* His words brought her comfort as she closed her eyes, forcing the images away.

"You'll forget all about them," he said softly, the strength of his voice waning, "when we get out of here—" He coughed feebly. "Somehow."

His words struck her. Here she was, wallowing in her own misery, when Endlebridge, who'd gone through nearly exactly the same pain and anguish as herself, and despite his injuries, whatever they may be, still had the courage to hope. *How dare I—* Tears filled her eyes, her throat tightening at the thought. *How dare I give up and leave him to his fate?* If it was true they were being brought to the Sornians, there was no knowing what would become of them after that, but judging by her past experiences with their kind, she knew it wouldn't be good. Endlebridge might not survive it, being already wounded. For better or worse, they were in this together, and they'd have to get out of it together. He likely wouldn't be able to do it alone. Silently, she resolved to find a way, if only for his sake.

At the sound of footsteps coming from the companionway, Adella sat up. By now, her eyes had adjusted somewhat to the dim light of the hold, and she squinted at the brightness of an approaching lantern. Soon, the crewman stopped at her cell door and unlocked it with a loud creak.

"Can you understand my language?" she asked as he emptied her chamber pot into a bucket. He didn't so much as glance in her direction. "Do you speak Modern Andolinian?" she tried again. He merely locked her in again and turned his attention to Endlebridge's cell on the other side of the hold.

"Ask him where they're taking us," she urged, grabbing the cold iron bars as she sat up.

While the man emptied his chamber pot, Endlebridge uttered a few words to him in Madorran. The crewman grunted a short answer, then shut him back in and left.

"What did he say?" she asked eagerly.

"He says we're heading north," Endlebridge replied. "They're taking us to..." He paused in thought. "Someone."

Adella's brows drew together. "Who?"

"I have no idea," Endlebridge replied. "I thought he said something about..." His voice trailed off to a faint whisper. "Never mind. My Madorran must be worse than I thought." He lapsed back into silence.

Adella closed her eyes. And yet, all that awaited her in the absence of her nightmares was the heart-rending pain of guilt and loss. In place of Matei's face, she saw Greywood Manor, stark and bare with its trees stripped away, and the rest of Elldon, abandoned. Gone was her beloved horse, Shy, James and his mother, Rosalind and the others. Between her more recent grief and the older, persistent ache of her parents' absence, everyone and everything that she'd ever known and loved had been lost. She missed them dearly; their voices all echoed in the hollows of her heart. Worst of all was the sight of James' headless body, strapped to his horse's saddle, which played over and over in her mind like an animal gnawing at a wound any time she let her thoughts roam. Then, of course, the recent battle, each moment of which had been burned into her memory, down to the blank stare in Holcomb's dead eyes. All of her choices that led up to that event, every mistake that she'd made—surely every decision she'd made had been a mistake, to bring her here—hammered in her brain. She hated herself for them. In the dark solitude of her prison, guilt and horror ate away at her. And in the quiet, small moments when she managed to sweep the agonizing memories aside, all that was left behind her closed eyes was the endless sea, cold and ever-present, with its rippling swells and moon-dappled waves billowing softly in the night, beckoning to her.

Retreating into slumber once more, her eyes flitted back and forth beneath closed lids while the crash of waves filled her ears, along with the muffled burble of movement deep below the surface. In her mind's eye, she sank into the depths as shadows darted past her in the inky water, long and strange, doubling back to weave around her limbs. *Pelkimund, haramund,* shark, and eel all swam fleetingly by. Then, a single vast, undulating form emerged in the murky distance, weaving forward to wrap its enormous, snakelike body through the blue space around her. Its head, island-large, led coils so massive the creature seemed vast enough to wind itself around entire cities.

All is set in motion, resounded in her head as the voice boomed through the water, carried to her from every direction. ***The Guardian has awakened.***

17

Unfinished Business

Kol stood on the weather deck, rain spattering in his eyes while he kept a watch on the horizon, his hands still busy with the file and shell. After several hours, his little carving was beginning to take shape. There had been no sight of the sea serpents yet that morning, and he'd started to wonder if perhaps he'd been wrong to argue with Declan. After all, he had many years of experience, whereas Kol was new to sailing. He wouldn't even make for a good deckhand. *Why would I think I knew better than the captain?*

Wandering toward the rail, he bit his thumbnail, absently watching the dark, churning waves that stretched to the horizon. Again, his thoughts turned to Adella and the fate of Elldon, wondering if they'd faced the Sornian army in battle yet or if it awaited them still. Deep in the corners of his mind, an unspoken fear rose to the surface. *Is she even still alive?* If the Sornians had come, it was possible she'd already fallen at the hands of the enemy, or worse; she could've been captured. *Stop it!* He shook his head to clear the thoughts away. His worrying wasn't going to help her; he'd just have to have faith in her capabilities despite her predisposition for throwing herself headfirst into danger. He sighed. *Easier said than done.*

Kol pocketed his things and was headed for his cabin when a loud shuffling, accompanied by grunts of exertion, came from the forecastle companionway. He turned to see a group of sailors dragging something heavy across the deck, wrapped in a hammock.

"Stay back," one sailor ordered as they hauled the heavy bundle past him. "Or you'll catch it next."

"What is it?" Kol asked, brows knitting.

"Ship fever," the sailor replied as they lowered the canvas-wrapped body by the rail. "Or camp fever, or war fever... Whatever you want to call it. It came aboard with those from Raymouth."

Kol frowned at the mention of camp fever. "How many?"

"Four, so far," the sailor replied.

Kol let out a breath. "If only four are sick, that's not so bad."

"Not four sick," the sailor corrected him. "Four dead. There are well over twenty stricken with it."

Kol's stomach dropped at the news. He opened his mouth to ask more questions, but the sailors strode off quickly, disappearing below decks.

Returning to the great cabin, Kol found his father and Kerchaw seated at the table, helping themselves to fragrant tea from a blue and white set of porcelain. "It's ten already?" he asked, taking a seat.

"What goes on out there?" Seaborn asked, mouth full of biscuit.

"There's a fever," Kol replied, reaching for the teapot, "spreading through the forecastle. It'd be best to stay in the cabin." While he wasn't pleased to be on a ship with sickness aboard, it at least gave him a reason to keep his father hidden from Declan. He took a sip of the steaming liquid, pressing his lips together thoughtfully. "Kerchaw," he began suddenly. "The captain mentioned needing the ballista balls later. Do you know what he might've meant?"

Kerchaw quirked his mouth. "Perhaps they mean to go privateering."

"But his commission is expired," Kol replied. "The captain admitted as much."

Kerchaw shrugged. "Though they sail under commission from the Crown, they are reavers still; don't forget that. They're a dangerous lot that don't rely on her leave to do what they do. The Queen needs them, and they know it. Which means they can get away with much."

"Great," Kol muttered. And here he was, stuck in the cabin without a say over what happened aboard his ship. Now that he had the greatest stake in its preservation, it seemed he ought to have more control over the situation. Declan's arrogance could get them all into trouble, but at sea, the captain's word was law. "And this was the crew you wanted to hire?"

"They have the skills to protect our interests. Besides," Kerchaw added off-handedly, "it's a very nice ship."

"Reavers, you say?" Seaborn interjected, rubbing his chin. "What was the captain's name again?'

"Uhh..." Kol looked to Kerchaw for help, but the agent only hid his face in his teacup. Voices arose from the sterncastle above, cutting through the silence, and Kol gave a sigh of relief. "I'd better go see what's going on," he muttered and hurried out the cabin door.

He crossed the rain-slick deck and approached the rail, where his breath caught in his throat. In the sea all about them bobbed pieces of flotsam. Barrels, broken planks, and sections of masts still clinging to the remains of canvas littered the waves, silently revealing a tragic tale of shipwreck.

Climbing up the aftcastle ladder, Kol came to the taffrail, where Declan peered through a brass spyglass. Far in the distance, nearly upon the horizon, a dark shape played upon the waves. "What is it?" Kol asked, shielding his eyes from the rain.

Wordlessly, Declan passed him the glass. Through the water-speckled lens, a serpentine creature came into view, its massive, bulky form dwarfing the sea swells as it raised a pointed snout high in the air. A black crest of fin-like spikes ran down its spine.

Kol shivered in the rising wind, ice flooding through his veins. "I've never seen one so large..." he breathed. "Is it—" He raised the glass for another look, and his heart dropped with foreboding to see it had drawn closer. He could now see its shape clearly in the distance, leaving a wide wake as it swam. "Is it following us?"

"I don't know," Declan remarked. "But we should prepare for the worst. All hands on deck!" he shouted, cupping his hands around his mouth. Soon, the ship's bell clanged loudly in answer, ringing over the weather deck.

"Stop!" Kol shouted, passing the glass back to Declan. "Stop the bell!" Running across the stern deck, he rushed down the ladder and made his way hastily toward the bow. Shoving aside the hapless sailor who stood clanging the large brass bell with a rope, Kol seized the clapper. "Be quiet!" he hissed.

All around, everything fell still, save for the howling wind and the spray of rain hitting their faces. All eyes were on the undulating shape in the distance. Slowly, Kol stepped toward the starboard rail, squinting at the grey sea and sky, as the great beast dove, slipping beneath the waves.

For several moments, he stood frozen, his gaze fixed on the water where the creature had vanished. Finally, when there was no further sign of it and it seemed the beast would rise no more, he let the tension fall from his shoulders. He turned and was just about to return to the cabin when a loud splash came from behind.

He looked over his shoulder as a massive head rose from the water, draped in kelp, tainting the air with the stench of rotted fish. It was an island in animal form, with jaws large enough to swallow *The Tigress* whole. Kol had never even imagined a living thing of this size. During the time it had gone unseen, the beast had closed the distance, apparently diving deep down along the seafloor to break the surface a mere stone's throw from the ship. Its bony jaws, long and lipless, parted to reveal curved fangs as the creature let out a throaty, gurgling growl that reverberated through the air all around the ship. A large eye, black and lidless, stared at them as it tilted its head to one side.

"Make ready the ballista!" Declan ordered.

"No!" Kol stepped in front of him. "That beast is too large, that'll only anger it. Give the order to set the rest of the sails," he urged. "Perhaps we can outrun it—"

Declan stepped around him. "Take aim!" he shouted to the crew.

Seeing his words disregarded, Kol gave up and went toward the rail, eyes fixed on the beast ahead.

"Release!" Declan shouted. A large bolt ripped through the air from the forecastle, becoming a speck of black in the spattering rain before disappearing into the flesh of the massive creature, just below the wide, staring eye.

The huge serpent didn't even react. It was as though the dart were merely another drop of rain. Its nostril flared. As it drew breath with a loud huff, great gills, lined with red, parted behind its jaws, and again the beast bellowed in their direction.

"Load the balls!" Declan's voice cut through the air. "Release at will!"

For a moment, Kol was surprised at the order given the captain's earlier aversion to using the ballista balls, but one by one, the heavy stones flew through the air, striking the beast's snout like pebbles as it drew slowly nearer to the ship. Kol's stomach dropped into his gut as he gripped the rail. *That's not helping!* As captain, Declan held supreme authority over the ship, but by his orders, they were wasting ammunition and attracting the animal. Kol had no right to challenge him, but the man didn't seem to be thinking clearly. If he didn't intervene, there would be no ship left to defend.

"Stop!" Kol ordered, voice carrying over the weather deck. "Stop the ballista! Set all sails!"

Declan rounded on him, open-mouthed. "How dare you—"

"Listen," Kol interrupted, pointing a finger at him. "You can see that wasn't working. I'm just trying to save our hides."

Declan's face burned red as he pressed his lips together, drawing a long breath through his nostrils.

"We need to leave a decoy," Kol proposed, taking advantage of the captain's speechlessness. "Fill the ship's boat with our scent, then cut it loose while we sail away."

"And give up one of our boats?" Declan snapped. Turning back to watch the beast, which was still huffing air as its jaws slowly parted, dripping long strings of spittle, Declan lowered his brow. He fell silent for a moment while all the crew stood by, waiting on his command. Ahead, a shrill, pulsating roar emanated from the creature's open mouth, resonating through the ship and rattling their bones.

"Use that one," Kol said, pointing to the small tender turned upside down on the foredeck.

Turning suddenly to face the crew, Declan's voice boomed over the ship, "Ready the skiff!" Then, he turned back to Kol. "And just what do you propose we fill it with?"

"Uhh..." Kol hesitated; he hadn't thought that far ahead. "Anything that bears our scent. Soiled clothing, waste, kitchen scraps," he replied hopefully.

As the crew manned the davits and quickly lowered the boat into the choppy waters, Declan's eyes searched the decks. "The dead!" he shouted, pointing to the bodies wrapped in hammocks along the rail, awaiting their funeral service. "Throw them in and cut it loose!"

"No!" a voice shouted from the crowd that had gathered at the rail. "Captain, please," a blue-clad sailor begged, stepping forth with strained expression. "To use these people as fodder..." Heartbreak shone through the tears in the boy's eyes. "Have a heart." It was the same cheery young man who had often come to Greywood, a relation of Adella's. *Yul Childric*, Kol recalled. His heart ached at the pain written so plainly across the youthful face.

Declan opened his mouth, then paused as he considered it. Slowly, his brow lowered, setting with determination. "Do as I said," he ordered.

Kol's stomach clenched as the crew grabbed the bodies, still wrapped in their hammocks, and slung them into the small boat, carelessly piling them one on top of the other. Yul turned away, and Kol grimaced. While it seemed disrespectful to the dead, Declan's tactic seemed sound and likely more effective than anything else they could throw overboard.

As the crew cut away the ropes, the boat, laden with the bodies of those who had succumbed to the fever, drifted loose beside the ship. The great beast, head still high above the waves, flared its serrated gills as it watched them, the pink of its inner flesh flashing briefly against the dark form. Its gaze remained fixed onto the weather deck as it continued to draw nearer.

Kol's pulse echoed in his ears, pounding in his neck and temples as he looked on, silently pleading for the animal to turn its attention away from *The Tigress*. His fingers tensed, stretching toward his cutlass hilt. Pinned by the gaze of the creature, around him the crew stood silent, waiting with bated breath.

Without warning, the massive, snakelike head dove down into the water, disappearing into the inky waves.

Declan clutched the starboard rail as he peered into the depths, mouth agape. "Has it gone?" he asked.

"Be quiet!" Kol warned under his breath. Tension locked every muscle in his limbs as the ship's boat drifted farther behind in their wake. A faint, burbling splash came from the larboard, but he dared not so much as twitch a finger. *The beast must still be down there somewhere, just below the ship.* He searched the waves for any sign of it, but none came. His heart sank as the corpse-laden boat disappeared from sight behind a swell. *It didn't work.*

Rigging and timber creaked loudly in the mounting gale as rain slashed across the decks. Something dark flickered through a wave trough a short distance off the starboard quarter. "Set all sails!" Kol ordered, turning to meet Declan's eye.

All around, the crew remained motionless, still, grey figures in the rain. Declan's brows quivered, almost imperceptibly.

"Set all sails!" Declan repeated, and the crew burst into motion. "Set the topgallants and staysails!"

It wasn't long until the canvas had full purchase of the storm winds with *The Tigress* coursing through the foamy waves like an unbridled horse, bow and stern bucking wildly. The ship's boat was only a dark speck on the waves behind them, but still Kol continued to scan the inky depths, waiting for the creature's return. Finally, the great beast broke the surface again, far behind them. He watched it swim wide circles in the sea around their grim bait and slowly let out a sigh of relief.

With the threat behind them, Declan rounded on Kol, striding directly over to him. "Never challenge my command again," he demanded.

Crossing his arms sullenly, Kol leaned against the rail. "We're still alive, aren't we?" he countered.

Lowering his brows, Declan drew breath to speak, but a loud creak sounding over the decks cut him off. Behind him, the foremast strained under the heavy winds. "That's good enough, take in sail now!" he ordered. Removing his hat, he pushed back the blond strands that blew in his face. "Good work, all! I think that beast is well behind us," he called out, overlooking the crew. He paused for a round of cheering. "Now, we must prepare for what lies ahead."

"What do you mean?" Kol asked, following Declan as he headed for the great cabin. Kol quickened his pace, stepping in front of him just as they reached the door. He pressed himself against it, blocking the entrance. "I think it's time you explained what's going on."

Ignoring his comment, Declan pushed past him and entered with Kol at his heels. Inside, Kerchaw sat at the table alone, working at his ledgers; Seaborn was nowhere in sight. Kol glanced frantically around, wondering where his father could be, until he noticed the large shape under the bundle of blankets on the mattress rose and fell gently. *That must be him,* he realized.

"I didn't want to let fear brew too long among the crew," Declan explained, striding toward his desk, "but the Capital is under siege; that's why the Queen has summoned all vessels. We are coming to their aid."

"Under siege?" Kol asked, tucking the spare knife under his belt. "By whom?"

Declan looked him hard in the eye. "Your people." Rifling through his desk, he pulled out a large, folded canvas and cleared a place for it on the table with a sweep of his arm. Shaking it out with a flourish, he laid it across the table before them, revealing a map of Belgrand Bay.

"The time has come," Declan began precisely, giving Kol an appraising look this time. "You're a skilled fighter; I'll need you in the boarding party. The Queen," he went on, placing a finger in the northern quarter of the map, "has sent a summons throughout Valenna for all ships to converge on the Capital. King Berento of Sornia—" He slid his finger to the southwest. "—has amassed his navy and laid siege to the harbor there. He's no idea her summons made it through the blockade." A grin played on his lips. "They won't be expecting us; all his attention will be on the palace, just north of the harbor." He moved his finger to Raymouth, then swept it across the Bay.

"According to the information in the summons," Declan continued, "we'll be arriving a few days into the action, and we'll have surprise on our side. Joined by other Valennian ships, heavens willing," he added hopefully, "we'll attack the enemy formation from the rear. All we need to do is take out their flagship—cut off the head of the snake—before the Ansebulet falls to their troops, and the siege will come to an end. So, what do you say?" Declan asked, raising a brow. "Will you be a part of the action, or would you rather hide away here in the cabin?"

Kol pressed his lips together, eyes fixed upon the map. "I'm in," he said resolutely. "Let's save Valenna."

"Excellent," Declan replied. "If the wind keeps up, we should arrive by this evening, so prepare yourself." With that, he turned to leave.

"Uh, Captain," Kol blurted out, unable to hold it back any longer. Reaching into his haversack, he pulled out Adella's letter. "There's something I've been meaning to give you," he said, handing it out to him. Though it pained him to deliver it, he wanted to do it now, while he could. With the looming battle, he wasn't sure he'd get another chance. "It's from Adella," he added.

A crease formed between Declan's brows. Then he nodded. Taking the letter, he left the cabin.

"What did he just say?" Seaborn asked, sitting up as the door banged shut and pulling the blanket off his head. "I was half-asleep for the first part of it, but it sounds like we're heading into battle."

"That's the look of it," Kol replied darkly. "But you two just stay here; bar the doors if things get rough."

"Right," Kerchaw agreed quickly, flipping through his ledger. "Can do."

"Not so fast," Seaborn interjected. "I can fight; just give me a sword."

Kol shook his head. "We can't risk that. The crew knows me by now, but not you. They'll think you're the enemy." It was a good excuse, he thought, with his father still bearing a heavy Sornian accent. But in truth, Kol was amazed he'd managed to keep his father and Declan apart thus far. He didn't want to find out what would happen if they met; he had a feeling there was more to the story than his father had let on.

"But—" Seaborn began.

"Just stay here," Kol interrupted. "Let the crew handle it."

18

Old Friends

Clinging one-handed to the rigging, Kol perched in the crow's nest high above the decks, eager to catch the first glimpse of the impending fight. Though he was much more comfortable at this height now than the first time he'd climbed the rigging back in the spring, an uneasiness still lingered as he kept a lookout ahead. Taking a watch certainly wasn't expected of him as the ship's owner, but since a few of the crew had been stricken with the fever that had come aboard among the passengers from Raymouth, he'd offered to help, knowing they'd need all the rest they could get for the fight ahead. Because of his lack of sailing experience compared to the rest of the crew, they'd given him the easiest of tasks—the crow's nest was usually appointed to novice sailors as it required little skill other than a willingness to brave the height. Though he'd been perched on the little platform for some time, long enough for his muscles to cramp, Kol wasn't sorry to be manning the post. It gave him something to do. Blinking at the horizon, he rubbed his eyes, wishing he'd slept better the night before.

The frequency of his nightmares had dwindled during his time in Elldon, despite the threat of war. That kind of danger wasn't new to him, but the feeling of warmth and belonging that he'd come to know was, and it made all the difference. Now that he found himself far from his newfound home and at the mercy of the sea, the dreams had returned with renewed intensity. Every night, he relived the same desperate, helpless moment from months before, when Adella had been swept from the deck of *The Accord* and into the jaws of the sea serpent. No matter what he did or how hard he tried to push the memory away, it played over and over, filling his sleep with terror. Even now, he could see it happening within the dark recesses of his mind. He shook his head, blinking the images away, and forced his attention back to his surroundings.

Soon, the rain tapered off, clearing the air beneath the heavy grey storm clouds. It would be a brief respite, he knew, as the skies only grew darker ahead. He gazed over the sea that surrounded him, taking in the endless, deep blue swells that caused the ship to dip and rise, rocking him gently forward and backward, and turned aft. A pale shape struck his eye far behind *The Tigress*. Its angular, unnatural form was easy to recognize.

"Ship!" Kol shouted over the steady wind. "Ship astern!" Another pale shape crested a swell, not far behind the other. "Make that 'ships,'" he corrected himself.

"How far?" came the captain's hearty voice below.

"About three leagues; maybe four," Kol guessed, judging by his vantage point. Bracing himself against the masthead, he lifted his spyglass. He could just make out a small patch of red flickering above the sails of the oncoming vessels. "They look to be Valennian!"

"How many?" Declan called up.

"Two—" Kol peered through the glass again as another shape materialized through the haze, far to starboard. "No—three," he called down.

"That's good news." Declan crossed his arms behind his back. "Are you sure they're Valennian?"

"Reasonably so," Kol replied. "They're flying scarlet colors, and not a caravel in sight."

"Excellent." Declan grinned. "Looks like we won't be going in alone."

It wasn't until some hours later, when the sky had dimmed to slate beneath the heavy cover of rain clouds, that Kol returned to his cabin for a quick meal, but he was almost immediately interrupted by urgent shouting that rang over the deck. He shoved a piece of hardtack in his mouth and rose from the table. Seaborn jumped to his feet.

"Stay here," Kol ordered, raising a hand.

"But—" Seaborn began, looking crestfallen.

Lifting his brows meaningfully at Kerchaw as he strode past him, Kol made his way back to the weather deck.

Outside, lightning flashed in the distance as he passed sailors running frantically to and fro, adjusting the rigging and clearing the decks. Far beyond the prow, a head of land rose from the sea, crowned by a sprawling palace with stone turrets stretching toward the black clouds. At its foot, the city sloped down toward the crowded harbor. Though he recognized the Valennian capital, the water had risen much higher along the shore since last he'd seen it. Various ships, mainly caravels of different sizes flying green and orange ensigns, littered the waters, locking in the Valennian barques and schooners that moored at the nearly-flooded docks. At the heart of it all, one massive, gaudily-painted Sornian caravel rode at anchor; the largest ballista that Kol had ever seen perched on its forecastle.

At their approach, two caravels with green and orange pennants fluttering from their masts broke away from either side of the formation—their large lateen sails making the vessels more maneuverable in the rising squall than *The Tigress*—and headed their way.

"Damn," Kol muttered, heart plummeting. He wondered if Declan had accounted for this in his plans.

"Make ready, men!" Declan shouted. "They're coming to meet us. Marley!" He cupped his hands around his mouth to be heard over the distant thunder. "Prepare the ballista with stone!"

Kol glanced astern; the larger of the Valennian ships had gained significantly on them, approaching on their starboard quarter. As *The Tigress* held a single ballista on the forecastle, the captain would have to choose which side to defend and which would be left vulnerable to the oncoming assault. But if the other Valennian vessel caught up soon, perhaps it could draw the enemy's attention in time to spare *The Tigress* a double-sided attack. "Captain," Kol said, motioning toward the approaching ship.

Declan pulled out his spyglass and squinted through it. "That's *The Warbrand*," he replied with a grin. "Old friends of ours, and making good time. Marley," he shouted, tucking his spyglass into his waistcoat. "Take aim at the waterline of the larboard vessel!"

"Yes, Captain," came the faint reply, nearly swallowed up by the wind.

A silence fell over the decks, save for the creaking timbers, as all waited breathlessly, watching the two enemy ships converge upon them. Thunder clapped and a sudden deluge of rain swept over the ship, battering their eyes.

The enemy ships drew closer, preparing to hem them in on both sides, and a dark shape shot through the air toward them from the deck of the larboard caravel.

"Down!" Declan shouted, dropping to his knees.

Kol threw himself onto the wet deck as it whistled over their heads and tore through *The Tigress's* striped sails, leaving the canvas hanging in tatters from the spar. His eyes widened. It was far more damage than any bolt or ball could have done. "What was that?" he asked.

"Chain shot," Declan grumbled, rising to his feet and straightening his jacket. "Release!" he called out. The ballista gave a loud thump as a stone flew from the forecastle and smashed into the hull of the small caravel with a spray of wood and water. "Ha!" Declan said triumphantly. "Good luck plugging that one." From the enemy deck, silhouettes rose against the darkening sky, forming a line along the rail. "Take cover!" Declan shouted, ducking behind the mainmast as the crew about them scattered.

Kol ran, shielding himself behind the forecastle ladder just as something whizzed behind his head. All around them, a volley of arrows rained down over *The Tigress*, their steel tips biting into the decks with a series of sharp twangs. One sailor let out a cry and fell to his knees beside the rail, clutching his belly.

"At least they're not fire arrows," Kol muttered.

"Shut up," Declan hissed. "Don't give them any ideas."

Behind them, the other caravel closed in on *The Tigress*, with *The Warbrand* overtaking it quickly on its far side. If the oncoming enemy ship were to likewise release a volley onto *The Tigress*, there'd be nowhere to hide. "Declan," Kol warned, nodding to starboard.

"Marley!" the captain shouted, taking his meaning. "Aim low to starboard vessel! Release at will!"

The crew of the caravel, nothing more than black figures against the grey of evening, ducked out of sight as Marley rotated the front of the ballista in their direction. He pulled the lever, releasing the shot with a heavy thump. A spray of water burst up from the sea between the two vessels, missing the hull entirely.

"Damn it," Declan spat.

Kol braced for another volley of arrows, wincing in anticipation; a loud crack rang out from behind him. He jerked around to see a blossom of splinters erupting from the base of the second enemy vessel's foremast and spotted *The Warbrand* close behind it, the sailors at the prow quickly reloading their ballista. As he watched, the great timbers of the Sornian caravel groaned and split, drawing all eyes before the mast crashed violently down upon the ship's deck like a fallen tree, tearing down rigging and crushing sailors beneath its spars. Muffled screams carried over the water.

Leaving both enemy ships badly damaged in its wake, *The Tigress* sailed on toward the main fray, with *The Warbrand* following closely. The enemy flagship, grander than the others and bearing a large, green ensign, lay dead ahead, straining against its anchor rodes in the rough, dark waves. Spurred onward by the gusting winds, *The Tigress* sailed straight toward it, headed for collision.

"Captain, what are your orders?" First Mate Jon called out from the helm.

Standing motionless, Declan stared into the distance. "Steady onward," he replied. "Prepare for impact."

"What?!" Kol shouted, eyes widening. "No—"

"Captain, did I hear that right?" Jon called out. "You mean for us to ram the ship?"

"I said, steady onward," Declan repeated. His voice was brittle and hollow.

"That's madness!" Kol shouted. "You'll wreck us!"

Declan stepped toward him, spine straightening. His eyes held a dark, distant look, and his mouth was grimly set. "*The Tigress* is the larger vessel, and built for combat. She can handle it. Her high prow will cleave into their low side like an axe."

Kol opened his mouth to protest again, then, thinking better of it, shut it. He narrowed his eyes at Declan's retreating back. Something about the way he said it gave him pause, though he couldn't say exactly why. *Maybe I just don't like him playing war games with my ship*, he reasoned to himself. He tried to shake the feeling off; there were more important matters at hand to contend with.

With worrying speed, *The Tigress* drew closer to the ships in the harbor. Wind filled the barque's tattered sails, bearing it swiftly toward the gathered fleet until it was too late to turn aside. Narrowly avoiding the prow of one ship, *The Tigress* barreled through a gap in the Sornians' formation and straight on toward the flagship.

"Brace yourselves!" Kol shouted, grabbing the shrouds beside the rail. As they rapidly approached the broadside of the gilded caravel, the crew, who had been staring agape, at a loss of what to do, sprang into a flurry of panic.

A deafening, bone-rattling boom shuddered through the ship, reverberating through the hull. Kol was flung forward, his legs flying out from under him. Only his grip on the ratlines saved him from being thrown across the deck, and pain flared through his hand at the jarring of the impact. Those of the crew that didn't have time to grab onto something slid helplessly across the wet planks; barrels that had been stowed on deck tore free from their nets and bounded forward, barely missing one hapless sailor before cracking against the forecastle.

Kol pulled himself to his feet and wrung the pain from his hand. "What are you doing?" he shouted, rounding on Captain Delcan, who remained standing, jostled but unmoved by the collision. "Are you out of your mind?" Kol's voice was drowned out by the groan of splitting timber as the sea pounded against the hull, driving *The Tigress* further into the caravel.

"Prepare to board!" Declan shouted. Loud voices filled the air around them as the crew recovered their footing and obeyed.

Behind him, an eerie, high-pitched shriek cut through the storm. A flash of lightning illuminated the dark sea beyond, revealing sinewy, serpentine forms rising and falling among the rolling waves.

"Oh, no..." Kol muttered to himself, wondering if anyone else had seen it.

"Attack!" Declan bellowed, hoisting his cutlass in the air. All around, the crew charged forward, storming up the forecastle toward the caravel ahead.

* * *

Adella had just finished choking down the last of the hard, dry biscuits that had been left for her when voices rose on deck, with shouts of what seemed to be orders from the captain.

"Endlebridge," she whispered. "Listen." His sleeping form stirred on the pallet of furs in the next cell. "What are they saying?" she asked eagerly.

He groaned and rolled over, then carefully propped himself up on an arm. "That's odd; it sounds like we're anchoring, but..." He tilted his head to listen. "They're readying for battle."

"Battle?" Adella's mouth went dry at the thought of them being locked in the hold while enemy ballistas crashed holes in the hull. "We have to get out of here," she urged, silently berating herself for not acting sooner. "If anything happens, we'll be the last thing on their minds." Jumping to her feet, she frantically shook the iron bars. They rattled but held fast.

"I can't," he replied softly. "You'll have to leave me behind."

"No." While she had nothing to go back to, only a faint hope of ever seeing Kol again, she couldn't let Endlebridge die like a bilge rat in the hold. He was the one who had pulled her from the water when she had been swept away by the sea at Pentz, and his agreement to send his cavalry troop to Elldon's aid, despite what he himself had been through, was a kindness she could never forget. She wouldn't let this be his end. "I'm not leaving you behind."

"I'm injured," he countered, a wince in his voice. "I'll only slow you down."

Adella opened her mouth to argue, but their conversation was interrupted by footsteps in the companionway. Soon the space flooded with light as a sailor approached, jangling the keyring in his hand. A large knife glinted from his hip, tucked beneath the woven sash on his waist. She backed away as he approached her cell door, unlocked it, and entered. Crouching at her feet, he searched through the various keys on the ring, then tried one in the lock of her ankle-fetter. It didn't turn. Dropping it, he rifled through them again, peering at each one closely while Adella waited motionless. *He means to bring me above decks?* Her pulse raced as she wondered what it might mean.

His hot breath filled the space, smelling of nutmeg and gin, as he fumbled with the keys. All of his attention was on the keyring, and as Adella watched him struggle, time seemed to slow. Her eyes shifted to the porcelain chamber pot beside her, fingers twitching.

"I'm really sorry about this," she muttered. Grabbing the heavy chamber pot, she crashed it over his head. Her stomach flipped at the stench as the porcelain shattered, falling over his shoulders in large shards. She held her breath as the man froze in mid-action, fingers hovering over the lock. Then, his eyes rolled back into his head and he fell onto his side.

She let out her breath and grabbed the keyring. Fingers fumbling with haste, her pulse pounded wildly in her ears as she tried one key and then another in the lock until finally one turned. With a satisfying click, the iron band around her leg swung open.

Taking the knife from the sailor's side, she slipped it beneath her belt and hurried out the cell door that had been left ajar. As she stepped into the open hold, the ship lurched violently as a loud boom shuddered through the hull. Her legs, unsteady after days of disuse, collapsed under her and she landed roughly on her stomach. The keyring slid over the planks of the sole. Across the hold, the sound of rushing water filled her with cold dread. *The hull has been breached!*

"Leave me," Endlebridge urged. "Go, before it's too late."

Ignoring his plea, she picked herself up and scurried after the keys, then ran to his cell door. There were so many keys of different sizes and shapes. Moments passed like hours as she tried one after the other unsuccessfully, all while the shouts from above grew louder and more urgent. Finally, one key turned in the lock and she threw the door open wide. Kneeling at his feet, she started the process all over again, this time with the lock of his ankle-fetter.

He put a hand on hers as the key turned. "My ribs are broken. I won't make it. Go!"

"Lord Endlebridge," she began sternly, looking up at him as the lock fell open. "When the wave hit Pentz, and I was swept out to sea with so many others, did you leave us behind then?" Tears rose in her eyes as she relived the fear and despair of that terrible night, floating on the dark, endless sea and believing it would be her last. She would never forget the sudden hope that came in the form of a ship among the isles. "Did you?" she repeated, rising to her feet.

"No," he uttered under his breath.

"No, you didn't. And I won't leave you behind now. Come on," she said, lifting his arm over her shoulder. "Let's get out of here."

He groaned loudly, grabbing his side as she helped him to his feet. Leaning heavily on her, he hobbled along as she headed for the companionway, water already pooling at their feet and rising quickly.

It took all her strength to support him as they slowly worked their way across the flooding hold. As she panted with exertion, the stench of filthy bilgewater mingled with fishy brine burned her throat, and her muscles strained to keep the man upright.

Reaching the companionway, she half-pulled him slowly up the steps, the water lapping behind them, but before they reached the top, the ship shifted, listing sideways. Already unsteady, Endlebridge lost his balance and stumbled, falling back down a few steps until Adella caught him by the arm. Throwing her weight backward, she managed to pull him up once more, eliciting another painful groan from him along the way.

When they finally emerged above decks and stepped out into the driving rain, Adella's mouth fell open. Their galley ship was surrounded by a fleet of Sornian caravels, their colors flapping brightly in the rising wind. The crew had stowed their oars and were preparing for battle. At the bow, several crew members gathered around a large ballista, loading iron balls into the barrel. Their ship faced a line of larger warships protecting the harbor beyond, their pennants of Valennian Scarlet fluttering in the rain.

"Heavens, have mercy..." Endlebridge uttered solemnly.

Further up the gently rising bluffs of the shore, the stone towers of a citadel loomed over the stormy landscape. Adella's heart leapt into her throat at the sight of the familiar skyline. *It's the Capital!* But her elation lasted only a moment; Valenna was under attack, and they were sailing straight into the heart of the battle.

Something whizzed across the deck just in front of her, smashing through the benches and into the larboard rail, and she jumped back, bumping into Endlebridge. Splinters rained down through the air. In the chaos, Adella spotted the ship's boat, stored upside-down amidships, but she dismissed it at a glance. Even if Endlebridge could manage it with her, it would be impossible for them to place the boat into the water, surrounded as it was by the crew at the benches. The sides of this galley ship, however, sat low in the water to accommodate the reach of the oars. *Perhaps we could just jump overboard and swim to shore... No,* she put the thought aside sadly. *Endlebridge can hardly walk; he certainly can't swim.* Even if he could, there was no knowing what lurked beneath the water.

A harsh shout from behind startled her, and hands clamped down around her arms before she could turn around. "Let go!" she shouted, pushing against them. "Surely you have bigger problems—" Rough hands took the knife from her belt, and they dragged her and Endlebridge to the galley's starboard rail amidst the bark of orders coming from across the deck.

Unable to move with her arms pinned behind her, Adella watched as a section of oars was brought up and a small group of sailors unfastened the ship's boat and hoisted it over the long benches, lowering it by ropes over the side and down into the water. With the galley ship riding so low, there was very little freeboard, and in lieu of a ladder, the crew climbed easily over the rail and dropped straight down into the boat. Next, they lowered Adella over the rails, then Endlebridge, who groaned sharply through tight jaws at the movement, depositing them into the hull of the small boat as it rocked side-to-side in the dark, sloshing waves.

The sailors manned the oars, working furiously in the turbulent water as they left the galley ship and the rest of the crew behind.

Cold seaspray hit her face. "What's happening?" she asked, turning to Endlebridge for translation. He didn't answer, only lay back against the thwart, his face tightened into a grimace. She frowned. Being handled so roughly had obviously caused him great pain.

The Madorrans rowed onward through the storm, guided by the man Adella assumed was their captain, judging by his opulently jeweled clothing, and passed between a number of much larger ships bearing Sornian colors. Soon, they drew alongside one caravel that was noticeably grander than the rest, with gilded carvings along ornate gallery windows at the stern. The Madorrans hailed its crew in their foreign tongue, shouting over the roar of sea and storm, and after a long, breathless moment, a rope ladder unfurled over the side. Adella was forced up first. As she clambered over the side onto the deck, sailors in green grabbed her violently, taking hold of her long hair. She let out an involuntary gasp as her head was tilted forcefully back, face skyward. With raindrops blinding her, she could see nothing but a bleary grey and knew only by the cries of pain that Endlebridge had likewise been hauled aboard.

19

Madness

Kol ran forward with the crew and the Royal Guard. Whatever his feelings regarding the situation, he still counted himself a Valennian, and would abide by his duty to his country as one of the crew. With his red jacket and dark hair pulled back in a tight queue, he blended in easily with the group, looking as though he belonged among them. His heart rose in his chest at the thought, proud to defend the place he now considered his home. Pressing forward with the crowd, he clambered over the forerail at the prow of *The Tigress* and dropped onto the deck of the caravel below. The hard landing jarred him, throwing him off balance, and he caught himself with a hand on the planks. Jumping up, he drew his cutlass.

Immediately, they were met by Sornians in emerald, swords swinging and metal clanging with each frantic parry. Kol slashed his blade, turning it this way and that, to meet and block the strikes that flew at him from all sides. Jabbing forward, he skewered one soldier in the gut and, stepping over his crumpled form, pressed onward.

With the crew of *The Tigress* fighting fiercely alongside him, he cut down one, two, then a handful of enemy soldiers until he lost count. Glancing around, he saw the familiar faces of *The Tigress's* crew doing the same. Though the Sornian numbers were greater, they couldn't match the ferocity of the Valennians, who were pushing back the enemy in a slow sweep of bloodshed as they gradually made their way toward the bow. Kol understood his comrades' passion deeply. Having been on the other side, he knew the Sornian soldiers were travel-weary, overworked and underfed, many of them fighting merely for a lack of better opportunity. They had no great love for the Sornian royal family, who ruled without compassion. But the Valennians, and now he, had willfully chosen this path for their lives, taking up arms to defend their homeland. Many of them were there as commissioned privateers, well paid by the Queen, and all were fighting for more than just their lives; they were fighting to defend their families from the threat of foreign rule.

Knowing he'd forged this path for himself strengthened his resolve and invigorated each slash and parry of his blade. One by one, soldiers in green fell at their feet until the enemy on deck found themselves outnumbered.

One man, standing head and shoulders above the others, stepped forward from those who remained and faced Kol with grim resolve. His emerald coat was opulently trimmed in gold braid about the chest and shoulders, and his hat boasted even more trim along the edges than an ordinary sea captain. This clearly was a man of rank, and Kol knew one didn't rise so high in the Sornian Navy on navigation skills alone. *A commodore. He must be the one who brought the fleet to Valenna's shore.* Kol swallowed, his throat suddenly tight. Given the way the man was looking at him, he could tell his adept swordsmanship had caught the man's attention, singling him out among the Valennians as the greater threat, though he was sure his own training was nothing more than basic compared with the skills this man surely had. A quick glance around revealed that *The Tigress*'s crew and Royal Guard were all preoccupied still, facing small groups of haggard Sornians, and Kol realized with a sinking of his heart that this fight would be his alone.

He focused his attention on the cutlass in his hand, felt its familiar heft grounding him, steadying his breath. A trusted companion, the blade was worn from countless skirmishes, though its edge was honed sharp enough to bite through bone. With his boots firm on the wet deck, he lowered his stance, centering his balance, eyes never leaving the man before him—a hulking shadow outlined against the stormy sky.

"Give it up," the man growled, his voice like flint. As he stepped forward, a bolt of distant lightning flashed off the cold metal of his wide cutlass. "It's over; you're too late."

"It's never too late to act with honor," Kol replied, readying his cutlass. "You're breaking a century of peace. Put Valenna behind you, and go home."

"*Home?*" the commodore repeated, emphasizing their shared accent. "Seems you're the one who has no honor." His expression fell from a sneer to a hard scowl. "Traitor!" he shouted, his voice echoing across the decks.

The man lunged, his sword swinging in a vicious arc toward Kol's throat, driving the blow with the full weight of his massive body. But Kol expected the move. He shifted to the side, leaning back to avoid the blade, though he still felt the breath of the strike as it passed him by. *Too close,* he chided himself as he brought his cutlass up in a smooth, practiced counter, deflecting the commodore's blade with a sharp clash of steel.

Though the force of the parry sent a jolt through his arm, Kol held firm, shoving forward to free his blade for the riposte. He pivoted on his back foot, bringing his cutlass down in a tight, controlled arc aimed at the commodore's exposed flank.

The man groaned—a deep, rumbling sound—and twisted just in time to block the blow, their swords ringing again. With a snarl, the commodore shoved Kol back to prepare for another attack.

But Kol was already moving, his feet light on the deck, his body always just out of reach of the blade. Though the man's sword cleaved the air with every swing, Kol kept one swift step ahead, parrying with precision, countering with deadly intent.

Soon the commodore, who was much older, panted with exertion, his breathing growing more labored with each heavy-handed blow. Kol wasn't sure how much of the water running down the man's face was sweat rather than rain. But though his strikes grew slower, they became all the more forceful, his mounting rage and desperation written plainly in the deepening lines of his face.

One hard parry knocked Kol off balance, sending him staggering backward. His foot slipped on the wet wood, and his back hit the deck. The commodore was immediately upon him, his blade swinging down toward Kol's neck, throwing the entire weight of his body behind it.

Instinctively, Kol rolled sideways as the tip of the commodore's blade bit into the deck close by his head. For an instant, the man's side was left unguarded. With a quick thrust, Kol drove the tip of his cutlass into the commodore's abdomen, his blade sinking in just beneath the rib cage. The impact sent a spasm of shock through the man's body, and he looked down, his eyes widening in disbelief.

In one sharp motion, Kol twisted the blade up, and the commodore's breath caught. The commodore choked on his own blood and collapsed to his knees, his grip weakening until his cutlass finally slipped from his hand.

Kol shoved the man's body away as it fell toward him, briefly groaning at the sheer weight of it, and hopped quickly to his feet. All around, the fighting stilled as the few remaining Sornians pulled back from the fight to stare open-mouthed at their fallen commodore. Then, still at the mercy of the Valennians' blades, they dropped to their knees in surrender and Kol heaved a sigh of relief. With their leadership gone, the battle was over; the Valennians had won.

Wiping the water from his forehead, Kol let the long-held tension in his body finally fall away. Surely, with their flagship captured, there was nothing left for the remaining Sornian vessels to do but make a hasty retreat. Satisfied with the outcome, he began to sheath his cutlass when a strange light caught his eye.

Across the ship, an unnatural glow, as cold and white as moonlight but far brighter, filled the harbor, illuminating the dark. Shielding his eyes against the glare, Kol squinted, but was unable to descry the source. Then, movement beyond the ship caught his attention; revealed starkly in the eerie light of the crowded harbor, dark figures were climbing over the rails of the surrounding vessels, making their way down rope ladders and disembarking into small boats that waited in the waves below. Many were already rowing to shore. His eyes widened, and a chill fell over him. The fight wasn't over yet. *They're attacking the Capital!*

Before he could act, the peculiar glow changed, darkening to an eerie green, casting everything in an uncanny shade of emerald. Finally, Kol spotted the source; a figure strode across the deck in confident, gliding strides that clearly betrayed a highborn life. Oddly, the light seemed to be moving with him. The figure lifted a small object above his head, revealing the origin of the eerie light. *A stone...* Kol squinted again, trying to make out the angular shape. *A crystal.*

A deep, pulsating hum emanated from the direction of the oncoming figure, whose strides slowed as he drew amidships, then stopped beside the main mast. The air was alive with a crisp, frenetic energy that caused the hairs on Kol's arms to tingle and stand on end. Behind him, something shuffled languidly on the deck, but the spectacle before him held him rapt. All at once, the crumpled forms of those who'd fallen during the fight began to stir. With small movements at first, then with the hissing of breath burbled with blood, they rose unsteadily to their feet, weapons in hand. Kol's gut sank. Panic shook him from his daze of astonishment and he spun around; behind him, the slain commodore, mouth stained ruby, lurched onto his side. Then, with a silent, unnatural movement, he reached for his sword and staggered to his feet. His eyes still held the vacant look of death, blood weeping from his parted lips.

Kol's mouth fell open as frigid, gut-wrenching dread flooded over him, sapping the strength from his limbs. *How? How is this possible? I just killed this man...* His mouth went dry despite the humid air, a swallow catching thickly in his throat. This one, he was certain had been dead.

"What in the blue hell—" Declan murmured from somewhere behind him.

The fallen, in all colors—the scarlet of the Valennian Royal Guard, the blue of Declan's crew, as well as Sornian emerald—arose and turned their weapons against those who remained of the boarding party. Before him, without groan or breath at all, the commodore silently lifted his sword to strike, like a poppet at the whims of its master.

The power behind the man's blow hadn't dulled with death, and his blade clanged just as harshly against Kol's cutlass as it had done before. Yet, something had changed in the process. Again and again, the resurrected form hacked and slashed at him, but there was no intelligence behind the rote movements. Instead of his opponent's skill, it was the relentlessness of each strike, without so much as a pause between them for a riposte, that wore down Kol's stamina. His muscles burned with each flash of movement, ached with the strain of every impact. Holding one particularly heavy parry for too long, his arm gave out. Mustering all his strength, shoved the enemy blade away, directing it away from his body as he released the block. Still, the sharp edge ran across his shoulder, slicing through his coat and into flesh.

Though he reeled from the stinging pain, the move left the commodore's front open for a strike. Roaring through clenched jaws, Kol lunged with everything he had left in him, plunging the tip of his cutlass deep into the broad belly.

Unflinching, the dull-eyed commodore swung his sword around for a downward strike. Kol barely had enough time to draw his cutlass from the massive body to block the blow overhead. Stumbling backward from the force, he retreated from the fight, his courage failing at the realization that this enemy would never yield.

In the eerie green light all around, his shipmates faced the same plight, each hacking and stabbing relentlessly, ineffectively, at the animated bodies that closed in around them. United in mind and movement, controlled by some unseen force, they were so numerous that the decks were crowded with them, leaving *The Tigress's* remaining crew vastly outnumbered. In a matter of moments, the tides of war had turned against them.

"Fall back!" Declan shouted, voice ragged with fear and desperation as he kicked a lumbering soldier in the gut. "Retreat to *The Tigress!*"

Kol followed the others as they retreated from the fray, scrambling toward *The Tigress's* prow that loomed overhead. Those who had remained behind to guard the ship now threw down ropes for him and his fellow survivors on the caravel below. Beneath the dangling ropes, Kol turned to fend off the pursuing dead, who encircled around him and Declan as the crew, hampered by their exhaustion, their wounds, and the driving rain, made their way up to their ship. The cut in Kol's shoulder stung sharply with each strike, and for a brief moment, he envied the animated corpses that pressed in on him, who, though hacked to red, ragged shreds of walking flesh that hung sickly from exposed bone, apparently harbored no such pain. Their faces, dead in both body and expression, did not so much as twitch when he ran his blade through their unfeeling flesh. The hardest to deal with were the faces he recognized, crewmates from *The Tigress.* Even as he fought back against their onslaught, his heart ached for them, made into traitors against their will. Whatever had the power to do such a thing, he couldn't imagine, but the thought filled him with a foreboding that turned his stomach.

Movement caught his eye off the larboard rail. In the surreal green glow that seemed to cut every shadow with a stark edge, filling the air with oppressive heaviness, a vast, dark shape rose over the waves. Towering on a great black stalk of a neck, the grotesque, predatory head of the *pelkimund* turned in their direction. Nostrils flaring as it huffed the air, a low growl reverberated from deep within its throat.

Icy terror gripped Kol's gut. With a desperate swipe of his blade, he pushed back the dead once more just as the ropes were cleared for Kol and the captain to ascend. "Go!" Kol shouted, shoving Declan's shoulder to urge him onward. With one last kick to the nearest lumbering attacker, he turned to the rope and, leaping up to grab it, climbed quickly, ignoring the surge of pain in his shoulder. His boots scraped against the slick wood of the ship's prow as he pulled himself onto the forerail.

"Cut the ropes," Declan ordered to the surviving crew. "And hold them off as long as you can!"

Hurrying down the forecastle ladder, Kol followed Declan to the main deck, where they were met by those who had remained behind to man the ship. "We must get *The Tigress* out of here—" the captain shouted. Sailors scattered to their respective stations.

"Kol!" a craggy voice broke through the commotion. "Son! Are you alright?"

Kol spun around to find Seaborn running toward them. "What are you doing out here?" he muttered gruffly, grabbing the man by the shoulders and turning him around, propelling him forward. "I said to stay in the cabin—"

Before he'd taken two steps, they were interrupted by a loud, haggard gasp. Declan threw out an arm, face pale as he blocked their path. "It can't be," he uttered, as if to himself. "And yet, here he is, right before my eyes."

Kol dropped his hands from his father's arms as the captain stepped forward, eyeing Seaborn up and down. In one swift move, Declan drew his cutlass, and the ring of metal echoed through the night.

Declan's eyes narrowed as he spoke again, louder this time, leveling his sword. "How does the man who butchered my father, spilling his guts upon this very ship, dare to stand before me now?" he demanded, voice booming over the decks. He shot an accusatory sideways glance at Kol, who winced at a sudden pang of guilt.

Seaborn stared blankly at Declan, his face full of surprise. Then, recognition slowly dawned and spread across his features.

"You," Seaborn uttered under his breath, his brow falling heavily over dark eyes. He drew his sword likewise, leveling it at the captain. A few of the crew stepped forward, but Declan waved them back.

"You!" Seaborn's voice rose, booming over the ship. "Son of my enemy. It was *your* father who took my family from *me!* He deserved to die like a dog. Now all that's left for me to do," he said, spitting the words, "is to cut you from this world, and I'll have my revenge!"

At a loss for words but giving voice to his rage nonetheless, Declan screamed a piercing, beastly growl, then burst into motion, slashing at Seaborn with his blade. Seaborn jumped back, and steel clanged loudly against steel as the old man struggled to parry each blow that beat him backward step by step.

It was far from a fair fight; Declan clearly had the upper hand, and as Kol watched, it was obvious he had no intention of holding back. "Stop!" he shouted, reaching out to stay Declan's hand.

It was too late; with one sudden thrust, Declan drove his blade deep into Seaborn's belly. The old man sputtered, stumbling backward as the captain withdrew his cutlass, leaving him crumpled against the rail. Clutching the wound, a gush of dark blood spilled through his fingers onto the deck.

"Father!" Kol cried out, falling to his knees beside him. "No..." he muttered, staring helplessly into Seaborn's face as the light in his grey eyes grew dim. Hands shaking, Kol reached for the pierced flesh, pressing it tightly in an attempt to stop the bleeding, but the wound was too great. With his last breath, Seaborn slumped forward, falling limply against Kol's shoulder.

Every bleak, cold night of his childhood that he'd spent alone, wishing for a family and a home, returned to him. The rain fell heavily over him, taking his thoughts back to the wet streets of Hedda, where he stood shivering with holes in his stockings and hunger gnawing in his belly, watching from the outside as the warm light of happy hearths danced in the windows. "Father..." he repeated, the word now merely a murmur of breath on the wind. A tear rolled down his cheek as he pressed his forehead against the old man's storm-chilled brow and realized there was nothing he could do; he was an orphan once again.

"Your father?" Declan asked with cold wrath in his voice. The captain's icy tone drew Kol back to the present, followed by the feel of cold steel beneath his chin.

"Draw your sword," Declan ordered, pressing the edge of his cutlass into his neck.

Kol took a shuddering breath, blinking away rain and tears as he raised his blood-stained palms and slowly stood to face the captain, the blade still pressing into his skin. "There's no need to do this," Kol reasoned. "We have enough enemies—"

"What was that man doing on my ship?!" Declan screamed, spittle flinging from his lips as his face turned crimson. "You brought him here!" Arcing his cutlass around in the air, he swung it downward with vicious force. Kol hardly had enough time to draw his sword and deflect the blow, the blade slicing over his knuckles as he stumbled backward. The wound in his shoulder panged sharply at the motion, echoing the fresh sting in his hand.

"Stop," Kol pleaded. "We're on the same side—"

"Sornian!" Declan spat, pressing into him. "Your kind always knows how to profit from the chaos they sow, don't you?" Metal clanging, he shoved Kol backward again, then drew back for another strike. His voice lowered to a growl, "First my ship, now her..."

Kol's heart leapt into his throat at the accusation. "It's not like that—" he tried to explain, but another powerful blow knocked the breath from his lungs as he parried, the clash of metal ringing in his ears.

"Your lowborn manners are too rough for a fine woman like her," Declan interjected, clipping the words out through a tightened jaw, and drew back again for another strike.

Kol's face burned at the insult. "You're wrong," he snapped, unable to hold his tongue any longer. "Turns out, she likes things a bit rough," he countered archly, his tone as lewd as he could muster in the moment. Whether it was true or not didn't matter; the insinuating remark was a blow aimed at Declan's heart. The look of shock on the man's sun-weathered face told him he'd hit his mark.

"You filthy, Sornian bastard!" Declan shouted, turning a deeper crimson. "Just like your father!" Lightning flashed, briefly illuminating the captain's twisted grimace to reveal tears streaming down his cheeks, mingling with the rain. "You've taken everything from me!" His screams contorted into heaving gasps as he continued his onslaught, hacking at Kol with strike after strike, insensible to all around him. "You traitor! You don't deserve her!"

Kol groaned, holding his cutlass fast against the repeated blows. The strain in his wounded shoulder shot pain through his arm, sapping his strength until a savage attack sent him stumbling backward again. He caught himself on the shrouds, yet still Declan pressed in on him.

Kol didn't want to fight the man, but as he blocked strike after strike, he felt an indignant rage slowly stoking inside him. *Why am I the one under attack here?* When they'd first met, the captain had everything Kol had ever wanted: wealth and honor, the respect of his countrymen, even Adella's affections. *All I wanted was to be like him.* Now, the roles were reversed, and Declan couldn't stomach it. This man, who'd always seemed so arrogant and so careless with Adella's feelings, was now trying to blame it all on him. Kol knew very well his father wasn't an innocent man, but every reaver on that ship had blood on their hands. Captain or not, it wasn't fair for Declan to make himself judge and executioner; he was no better.

Clenching his jaw, Kol roared through his teeth as anger and indignation flooded through him. Ignoring the pain that surged in his shoulder, Kol pushed with his blade, ramming it into Declan, who lurched backward at the sudden force. Rounding his cutlass on him,

Kol slashed at his middle; Declan just barely caught the blow in a hasty parry.

Shoving away, Kol slammed his elbow into Declan's mouth, his teeth cracking loudly as blood splattered through the air and sending him reeling backward against the rail. With Declan momentarily stunned and his middle open, Kol drew back his cutlass for the final blow.

He paused, blade in midair. Despite everything that had passed between him and Declan since their first meeting—the jealousy, suspicion, and hate—he still didn't want to fight the man. Valennians valued honor above all else, and he wanted nothing more than to be worthy of his new homeland. He'd been given a second chance here, had been given a new life, a ship, and a mercantile. Fighting his own countryman, his own ship captain, wasn't right. *Traitor.* The word seared through his heart. *That's what I was, before.* He'd come to Valenna with the hope of becoming a better person, and he was about to ruin it all in anger. Whatever came afterward, Kol knew he couldn't let himself be that man anymore, that worthless, helpless traitor that Adella had found in the Campos, rain-soaked and awaiting death like the criminal he was. Acting on his anger, envy, and fear had brought him to that point, but in that pivotal moment outside of Greywood Manor when he'd decided to abandon his previous life, to part ways with who he once was, he'd promised himself that someday, he'd be a better man. That someday would have to be now. Adella would never forgive him if he gave in to his anger and killed her previous lover out of spite, and he wouldn't risk losing her forever, not as long as they had a chance of finding each other again. For once, he wanted to do what was right, even if it hurt. For her, and for himself, he had to be the better man.

"This is madness," Kol said, biting back the flood of emotion that threatened to overwhelm him. "It isn't right for us to turn on each other; we have enemies enough as it is." With the tip of his sword, he pointed to the forecastle where, beneath the swirling darkness in the twilight-green sky, the awakened dead broke through the line of Valennians at the prow and crawled over deck like ants, the waters below churning with the coils of the *pelkimund*. Turning back to meet Declan's steely gaze, he sheathed his sword. "I won't fight you."

"No!" Declan shouted, struggling to regain his feet. "You coward!"

Kol flinched at the word but stood resolute. "If you must strike me, then do it. But the Declan I know wouldn't turn his blade on an unarmed opponent." He straightened his back. "He has more honor than that."

Declan's face burned with rage, eyes bulging, as he let out a feral growl and raised his sword to strike.

Lightning flashed, glinting off metal. Thunder cracked through the heavens as steel plunged into flesh, ripping through cloth and skin.

2 0

Something Recovered

"So," a gravelly voice began, the dark tone cutting through the air like a knife. "Here you are at last." A firm hand grabbed Adella's neck, its long, cold fingers digging in and leeching the warmth from her flesh. Horror flashed through her as she recognized the voice. *Matei!*

He said something in Madorran, and metal jingled. The hands released her. Blinking the water from her eyes, she caught a glimpse of a small drawstring purse as Matei handed it to the Madorran captain, who slipped it into the pocket of his rich clothing. Her breath caught in her throat as she recognized the naked blade that hung from the captain's belt. *That's my father's saber!*

"What's this about?" she demanded. Matei turned toward her. She stifled a gasp at his strikingly bloodshot eyes. Bright scarlet surrounded flint-grey irises, and an unnatural coldness lurked in his gaze, like the eyes of a corpse. Though he met her stare, his gaze seemed to go straight through her. In one hand, held protectively over his heart, he clasped something tightly, an unusual white glow emanating from within his grasp.

He caught her by the jaw, fingernails digging into her cheeks. "Shut up," he snarled, his face mere inches from hers. The stench of his foul breath hung so thickly between them she could taste the tang of decay

236

on her tongue, and her stomach heaved. "I'm just taking back what's mine."

An ear-splitting crack, loud as thunder, shattered through the din of the storm. The ship suddenly rocked sharply to one side, throwing the entire party off their feet. Adella flew sideways, landing roughly on her left side a few feet from Matei. The object he held in his hand was knocked from his grip. It slid across the deck and lay uncovered in the rain near the far rail, a soft, blue-white glow illuminating smooth, angular planes to reveal a double-pointed crystal, clear as glass. Matei cried out in surprise and crawled toward it on his elbows as the green-clad crew about them flew into a panic of motion.

Adella's jaw fell open when she noticed what he scrambled after. *That crystal...* she realized, pulse surging through her veins as she re-called the glowing jewel depicted upon the pages of the Codex, rays of golden ink radiating from its facets, *it's the Heart of the World!* Guilt struck like a blow to the gut; he held the legendary object only because of her. *I should've listened to Kol all those months ago while we were travel-ing across the Campos,* she berated herself. He'd urged her to turn back, but she didn't listen. It was she who'd brought Leveret's Key to Sornia; it was her fault Matei now held the powerful object.

The desperate urge to try to take it from him nearly overwhelmed her, but Adella pushed herself up and looked astern for the source of the noise. She let out a sharp gasp to see the bow of a great ship had smashed through the rail, splintering the hull and biting deep into the weather deck. From the oncoming prow that loomed over-head, sailors in scarlet dropped down onto the caravel and drew their swords. They flooded the deck, cutting down any unfortunate Sorni-ans in their path. High above, sails with red and black stripes hung from the masts of the attacking vessel, with one tattered and flapping.

"*The Tigress!*" she blurted out in surprise. There was still hope. She searched around for Endlebridge and spotted him still lying by the rail, bracing his ribs. Running to his side, she grabbed his arm and helped him to his feet. A scream rang out behind her; a backward glance revealed the Madorran captain now clutched his belly as a Valennian in scarlet drew back a bloodied cutlass.

If we can just make it aboard The Tigress, *we might be safe.* Given that Kol had set forth to purchase the ship, there was a good chance he was on board. *Or even part of the boarding party.* Adella's heart leapt at the thought of seeing him again. She searched the chaotic scene for a sign of him, but all about her was a blur of rain and confusion. No sight of him left her torn between relief and worry, but there was nothing for it; she needed to get the injured Endlebridge to safety. Stopping beside the fallen Madorran, she pulled her father's saber from his hand and slipped it carefully under her belt. From his bare neck, her mother's ruby glistened in the dull twilight. Grabbing it, she snapped the chain and, pocketing the necklace, returned to Endlebridge's side. "Come," she urged, carefully pulling him up by the arm. "Now's our chance."

Leaving Matei scrambling for the crystal in the confusion, they stumbled across the deck toward the prow of *The Tigress.* The planks beneath their feet groaned as the larger barque, driven by tide and wind, continued to wedge into the Sornian hull. Finally, they stepped beneath the bowsprit as sailors threw down more lines and continued to swarm the caravel.

When a sailor in red dropped onto the deck before her, Adella came forward. "Please," she began, then shrieked as he rounded on her, drawing his blade. "I'm Valennian!" she shouted above the noise and confusion, putting her hands in the air.

Beneath a wide cocked hat, the sailor's brow furrowed. "Is that you, cousin?" a youthful voice asked in disbelief, strands of wet blond hair clinging to his face as he looked her up and down from saber to jacket. "I thought you were a sailor."

"Yul!" she exclaimed, letting out a breath. "Oh, thank goodness." In a wash of relief, she wrapped her arms hastily around the boy for a brief moment. "This is Lord Endlebridge of Pentz," she said as she drew back, gesturing to the man beside her. "He's hurt; we must get him aboard somehow."

Yul nodded and turned to grab a rope. Working quickly, he tied it in a loop and lowered it around Endlebridge's waist, positioning it like a seat at the back of his legs.

"Haul up!" he shouted, and soon the rope rose in the air, hoisting Endlebridge slowly up the prow.

"Stop them!" Matei's voice cut through the rain. Adella turned to see a flood of green-clad men rush forward at his orders. They appeared to be a new class of soldiers, with various blades hanging heavily on their belts, unlike the more sparsely armed Sornian sailors. Behind them, Matei slowly stepped through the din, stalking across the crowded deck toward her, the crystal glowing brighter in his hand with each stride.

"Go," Yul urged, passing her a rope. He readied his sword. "I'll slow them down."

Adella shook her head. "No—"

"This is my duty," he interrupted, pressing her hand tighter around the rope. "Yours lies elsewhere. Now, go!"

Reluctantly, she obeyed, and, taking the rope in both hands, began to climb. Catching it between her feet, she forced her aching arms to pull her upward bit by bit. As she crept up the side of *The Tigress*, the air around her darkened further, suddenly taking on an eerie emerald hue. Adella paused to give her sore muscles some relief, dangling precariously over the Sornian deck, and glanced at the turmoil below.

Amid the clash of Valennian Royal Guard, sailors and Sornian soldiers, bodies clad in emerald, scarlet, and blue lay where they had fallen, motionless on the deck, surrounded by puddles of crimson. *So many dead.* She shook her head.

Yet even as she watched, the slain suddenly began to revive. Moving as one, they rose to their feet, the whites of their dead eyes flashing brightly in the gloom. Wounds gaped, fresh and ragged, as blood continued to pour from them, darkening the rain at their feet. Slashes, like misplaced smiles, marked their necks and brows as the dull-eyed dead, wearing all colors, picked up their weapons once more. Some resumed their fights with the few surviving sailors, but many trudged single-mindedly toward *The Tigress*, swords clutched firmly in their hands.

Adella's heart plummeted, her head swimming with sudden dizziness at the surreal sight. For a moment, her grip on the rope slackened as terror flooded through her from head to toe. "How...?" The word escaped her lips, barely audible over the shouts and groans, the rain and wind.

Below, a steely gaze tinged with blood caught her eye; she looked down to see Matei grinning cruelly up at her, the stone in his hand glowing brightly. But the larger scene still demanded her attention; for every soldier or sailor that mortally fell among the fray, another body arose. Driven by unseen forces, they shuffled ominously forward, making their way toward her and Matei. She shook her head again, trying to make sense of the scene before her. *How is this possible? What has Matei done?*

Movement directly below drew her eye again. Dangling from her rope, Adella watched helplessly as Matei closed his eyes and lifted the stone high over his head. Its verdant light increased, flaring so brightly that it cast shadows on the deck below her. The enlivened dead flooded toward the prow of *The Tigress*, heedless of the Valennian sailors' blades that hacked and stabbed at them as they went.

Stifling a scream, she turned her attention to the rope again and furiously climbed until she finally came to the ship's forepeak. She grabbed the bowsprit netting and hauled herself onto the headrails of *The Tigress*. Cringing inwardly at the stench, she crawled on her elbows over the grating through the seats of ease, where the sailors relieved themselves, and tumbled onto the foredeck.

Above *The Tigress*, black clouds hung low over the battered red and black sails. Lightning flashed, briefly illuminating the decks in bright white. Pushing past rushing sailors, Adella paused beside the forecastle ladder to catch her racing breath and searched through the tumult.

Kol is here somewhere, she told herself, desperately hoping it was true. *He must be...*

For the moment, she brushed that thought aside as she owed it to Lord Endlebridge to make sure he was safe. Near the companionway, he was being escorted by sailors in red. Quickly, Adella picked herself up and hurried after him into the dark of the below decks.

"Put him in the captain's quarters," she ordered. It didn't matter who might be berthed there, whether Kol or Declan; it was the best place for the injured man to rest.

"What's going on out there?" a strange voice demanded as the door opened. An old man rose from the table, grey hair hanging limply over dark eyes. His Sornian accent was much like Kol's. Beside him sat another man, nervously whittling a seashell.

"There's a battle going on," she replied, eyeing them reproachfully as the sailors helped Endlebridge to the captain's berth. "Arm yourselves and get up there." Shouldering past the old man as he rushed out, she went to Endlebridge's side.

"Go," he insisted, patting her hand. "I'll be fine." His breathing was labored and he winced with each word.

"You'll be as safe here as anywhere," she said, glancing at the open door. Heavy, haphazard footsteps came from above decks.

"Let me rest," he replied. "There's nothing more you can do for me."

With that, Adella spun on her heel, hand moving to her saber hilt, and rushed above decks. Metal against metal rang loudly from starboard, and she whirled around. Lightning flashed again, revealing two sailors in combat. One man gripped the shrouds at the rail as he parried his sword against the other; the man bearing down on him with his cutlass wore a large, cocked hat. *The captain's hat,* she realized. *That's Declan!*

Before she could move, screams erupted across the ship. Spinning again, her mouth gaped at the sight of the risen dead now flooding over the bow in a surge of writhing limbs. The crew that had held them back from overtaking *The Tigress* were forced aside, some fleeing in terror across the deck, others turning to fight against the on-slaught.

Another clang of metal brought her attention back to the two fig-ures to starboard who were still locked in combat. The man pressed against the rail, dressed in the scarlet jacket of the Royal Guard, quailed beneath the ferocious blows of the captain's cutlass, his strength clearly wavering with each harried strike. Adella squinted, trying to make out his face. *Who is Declan fighting?*

With a violent kick out, the man at the shrouds forced Declan to retreat back a few steps. Pushing off the rail, he rose, revealing his full height, and leveled his sword at the captain. Adella's eyes quickly traced the line from the blade up to the man's face. A heavy weight dropped into the pit of her stomach as she recognized his features. *Kol!*

Frozen in place, she held her breath as he turned his arms outward, pointing his blade away from Declan's face.

"I won't fight you," Kol's voice carried through the rain as he sheathed his weapon.

Slowly, Declan stalked forward, raising his sword.

"No!" Adella shouted, but her cry was swallowed up in the din of the storm. Bursting into motion, she ran frantically toward them, drawing her father's saber from her belt.

Declan slashed his blade through the rain.

Lightning flashed on metal as steel sank into flesh, and a ragged scream rang out over the decks of *The Tigress*.

21

The Tower

Armand awoke shivering on the hard floor. He had dreamed of Elldon again, and his peaceful little cottage on the grounds of Greywood Manor. The dream had been so pleasant that it took him a moment to recall where he was. *Oh, right,* he groaned to himself. *Locked in the tower.* His cottage was gone; it had long since burned to the ground in the war with Sornia. He sighed, rubbing the sleep from his eyes.

He'd been in the tower for days now, maybe weeks. He wasn't sure. The thought was beginning to settle into his mind that perhaps help wasn't coming after all. It'd been so long that the lidless brass chamber pot, which had been clean when he'd arrived, now reeked foully. Each time the door to their prison opened, his hopes momentarily rose that it would be the Queen, or Margo's husband, Lord Rolan, or even Miss Adella—anyone—coming to release them, but it always turned out to be just a Royal Guard stopping in only to slide a pewter plate of food beneath his door, along with a fresh canteen of water. He was grateful for that, at least. Wincing at the pain that flared in his back, he sat up.

"Are you awake?" Margo's gentle voice asked from across the dark space.

He murmured a groggy reply as he sat for a moment, letting his brain grapple with the disappointment of waking to the same surroundings again. "Won't Rolan find out you're in trouble?" he asked at last. "I'm sure he could get us out of here."

She sighed heavily. "I don't think so. He's still with the children in the Hartwicks. It will take some time before he realizes I'm not answering his letters. Ugh," she groaned. "I wish I'd been more prompt with my correspondences."

Rising to his feet, he lifted up onto his toes and pulled up on the stone ledge of the window until he could just see over the edge. He peered through the bars of his window, down over the rooftops of the palace and surrounding town, all the way down the gently sloping bluffs beyond the Royal Palace and out to the overly full harbor. Outside the city, strange ships had gathered across the water, crowding the Valennian vessels moored at the flooded docks. Some were still arriving, their shapes merely black shadows in the distance. It was too far to make out the colors of their flags. *Could they all be Valennian?* Armand doubted it. But he kept his observations to himself. He couldn't be sure, and there was no need to worry Miss Margo for naught.

"What of the war?" Margo prodded, seeming to read his mind. "Do you think it'll amount to anything?"

"Eh," he muttered, shrugging as he lowered himself back to the floor, wincing on the way down. "Sornia's been at odds with Valenna for ages. Nothing ever comes of it." Yet even as he said it, he frowned. His mind slipped back to the crowded harbor. This time, something seemed different somehow. He didn't want to frighten her, though, and held his tongue.

"I hope you're right," she said softly.

"You know, this reminds me of the time your mother was locked in the dungeon," Armand mused, grasping for a change in subject as he wrapped his arms around his knees for warmth. He'd heard the note of despair in her voice; perhaps a story from home would comfort her.

"I haven't heard that story since I was little," she replied, voice brightening. "What happened? How'd she get out?"

"Well..." he began with a smile. "It was a long time ago, right after King Rickan's coronation. Your father, Lord Grimless, had only met Kat about a month before, but he was already smitten with her beauty. Thick as thieves they would eventually become, but at that time, they barely knew each other. He only knew that, for him, it was love at first sight.

"But even back then, Lord Hollen was making trouble," he went on, warming to his tale. "At the time, the High Council was for the King and Lords only; women weren't permitted to attend, not even Queen Ellinora. It was eventually due to her persuasion that a lot of the laws of inheritance and such were changed, which led to the office of Queen having far more rights and responsibilities, including the ability to sit upon the throne herself if need be. That's how she became regent after both Rickan and Harrian died. Some people resented that move, believing Lord Hollen was the better choice as Harrian's cousin; they claimed she had no right to the throne because she was Queen by marriage, not by birthright..."

"Armand," Margo interrupted gently. "I realize we're stuck here indefinitely, but please, get to the good part."

Hearing the smile in her voice, he let out a chuckle. "Right. So, as I said, things were different back then. Queen Ellinora's reach was restricted—but that didn't mean she was without her own resources. Due to illness, Queen Ellinora had to remain in the Capital during King Rickan's coronation tour. With Kat being cousin to Harrian, she was also good friends with the Queen, so she hired Kat to spy for her. Your mother went covert, pretending to be a supporter of Lord Hollen's. Unfortunately, her deceit was discovered, and Lord Hollen had Kat imprisoned in the dungeon and charged with treason. He left her there, awaiting punishment, which was scheduled to take place before the King's return.

"Your father was determined to get her out, and soon enough, he came up with a plan—one that also involved me, of course. At the time, the Capital had this fierce old woman overseeing the scullion maids, whose duties included scrubbing the prison floors. One day, while I took the old woman to *The King's Garters* and got her blighting drunk with rounds of gin, Grimless snuck into her chambers and put on her clothing, lace cap and all, and when it came time to clean the dungeon cells, he snuck Kat a scullery disguise. They both walked out with no trouble. The best part about it is no one was any the wiser, even with his full mustache," Armand chuckled. "Soon after, King Rickan returned to the Capital from his travels abroad and had her pardoned."

"That was a ridiculous scheme for you two to try with her life at stake," Margo replied with a laugh. "I can't believe that's the whole story."

"Sure it was," he countered.

"I miss him," Margo said after a brief silence, sadness weighing down her words. "Father. And Mother, too. I miss them both."

"So do I." Armand sighed. He'd lost many friends in his years, but none as fine as the friend he'd had in Grimless. *At least I still have the memories.* The truth was, many years had passed, and sometimes tales changed in the telling. But he would keep telling those stories as best he could, for they were all he had. The thought struck him painfully. *In the end, our stories are all that's left.*

* * *

"Armand," Margo whispered. "Do you hear that?"

His eyes blinked open in the darkness of night and he paused, listening. A distant murmur of crashing waves filled the silence. Strange ships still filled the harbor outside, infusing the entire Royal Palace of the Ansebulet with a sense of tense anticipation. He didn't blame Miss Margo for being on edge. He was, too. "It's just the sea," he said gently, hoping to ease her worry.

"No, not that," she whispered urgently. "Listen."

He cocked his head and listened again. Faintly, between the distant roar of waves, voices rose in the night. "It sounds like—" An orange light flared beyond the window above his head, followed by the crash of breaking stone. He rose slowly to his feet, lower back panging sharply from so many days spent on the stone floor. Straining up onto his toes, he grabbed the cold stone sill and pulled up. Peering out between the iron bars, an odd glare hit his eyes. At the docks, an eerie light hung over the Bay, though he couldn't descry the source.

"What can you see?" Margo asked, but Armand didn't reply. Up the steeply rising shoreline, just outside the walls of the palace, he watched as the gable of a townhouse blazed with fire; with each gust of wind, the flames spread further along the roofline. His stomach dropped. In the distance, from seaward, a ball of light arced through the air, then landed in the street before the palace gates, catching wooden carts and signs ablaze. Screams of people fleeing its path pierced the night.

Stone rumbled as their tower shuddered from another blow, and Armand fell back onto the floor, groaning at the pain that flashed up his spine. From across the musty space, iron squealed, and the door burst open and two shadowy figures strode in silently.

One, a woman in voluminous skirts, approached his door with the jangle of keys. A golden flash shimmered on her brow. "Come," she whispered, inserting a key into the lock as her companion stepped beside her. "Let's get you out of here." The barred iron door of Armand's cell swung open, and her companion's strong hands helped him to his feet.

"Wait," Armand said urgently, nodding across the space. "Miss Margo."

The figure with the keyring went to the other cell and quickly unlocked Margo's door.

"We have to get out of here," the strange woman ordered, her voice craggy with age. "The Capital is under attack; they've got the palace surrounded." Orange light lit the windows again, revealing a golden crown glittering upon her head.

"Queen Ellinora," Margo said with astonishment as she joined them, then made a hasty bow. "Your Majesty—"

"No time for that," the Queen interrupted, stowing the keyring in a large haversack before tucking it protectively under her arm. "We must hurry."

They hurried down the spiral staircase, now filled with the smell of smoke; the arrow slits in the thick stone walls revealed bright flashes of fire as Queen Ellinora led the way into the darkness. The man before Armand, his dusky skin shining in the scant, intermittent light from outside, felt both foreign and familiar; when he glanced back at them over his shoulder, Armand recognized the stout, lined face of Captain Jago. He had met Jago that spring, upon the island of the Cairn, where the old Andolinian refugee had spent many years as the queen's personal guard. *Of course,* Armand recalled; *the man would never leave her side.* Jago had clearly taken his Royal Guard duties to heart.

Dodging armed guards that ran to and fro in a panic, shouting orders to each other, the four made their way through the dark halls with Queen Ellinora guiding the way, turning them down one corridor after another. Finally, they came to the vast, columned antechamber outside the throne room, softly illuminated by sconces that lined the walls, and approached the large pair of doors leading to the palace entrance.

Suddenly, a thunderous pounding struck the doors from the outside. Armand and the others were pushed back as a group of Royal Guards ran in from the far hallway and rushed forward, bracing themselves against the heavy wood. Another crash came from the outside, slamming the doors into the shoulders of the guards pressed against it. Wooden splinters bristled around the thick, iron latch and the hinges on both sides as the doors bowed inward, threatening to give way. With one final, powerful blow, Sornian Soldiers burst through, flinging open and throwing the guards to the stone floor. A sea of green jackets spilled into the antechamber. As emerald and scarlet collided beneath the hanging banners, swords glinted in the dim light amid cries of rage and pain.

From their position in the shadows, Jago silently waved a hand. "Go back," he ordered in his heavy accent, keeping his voice low. "The way we came."

A bolt whizzed by Armand's head as he turned, just missing his scalp. "Go!" he urged Margo, propelling her forward by the shoulder. They fled as more bolts flew in their direction, missed shots clattering loudly as they skimmed across the stone floor.

After a few twists and turns, Ellinora began to slow, her breath coming in ragged gasps. Armand and Jago exchanged a glance, then stepped toward her, both offering her their arms. "That way," she ordered, her voice weak as she pointed down an adjoining hallway. Nearly lifting her from the floor, they carried on, Ellinora leaning heavily on them for support.

Soon they came to a long, dark corridor lit only by the outside light from the high windows, its walls lined with decorative gilt molding. Halfway down, Queen Ellinora spoke again. "Stop here," she ordered, her labored breath now coming in panting hitches. She released their arms and placed her palm against the wall, slumping heavily forward while her other hand pried at the corners of the molding nearby. Finally, she turned a small piece of carved wood, and with a click, a section of the wall swung ajar. "There it is," she breathed, leaning her shoulder against the wall for a moment before sliding to the floor.

"Ellinora," Jago uttered, voice thick with worry as he knelt beside her.

"You must get them to safety," she said softly, her arms wrapped around her abdomen. In the scant light beneath the window, a dark liquid seeped through her fingers.

"What is it?" Jago asked, more of a demand than a question, as he pulled her arms gently away from her belly. Embedded deep in her gut, the butt of a crossbow bolt stuck out from her flesh, staining the golden silk of her bodice. "No," he gasped, horror in his voice.

Dropping to his knees on Ellinora's other side, Armand's heart hammered wildly. *Not the queen...* he pleaded silently. *Not now.* Beside him, Margo let out a gasp, the sound tapering off into a shuddering sob.

With a meaningful look at Jago, Ellinora pulled her haversack from over her shoulder with a grimace. She looked up at Armand, then pressed the weighty object into his arms. "You must get this to Lady Grimless," Ellinora said faintly, her eyelids fluttering. "She'll know what to do."

"No!" Jago cried, reaching for her hands. "I won't leave you."

"Jago," she began gently. With an effort, she raised a hand to his cheek, wiping away a tear with her thumb. "You've spent too much of your life by my side; I won't have you die that way." She flinched as she bent forward, extending her other arm. "Dear friend," she whispered, touching her forehead to his as he leaned in to meet her. "I need you to continue on, to see this through to the end."

"I can't—not without you—" he began, emotion choking off his words.

"You must," she replied, her voice fading to a whisper. "You, more than anyone, know what's at stake." With a gasp and a small cry, she leaned back against the wall. Her eyes fluttered closed, and she gave a small sigh. Her head fell to one side and the narrow golden crown that had glistened on her brow slipped from its perch, clattering loudly onto the stone floor.

"*No!*" Jago screamed, a deep, guttural shout rising from within him. Face distorting with grief, he grasped both her arms, then reverently cradled her head in his hands, kissing her forehead as tears poured down his face.

Behind him, Margo stifled another sob as voices echoed down the hall.

"We've got to go," Armand urged, feeling the tightness in his throat as he held back a sob of his own. He glanced over his shoulder as the shouts grew louder. Rapid footsteps approached, and the slither of metal against metal carried down the hall. "Now!" He slung the haversack over his shoulder and, prying the man's arms from the Queen's form, grabbed Jago and pulled him to his feet, shoving him toward the secret opening in the wall. "Go on," he said, urging Jago into the dark space just as a loud boom shook the walls, raining bits of plaster and dust down on their shoulders.

"Uh," Margo began hesitantly. "Are you quite sure—"

"Get in," Armand ordered, pushing her into the passageway before slipping inside himself. He pulled the panel shut behind them and it locked into place with a click just as the sound of footsteps rounded the corner.

"No," Jago moaned, pressing against the hidden doorway. "Ellinora..."

"We have to keep going," Armand said urgently, taking him by the arm and pulling him down the black passageway.

"I can't see," Margo whispered.

"No need to see," Armand instructed. "Just stick your hand out and follow the wall." Earlier that spring, only a few months ago, he'd come down this very passage, sneaking into the palace behind the Queen, along with Adella, Kol, Jago, and the others from the Cairn on a mission to reclaim the Valennian throne. At the time, he hadn't even realized who Ellinora was. It had come as quite a surprise to discover she was the Queen as they fought off Lord Hollen and his supporters.

Leading the others, Armand crept carefully through the corridor in total darkness, the ground rising and falling beneath their feet as they walked. The air was damp and chill, sinking into his bones and sending shivers down his back. From time to time, a rumble would emanate from the stone above their heads, and bits of rock and dirt fell, littering their shoulders. Each time, he cringed, wondering if the whole palace would collapse upon them, crushing them inside the tunnel.

The way through the passage felt longer than Armand remembered, but soon, he stubbed his toes on something solid. Falling forward, he caught himself on rough stone and, feeling steps beneath his hands, began to climb upward. When the empty space above his head gave way to a wooden platform, he pressed upward against it, shoving it aside.

As he pulled himself up through the small opening in the floor, faint light spilled in from around a door ahead that opened to the outside world. Just as he recalled from his last time there, they had emerged inside a small, musty woodshed.

Quickly, he reached down to help Margo and Jago out of the square-shaped hole, then replaced the wooden covering and flung the dusty rug that had been displaced back over it, concealing the tunnel beneath. Carefully, he pushed open the shed door, and they stepped out into the open air beyond the Ansebulet's walls. Thick smoke immediately stung their throats even through the heavy rain, and Armand coughed, eyes watering as he put his sleeve to his nose and peeked through the branches of the tall cedar trees that surrounded the shed.

Before him, the harbor lay spread out as the land sloped downward toward Belgrand Bay, the shoreline littered with ships of varying sizes, all crowding the waters haphazardly. In the orange light of one burning vessel, a familiar pattern caught his eye—red and black stripes. *The Tigress!* The prow of the Valennian barque seemed to be embedded into the side of a Sornian caravel at the edge of the fray; beyond it lay open sea. *If we could just get to* The Tigress *somehow...*

"Come on," he said, turning back to the others. "We need to get to the docks."

"Are you daft?" Margo exclaimed. "You'd be running straight into the fight! Come with me," she pleaded, taking his hand and tugging gently. "I've got to get back to my family in the Hartwicks, beyond the north gate." She nodded in the other direction.

Armand shook his head. "I can't. The Queen commanded me to take this to Miss Adella," he said, lifting the laden haversack. "*The Tigress* is my best chance to find her."

"Then..." Margo began, her lips turning downward, "We must part ways here."

"You can't travel alone!" he countered sharply. "It isn't safe. Come with us."

"I know the Capital by heart," she replied. "I could make it with my eyes closed. I must get to my family and see that they're safe. Please," she pleaded, dropping his hand and throwing her arms around him, "take care of my sister, and yourself."

"I'll do my best," he replied, tears springing to his eyes as he squeezed her tightly in return. "Like always." Reluctantly, he released her. "Now go on," he urged, "and be careful!" A burst of firelight from the Bay illuminated her back as she disappeared into the shadows beneath the tall evergreens on the other side of the shed.

"Come on," Armand whispered to Jago. The man followed numbly behind him as he led them toward the churning water and the clash of battle in the Bay, the ongoing fires in the distance lighting their way. They hurried through the streets, now filled with battle rubble and scattered, lifeless bodies, ducking behind abandoned carriages and merchant crates whenever a group of Sornians, announced by their foreign accents, ran past.

Only two now, they drew no attention among the fervent disorder of the harbor as they hurried along the wharf. Armand frowned as a strange, green light settled over them, casting their surroundings in an unnatural glow that grew in intensity the closer they got to the docks. The light seemed to come from one ship in particular, far out among the many vessels that littered the waters—the very one into which *The Tigress* pressed her prow, slowly displacing it from its anchorings. He squinted, then deepened his frown. By the rig of its sails, it appeared to be Sornian.

Coming to the eastern end of the wharf, he spotted one small boat that had been abandoned in the turmoil and headed straight for it. Slinging the haversack from his shoulder, he set it inside, then turned to Jago, urging him in.

"No—" Jago's voice broke as he resisted. Shaking his head, he crumpled to his knees, the Queen's red handprint still staining his cheek. "I can't. Not without her."

"You must. Do you think she'd want you to die here?" Armand pleaded. "She wouldn't, and you know it. Now get up," he ordered. "I need your help."

Reluctantly, Jago allowed himself to be led onto the boat. Taking up the oars, they rowed between the larger ships, weaving precariously through the channels between massive hulls, passing beneath boarding parties rushing across gang-boards. Cringing at the thought of being crushed between vessels, Armand rowed faster while all around them, ballista balls flew, raining down into the water with loud splashes or cracking into the tall ships that loomed overhead.

"Where to?" Jago called out over the thunder of sea and storm. Armand looked quickly about. All was confusion and shadow, flickering lightning and the clash of steel. Then, as they emerged beyond the prow of one large caravel, painted sails rose above them; though tattered and ragged with holes, their red and black stripes could still clearly be seen, whipping like a battle flag in the stormy wind.

"There!" Armand shouted over the din. "Head for *The Tigress!*"

2 2

Unraveling

Declan's blade sliced through the air as Adella lunged between him and Kol, plunging her drawn saber deep into Declan's thigh. Letting out a ragged scream, he staggered back a few steps, then twisted in her direction, pushing off his uninjured leg to throw his elbow into her chest, toppling her backward onto the deck. Her teeth jarred together at the painful impact, and her saber slipped from her hands, sliding out of reach.

"Adella!" Kol shouted, drawing his sword as Declan rounded on her with his cutlass.

"You," Declan snarled down at her through clenched jaws, his once-handsome face now twisted with rage. She scrambled backward on her hands, pulse surging through her veins as he approached. Just inches from her fingertips lay her saber, its silver steel gleaming in the green twilight.

Adella glanced back at Declan, who hadn't noticed the blade so close. "You were supposed to be mine!" he shouted, raising his cutlass high above his head, poised to strike. "Along with your gold," he added, "so I could buy back *The Tigress*. But you had to go and ruin all of that, didn't you? By choosing *him!*" he shrieked, voice so full of fury that each word struck like a blow.

She shrank back from the assault. Tears sprang into her eyes with the full meaning of what he'd said. *He never really wanted to marry me at all; it was only about the money...* Anger rose within her at the thought. She felt like a fool. Naively, she'd given herself to him on more than one occasion, believing the sentiment between them to be mutual. *And the whole time, I was no more than a means to an end for him.* Blinking back her tears, she slid her fingers quickly over the rough wood planks until she touched cool metal.

Declan sprang into motion, throwing himself forward and sending the tip of his cutlass plunging toward her chest. Quickly, she wrapped her fingers firmly around the hilt beside her and hoisted the blade upward. His momentum gave him no time to react; the weight of his broad body drove the wet steel through his wool jacket and into his shoulder as he fell. Adella's arm drew back as metal sliced toward her, and she turned away, holding firmly onto the hilt of her blade even as the edge of his cutlass grazed the side of her neck.

Before Declan could regain his feet, Kol slammed into his side, sending them both sprawling over the deck, tearing her saber free from Declan's body and leaving the bloodied blade in her hand. A volley of lightning blazed through the dark sky as the two wrestled relentlessly in the downpour, followed by a deafening crack.

She jumped to her feet, struggling to see through the rain until another flash illuminated their surroundings, then gasped to see a long, spiny shape rising out of the water and above the rail behind the two men, coming at them from the sea beyond. The *pelkimund*'s gaping jaws revealed long, jagged rows of fangs as it huffed the air, nostrils and gills flaring widely.

"Stop!" Adella ordered urgently, trying to make herself heard over the storm while keeping her voice low. "Don't move—"

Still entrenched in their fight, her warning came too late. Before the two could turn around, the beast's head shot over the rail and snapped around Declan's shoulder and arm. Panic filled his face as his free hand flung out, grappling for something to hold on to. Coming up empty, he let out a pained scream. The crew of *The Tigress* watched open-mouthed as the creature drew the captain backward and up over the rail, disappearing into the sea below.

Sucking in a ragged breath, Adella ran to Kol's side, dropping her weapon to the deck as panic flooded over her. "Are you hurt?" she asked, hands fluttering from abdomen to brow as she anxiously looked him over.

He propped himself up, wincing as he grabbed his shoulder. "Not much—"

"Thank goodness," she breathed, throwing her arms around his neck. Slowly, Kol wrapped his arms around her in return, drawing her close.

"Adella." He pulled back to look her in the eyes, placing a rough palm on her cheek. "I can't believe you're here. You found your way back to me."

"Of course," she murmured, giving him a gentle smile. "You said it first. 'Wherever you go, I will go with you.'"

Holding her gaze, he nodded, the edges of his eyes glistening, then leaned forward to kiss her forehead, then her cheek. Then, softly, he pressed his lips to hers. She melted into his arms, letting his body warm her flesh through her cold, rain-soaked clothes, until the clash of metal and cries of pain from the rest of the ship finally drew their attention back to the battle.

Kol rose slowly, the bronze of his face growing ashen as he turned to take stock of the scene aboard *The Tigress*. Collapsing in a puddle of his own blood, a Valennian dropped to his knees by his reinvigorated, dead comrade. He lay still for a moment before lumbering slowly upward again, grabbing his dropped sword. As Adella and Kol watched, the two dead soldiers slowly spun, turning in their direction.

"Shit!" Kol hissed, glancing around for his cutlass, thrown from his hand when he'd launched himself at Declan. "Why is this happening?"

"It's Matei," Adella replied, darting across the deck to grab his blade from where it had slid along the deck, then quickly retrieved her own saber. "I think he's doing this somehow with the Heart of the World," she said, handing him his weapon.

He leveled his cutlass protectively, stepping in front of Adella as the two risen bodies shuffled toward them. "What do you mean?"

"He's controlling them with it," she explained. "He's using it to awaken the dead, though they're not themselves."

"Matei?" Kol muttered, searching widely over the battle scene. "He's the one behind this? Then we need to distract him."

She shrugged helplessly, gesturing at the two dead soldiers still lumbering toward them. "But how?"

"Come on," he said, reaching back to take her by the hand. "There's no use in trying to fight them. If we want this to end, we need to get to the ballista."

"But—that's at the bow—" she protested, running to keep up as he dragged her along beside him. "That's where they're coming aboard!"

Giving her a grim smile, Kol led her across the deck, dodging and parrying the slow-reacting dead. At the forecastle ladder, they spotted a sailor in scarlet making his way down. Kol readied his cutlass, prepared to strike.

Stepping down onto the deck, the sailor turned and raised surprised, blood-smeared brows at them.

"Jon!" Kol sighed in relief.

"The Capital has been taken by the Sornians," Jon said with a frown, panting. "The Sornian flag now hangs from the ramparts of the city; Valenna has fallen. The battle is over."

"No!" Adella's heart wrenched.

"Where's the captain?" Jon asked, eyes searching the ship. "He needs to know."

"He's gone," Kol replied, his words heavy with meaning. "You're the captain now. Get us out of here."

Solemnly, Jon removed his hat and placed it over his heart. He gave a brief nod before heading astern.

Releasing Adella's hand, Kol turned toward the ladder. "Hurry," he urged over his shoulder as he began to climb. "We may be too late for Valenna, but we can still save *The Tigress*."

She followed him over the foredeck, and they ran to the ballista just as a figure climbed over the prow. A sailor in red stumbled toward them, clutching his side; a red smear marred his otherwise smooth brow, his young face framed by loose strands of wet, blond hair.

Adella froze, her heart plummeting at the sight of her injured cousin and friend. "Is he—" Unable to finish the thought, she glanced at Kol, who slowly raised his cutlass in response.

"Cousin," Yul uttered, then swayed forward.

"Yul!" Running to meet him, Adella caught him in her arms as she let out a breath. "You're alive!" Drawing back again, she steadied him, then urged him toward the forecastle ladder. "Go; get to safety!"

She returned to Kol's side to view to the Sornian caravel below, where the strange, green light emanated from a dark figure standing amidships. Seemingly heedless of the chaos that surrounded him, Matei gazed over the water to the palace in the distance. In his hand, he clutched the source of the uncanny glow, which burned like an ember of vivid green.

"There he is," Adella said, pointing. "Holding the Heart of the World."

Kol's gaze settled on Matei, illuminated in green and standing alone. "Now's our chance," he muttered. Grabbing a long, iron bolt from a barrel at the base of the ballista, he loaded it into the groove. Together, they grabbed the side cranks and turned them fervently until the bolt was fully in place. "Help me aim." Crouching, he pushed the rear support forward, lowering the stock.

As the front of the ballista sank down, Adella squinted down the stock until Matei came into view, the side of his fiendish face checkered with black shadow and emerald light. "Stop there!" she called out as the bolt lined up with its target. She stepped back. "Release!"

23

The Golden Crown

With the crystal singing in his palm, the dead around him rose, obedient and malleable. *Fight,* Matei ordered, and he felt their slow-moving flesh shuffle into motion. As with the corpses in the graveyard, he could feel each death-stroke they had suffered. Though it was phantom pain which caused him no physical harm, many of them had died brutally, and together, their combined anguish stabbed through him, nearly overwhelming his senses in a flood of pain. For a moment, his control slipped, and all at once, the sights and sounds of the battle engulfed him: The screams of the injured and dying, the clang of metal, the crack of lightning, and the pummel of driving rain all came at him through a multitude of empty minds, bursting into his own with feverish intensity. He could even sense the sharp minds of hungry sea creatures deep below, gathered in large numbers beneath the ships in the harbor, drawn by the scent of blood. He reeled for a moment at the onslaught of sensory input, struggling to maintain his hold. Though he'd practiced relentlessly his connection with the Heartstone since it had come into his possession, he'd never before attempted it while faced with this level of turmoil before.

Closing his eyes, he gripped the crystal tightly, allowing its familiar, smooth facets to calm and orient him. Breath by breath, his control returned, and soon the pain of the dead ebbed until he was able to push it aside with his mind even as the battle raged on.

With the dead in his command handling the living that surrounded him, he sent his mind beyond the chaos that filled the harbor and up the hill, into the minds of those still protecting the Royal Palace. An evil grin played on his lips as he witnessed the bloodshed there. At this rate, there would be no Valennians left by the time he took the throne.

Suddenly, through it all, he found one beacon of energy that stood vividly out from the rest. This person wore a crown. Or they had, at least, until recently. He received brief flashes of an opulent life, spent in glittering, silken courts, before it was interrupted by a sharp pain that pierced through the body, echoing in his own abdomen. *A king... No, a queen.* He groaned as the scenes continued to come, feeling an intense, aching love for her people and her homeland throughout his whole being. Involuntarily, he clutched his own stomach and doubled over, unprepared for the sudden onslaught of emotions—feelings he'd longed for all his life but had never really come to know—along with the pain of her death-blow.

Again he felt for the crystal in his palm, allowing it to ground him as he shoved the unfamiliar emotions away. He replaced them instead with the burning hatred that so often consumed him, focusing on what the scenes he'd seen meant. *Their queen is dead. The throne is empty.* Alongside his rage, a surge of elation swept through him. The throne was his... almost. There was only one thing left.

He returned his attention to his surroundings aboard *The Fury*, where the dead still obeyed his will. They hacked and stabbed at the enemy as they turned to retreat. Across the water on a nearby Sornian caravel, his father stood by the helm, shouting commands from the weather deck. Lightning split the dark night, illuminating his stout silhouette. *Father,* he sneered to himself. *Some father you've been. You only wanted me when you had nothing else.* Thanks to King Berento, Matei had spent his life locked away, forgotten and alone; it was only after the death of his half-brother that King Berento had shown any interest in him. He didn't seem to suspect Matei at all.

However, any goodwill he'd extended was too little, too late. It was time for his father to pay for his misdeeds. *I should be the one to rule Valenna anyway. Look what I've done to earn it!* Any fool could see Sornia's achievements were thanks to him and his efforts with the crystal. If it were up to his father, they'd still be back where they started. *But it doesn't matter whether I'm Crown Prince Matei or not,* he fumed to himself, remembering past injustices. *They still see me as "Matei the Bastard."* Anger surged through his heart, heating the blood that tingled through his veins. He gripped the crystal more tightly against his palm. *Even now, they still can't see that I'm the one holding all the power.*

Taking a deep breath, Matei closed his eyes, forcing himself to focus as he sent his mind out through the dark, murky waters of the harbor, alive with the thrumming vitality of countless creatures. He was searching for one in particular. Not quite fish nor serpent, the *pelkimund* sang with an ancient savagery that no other living being bore. Connecting to it felt like taking the reins of the very soil beneath his feet, or forcing the hand of *Mundil* herself. With the battle raging on the decks above, the whole bay was filled with the primal chorus of their ferocious minds, so focused on their feeding that their awareness of him was fleeting. One after another, they darted their long, lithe bodies up out of the water, snatching at unfortunate sailors who stood too close to the rails.

Focusing, Matei found the mind of one specific beast, its belly still ravenously empty as it approached the battle. Quickly, he sent his awareness into the creature's mind, and the connection snapped into place. Fangs flashed in his mind's eye as a sharp hunger clawed his gut. *Got you,* he smiled to himself. The creature's eyes were his eyes, its limbs his own, and he paddled with small, dull flippers through the chilly depths beneath the ships, weaving his long, massive body between the anchor rodes. He surfaced beside several smaller boats, all filled with the musky scent of man. The piercing smell of fresh blood, and the tang of metal permeated the salty air. The *pelkimund* he possessed sniffed the wind, and his stomach grumbled.

Don't get distracted. He willed the creature onward, searching just above the surface of the water with its large, flat eyes, seeking the distinct prow of his father's ship. The animal blinked, then focused. It was harder for it to see detail above the waterline, but soon, Matei found what he was looking for and directed the creature forward.

Lifting its head high above the surface this time, the *pelkimund* snuffed the air. On the deck of his father's caravel, sailors scattered, their shouts of alarm reverberating through his brain. One man stood resolute, though whether his father's resolve stemmed from surprise or hubris, Matei couldn't guess; the stench of fear seeped from him just as thickly as every other human aboard.

Staring at his father, his anger suddenly mounted. With a cry of righteous vengeance, voiced as a massive roar from the throat of the creature he possessed, Matei sent the *pelkimund* lunging toward the deck, jaws snapping. King Berento's terror-stricken face was the last thing Matei saw before he released his hold on the creature's mind, leaving nature to take its course.

Returning to his own body, Matei grinned darkly. Now nothing would stand between him and the throne he'd rightfully earned.

He returned his attention once more to his own ship, already contemplating who he would take ashore with him to claim the throne, when the hairs on his neck suddenly rose. *Adella.* He knew it was her without looking; her presence called to him, like the dance of an insect on a single strand of a spiderweb. Even the gentlest touch summoned the spider.

He turned in the direction he sensed her presence. A dark shape flew through the air toward him, slicing across his flesh in a blinding burst of pain, knocking him backward. A scream tore from his lungs as Matei collapsed to the ground, grabbing at his face with both hands as the crystal fell to the planks at his feet. His connection to the Heartstone broke at once, its eerie light snuffing out like the flame of a candle, leaving darkness all around. Across the decks of the caravel and the ship above, the dead he'd commanded suddenly dropped where they stood, surrounding him with the simultaneous thud of fallen bodies.

Clutching his face, he looked up between fingers covered in blood. Ahead, staring down at him boldly from the prow of the enemy ship, was that damned Valennian woman. He spat a mouthful of blood to the side, watching as she and some nameless soldier darted out of sight.

He prodded his wound gently, feeling a large slash deep through his left cheek, revealing peaks of jagged, broken bone. *My face! It's ruined.* Hatred curdled his stomach as the warm blood spread through his fingers, dripping down his wrists. For a moment, he wavered, torn between the desire to go after her and capture his wayward property and the imminent victory that lay before him.

Maybe I can do both. Gritting his teeth against the pain, he knelt down and grabbed the crystal again, clutching it to his chest as he stood. Tentatively, he reached for it with his mind, but each time he tried, the searing pain in his face stole his attention away. The slash throbbed with the sting of rain and wind upon open flesh. The thought of Adella landing a blow that would leave a mark upon his face forever filled him with indignant rage, clouding his mind; despite his desire to enact his revenge as soon as possible, he was unable to focus. For the moment, he was powerless. *Forget it,* he sneered to himself, pocketing the stone. *There will be time to deal with her later; I have greater matters to attend to right now.* He turned his gaze northward. In the distance, the imposing fortress of the Royal Palace rose high above the sea. Though they'd fought a hard fight, the Valennians had lost, and now their throne was empty. With his father now dead, it was his for the taking.

"Ready the boat!" Matei shouted over the roar of the storm. Striding across the wet deck, he entered the main cabin of the sterncastle, where Lucas and Teressa awaited him. They jumped up at his entrance.

"It's done," Matei said flatly as the door fell shut behind him.

"Your face!" Lucas gasped. The color drained from Teressa's cheeks as she put a hand to her mouth, gagging.

"Never mind that," Matei replied, wiping the blood with his sleeve. He grabbed a cloth that lay on the berth, tore it, and pressed a strip to his cheek. "Valenna is ours. Come," he ordered with a flick of his hand.

They followed him above decks, where lightning flashed over the dark harbor. The ship's boat, which had been ferrying marine soldiers to shore, drew alongside *The Fury*. The weather deck had been cleared of fighting; the few Valennians left had retreated to the prow of the Valennian barque that loomed above them, which was slowly drawing backward from the battered caravel. *Let them go,* Matei told himself. *They won't get far.* Adella was still on board, he knew that much; he could sense her distinct energy signature without even trying. It was different from the others, and not only for being a woman. Something about her entire being felt diametrically opposed to his own, as though fate itself had formed her solely to be his enemy. As badly as he wanted to put his hand around her throat, especially now that she'd left this gruesome mark on his face, it would have to wait until after he had the throne. *No matter,* he consoled himself. *She can't hide from me.* He reached for the weight of the Heartstone in his pocket; its hard surfaces felt still and cold.

Matei climbed over the rail and down the rope ladder into the ship's boat, taking a seat on the thwart as Lucas and Teressa joined him. The crewman who worked the oar beside him wore a scabbard at his side. "Give me that," Matei ordered, eyeing the weapon. Though he felt certain his inability to access the crystal's power was temporary, he felt oddly vulnerable without it. *A king should wear a sword,* he bolstered himself. He extended his hand. The marine shot him a puzzled look but obeyed, handing it over.

"My father has fallen," Matei announced loudly, buckling the soldier's sword belt around his waist. "In battle." He tried to muster a look of remorse, but his face pained him too greatly to display much sentiment, especially one he didn't feel. "The thrones of Valenna and Sornia now pass to me." He looked haughtily around the small boat, catching a few looks of surprise from the crew before they quickly averted their eyes.

"I'm sorry," Lucas replied solemnly, placing his hat over his heart. "May the King rest in peace." Beside him, Teressa muttered likewise. "Will you be able to continue this without him?" Lucas asked gently.

Frowning, Matei turned his gaze to the palace in the distance, a menacing black shape outlined against the ink-dark clouds. "Of course."

"The palace has been cleared for your arrival," one of the marines informed him, "Your High—" The man sputtered nervously. "I mean, Your Majesty. The throne awaits."

The crew rowed for the docks, and they soon disembarked upon the eastern wharf. Though it wasn't Matei's first time on Valennian soil, it felt different now. This time, he arrived as a conquering king, rather than the unwanted bastard prince he'd once been, hiding in the shadows of some greasy inn. Finally, his years' worth of destabilizing Valenna by plague and political unrest would culminate in victory.

He made his way through the empty cobblestone streets. The ballistic onslaught had left broken walls, smashed roofs, and crushed bodies behind, and it appeared the city's surviving occupants had either fled or were in hiding, perhaps silently watching him pass from the dark windows. However, he was joined now and then by groups of soldiers in green who knelt before him, lowering their heads as he went. To all who called Sornia home, the silver circlet on his brow, the gold-trimmed velvet cloak at his shoulders, and the careless self-assuredness of his stride clearly announced his newfound kingship.

Matei and the others stopped before the gates of the foreign palace, with its strange architecture and unfamiliar roofline, and the Sornian soldiers on the other side swung them open and bowed low. Beside him, Lucas cast an uneasy glance at Teressa, whose freckled brow was furrowed, a look of sadness in her eye. Catching the look, Matei wondered briefly what it must feel like for them, arriving in their old homeland under circumstances that likely felt somewhat like treason. *No, not treason,* he corrected himself. After all, the Andolin Empire was mother to both nations; he was simply restoring it to its former, glorious state. *It's the opposite of treachery—it's loyalty. To the Empire, and to me, the rightful heir of Andolin.*

"All hail King Matei!" one soldier shouted, hand over his heart, as though he could sense Matei's thoughts. "Emperor of Sornia and Valenna!"

"Emperor of Andolin," Matei corrected him. Drawing his sword, he stepped inside the gate.

Making his way through the antechamber, where his marines dragged bodies out of the way, he came to a set of wide, curved steps that led up to a grand doorway, the opulence of its gilded beauty revealing its importance. *The throne room.* He pushed open the door.

Inside, large, intricate tapestries hung from the walls. On the far side of the vast space, a second, double-winged staircase led to a balcony that overlooked a raised dais, upon which sat an ornately-carved, gilded throne. Resting on the velvet seat of the throne, in the light of the melting candles of the chandeliers overhead, glittered a thin, golden crown.

Two red-clad Valennians stood beside the throne, an old, hollow-eyed man and a beautiful woman whose lustrous black hair was piled high atop her head and adorned with feathers. Though the fashion of their clothing was foreign to him, they were both clearly dressed in the opulent style of court. Striding quickly across the ancient carpets, Matei approached them.

The man muttered formalities as he hastily lowered into a bow. "Welcome to Valenna, Your—"

"Are you Lord Hollen?" Matei interrupted. "The one I've been corresponding with?"

The man straightened quickly and nodded. "Y—Yes, Your Majesty," he sputtered. "It was I who—"

Matei's blade sank deep into the man's gut before he could finish speaking. Lord Hollen collapsed, arms and legs askew on the ancient carpet as pink foam burbled from the corner of his mouth. The woman stood open-mouthed for a moment, gaping at the blood that pooled at her feet, then turned and fled.

"After her," Matei ordered.

Two of his Royal Marines nodded and ran out the open doors as Lucas and Teressa walked in. Taking in the scene before him, Teressa's green eyes widened in shock, and she put a hand over her mouth, stifling a gasp.

"After so much blood has been spilled," Matei said with a half-shrug, "what's a little more?"

"That's a bit harsh," she managed to say, her voice faint. "Don't you think?"

"He was right to do it," Lucas interjected. "Or they'd always be working in the shadows, trying to take the throne."

Matei gave him an appraising look. "This is yours now," he said, lifting the silver circlet from his brow. "You will sit upon the throne as my viceroy when I return to Sornia." Extending his arm, he handed it to Lucas, who gave him a searching look before taking it wordlessly, struck silent by the unexpected gesture.

Matei's footsteps grew louder as he approached the throne, rising deliberately up the dais step by step. Holding his breath, he reached out for the golden crown that awaited him, setting his fingertips gingerly around the glistening metal. It was still warm, smudged with fresh blood.

Turning to face the crowd of emerald that had quietly gathered behind him, he slowly and deliberately placed the Valennian crown on his head, surveying the room. All bowed.

Sweeping his cloak aside, Matei sat down upon the throne, taking the moment in. *My empire.* Finally, he had what he'd always longed for. The cushion barely provided any comfort, worn thin as it was after so many years of use, and the room before him was much quieter than he'd imagined. There were no Valennians present to witness it, save for the ones he'd brought with him, and no cheering or flattery from courtiers. Instead, the moment was solemn, a silent lowering of the Royal Marines as they knelt before him.

Taking the cue from the others, Lucas and Teressa bowed likewise until Matei ordered them all to rise.

"You did it," Lucas said admiringly, looking around the throne room. "You've united our countries. Now what?"

Matei gave a smirk, though it fell away quickly as the motion sent a burning pain through his cheek. "It's not finished yet. We still need to take Andolin proper, the mother country. We have outposts in the south, but we have yet to command the lands there fully." The ancient land of Andolin, for which the empire was named, was a mere shadow of its former glory, its people diminished to a few remaining bands among the ruins. Now a desolate wasteland, the region was often left off modern maps of Belgrand Bay. He shrugged one shoulder. "But that place is wild, not many people left. It won't take much. However, there is something else I want," he went on, raising a finger, "that may prove much more difficult to obtain."

Lucas raised a brow. "What's that?"

"A queen, for my kingdom," Matei replied. "An empress, for my empire..." His fingers found the ragged edge of flesh on his left cheek, which still wept openly with blood, though it no longer poured forth as profusely. Pain flared through his face at the touch. He winced, then lowered his brows. "One, in particular," he added. He'd always intended to take a Valennian woman for his bride, to unite the bloodlines of both kingdoms; now that the empire was his, it was a mere matter of formality. But beneath all that, it was revenge he longed for—revenge on his fated enemy, the one who still eluded him, the one who'd permanently marred his noble face. He gave Lucas a piercing look. "Your sister."

24

Lament

"That's Armand!" Adella called out, leaning over the rail. "But who is that with him?" Below, a small boat, guided by only two oars, had drawn alongside *The Tigress*, which, under Captain Jon's orders, was slowly retreating from the harbor. Two figures climbed up the rope ladder toward her. She recognized Armand by his bushy grey sideburns, but the other man, climbing after him, she didn't recognize. He certainly wasn't Valennian; his bald head glistened like wet leather.

Beside her, Kol extended an arm to help Armand over the rail. As soon as he regained his feet, Armand flung his arms around him. "Bless me, it's good to see you two," Armand muttered into Kol's shirt. Releasing him, he embraced Adella next. "I must tell you," he began, pulling back to meet her eyes, "the Queen—" His voice broke before he could finish and, removing his hat, he placed it over his heart.

"No," Adella uttered as the meaning behind the gesture struck. She closed her eyes as the pain of grief flashed through her. Opening them again, she became aware of the other man who'd boarded with Armand, and, looking his way, her mouth parted in surprise at the sight of Captain Jago. Though she knew him at once, the man's face was barely recognizable now. The expression he wore was beyond grief; his eyes stared dully at nothing. He didn't speak, or even look up to greet her; it was as though he wasn't even there at all.

"The Queen, she, uh—" Armand tried again. He gave a loud sniff and pulled a haversack from his shoulder. "She wanted me to give this to you."

Furrowing her brow, Adella took the bag from him and felt hard metal within. Opening the flap, she let out a gasp. Inside was an iron lockbox. "Oh, Armand..." she sighed. Having seen Matei with the crystal, she knew there was no chance the box still contained the Heart of the World as when she'd first found it in the cave beneath the Campos. Still, at least one of them had succeeded in their mission. She tucked the small, iron box safely beneath her arm.

In the distance, the high towers of the Ansebulet overlooked the wreckage below. The roofline fires no longer burned, only smoldered beneath the ongoing rain. In the waters of the harbor, *The Fury*, the Sornian flagship at the center of the battle, listed heavily to starboard. *The Tigress* had taken a hit, too, with a breach in the hull the crew had hastily plugged with oakum. The Madorran vessel she'd arrived on was nowhere to be seen, but all around the remaining ships, the waves still writhed with the undulating coils of the *pelkimund*, bringing the waters to life with hungry violence as they preyed upon the dead, snatching the bodies boldly from the waters and the decks.

As *The Tigress* changed tack, turning about more slowly than usual with its damaged hull and mainsail, Adella put the gruesome scene behind her, directing her gaze to the south. Before them, the wide, white sails of *The Warbrand* led the retreat. It was over; Sornia had won. Her heart panged at the thought, though it all still hardly seemed real.

Beside her, Kol wrapped an arm around her shoulders, and she leaned in to his solid warmth. "I'm sorry," he said quietly, his breath forming white curls in the chill air. "About the captain."

She shook her head against his chest. "That wasn't the man I knew," she replied, even as loss and guilt sent another pang searing through her. She couldn't help but recall Declan's death vividly: The flash of the blade as she stuck it into his leg. The feel of the saber sinking into his shoulder as he fell over her. Each memory burned like a brand on her heart. Though she couldn't bring herself to regret it—the moment she'd realized Kol was in danger, she'd acted, with hardly a pause to think her actions through—the violence she'd done to one who never should've been her enemy had left its mark. *It was by my hand...* The image of the *pelkimund* clamping down around his injured body and the wild terror in his eyes as it pulled him into the dark sea would be with her forever. Yet, if she had that choice set before her again, she knew she would do it all the same. She would do whatever it took, if it meant saving Kol.

* * *

Kol stood at the rail, the frigid wind whipping rain into his eyes, as the many bodies of the fallen, wrapped in their hammock-shrouds, were solemnly hoisted, one by one, and slipped into the night-black sea, all while Captain Jon spoke their solemn farewells.

Kol's own father, the only family he'd ever known, was among the dead. Though he'd known the man only briefly, a knot still formed in his throat when Seaborn's body was brought forth, and he swallowed hard against it. Adella had been right when she'd warned him not to be hasty aligning himself with a stranger, blood ties or no. From the beginning, it had been clear that his father wasn't a good man by any stretch of the word, but he'd wanted so badly to believe otherwise that he'd brushed those past misdeeds aside. It stung deeply to think that both Seaborn and Declan had paid for his bad judgment with their lives.

Beside him, Adella reached for his hand, her soft fingers weaving between his, bringing him comfort. He wasn't sure what lay ahead, but whatever it was, there was no doubt they'd face it together. *'Wherever you go, I will go with you.'* The words echoed in his mind, and, plain though they were, their earnest meaning sang through his heart. He squeezed her hand.

Captain Jon continued with his eulogies. The incessant rain turned to heavy white snowflakes, settling over the ship in a dusting of white.

When Jon had finished honoring the last life that had been lost in battle, and a silence fell over those gathered, Jago stepped forward, grief etched into the lines of his face. "We have one more farewell to give this night," he began, his Andolinian accent heavier than usual as it carried through the cold night air. "To Queen Ellinora, consort to the former King Rickan and mother of the late King Harrian of the Haspen dynasty. But she was more than merely a queen. She was a friend. And that's the greatest thing one can be." He placed his hand over his heart. "Farewell to our beloved Queen. May you find rest among the stars until we meet again."

Adella's throat burned with emotion as she mirrored his gesture, placing her hand on her chest. "Farewell," she murmured softly as a lone tear escaped, its wet warmth warming her cold cheek briefly before rolling down.

* * *

In the great cabin, Adella rifled through a sea chest for spare blankets. Outside, the heavy rain that had beat in their faces all day was now falling in large, white flakes and had begun to gather on the window frames. *The Tigress* would continue on through the night, following *The Warbrand* wherever it might lead, but she hoped they'd make landfall quickly. Not only was the hull in need of repair, there was still a bad spate of fever aboard as well. Two more had died. *More death after so many others...*

Judging by their heading, Adella wondered if *The Warbrand* might be leading them to Smuggler's Port. *If it's still there, that is.* She frowned. With the destruction of the Campos, it seemed there was hardly anything left of the world, at least to her. The Campos, after all, had been her whole world. And now it was gone. Between that and the recently rising waters, there were hardly any safe harbors left on the Valennian coast, especially now that Sornia had invaded the Capital. With Matei in charge, they'd likely set up garrisons at every remaining port in the Bay.

The door banged open, jerking her out of her lamentation, and Kol walked in, followed by Armand and Jago. The trio approached the table where Kerchaw was already seated; a blue-and-white porcelain tea service sat before him, steam rising from the pot's delicate spout.

"Were you in here this whole time? Since before we entered battle?" Kol asked, pulling out a chair.

"Of course," Kerchaw replied, calmly flipping a page as he reviewed his ledger. "You told me to stay here."

Bending down to pull out the last wool blanket, Adella glanced down at her arm. The blisters that had been left behind by the foreign plant had faded completely; not even a bit of redness remained. Remembering the lingering, stinging pain it had caused her, she wondered if the comfrey she'd placed over it had aided in the healing process. *Like that strange voice said in my dream,* she mused, *'Each calamity has its cure.'*

Rising, she closed the chest and placed the pile of blankets on top, pausing to drape one over Endlebridge. His eyes fluttered open. "How do you feel?" she asked, leaning toward him.

"Terrible," he replied with a wan smile.

She let out a small laugh, then searched in her jacket pocket and pulled out the ruby necklace. It dangled partly from her fist, glittering gold in the candlelight. "I believe this belongs to you," she said softly.

He shook his head. "No. It's yours."

"You can't—" she replied, raising her brows. "I gave it to you as payment."

"It means more to you than to me," he replied firmly, closing her fingers around the jewel. "Besides, what need do I have now of rubies?"

he muttered, turning his head away and nestling into the pillow. "It's over; we lost." He shut his eyes. "Valenna is no more."

Leaving him to rest, she joined the others at the table beneath the flickering light of the chandelier. Her foot bumped her haversack below the table, which she bent over and set on the table before them. At the heavy thunk, Jago's gaze focused, drawing him out of his daze of grief. Gently, she removed the iron lockbox, its strange pictographs covering its surface.

"So... Now what?" Armand asked, breaking the somber silence. "Go back to Elldon?"

"We can't." Adella's fingers tightened around the ruby on its chain. "There is no Elldon left. The bridge is burned; the Campos has fallen into the Bay. Along with so many of us—" Her words caught in her throat as the grief burned up from her heart, tears rising. She thought of Holcomb, Rosalind, her beloved horse, Shy, and all the others lost to the sundering sea, and clapped a hand over her mouth to stifle a sob. "It's all gone," she finally managed. "Destroyed. I don't know why I thought I could take my father's place—" No longer able to hold the emotion back, tears flooded her eyes. "I'll never be like my father," she said, voice breaking. Shoulders heaving with each shuddering breath, she draped herself over the table, burying her face in her folded arms. "I've failed everyone."

"You're wrong," Armand countered a moment later. "Do you think your father won every fight he was in? Do you think things were always easy?" He shook his head. "No. They weren't. Nor did we have to face an outright war back then." He pointed a finger at her. "If there's one thing I know for sure, you are your father's daughter. You're every bit like he was. I know he'd be proud of you for trying, and for making it this far. As I am." He waved his hand dismissively. "So no more of that talk."

As Armand spoke, Adella realized just how badly she'd needed to hear those words, and her tears overflowed again. Unable to find her voice to reply, she gave him a teary smile, then nodded and wiped her eyes with her free hand. In her other hand, the ruby seemed to shine more vividly, a sparkling Valennian scarlet. Looking down at it, memories of seeing it around her mother's neck, glistening at the table during supper or as she sat at her desk writing letters, returned in vivid detail. Her mother's presence was so strong that Adella could nearly feel her in the cabin, along with her father, taking his usual place alongside her mother. The sensation of his presence was bolstered by his saber, which hung at her side. Between the ruby and the blade, she felt a little less daunted by the future, as though her parents stood behind her even now.

"Don't you all see what's happening?" Jago suddenly interjected, his unusual accent warping his words. He searched his companions' faces. "The Twelve Calamities are upon us; the world is falling apart. We have to find a way to stop it." He looked Adella sharply in the eye, his own expression filled with fire. "I promised the Queen I'd see it through to the end, and she said you'd know what to do." He pushed the sealed lockbox closer to her. "We've taken it to all the locksmiths in the area, to every tinkerer and blacksmith we could find, to open it. For months we traveled..." A frown crossed his face, his grief written plainly once more.

"That must have been when my letters to her went unanswered," Adella guessed, pocketing the ruby.

Jago nodded. "No one knew where we were. But there's more to it than that. Lord Hollen had returned to the Capital," he went on, his voice lowering. "He'd gone into hiding after the Queen came back to Valenna from the Cairn, secretly brewing a conspiracy against her—there were even whispers he had ties to Sornia. Ellinora hadn't been back on the throne long when we'd heard rumors of his presence again, and then an attempt was made on her life—" His expression twisted into one of fresh pain at the memory. "Because we couldn't find the culprit, we deemed it safer to travel than to sleep in a den of hidden vipers. But we never did get the lockbox open." He shook his head.

"I'm not surprised," Adella replied. "According to legend, only Leveret's Key can unlock it. But it doesn't matter now. I know it's empty. It used to hold the Heart of the World, which Matei now has; he's had it all along. Somehow, he found a way to remove it during the battle on *The Accord*. He had the Key on him, after all, so it would've been easy for him to do without any of us being the wiser." She looked at the faces around her, expressions varying from shock to grief, and sighed. "We brought the lockbox to the Capital empty." Her heart sank at the admission, and the weight of guilt settled once more over her shoulders. She stared down at the iron box on the table, her eyes fixed on the strange symbols adorning its surface. She wrapped her arms around herself and shuddered, thinking of Matei. "I've seen the crystal in his hand. It's given him..." She pressed her lips together. "Strange abilities."

"He can command the dead," Kol clarified, brows lowering.

"More than that, I fear." She swallowed thickly. Too many of her nightmares had bled into reality to believe her visions of Matei were merely dreams. "I think we've only seen a glimpse of what's possible with the Heartstone in his possession."

Flotsam

Morning's winter-grey light filtered through the falling snow, mottling Matei's view of the dark, churning Bay with specks of white. The turning tide brought bodies that had begun to float in the days after the battle, returning them to shore. He'd come out to the beach each morning since he'd taken the throne; something out here called to him, though the feeling grew fainter as each day passed.

With one hand clutching the Heartstone inside his waistcoat, Matei closed his eyes and opened his mind to the energies all around. There was much here to sort through between the multitude of wild creatures and the memories of the recently dead. Amidst it all, though, one spark of life cut through the noise, dim though it had become since he'd first felt it call to him in the night's darkness. Neither fully dead nor exactly alive, the intensity of the unique feeling was reminiscent of a vibrant and powerful will, perhaps one much like his own, bearing feelings of avarice, anger and a fervent sense of superiority over the other beings of the world. At the very least, whatever it was seemed to be attracting him, as like to like. This was, he felt sure, something that would prove useful.

Scanning the eastern beach, where thin drifts of snow collected on the rocks, he searched for the source of the strange, energetic call. The frigid winds, so strong here by the shore, bit through his clothing. Searching from one dark mass to the next, he watched the flotsam that had washed up with the rising tide.

"Search the bodies," Matei muttered, giving the order with a wave of his hand. "Look for survivors." At his murmured words, the soldiers flanking him scattered, flooding over the lapping shore to stoop at the forms that littered the rocky beach. Their jackets, still the bright scarlet of Valenna rather than the usual Sornian emerald he was accustomed to, clashed starkly with the dull colors of the landscape.

He'd ordered the same search the day before, and the day before that, so he wasn't sure what he expected. He only knew that as long as he still felt the unusual call, he had to keep looking. Since he'd taken possession of the stone, the world had become filled with strange energies that were now growing familiar: the *pelkimund* and their voracious hunger, the recently dead and their brief flashes of memory, and the myriad other living beings, both animal and human. Of them all, this one that called to him was different, stood out.

An energetic pulse, invisible but catching his attention like a flash of lightning, drew him from his contemplation. "Look there," Matei called out, bracing his injured jaw and bandaged face with his hand against the pain that flared as he spoke. He pointed beyond several large boulders that obscured his view to the left. "Behind the rocks."

The soldiers scurried over to the area and soon were pulling a dark shape into view. Dragging the heavy, water-logged thing over the pebbled beach, they brought it before him. It was a man—or rather, the body of one. The seawater that ran off the limp form was tinged red with blood; an arm was partly missing, with shards of splintered bone peeking through the open muscle and torn jacket. The soldiers turned the figure over and its face turned upward. Matei let out a gasp. Deep, ragged slashes, rather like the one that marred his own face, cut through the waxen flesh of the jowls and brow, slicing through the thickly-bearded chin. Instinctively, Matei put a hand to his own cheek, fingertips brushing the bandages that covered the gruesome wound left by a ballista bolt. Even now, it pained him greatly, tugging on his skin and limiting his speech. It still hurt too much to eat and drink, though he forced himself to choke down water now and then.

Staring into the disfigured visage at his feet, he felt the connection that had been calling to him softly. *This is it*, the thought came to him with a sudden certainty. *This is what I've been searching for.* The energy was much stronger now, with the man before him, and the air around him was vibrating with electrified energy. He felt for the crystal only to realize he didn't need it; what he felt from this man was an emotion he already knew well. *Rage. Hatred...* Whoever this man had been, even now, after his death, his soul called out for revenge.

As the snowflakes landed softly on the corpse-still face that lay upon the ground, an eyelid twitched.

"He's still alive!" Matei muttered, almost to himself, shoving aside the pain he felt in his face at his own words. His gaze shifted to the sword that hung from the nearest soldier's waist; surely, it would be kinder to let this man's suffering end. And yet, the strength of his will, still tethering life to his mangled body, was impressive.

"Bring him to the palace," Matei ordered, mustering his voice enough to command the soldiers around him again. He turned and led the way up the hill, pulling the Heart of the World from his pocket as he made the ascent. Glancing down, he was surprised to see it glowing a bright, cold blue. He narrowed his eyes against the glare. Whoever this man was, it was clear that his fate wasn't over yet.

To Be Continued...

Acknowledgements

For the Legends of Andolin Series

Firstly, I want to thank my sister, Alyssa, for giving me the idea that I could write a book. Before her encouragement, I never would have attempted such a thing. And of course, I am ever grateful for my husband, Philip, and his support through the many years of writing thus far and yet to come—for being my alpha reader, for helping me get Kol's perspective, as a man, just right, and for the countless rereads of every draft. I couldn't have done this without you.

I'm also extremely grateful to my tireless editors. When I met Julie McKay Covert aboard the *Huron Jewel* (of which she is First Mate) for the fudge cruise on my birthday, I had no idea what a blessing I had come upon. I'm so lucky she agreed to edit my books. She had a hand in shaping all three of the books that have been published so far—anything I get right about sailing is due to her knowledge. Then, while creating the second edition of *Adella of the Campos,* I was fortunate once more to find Erin Leigh, who helped me add depth and emotion to the first book, and then again in this third installment. Without the two of them, the series would be a mere shadow of what it is now. As it was up to me to implement their edits, any errors found in these books are solely my own.

Above all, I thank God every day for the privilege to be able to spend my time doing something I love. And to every reader who has been following Adella on her adventures,

Thank you.

Kol's Switchel Recipe

1/2 gallon water

1/2 cup honey

1/4 cup apple cider vinegar

1 tablespoon powdered ginger

Mix well